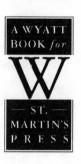

A WYATT
BOOK *for*

W

ST.
MARTIN'S
PRESS

CLEO

JEAN BRODY

A WYATT BOOK for ST. MARTIN'S PRESS
NEW YORK

For my teachers

Design by Sara Stemen

LIBRARY OF CONGRESS CATALOGING-IN-PUBLICATION DATA
Brody, Jean.
    Cleo/Jean Brody.
        p.   cm.
    ISBN 0-312-11761-2
    I. Title.
PS3552.R625C55   1995
813'.54—dc20   94-40978
                                                                     CIP

First Edition: February 1995

10   9   8   7   6   5   4   3   2   1

I wish to thank the National Endowment for the Arts for support during the writing of this book. Gratitude is due Nancy Nordoff for a three-month stay at her writers' retreat, Cottages at Hedgebrook, and to the Cambria Writers' Workshop for helpful criticism. I am also grateful that Alexandra David-Neel saw fit to write a book called *My Journey to Lhasa,* which gave me not only pleasure, but inspiration.

 PART I

I send you forth as sheep in the midst of wolves;
be ye therefore wise as serpents, and harmless as doves.
—MATTHEW 10:16

1

I WAS BORN IN THE LATE FALL OF 1912 ON a two-cow farm just north of Robina, Oklahoma. When I was fifteen I left home, old for my age and able-bodied. I had a cardboard satchel of my belongings, twenty dollars of egg money my momma had saved up, and the trumpet my daddy gave me along with his blessing.

That's not the whole truth. It's the truth I strained through life's sieve, leaving kernels of my heart's desire. I stole the money and the trumpet, and I divined the blessing from Daddy, who had passed on the previous summer as the result of a dispute over a poker hand with a blood Shawnee. I mourned my daddy but I didn't leave because of his death. I left home because of something I read in a book from the lending library in Robina. This is how it went: "I craved to go beyond the garden gate, to follow the road that passed it by, and to set out for the unknown."

It was the early spring of 1927. I'd come into town on the mule to do shopping and errands for my momma and my grandmother, which I did every other Saturday. As was my habit, I took back the books I'd borrowed and checked out three more, which was all that was allowed on a single visit. By the time I returned a book I knew most of the good parts by heart.

Miss Emma Hawkins, who treated books like they were fertile eggs and she the last setting hen in Robina County, always had something special waiting for me on her desk. That Saturday it was *My Journey to Lhasa* by Alexandra David-Neel. Miss Hawkins smiled at me and said it had just come in.

She said, "It has your name written all over it, Cleo."

Miss Hawkins had come out from Raleigh, North Carolina, with her brother, who established the Robina Pharmacy and Notions. When she discovered that Robina had no public library, she put her own considerable collection at the disposal of the citizens. I was her first customer: *Life on the Mississippi, Rebecca of Sunnybrook Farm,* and *Prisoner of Zenda.*

Miss Hawkins changed my life. The only book we had at home was the King James Bible, which I had read cover to cover three times at my momma's urging. I was nine years old when Miss Hawkins came to town. Six books a month times twelve months times six years adds up to 432 books under my belt when I left Robina. Plus Webster's Dictionary and the Sears Roebuck catalogue, and whatever newspapers and magazines I could lay hands on. Plus books read on the library premises. Miss Hawkins had a wall of shelves built down one side of the room, which separated her library from the store proper. There was a potbellied stove with a steaming teakettle in the wintertime, and two armchairs besides the one behind Miss Hawkins' desk—an invitation to sit awhile and talk over what you'd read. In the summer there was a bottomless pitcher of ice cold lemonade, free to library patrons. This lemonade was said to be largely responsible for the high degree of literacy in Robina County.

I commenced to read on the way home, letting the mule have his head. By the time we got to the turnoff I knew I was destined to go to Lhasa. There was even a map provided. I could follow in Alexandra David-Neel's own footsteps through the wild hills, the deserted steppes and impassable glaciers! An honest traveler, she said, has the right to walk as he chooses, all over the globe. You went first to Peking, China, where you hired a mule and a holy man. Then you went south and west to Lanchow, then due south to Suifu on the Yangtze River. Likiang was the next stop, then bear north to Giamda, which appeared to be just a ways down the road from my destination. The only hitch I could see was the Himalaya Mountains, which I knew from the *National Geographic* magazine to be of a good size.

I began to make my plans.

The way I saw it I didn't have any choice. Alexandra David-Neel had revealed to me my own deep craving for the unknown. And I knew if I stayed in Robina much longer, Willis Henderson would succeed in his mission to get my drawers down around my ankles, and first thing you know we'd be married and have three or four kids and would've worn out our welcome with one another. It's one thing to rub up against the sweet hardness of a hot-eyed boy, to feel his mouth and his hands open you up like a crocus impatient for spring. It is another thing altogether to make conversation with him for as long as you both shall live.

4

That evening when I went to milk the Jersey and close up the chickens, I snuck out my belongings and hid them under the house. After the supper things were cleared away, we all gathered around the kitchen table and Momma—as was her daily habit—read to us by kerosene light from the Old Testament. There were four of us: Ethan, Sarah, me, and Baby Fidelity, who was six years old at the time. She wasn't a baby anymore but that's what we called her. When Momma was big with her she caught Daddy bare-assed in the rumble seat of Aggie Littlefield's new Pierce-Arrow. She snatched Aggie practically bald-headed, and named the baby Fidelity as an ever-present reminder to Daddy of the sanctity of the marriage bed. I was young and innocent at the time and didn't know enough to be mad at him or ashamed. And he was always so good to us kids. He brought us presents and made up games and taught us to play his horn—although I was the only one with a gift for it. He was more like a playmate than a father. We made no secret of the fact that we preferred his company to Momma's.

Now, with him gone, Momma had doubled her efforts on her children's salvation. She turned up the lamp, opened the Bible, and sent her finger swooping down on a passage like a redtail with a bead on a rabbit. The words she caught were to direct our footsteps on the path of righteousness over the following day. She lifted her chin and gazed around the table to make sure she had our attention. Then she commenced to read:

"And they took their journey from Elim, and all the congregation of the children of Israel came unto the Wilderness of Sin."

Sarah tugged at Momma's sleeve. "You mean sin is a place?" she asked. "You mean sin ain't something you do?"

"Both, Sarah," said Momma. "Isn't." And she went on about how the children of Israel were put out with Moses and Aaron because there weren't any fleshpots or any bread to eat since they'd left Egypt. After Momma read the part about how God said the bread would rain from heaven, she stopped and pulled her face into a frown. She began to riffle the pages as she often did when God's words were at odds with her own philosophy. It was all right with Momma for Him to give spiritual guidance and inspiration, but not material goods. She believed that anyone in authority—including God and the Democrats—should help only those who helped themselves.

"Ahhhh!" she said, her finger lighting on a spot. "And the Lord went before them in a pillar of cloud, to lead them the way; and by night in a pillar of fire, to give them light. He took not away the pillar of cloud by day, nor the pillar of fire by night from before the people."

She closed the Bible and patted it with affection. It had not failed her. My brother Ethan, ten months my junior, nudged me under the table and we gave each other a private grin. We understood that Momma didn't always get her rabbit on the first try.

She folded her hands and looked over her spectacles. "Now then," she said. "What that means is that God is with you at all times, casting his light on your path." Her words were comforting but her tone gave us to understand that in fact He had His eye on us personally, the brood of a poor widow, night and day. Momma had as many ways to make her point as summertime has chiggers. For example: She always baked a Bible saying into the cornbread muffins she packed in our schoolbuckets. One fine day Willis Henderson and I were having our picnic out on the grass behind the schoolhouse. I broke open my muffin and there was this message: "For by means of a whorish woman a man is brought to a piece of bread. Proverbs 6:26." And: Ethan came home drunk the night after Daddy's funeral service. His muffin told him: "They are drunken but not with wine; they stagger, but not with strong drink. Isaiah 29:9."

Which tells you something about my momma's weakness for her favorite child. If it had been me, she would've really let me have it with "The drunkard shall come to poverty" or "A drunkard staggereth in his own vomit."

Now she leaned forward, tense with the divine instruction forming inside her. "The light comes from the Lord, that's true, to any and all who raise up their eyes. But your daily bread is not going to rain out of the sky, I can tell you that right now. Faith is one thing. Personal industry is another."

After a decent interval for reflection I asked Momma if Egypt was anywhere close to Lhasa.

"Well, I don't know about Lhasa, Daughter. Where is Lhasa?"

I shrugged. "Close by India, I think."

Momma looked off in the distance. "Yes," she said. "I believe Egypt is somewhere close to India. Why do you ask?"

I shrugged again. I wanted to tell her. I wanted her blessing on my journey. But I knew she'd have some evidence from On High as to why I should stay put, some version of how we sit by the rivers of Babylon weeping for Zion. "Just wondered," I said.

"Close to the Wilderness of Sin?" asked Sarah. Sarah was twelve at the time and had developed a consuming interest in certain aspects of that subject.

Momma nodded solemnly and told us the Wilderness of Sin was close to everywhere, especially after the sun went down. To avoid blundering into it we had to keep our eyes trained on the pillar of fire.

As the eldest I had my own room, which was our add-on of many uses. It was separated from the house by a screened-in walkway where Momma dried herbs and flowers she used in her curative business. The house was built of hewn logs and lime cement; the fireplace was a great beauty made of jam stones from the creek, but with no damper or baffle plate, so the heat went right up the chimney. And when a strong wind came down from Kansas the house would fill up with smoke. There were two rooms, besides the add-on: the kitchen, which was all the parlor we had, and the bedroom, which Momma shared with the girls. Ethan had a cot he unfolded by the stove in the winter, and out on the front porch in good weather.

That was one of my problems. It was good weather and Ethan was sleeping on the front porch, which I had to pass to get to the road. And there were the dogs; two yellow hounds that could hear grass growing in a thunderstorm.

The clock chimed three times as I crept into the kitchen. I took the crock where Momma kept the egg money, and a handful of biscuits left over from our supper, and I stole—like the thief I was—back to my room. I lit my lamp and counted out twenty dollars in change and ones which I stuffed in my pocketbook.

Then I got dressed. In order not to attract the wrong kind of attention to myself, I took a strip of tea towel and wound it around to flatten my chest some. This chest was famous in Robina County, its true wonder, however, a mystery to all but Willis Henderson. Cleo's wonders, that's what he called them. I put on my Sunday outfit; navy crepe dress with a wide lace collar, white straw hat with pink grosgrain ribbon, white gloves with pearl buttons. I carried a pair of sad brown brogans, which were all the shoes I owned.

As I mentioned, I was old for my age and could easily pass for eighteen, maybe even twenty in dim light. I was of average height and tended to be wiry where I wasn't filled out. I had my momma's Indian hair and narrow hands, and my daddy's light brown eyes with flecks of gold and green. I was not the prettiest girl in the tenth grade, although there were those who would dispute that, but I was without question the most developed, in both body and mind.

The hounds got up and stretched as I came around the corner of the house. I gave them the biscuits and told them to stay; then I collected my belongings from where I had hidden them and started off. I could hear Ethan snore as I skirted the porch; I could hear the dogs chomp on the biscuits; I could hear my heart pound like a thrashing machine on its last legs.

I did not take a deep breath until I got to the road, where I sat down on a log and put on my shoes. I stood up and looked back at the house where I'd lived my whole life. I thought about my feather comforter and hot food on the table and all my daily blessings. Then clear as day I saw my daddy come in from the field. He gave me a wide smile and called out to me—said the wind would be at my back—said the road would rise up to meet me. I hoisted my belongings and headed for the unknown.

It was dawn when I hitched a ride with a tie salesman just north of town. I looked him over before I got in. He had soft pink hands and a grey complexion, and I knew I could whup him if it came to that. I told him I was going to Kansas City to look after my sick auntie and could he recommend a modest hotel near the train depot in Tulsa where a lady could safely spend the night. He let me off at a hotel on North Main. He said it was cheap, but clean and well regarded. After he was out of sight I turned the corner and found another place a couple blocks away. I was laying a trail of false bread crumbs in case Momma sent Ethan to fetch me home. I knew she wouldn't come herself as, in her view, the city of Tulsa lay just on the outskirts of Gomorrah.

I got a room on the first floor of the Robinson Hotel—paid in advance—unpacked my belongings, and set out to find a busy street corner where I could set up my business. I was bowled over by what I saw; more tall buildings than you could shake a stick at. Tall! Maybe ten-twelve stories high! And all kinds of stores stacked up against each other. There were stores that specialized in just one item. A store for shoes, one for men's shirts, one for books, even one for ladies' dainties and them displayed right there in the window. My momma would've had a few thousand Bible words to say about that. And there were automobiles whizzing up and down the streets like they were off to a fire. And people going past you at a fast trot without so much as a nod of the head.

I had to stop in a café to regain my strength and purpose. I had never been out of Robina, which had maybe eleven hundred souls, dead and living, and here I was in Tulsa, the Magic Empire, the Oil Capital of the World with a population upward of one hundred thousand, according to the tie salesman. Fortified with sausage and eggs and grits and a big slice of berry pie, I took to the streets again.

I walked for hours and was beginning to entertain notions of going back home, tail between my legs, when suddenly I was given a sign—a literal sign. There it was, shining like a beacon in the early dusk. The Gusher, it said in bright violet-blue letters, which I knew later to be made of neon gas but gladly accepted at that moment as the pillar of fire.

I hurried back to the hotel and got into my costume, which was composed of a pair of Ethan's worn-out overalls, the top part of my winter underwear, a red kerchief, and an old brown fedora I had borrowed off one of Gideon Warwick's scarecrows. I tucked my hair up under the hat and smeared my face with some ashes I'd brought along in my cardboard satchel. The idea was to look like a tramp who'd just got off the Frisco.

I'd done this act many times at community functions in Robina and was always well received. I'd walk on stage with a stick over my shoulder, to the end of which was tied a small gunnysack. I'd stop in the middle of the stage, pretending to be dumbfounded to find an audience out there, and I'd put the stick down and rummage around in the

9

gunnysack for—you guessed it! My trumpet! I'd pull it out, shine it up with spit and the red kerchief, then I'd launch into W. C. Handy's "St. Louis Blues."

People would holler and stomp when I finished; then they'd shout out requests. I played by ear, only had to hear a piece once and it was mine forever. I always closed my act with "The Battle Hymn of the Republic," and the audience would come in on the chorus. "The Battle Hymn" is probably the greatest song ever written for the trumpet. The lyrics don't make much sense, and as Ethan said, you can't dance to it, but people do love it. Amazing how a few glories and a little hallelujah will stir folks into an emotional frenzy. Afterward, I'd bow and smile and remove my hat to show off all that shiny black hair, then pack up my horn and mosey off stage to ride the rails into the sunset.

As I got into my costume that first evening in Tulsa I knew I would have to alter my act if it was to be profitable. I considered taking off my hat after that last hallelujah and holding it out so folks would get the idea, but I knew that would mortify Momma if she got wind of it.

"Thank you, kindly, I'm sure," she told the ladies from the Beulah Baptist Auxiliary when they brought groceries after Daddy passed. "We do not take charity here." Momma was part Creek Indian, descended from royalty. She would rather see her children starved than humiliated.

No. What I needed was a little kettle like the Salvation Army used, a small tasteful vessel that would fit in my gunnysack. I settled for the chamber pot from under my bed, took my lipstick, which was my sole item of luxury, and printed REQUESTS on it in big letters.

I told myself Momma would approve of my sense of personal industry.

The Gusher was a busy place, with people going in and coming back out later in inordinate good humor. I knew that somewhere in its entrails they were serving bootleg hootch. I also knew that folks with a couple of drinks under their belts tended toward generosity. And just down the street there was a movie house. Earlier I had checked for the times so I could start my performance when the picture show let out.

This was the first time I could remember being nervous before my act. Always before there was a friendly audience seated and expecting me, and this time I had to gather them up like Texans herding steers to Kansas. I searched my mind for a plan. And then it came to me. I stood square in front of the double doors to the Gusher, set down the gunnysack, got out the chamber pot and my horn, which I pointed to the heavens, and played taps as sweet and sorrowful as it's ever been played before or since. I held the high note until my breath was gone, and by the time I'd been through it twice people were filing out of the Gusher to see where the funeral was. I gave them a sweeping bow and started right in on the "St. Louis Blues." There was no need for nervousness. Folks laughed and cheered and filled up the pot.

The end of the week I sent a letter by way of a woman going to Kansas City, to be mailed from that place. More false bread crumbs until I had a stake and was safely on my journey to the unknown.

This is what the letter said:

> *Dear Momma:*
>
> *Enclosed is the egg money and the price of the book I borrowed from Miss Hawkins' library. The other two books are on the crate by my bed. A Henry James and a Mary Roberts Rinehart. Please ask Ethan to return them for me as they will soon be overdue. I hope you will agree that Daddy's trumpet is rightfully mine since I'm the only one who can play it.*
>
> *Momma, I promise you this enclosed money comes honestly from my ability with this horn. I will send more to help out on a regular basis. Please don't worry about me, Momma. I am doing just fine. I have found the pillar of fire.*

2

I PLAYED MY HORN OUT IN FRONT OF THE
Gusher four nights running and collected thirty-eight dollars and two
bits in the chamber pot. At that rate I figured I'd be able to send home
at least twenty-five a month and still have plenty left over for my room
and board, and some to save for my journey to Lhasa.

I picked up a copy of the *Tulsa World* and checked the classified
section for rooms to rent. I had noticed that the girls who lived in the
Robinson Hotel slunk around in satin dresses and reeked of gardenia
perfume even before sundown. I had pretty much surmised the sort of
business they engaged in and figured I had stumbled into the wrong
pew.

I made a list of the places I meant to see the next day and then began
to get myself ready for work. This preparation involved a good hour in
the bathtub, which was the first one I had ever seen except for pictures
in the Sears Roebuck catalogue. At home we had a number three zinc
washtub that we kids filled with hot water every Saturday night, then
drew straws to see who got to be first. I lay in that hotel tub like the
Queen of Sheba, my head propped on a folded towel, and read about
Lhasa.

Alexandra David-Neel is in the Dokar Pass at its highest point and
she has just uttered a Buddhist blessing—"May All Things Be
Happy"—when she and Yongden (who is her combination guide and
holy man) are beset by a sudden blizzard. Darkness falls and they have
to camp on the mountain, clinging to their pilgrim staffs and each
other. She makes tea. (Alexandra always makes tea no matter how dire
the circumstances.) While she's drinking it she hears noises in the
bushes and sees the glimmering eyes of a large animal with a spotted
coat. A leopard!

I cry out to her: "Run, Alexandra! Oh Lord in Heaven, please run!"

But she's as calm as a creek in midsummer. She recalls another journey wherein she met up with a tiger, uneventfully. She is convinced
that no beast will ever harm her or those who travel with her.

This is what she said:

"Little thing, I have seen a much bigger prince of the jungle than you. Go to sleep and be happy."

I had to leave her there and get into my costume. While I dressed I thought about the man who came to the door of the Gusher every night and smiled at me. The first night he got things going by putting a dollar bill in the chamber pot and gesturing to the other folks standing around. I must have played a dozen requests that evening. The next night he did the same thing, started the onlookers in the right direction.

He was a tall, lank drink of water, a little on the homely side. He was maybe thirty—thirty-one, and he had that look in his fine brown eyes of a man who doesn't take life easy. The third night I looked for him first thing, and he winked at me like we were conspirators. The next night—the night I got in bad trouble with the law—he wasn't there.

This is how it happened:

I'd just finished "Limehouse Blues" and somebody asked for "Danny Boy." I was only seven years into my career as a trumpet player but I already knew that Irish lullabies tended to send folks off in search of strong drink. Still, the money had gone into the pot so I raised my horn to oblige when I felt a heavy hand on my shoulder. The hand belonged to the meanest-looking policeman I'd ever seen. He wanted to see my license.

"My license for what?" I said.

"Your business license," he growled, grim as the middle of January.

"I didn't know I needed one."

"Well, you know it now. You can't collect money on Tulsa street corners without you have a business license and permission."

I told him that a man who worked in the Gusher had given me permission, which I figured was true in a way.

"What man?" he said. He got out a notebook from his back pocket and a yellow pencil from inside his coat.

"I don't recall his name," I said. "But you could go inside and ask."

"How 'bout your name," he said. "You recall that by any chance?"

"Cleo . . ." I stopped right there. I could not give a policeman my momma's name, to be written down and put in any records of wrongdoing. "Alexander," I said. "Cleo Alexander."

"Address?"

"I am stopping temporarily at the Robinson Hotel," I said. I had read about stopping at hotels in Henry James and Edith Wharton.

He went steely-eyed and wrote furiously in his notebook; then he grabbed my arm and told me I was under arrest.

"For not having a license?"

"Panhandling and prostitution." He said the words like they soiled his tongue. Then he grinned at the man who had just put a quarter in the pot for "Danny Boy." "Don't that beat all," he said. "A whore with a cornet."

I drew myself up. "It's a trumpet," I said, although why I thought to defend my horn instead of my virtue is a mystery to me.

"And you are Miss Gabriel, right? Come down to save us all."

I argued that I was a professional musician, that I played my horn to earn honest money for my keep, but it was like trying to reason with some outraged rooster. I looked one more time toward the Gusher, hoping to see the long, lank friendly man, but the doorway was empty. The policeman gripped my arm tighter, then bent over and picked up the chamber pot. He shook his head. "If this don't beat all."

He brought me to the police station, to a big desk down in the basement. A man took the chamber pot and my horn and gunnysack, then wrote out a receipt. The receipt didn't say anything about the money in the pot and when I asked about it I was told it would be applied toward the fine. I said I needed my horn back so I could work, once I'd got this license business straightened out.

"We'll see," he said. "We'll see."

I didn't like the sound of that one bit. When Momma said "We'll see," it was usually something you wanted and she didn't want you to have and hoped you'd forget about.

I stiffened up my back. "And just what do you mean by that, sir?"

"Well, if you can't pay the fine . . ." He poked around in the chamber pot. ". . . and I can tell you right now this won't cover it. If you can't pay the fine then we'll have to take this horn against it."

Right then. That very moment. For the first time in my life I was afraid. Real fear does not strike the heart like they say in books. It hits the small of the back and slithers down the legs to the feet, turning them into Oklahoma bedrock. I thought about Alexandra and those spotted cats with the glimmering eyes. I would have given my soul to be in the Dokar Pass enduring blizzards and great beasts that prowled in the night.

Instead, I was taken to a big open room where there were maybe a dozen women, sitting and lying on army cots. The floor was wet like it had been hosed down, but the place smelled like a swamp after a long drought. I was pointed toward one of the cots and handed a blanket that Momma would have boiled and tore up for rags.

The woman on the cot next to mine raised up on one arm and laughed out loud. "What is it?" she said.

The matron told her "it" was panhandling and streetwalking.

"Streetwalking? In that getup?"

"I am a professional musician," I said, getting my legs back. "There has been a case of mistaken identity."

She went on laughing and all the other women joined in. I crawled under the blanket, pulled it over my head, and set to wondering what would become of me. I thought about home, about my brother and sisters and Momma all gathered around the kitchen table, Momma with her finger poised over a passage that would keep our feet on the path of righteousness. My throat got tight and I was afraid I would disgrace myself with loud weeping. I had not cried since I was a baby. Even at Daddy's funeral I was dry-eyed just like Momma, who regarded tears as self-indulgence.

One good thing about being fifteen years old is that hardly anything can keep you awake the whole night, not even thoughts about grievous loss and life imprisonment.

The next morning I woke up to the clanging of steel doors and the rattling of tin plates.

"What's this?" I asked the woman in the next cot.

"Oatmeal," she said. "More or less."

And the stuff in the tin cup was coffee. That's another good thing about being fifteen. You can eat almost anything, and adverse circumstances seldom affect the appetite. While the breakfast got cold (and stiff in the case of the oatmeal) they lined us up to use the toilets and the one sink, which had not seen any elbow grease for ninety-nine years. I had taken exactly one bite of my oatmeal when a woman came through the steel doors and called out my name.

I followed her down the hall to the desk where I'd been checked in the night before. There he was—as big as life when you're happy and twice as welcome—the long, lank homely man from the Gusher.

The officer shoved a paper toward me and told me to sign here. "Ed Shannon has gone your bail," he said. "You are one lucky girl."

I could see I was supposed to do a little jig of gratitude, but the officer's nasty tone of voice put me off. I lifted my chin and handed over my receipt. "I'll have my belongings," I said.

"Those will be kept to apply against the fine."

"But you said this gentleman . . ."

"That's the bail. We're talking here about the fine."

"What fine is that?" asked this Mr. Shannon.

The man, not the same one as the night before, shuffled some papers. "Says here panhandling and prostitution."

Mr. Shannon nodded slow and easy as if he was thinking that over. "Well," he said finally, drawing it out. "I think the arresting officer made an error. This young woman was providing entertainment for our customers at the entrance of our establishment. With our knowledge." When he said "our" it was as if he had Julius Caesar and Henry VIII lined up on his side.

The officer looked down at the paper and read through it, using his finger as a guide. "She'll have to take that up with the judge," he said finally.

Mr. Shannon moved closer to the desk. "She will need her instrument." His tone was mild as a spring day, but you could hear a storm gathering underneath it. "The instrument is her livelihood. You cannot deprive a person of her livelihood on the basis of a misdemeanor."

"Don't say nothing here about any misdemeanor. What it says about her livelihood is that she lives at the Robinson Hotel."

"Circumstantial. As a matter of fact Miss Alexander didn't know the nature of that hotel. She only recently arrived in Tulsa."

"I was planning to move out," I said quickly. "I have a list of places back in my room I was going to go look at today."

The officer frowned and shuffled the papers some more.

"I think you can let her have her things," Mr. Shannon said smoothly, as if something had been settled. "I'll vouch for the fine."

The officer pondered that. He then disappeared behind the swinging doors and came back with my horn, my gunnysack, and the chamber pot. "We keep the money," he said. "That's the rule."

Mr. Shannon nodded in a pleasant way, gathered up my stuff, and motioned for me to go ahead of him. It occurred to me that he was not only a man of obvious good breeding, but one of some considerable standing in this city.

Out on the sidewalk he handed me my horn and the gunnysack. He swung the pot back and forth by its handle. "I don't think you'll be needing this," he said. "You can play inside the restaurant and I'll pay you a weekly salary. There's a boardinghouse near the Gusher that has a room available."

I said that sounded swell to me; then I pointed at the pot, for which I had developed some affection. "I borrowed it," I said. "From the hotel."

"Then we'd better return it before you're accused of grand theft." He stopped beside an open automobile with red leather seats, which turned out to be a 1927 Packard. He opened the door and looked at me, hard.

"How old are you, Cleo?"

"Eighteen," I said, without blinking an eye.

"How old are you really? What is your true age?"

I thought about that. My true age? Fifteen going on thirty-five? A hundred and four in the shade? But I just covered the ground I stood on.

He sighed and put my stuff in the backseat. He asked if I'd like something to eat and I told him no thank you I'd had my breakfast. A person can accept just so much kindness in one helping.

"Did you leave anything at the hotel?"

"Yes," I said, thinking mostly of Alexandra David-Neel.

When we pulled up in front of the Robinson, Mr. Shannon asked me why I had chosen that particular place. I told him that the lobby had looked clean to me and had some nice ferns in it and that I'd never been to Tulsa before so I just had to go on appearances, which he said he hoped I had learned were not always reliable.

There was more trouble to be had inside.

The desk clerk said my rent had been overdue at eight o'clock that morning and they had confiscated my things to cover it. I swear, I had never seen so many people interested in my pitiful little accumulation of possessions.

Mr. Shannon dragged out his wallet again, and I held up the chamber pot. "I'll just return this to the room while you hunt up my things," I told the desk clerk. "I borrowed it."

I had hidden a five-dollar bill in the Gideon Bible, a safe place I thought at the time. It was gone, of course. My worldly lessons were coming thick and fast. And of course the desk clerk didn't know anything about it, but he handed over my satchel after Mr. Shannon paid for the one night that was due. I opened up my satchel. My clothes were all there but my book was missing.

"I had a book on the bureau," I told him.

He shook his head and said he didn't know anything about no book. "Our clientele don't do much reading," he said, tickled as he could be by his own smart mouth.

Then Mr. Shannon leaned across the desk and put his big nose in the man's face. "I'm sure the lady's book is back there somewhere. You've probably just overlooked it."

And that's when it happened.

In my childhood books I'd read about how the man on the white horse swoops down and rescues the fair damsel in distress. I had outgrown those books when I took up with Edith Wharton and Thomas Hardy and Gustav Flaubert. But I hadn't forgotten them. The feelings that began to surge through me were not base like what I'd felt with Willis Henderson. Instead, something selfless and uplifting came over me and settled into my very bones. Right there on the spot, in the lobby of a house of sin, I fell as far and wide in pure love with Ed Shannon as is possible in this round world, and I shouldered that burden with all the joy that was in me. It *is* a burden. Don't let anybody try to tell you any different. We're damn heavy, all of us are. We are bags of stones to those who love us. But there are high passes and wide plains where you cannot go without those bags of stones.

While I pondered that revelation on the nature of pure love the clerk hustled up Alexandra David-Neel from under the counter. Mr. Shannon took my arm and I stepped out beside him like a queen who has just alighted from her blooded steed.

He took me straightaway to the boardinghouse and handed me some money for my rent before we got out of the car. "Don't worry about it," he said. "I'll deduct it from your salary, and I'll see what I can do about the fine."

I thanked him and we went up the long brick walk to this three-story house where he introduced me to a Mrs. Figgs as one of his employees at the Gusher Restaurant. Then he tipped his hat, said he'd see me that evening at work, and walked away, whistling.

Mrs. Figgs looked me over and frowned—understandably—at my appearance. She made it clear at the onset that there was to be no funny business. Fifteen dollars a week included breakfast at 7 A.M. and supper at 6:30 prompt. No guest of the opposite sex was allowed in any room at any time for any reason. That included uncles and cousins and employers. Entertaining was done in the parlor, under, I was given to understand, her own watchful eye. No loud radios or Victrolas, and the door was locked at midnight. No keys were given out, so unless you wanted to sleep on the porch swing you came home in a timely fashion. There was a sign-in sheet in the hallway. The last person in locked the door, and if you didn't like all these rules you could go elsewhere. "You a waitress at the Gusher?" she asked, taking in my overalls again.

"No, ma'am. I'm an entertainer, a musician, this is my costume I'm wearing."

She relaxed a little and said I was to follow her to my room, which was on the third floor. The third floor! Mercy! We are talking here about a girl whose highest point of reference up to that time was the back of a mule. I climbed the stairs with some trepidation, keeping my eyes forward on Mrs. Figgs' backside, which was ample scenery indeed.

The room was in the front and ran the whole width of the house. There was a four-poster covered with a quilt I recognized as the Blazing Star design. Momma had made a little one for Baby Fidelity. It made me feel right at home. The claw-footed bureau had enough drawers for the possessions of my whole family. There was a swinging mirror in which you could see your whole self from head to toe in one viewing. This was, I believe, the first time I had ever seen myself in a full-length mirror, which is very different from a store window or a reflection in clear creek water. Even in my overalls, I was something to look at. An easy chair sat in front of one of the windows with a floor lamp next to it. There were two pictures on the walls. One of Jesus and one of that poor sad Indian on his pinto pony. On one wall there was a bookcase, filled with books. I couldn't help it! I threw my arms around Mrs. Figgs and told her I had for sure died and gone to heaven.

She disentangled herself and showed me the bathroom at the end of the hall. I was to share it with the two other girls who lived on that floor. Rosemary worked at the Rialto as a cashier, and Noreen waited on tables at the Gusher. I would meet them at supper. I was to clean up after myself and keep my personals like my towel and toothbrush in my own room. Mrs. Figgs gave me a sour look and said she would not tolerate tooth powder in the sink or hair in the bathtub drain. Then she reminded me about being prompt for supper, gave a quick sideways grimace, which I gamely took for a smile, and left me to get settled.

The bookcase was a disappointment on close inspection. *The Decline and Fall of the Roman Empire* was the only title I recognized besides a dictionary, a King James Bible, and three volumes of the Book of Knowledge. The rest appeared to be textbooks. I pulled out *The Speaking Telephone, Electric Light and Other Recent Electrical Inventions* by George B. Prescott. Melvin J. Figgs was written in a tidy hand on the first page. Since Mrs. Figgs hadn't mentioned him I divined he'd gone on in one way or another, and had been in a scientific line of work. If he was here, surely his books would be in his own room or in the parlor. I picked up a Book of Knowledge and flipped through it at random. My eye was arrested by the question: CAN A SPIDER'S WEB BE MADE INTO CLOTH? The answer was yes. Seems there used to be a factory in France where they raised spiders and turned their webs into gloves and stockings. The factory failed because of the expense and difficulty of rearing spiders, which tended to eat each other if not kept in separate pens. That was a revelation. Who'd ever think of penning up spiders? Seems that in 1830 a Mr. Daniel Rolt received a silver medal for inventing a spool attached to a little engine which in just two hours wound off eighteen thousand feet of web from twenty-four spiders. Amazing!

I put all three volumes on my bedside table for nightly reading since I was on my own now as far as my formal education was concerned. Then I carried the dictionary to the table under the window and propped it up like the big one that sat on its own stand in Miss Hawkins' library. It looked handy and important. I turned to the Ms. *Misdemeanor:* "Not as heinous as a felony." *Felony:* "Utterly odious or wicked." I was relieved to know my offense was less than wicked.

I unpacked my satchel, took off my costume, put it with my unmentionables and my tea towel in the lower drawer, then hung up my Sunday dress in the closet. I put on Momma's old chenille bathrobe and saw by the clock that it was five hours until suppertime. I was as empty as a dry well and regretful I hadn't accepted Mr. Shannon's offer of a meal. I supposed I could go for a walk and see if I could find a café but at that point I had only a one-dollar bill to last me until payday. I could go downstairs and look for Mrs. Figgs, ask her if there were any cold biscuits left over from breakfast. I decided against it, not wanting her to think I was the sort to ask for special favors.

So, I got my Lhasa book and settled into the chair by the window. The spotted cats were still there when Alexandra woke up in the morning, but they had not bothered her, just as she had known they wouldn't. They watched her and Yongden for a while, through the bushes, then went on their way.

If Alexandra could go through a whole day with nothing in her stomach but a cup of tea—climbing those tall mountains, digging in for a blizzard, fighting off leopards with only thoughts and blessings— then surely I could make it until suppertime.

There were seven of us at the table, including Mrs. Figgs. (I was right about Melvin J. He was nowhere in evidence.) I was introduced as the new girl in number five. Besides Noreen and Rosemary there were the men who lived in the three rooms on the second floor: an elderly gentleman named Mr. Roads (". . . Not like the chickens, not the Greek island, but like the road from here to Oklahoma City. R-O-A-D-S, got that, girlie?"); Amos, who worked in the kitchen at the Gusher; and the Reverend Endicott, who wore a spotless white suit and looked like a movie star.

Everybody smiled and nodded and said they were pleased to make my acquaintance, but their real interest was in what was on the table. I had never seen such a spread, not even at my grandmother's house on Christmas Day. A platter was piled high with fried chicken, and another with roast pork. Pork and chicken at the same meal! I couldn't get over it. And there were sweet potatos *and* mashed potatoes, with giblet gravy and biscuits with honey and butter, and maybe three kinds of fresh vegetables. Mrs. Figgs may have had a tight soul, but she sure knew how to set a table.

I sat next to Rosemary, the cashier at the Rialto, and it turned out she'd been working the day I came to check the movie times, and had heard me playing my horn out in front of the Gusher.

"I'll be playing inside tonight," I said, remembering the tin plates of oatmeal at the jail.

The preacher, who sat on Mrs. Figgs' right, patted his lips with his napkin and inclined his head in my direction. "You play an instrument?" he asked.

"The trumpet," I said.

"How nice." It was hard to tell if he really meant it, so polite was his tone. "Perhaps you could play for us some Sunday at the service."

"The Reverend," said Mrs. Figgs, "preaches a fine sermon at the little white church down by the duck pond." She glanced over at him with a mixture of respect and pure lust.

I'd seen that look a lot of times when the Baptists had the protracted meetings where people would come into Robina and camp for a week or so on the church grounds. As time went on the worshipers would get more and more wild-eyed—especially the women. They'd come down the aisle to Jesus, then disappear into the bushes for hours on end. Momma said the Baptists had it both ways. Once they were saved it didn't matter how they conducted themselves. Momma and Mam— my grandmother—were Presbyterians and held the fundamentalists in low regard. Momma allowed me to play my horn at the revivals because Brother Glover gave me two bits a night. I looked over at this preacher in the white suit and saw the possibility of some spare change.

"Do you know any liturgical music?" he asked.

I excused myself, went to my room, checked my dictionary to make sure I got his meaning, then took out my horn and went back to the head of the staircase. I did a chorus of "Bringing in the Sheaves," then enough of "Just As I Am" to break your heart. When I came back into the dining room I knew from the look on the preacher's face the job was mine.

"How about this Sunday?" he said.

I said: "I have a fee."

Mrs. Figgs took in her breath. "For serving our Lord?"

I gave her my earnest look. "I'm a professional musician, ma'am."

The preacher said he'd have to think about it; then he pulled out a gold watch, looked at it, placed his napkin just so by his plate, got up, and bowed low to Mrs. Figgs. "Splendid repast, madam. Indeed, you do filleth the hungry soul with goodness."

His teeth gleamed. I had never—in life or in magazines—seen a finer-looking man. His eyes were a lilac blue, and his hair, which was not slicked down with hog lard as was the unfortunate fashion, fell across his forehead when he bowed. That forehead was high and smart; his hands were long and slender, and had never seen an honest day's work. I could tell he would make one hell of a preacher.

He told Mrs. Figgs he would have his dessert later. "Apple pie! Oh, madam, how you do spoil us!" Perhaps they could have dessert together if she wasn't otherwise engaged after he'd finished work on his sermon? She'd be honored, of course. I felt a little sorry for her as I watched her watch him leave the room. Talk about hungry souls.

Noreen, at the other end of the table, started picking up plates and I jumped up to help. Rosemary put her hand on my arm. "We take turns," she said. "Mrs. Figgs puts up a duty list in the kitchen."

I sat back down. "Do you like it here?" I asked her in a soft voice.

"Oh my, yes," she said; then she put her hand over her mouth and leaned toward me. "Figgy is a trial, but it's clean and respectable and the food's very good, especially since Reverend Endicott moved in."

Noreen picked up our plates, then stopped in her tracks and stared at the clock on the wall. "Oh good Lord, Rosie, I'm late. Would you finish for me? Ed's picking me up."

"Ed?" Ed. Not *my* Ed. *Surely not my Ed.*

She touched her hair—which I noted was bleached and frizzy—the way girls do when they speak about a boyfriend. "Ed Shannon," she said. "The boss."

I went to work that night with a heavy heart. The man I'd fallen into pure love with was already taken. I told myself it was just as well, and I tried to concentrate on Lhasa and all the reasons why I wanted to go there. Himself greeted me at the cash register near the front of the restaurant. He smiled and looked me up and down. "Next time just bring your costume with you," he said. "You can keep it in the storeroom and get dressed there."

I nodded and wondered where I was to do my act. The place was crowded with round leather booths on two sides and had tables down the middle and on the far wall. Mr. Shannon told me to follow him and we went through the kitchen, then out a swinging door to a stairway. At the bottom of the stairs there was another door. Mr. Shannon knocked twice, paused, then knocked twice again. The door was opened by a big man in a tuxedo. Smoke billowed out; through it I could see booths like those upstairs, and a long bar with a big mirror behind it.

Noreen was there in the shortest skirt I had ever seen on a grown woman. She had a tray of drinks in her hand and when she leaned over to put the glasses down her tits like to spilled out of her blouse. I glanced sideways to see if Ed Shannon was noticing. He was. I wondered if it might even up the competition some if I was to dispense with my tea towel.

He introduced me to the man behind the bar and told him to keep an eye on me. The man—his name was Tully—grinned and said he didn't think anybody would suspect there was a girl under those overalls. Mr. Shannon said all the same he was to be watchful, that I was underage and he didn't want me in any trouble.

"I'm eighteen," I said. I have always been stubborn with my lies.

Mr. Shannon said sure thing and led me to the stage at the end of the room where a Negro man was playing the piano. It was a song I had never heard before but one I would make mine before the end of the evening. He finished with a two-handed flourish. I was impressed.

"Scat," said Mr. Shannon, "this is Cleo. I told you about Cleo."

"The new trumpet man, sure. How 'bout that."

Mr. Shannon said he would see me later, and Scat asked what I wanted to play.

"I like to do the 'St. Louis Blues' first," I said. "It's the introduction to my act." I looked around. "But I usually come in from the side with my gunnysack."

Scat looked dubious and rubbed his chin. I could tell he had some reservations about Mr. Shannon's sidewalk talent. I explained how I worked, being surprised by the audience and digging around in the gunnysack for my horn and all that.

"Sounds really nice, honey, thing is these folks is already about three sheets to the wind. I don't think they'd recognize such fine touches. This ain't the Cotton Club, you know."

"What's that?"

His eyes lit up. "Where the Duke's playing in Harlem. If folks talk or get rowdy during the show, they's asked to leave. How 'bout you just take out your horn now and give these people a tune. What key you doing it in?"

"I don't know," I said, my eyes on my feet. I was truly shamed by that admission. "I haven't learned keys." I was sure Scat would call Mr. Shannon over and tell him he'd made a big mistake. But he didn't. He told me to take off and he'd follow.

"And not too loud," he whispered. "These folks like to concentrate on their drinking."

So, we did it like he said. He was right about the audience. I'd had more attention out on the street. I told him how I usually asked if anybody had any requests. He said I could try that if I wanted. He said it was up to me. I went to the edge of the riser and held out my arms, but nobody paid me any mind. It was my first experience as a musician being part of the furniture. We played a couple more soft ones. He was so good, we were so good together, I started to feel frisky.

"Let's do 'Bill Bailey,' " I said.

He shook his head. "Nah. Too loud."

"Let's do it anyway. Just once. Please."

He shrugged in a what-the-hell sort of way. We did it. By the time we finished people were clapping and stomping and having a fine old time. Tully came over from the bar and said that would be enough of that.

"But the people liked it," I said, all hepped up on the attention.

"Sure. And they can hear you all the way to the sheriff's station. Listen here, young lady, this is a nice quiet private club where the customers can get quietly, privately drunk. That's the deal we've got with the law. Besides, if they listen, they don't drink. Got it?"

Scat just ran his fingers over the keyboard and grinned, but I snapped to. Tully was a little man, shorter than me even, with a big bald spot and little gold-rimmed glasses. He didn't look like much, but his voice had tall authority. "Got it," I said.

So, Scat and I played quietly. In truth, we entertained each other. We played some of the songs I knew, mostly old stuff. Then we started in on his. He'd play it through once by himself. Then he'd do the lyrics with me noodling along behind him. Then he'd back me and by that time I had the melody nailed shut. Scat shook his head in amazement and said he'd never heard such an ear before. Not even in New Orleans. Not even in Chicago.

Every once in a while I'd look up and catch Mr. Shannon watching me, his arms folded, his head keeping time to the music. A couple of times he even poked a customer and started up some applause. That night I learned "Can't Help Lovin' That Man," "Make Believe," "My Heart Stood Still," and "Thou Swell."

I played them all for Ed Shannon.

3

A MONTH LATER I BOUGHT A UNITED States postal order for twenty-five dollars made out to Momma. By that time, thanks to Mr. Shannon, the charges against me had been dropped, my confiscated earnings had been returned to me, and I was almost square with Himself. He was going on a business trip to Hot Springs, Arkansas, and I asked him to mail the postal order from there as a part of my bread crumb strategy. He took Noreen with him, which sent me into a deep depression. He didn't seem to notice I was a grown woman. He was bossy and protective like you are with a favorite little cousin. But at least he paid me some attention. Now he was to be gone for a whole week with a woman beneath him in every way possible.

The night after he left I read, as usual, from my Book of Knowledge, a volume full of such deep questions as WHERE DOES THE DAY BEGIN? WHERE DOES A THOUGHT COME FROM? and WHY DOES A TREE GROW STRAIGHT, AS A RULE? That night's question made me sad. The question was: WHERE DOES THE RAINBOW END? The answer is: It ends nowhere. That's not the sad part although it does set you to pondering your life somehow. A rainbow is due to tiny drops of water that reflect the sunlight in *one's own eyes.* It's not really there so it can't really end. And, no two people see exactly the same rainbow because no two pair of eyes are ever in the same place at the same time. Which means: You can never stand close enough to another human being so you'll see the same rainbow.

That's the sad part.

I played at the speakeasy six nights a week from eight until eleven, sometimes eleven-thirty depending on the crowd. During the day I got to know the city, fed the ducks at the pond, and studied *The Decline and Fall of the Roman Empire,* having abandoned, temporarily, my passion for Lhasa. Truth is, I languished.

The Reverend Endicott kept at me about playing my horn on Sundays at his church. First he tried to convince me I should do it as pay-

27

ment to the Lord for the gift of music that had been bestowed on me. Then he offered me a better deal. He said he would average the collections over the past month, and after I started with him, I'd get ten percent of anything over that. He said it was like working on a commission. I said, "You must think I'm feebleminded."

It wasn't that I objected to doing a little work for the Lord. I'd always liked church music, and I really missed "The Battle Hymn of the Republic," which Tully would not allow me to play at the Gusher. It was the Reverend himself and my reaction to him that troubled me. I was attracted to him in a way that was not seemly, and I was thankful I had my pure, uplifting love for Ed Shannon to keep me from giving this preacher consideration as a person of the opposite sex, and all the danger that entails. He would look at me out of those lilac eyes and I'd feel as naked as a horse chestnut tree in January. He would touch me on my shoulder, or worse, the bare part of my arm, and I'd have to go get myself a tall glass of cool water. No question, I had the toes of one foot square on the border of the Wilderness of Sin.

But I kept an eye on myself, and things probably would've worn themselves out, as things have a way of doing, and I would've moved on toward Lhasa. If Noreen hadn't opened her big mouth.

Scat and I were taking ten at the bar with her and Tully, listening to her twaddle on about long shots and how Ed Shannon could sure pick horses. Himself came in from upstairs and joined us. Noreen put her arm around him and shoved up against him. He patted her bottom like he knew it as well as his own, then smiled his cousin smile on me and asked how things were going.

"Just fine," I lied. "Thank you for mailing my letter."

He shrugged away that small favor. "Anybody giving you any trouble? You been looking after her, Tully?"

Tully gave a snort. "Trouble? She looks like she just came in from Sunday school. Who's to give her any trouble?"

Tully had demanded that I give up my tramp costume in favor of a dress. The only dress I owned was the navy blue crepe with the wide lace collar. Tully said I ought to spend some of my considerable salary on an evening outfit and some *shoes*. Every night he trained his little gold spectacles on my brown brogans and pretended to have a heart attack.

"I will. I *will*," I'd tell him. "I have financial obligations I have to tend to first."

So, without fail, Tully had some smart thing to say about my attire. That night I could see that Noreen didn't appreciate so much attention paid to me and my wardrobe. She tossed her head back and lifted her chin up like a movie star. That frizzy, bleached, dry mess of hair didn't even stir. She ran her fingers across Mr. Shannon's neck again and pushed so hard against him I feared for his breath. Then she pointed a long red fingernail at me and laughed out loud.

"Look at Cleo," she giggled. "Just look at that kid."

They all stared and I glanced down at myself to see if my slip was hanging.

She whispered in his ear but you could have heard her down on South Main. "Our little Cleo is sweet on you, Ed."

I almost died of mortification.

Noreen kept on stroking his neck, and the others stood there looking at me like I was a yearling doe caught in a leg trap. Mr. Shannon pondered his shoes and I knew he felt real embarrassment for me. I also knew that he regarded me as the fifteen-year-old virgin I truly was.

In a slow deliberate motion, he took Noreen's hand from off his neck, giving her a hard look that caused her to stop snickering. "Don't be silly," he told her. "Cleo and I are good friends. Isn't that right, Cleo? We're like family."

I bit my tongue and nodded that was right. At the time I had no idea of just how right it was.

The following Saturday morning Rosemary and I went to the Lerner's dress shop next to Kresses. Rosemary dressed real nice, and as I had no experience with store-bought clothes I had gone to her room the day before and humbled myself with that admission.

Rosemary was a friendly, straightforward girl, the product of a failed farm just like me. She'd been in the city for two years at the time I met her, was eighteen years old, and while she had learned city ways, she hadn't been spoiled by them. She sent money home just like I did, but did not feel obligated to send as much because her daddy got work from time to time in the oil fields north of Drumright. We were on our way to Lerner's when I told her about my bread crumb strategy, which I thought was pretty clever.

Rosemary stopped right in the middle of the sidewalk and gave me a disapproving look. "You ought to let your momma know your whereabouts," she said. "Folks feel a lot easier about their children if they can place them on a map."

"Not Momma," I said. "She thinks cities are evil places. She thinks God never travels any further than Wagoner, and then only on business." I shook my head. "I don't know where she gets it. Mam—my grandmother—prays and goes to church regular, but she's not, you know, silly about it. Maybe from my granddaddy. I don't know. Mam and Momma don't talk much about him. Mam says Momma was always stiff-necked, even when she was a little girl."

Rosemary nodded encouragement and we leaned up against a store window while I told about my family, a slippery item to contain in an explanation. How Momma was thirty-five years old when I was born—her first child. Most women had a houseful by then and she'd had offers but she regarded herself as a spinster by choice. She took pride in her curative business. People came to her with their own and their animal's illnesses. She even fixed wild creatures when they turned up maimed or sickly.

But one day my daddy blew into town, younger than her, tall, blond, with his light brown eyes with green and gold flecks—that handsome Irish devil, Mam called him—and swept Momma square off her feet. My daddy had come west looking for oil. Word was that it just seeped right into your shoes wherever you walked. But he didn't have the price of any likely land. My momma had her own land. Almost a hundred acres you couldn't raise a good crop of hell on. Mam said Daddy took a whiff and thought he smelled black gold.

"So they got married," I said. "Momma tried her best to bring him to God, but he never came. Every time he went off to play his horn in the city she'd tell him not to bother to come home. He always came home. She always took him in."

Rosemary smiled and took my hand in a friendly way. "See there," she said. "That proves it."

"Proves what?"

"That she'd want to know where you are even if she didn't like it."

Because of that conversation with Rosemary I began sending the postal orders to Momma with a Tulsa postmark. No return address, I wasn't ready for that, but postmarked honestly. In truth I felt much better about it. Rosemary always had a way of suggesting a thing that made you think you would have arrived at that very conclusion yourself if you hadn't been temporarily caught up in other vital matters.

The window of the Lerner's shop was crammed full of dresses and robes and even some unmentionables. I stood in awe and wonderment of so much beauty. Rosemary hustled me inside and started pulling things off the racks, holding them up to me, turning her head this way and that. Finally she collected about a half dozen prospects over her arm and steered me into a little curtained-off cubicle. We ended up with a couple that weren't so much dresses as extra skin. I told her they were so tight across my rib cage I'd not be able to get any wind into my horn.

"Tully said I should have an evening dress," I said. We took another tour around the store. Rosemary put her hands on her hips and said we'd need to go up to Miss Ada's, where the quality was higher.

It was almost noon before we found my new costume. Two identical satin dresses, one black and one white. In truth each one looked like a princess slip, except floor length and with a little train that dragged behind. They were cut low and had skinny little straps that were to have the full responsibility of holding up my wonders.

Rosemary pronounced me glamorous, and Miss Ada took all the money I had in the world. I asked why they cost so much seeing they were so plain. There were other dresses with fringe and ruffles and imitation roses that were not so dear. Miss Ada said those were for ladies that needed gelding. At least I thought at the time she said gelding, which necessity I pondered but did not pursue.

Rosemary said next week we'd shop for shoes and a long string of imitation pearls. Meanwhile she would treat me at the Kresses counter, where we ordered grilled cheese sandwiches and Coca-Cola, and I steered the conversation around to Noreen.

"She's from Oklahoma City," said Rosemary.

"You think she stays at Mr. Shannon's place those nights when she doesn't come home?" I said this in an offhand, disinterested way.

Rosemary shrugged. "Probably."

"She looks too old for him."

"Think so?"

"Don't you?"

"I hadn't thought about it. Depends on what you think is old, I guess. She's probably twenty-four, five, someplace in there. She has a little boy that stays with her mother."

I held my breath. "Mr. Shannon's?" I didn't want to hear the answer.

"Goodness no. She's been at the Gusher for less than a year. Her little boy is by a previous marriage. Sometimes her mother brings him to visit at the boardinghouse." She sipped her Coca-Cola and I saw a light go on in her eyes. "You interested in Ed Shannon?"

I waved that away, the furthermost thing from my mind. "Of course not. It's just that he's been so kind to me, and he's such a good sort I hate to think of him mixed up with somebody so trashy as Noreen. Anyway, I can't take on any extra baggage of affection just now. I have these plans to travel. I'm going to Lhasa when I have a stake."

"Lhasa?"

"It's close by India. I have this book about a woman who spent half her life trying to get there. She finally made it when she was fifty-five years old."

Rosemary looked thoughtful. "Then what?"

"What do you mean?"

"I mean what did she do when she got there?"

"I've not got to that part yet, but I'm sure she'll get there full of spunk. She's dyed her hair black with ink and dresses up like a beggar as a disguise because foreigners aren't allowed in Lhasa. It's a holy place. It's called the Forbidden City."

I suddenly felt a deep disloyalty to Alexandra, having let her slip from my mind that past month. I said: "I haven't had much time to read since I got to Tulsa."

"But why on earth would anybody want to go to India of all places? That's what I want to know."

I liked Rosemary a lot and I knew we had the underpinnings of true friendship, but I could see she would never understand the heart and mind of someone like Alexandra David-Neel. I turned the conversation back to Noreen. In an offhand way I asked if Mr. Shannon went around with anybody else. Rosemary said she didn't know, she said that Ed Shannon was regarded as something of a mystery. There were those who said he was a spoilt priest. Others said he'd been to Antarctica. He used to be high up in the police department, she knew that for sure, and that was why nobody bothered his speakeasy business.

"He left the department after the riots, that's all I know. There was some kind of trouble after the riots. Did this woman travel by herself all the way to this Lhasa place?"

"No, she hired a holy man to go with her. His name was Yongden and she adopted him later."

"A holy man? Like a preacher? Like the Reverend Endicott?"

I shivered. "No, ma'am, not like the Reverend one bit."

"Isn't he the most handsome man you ever laid eyes on? I could just fall in his lap every time I clear away his plate. I wouldn't of course, I mean, any fool can see that man is *dang*erous. And when he looks at *you*, Cleo! Doesn't it give you chicken skin all over?"

I agreed that the Reverend Endicott was a well-made man. I was not ready to share my true feelings about him, partly because I didn't understand them myself.

We finished our lunch and walked around town looking in the store windows. Rosemary said we could pick out my new shoes then come back next week and pay for them. But I told her I needed to stop by the public library and arrange for a card. I had made that decision while we sat at the lunch counter. Unrequited love was no good reason to neglect one's education.

"Why don't you come along and get one too?"

Rosemary shook her head. "Oh no," she said. "I just read magazines." She blushed and looked away. "I don't have the head for books, I only finished the sixth grade."

"I could pick out a book for you. I could pick out something you'd like just as well as a magazine." And as a matter of truth I did. I got her a Mary Roberts Rinehart and in no time at all she could figure out who committed the crime by page twenty-four and a half, and she soon went on to finer, deeper things. But at that moment, on that warm spring day in Tulsa, Oklahoma, Rosemary and I were still trying each other on to see how we fit.

She told how it was in Drumright, and I told how it was in Robina. I told her about Willis Henderson—not all of it—and she shared some of Tommy Ray Rickles. Rosemary wasn't as big as a minute. She told how when she was born her arms were so tiny her mother could fit her wedding ring on her wrist.

"The only reason I didn't die was because she wrapped me up and put me in the warming oven. I stayed in the warming oven for six weeks."

So I told about when my daddy got poked in the eye by the hay rake and my momma cured him with toad-frogs.

"She said the wound needed to be kept cool so it would heal. She sent us kids down to the pond to gather up a bunch of little frogs, then she tied their legs together. She spread a thin cloth over daddy's sore eye and applied a frog. When that frog got warm she just changed it for another one."

And we exchanged our genealogy. Rosemary told how her folks were French and German and had come to Oklahoma from Ohio. She said the famous French artist, Manet, was a distant cousin on her mother's side. On the spot I invented an Irish poet to be a close relation of my daddy's, and I told how Mam was Creek Indian and born in Oklahoma when it was still Indian Territory.

Then I told her something close to my heart. I told her how my momma had never once spoken my name.

"Why not?"

"She thinks it's a wicked name, because of Queen Cleopatra's behavior."

"Then why did she give it to you?"

"She didn't. My daddy did, had it written on the birth certificate without her permission. I don't think she ever forgave either one of us."

"What does she call you?"

"Daughter."

Rosemary pondered that and said, "No question she's forgiven you if she calls you Daughter. Mothers don't hold grudges against their own children."

We were as thick as Ali Baba's thieves by the time we got back to the boardinghouse. With frogs and warming ovens and family history, we had cleared the ground for the deeper knowledge and unspeakable deeds that would come later.

We went to the kitchen and checked the new duty list. Rosemary was clearing and I was setting table. Which meant I would have to take my bath early because I was now going to work at seven-thirty on

Saturdays, and Noreen had a snit-fit if I was soaking myself in the tub when she wanted in the bathroom.

I was gathering my towel and toothbrush when there was a knock on the door. Rosemary came in carrying a pair of black patent-leather pumps.

"See if these fit you." She held them out and I could see she was shy about the offer.

"But those are your good ones," I said.

"I can get along without them till next Saturday." She pointed at my feet. "You can't wear your pretty new dresses with those things."

It was true. "Those things" were worn and brown and laced up like a man's. In truth they were a pair my brother Ethan had outgrown.

"But you're so little . . ."

"Not my feet." She lifted one up as evidence. "Daddy says I would've been a proper height if so much of me wasn't turned under." She held out the shoes again. "Come on, give them a try. And put on these stockings, that'll make them go on easier. And the garters."

They were a close fit, but oh how they did shine. I accepted them gratefully and said I'd see her at dinner.

When I came back from the bathroom, having cleaned out the sink and checked the tub for hair, there was another knock on the door. I figured it was Rosemary again.

"Come on in," I said. "It's open." I had my towel wound around me like a Hawaiian native.

"Well. Well. Well."

It was the preacher and he surely did like what he saw. I stood there for a second, dripping from my wet head, then I lunged for the closet and spoke to him from around the corner of the door. "I thought you were Rosemary."

"No," he said. "No, I'm not Rosemary." He just looked at me, a slow smile spreading across his face. He said, "You are certainly pleasing in my sight," like he was giving a blessing, but the fire in his eyes could have melted all of Alaska.

"Mrs. Figgs says no one of the opposite sex in the rooms."

"Mrs. Figgs was not referring to a man of the cloth on God's business. I want to talk to you about the service."

"After supper in the parlor," I said. "I've got to go to work early and I'm setting table tonight."

He didn't move a muscle. Just stood there watching me right through the closet door.

My soul writhed and groveled: *Have mercy on me, O Lord, for I am weak. Psalms 6:2. Be merciful unto me, O God, for man would swallow me up. Psalms 56:1. Save me, O God, for the waters are come into my soul. Psalms 69:1.* Oh Lord, oh Lord, the flesh does have a mind of its own! I wanted him to see me. I knew that in my rotten heart. I wanted to step out of the closet and drop that towel like the last of Salome's veils. If there was ever a girl in need of one of her momma's cornbread muffins, I was her.

"After supper," I repeated, making the words as cold as I could under the heated circumstances. He smiled, having read my mind like a dirty book, and he took his sweet time leaving. I slumped against the door and sent up another request for my salvation. No question I had inherited my daddy's hot blood.

After supper, which was Figgy's speciality—catfish, breaded in corn meal, spuds, okra and green tomatoes, all deep-fried in pork fat—I met with Reverend Endicott in the parlor. He said his piano player was going to be gone for two weeks and he would deeply appreciate my filling in just on Sunday mornings. He had someone for the evening service. He said he would pay me a flat fee of ten dollars.

I gave it serious consideration. We were not talking about commissions and percentages now, we were talking hard cash. Because of my new costumes I was going to be dead broke until next Friday, and I would starve before I'd ask Mr. Shannon for an advance of salary. I realized I could've—*should*'ve bought one dress and put the other on layaway. Miss Ada said I could do that, but I had been overtaken by an attack of neediness from my past.

Sure, back home, we always knew there would be something to eat. At the very least a bowl of clabber and some cornbread with fresh butter. Our Jersey gave five quarts a day, half of that rising to the top. At the next to very least we'd have what Momma called gallimaufry, which was her name for a soup she made from potato water and whatever else she could scare up.

But when there was fresh pork from Mam's, we tended to eat it all at one sitting with no thought of tomorrow. And even though I could only check out three books at a time from Miss Hawkins' library, and she would warn me to make them last, I'd have all three gobbled up before the week was out. A person who has never been poor can't begin to understand poverty. It's the rich people who save some for a rainy day. Rich people starving in a lifeboat on the open sea would be more apt to survive than poor people. Say the rich man caught himself a fish. He'd put some of it by against rescue. The poor man would figure the odds against rescue on prior experience and fill up his stomach while he could.

I was giving that ten dollars my full attention when Noreen stuck her head in the parlor and said Tully was picking her up and did I want a ride. This interruption was an answer to my prayers for guidance, a sign from On High. I told the preacher I was sorry but I had other plans for Sunday morning. "I appreciate the offer," I said, politely, leaving the door open just a crack. For a moment I thought he was going to up the ante, but he just touched my shoulder ever so lightly and left the parlor. Where his hand had rested, the flesh sizzled. I swear.

"Well, are you coming or not?" Noreen had taken to treating me like a something underfoot. Like I treated my sister, Sarah. "Are you ready?"

"I just got to get my dress."

She rolled her eyes and I knew she was thinking about my poor pitiful navy blue crepe that had become the butt of so many jokes. I ran up the stairs, which progression no longer made me dizzy, got my new black dress and folded it into Miss Ada's pink box, along with Rosemary's stockings and garters and patent-leather shoes. I could hardly wait to see Noreen's face fall down around her knees when she got a look at me in my new costume. And Tully. And the customers. And my good friend, Mr. Ed Shannon.

As it happened, Mr. Shannon had gone off on another business trip, this time to St. Louis, this time without bleached, frizzy, mean-mouthed Noreen. This cheered me considerably.

I went directly to the downstairs storeroom, which Tully had turned into a place for me to dress. It had a couple of orange crates and a mirror that added about fifty pounds of wavy flesh. You had to hold your head just right to keep your nose out of your eyes. But I wasn't concerned about such trifles that night.

I had read in Edith Wharton about coming-out parties where a girl was presented to society in all her finery, and people commenced to take notice of her as a grown woman. This was to be my coming-out party. I stood in front of that wavy mirror in nothing but my drawers and stocking feet, and pulled the black satin dress down over my head. My nipples showed right through the cloth, which Rosemary had said was the general idea, but my drawers made creases around my hips. No question. They had to go. I shook my head to fluff out my hair like Rosemary said, then I put on the war paint I'd bought at Kresses. When I finished I faced a stranger in the mirror. I was that smoldering, sloe-eyed Egyptian queen my daddy had named me for.

Not without effort, I got my feet into Rosemary's shoes and sashayed into the club. Tully and Noreen just stood there with their mouths open, and there were whistles and catcalls from the regulars.

Scat took the transformation in stride. "Where's your horn?" he said, dry as a powder house.

I stopped dead in my tracks. "Oh mercy!" Had I forgotten it? Had I left it at home? Had I become so enchanted with myself as an Edith Wharton debutante I had clean forgot I had to work for a living?

"It's in the storeroom," I said, in a meek little voice. "I *hope* it's in the storeroom."

He motioned for Noreen and she came over with a look in her eye that would have wilted a cabbage. "Would you please fetch Miss Cleo's instrument from her dressing room?" Noreen went off in a huff and Scat gave me a little half bow. "We can't have you ruining your entrance, now can we?"

Noreen came right back with my trumpet and I thought for a minute she was going to bean me with it. "I ain't no lady-in-waiting, you know."

"I'm sorry, Noreen. Thank you. I'm much obliged."

She wagged her finger under my nose. "If Ed Shannon has in mind to do a little cradle snatching, that's his business, but don't expect me to pick up the pieces. You hear?"

"Yes, Noreen, I hear." Oh boy, did I ever hear. This was the first indication I'd had that maybe things were not all peaches and cream between them. No question it was the old green-eyed monster that had just put words in Noreen's mouth. Maybe Ed Shannon had been saying appreciative things about me. Maybe Ed Shannon spoke his innermost desires aloud in his sleep?

4

IN THE WEEKS TO COME I LEARNED FROM
Scat about Ed Shannon's mysterious past. Not all of it, of course, but
those parts Himself had been willing to share both on purpose and by
inadvertence. He was not a spoilt priest that Scat knew of, nor had he
been to Antarctica. When Scat had told me all he knew, or was willing
to tell, he suggested I visit the morgues of the three Tulsa newspapers
for further information.

This is what I learned:

Edward Hamilton Shannon was the only son of a famous Chicago
judge, now deceased. His mother—also deceased—was a Hamilton
from Roanoke, Virginia. He studied law at Northwestern University,
which accounted for his assured manner and the discussion about
"livelihood" and "misdemeanors" with the officer at the Tulsa jail
where I was wrongly incarcerated.

He had been sent to Tulsa in February of 1920 when he was only
twenty-seven years old by none other than the attorney general of the
United States at the personal behest of the lieutenant governor of
Oklahoma. He was sent because a mob had stormed the city jail and
hanged one of the inmates in plain sight of outraged Tulsa citizens.
Mr. Shannon's job was to correct "anarchy and police inefficiency," at
which, in spite of his relative youth, he had enjoyed considerable success in Chicago.

He had made progress in that direction when on June 1, 1921, the
Tulsa Tribune ran a short article with the headline POLICE NAB NEGRO
FOR ATTACKING GIRL IN ELEVATOR. The girl in question claimed that
one Dick Rowland, nineteen years old and a student at the local business college, had molested her on the way to the third floor.

At 7:30 that night, throngs of blacks and whites gathered outside
the jail where Mr. Shannon had placed the suspect for safekeeping.
There were rumors of lynching but the mayor believed them to have
no firm foundation. Ed Shannon was not so sure. He had the elevator
in the jail run up to the top floor, and he blocked the stairways with
armed policemen.

He then sent his Negro deputy, who he had worked with in Chicago and had brought with him to Tulsa on special assignment, to talk to the colored element of the mob while he himself attempted to reason with the whites. They had some success but did not rest easy. For that reason Mr. Shannon sent a secret telegram to the lieutenant governor asking for help, but the telegram arrived too late.

War broke out on Archer and Cincinnati, north of the Frisco tracks, and ended with the Greenwood District, called "Little Africa," burned to the ground. The papers reported some two and a half million dollars' worth of damage. The dead were variously estimated at between thirty and five hundred.

These are the words I read in the *Tulsa Tribune* dated June 25, 1921, describing how a grand jury, under District Judge Valjean Biddison, handed down the following decision: "There was no mob spirit among the whites (who assembled quietly) until the arrival of armed Negroes." The decision further noted that these armed Negroes were not representative of the colored community, but were a handful of "militants pressing for equal rights and social equality."

Judge Biddison said the best way to avoid such confrontations in the future was to prohibit the "indiscriminate mingling of white and colored people in dance halls and other places of amusement."

The editors of the *Tribune* were in agreement with the jury's findings. They said the uprising had long been in the "planning" and described the whites that gathered outside the jail as "largely a curious, good-natured crowd." They blamed the "bad element of niggertown" and the Negro newspaper, the *Tulsa Star,* for preaching "so-called equality" and stirring racial unrest.

The editors of the *Tulsa World* had another view. They laid the blame on the Invisible Empire—that is, the Klan. It was during my research into the mystery of Ed Shannon that I discovered the virtues of a town having itself more than one newspaper.

On September 21, 1921, all charges were dropped against Dick Rowland. The elevator operator had declined to testify against him in a court of law. This act further offended the leaders of the Ku Klux Klan, who had hoped for more blood. They began to draw their own. They would abduct somebody they had it in for, take them someplace in the dark of night where the victim would be stripped naked and flogged with a bullwhip.

Mr. Shannon's Negro deputy was one of those so treated. Mr. Shannon found him dead of his wounds, tied to a tree in the city park on Eleventh Street.

The next day, in broad daylight, 1,700 men in their white robes and hoods marched down the middle of Main Street. There was a picture in the *Tulsa World* of the three leaders on horseback, the one in the middle carrying an American flag.

Scat said Mr. Shannon arrested two Klansmen for the murder of his deputy, but they were out on bail in less than an hour. He gathered more evidence, got another warrant, and arrested the same two men again with the same result. That's when Ed Shannon gave up on law and order. He resigned his commission with the police department and went into the restaurant business. He opened the speakeasy, Scat said, because he believed Prohibition to be unconstitutional.

He would never speak of any of this to me. When I asked him about it, he would shake his head and change the subject. One of the questions in my Book of Knowledge was IS THERE A REASON FOR EVERYTHING THAT HAPPENS? The answer was Yes. That everything has a cause and that the consequences are endless.

In August, Noreen went off with a customer, a bootlegger from Coffeyville, Kansas. I was never so glad in my life to see somebody's shirttail flapping in the breeze. And for more than one reason. A woman of middle age, Mildred Ashcroft, moved into Noreen's room. Quiet and refined, she was from Boston and had come to teach English at Tulsa Central High School. We hit it off the day she moved in as I helped her bring up her belongings. She had three big boxes of BOOKS, which I was allowed to unpack and arrange in her bookcase. In thanks, she gave me *Lolly Willows* by Sylvia Townsend Warner, which a friend had sent her all the way from London. Besides that, I was able to go back to taking my long, comforting soaks in the bathtub and Miss Ashcroft never once banged on the door or yelled at me to hurry it up.

Noreen's absence made not a whit of difference in Ed Shannon's attitude toward me, nor had my high-priced costumes. His eyes did widen the first time he saw me in my black satin, but as far as I could tell the sight did not cause him any sleepless nights. He did, however, take a special interest in the customers who began to hang around the piano when Scat and I finished a set. He would amble over and engage my admirer in a spirited conversation about the weather or some current sporting event. When one of them would offer to buy the little lady a drink, Mr. Shannon would tell him solemnly that alcohol causes trumpet players to lose their lip. And he arranged for Amos to come down and tend bar while Tully drove me home after work. So we progressed all the way from favorite cousin to Dutch uncle in just under five months' time.

He did say one thing that let me know he was not totally blind to my physical attributes. When Tully said I'd be more in fashion if I would adopt the flat look and have my hair bobbed, Mr. Shannon pretended to look horrified and said, "What Providence has bestowed, let not high fashion take away."

All the same, Noreen wasn't gone three and a half minutes before Himself started bringing around another girl. She was of a finer sort than Noreen, but still not the kind a man with a middle name like Hamilton was apt to marry. I let that thought comfort me and went on about my business.

On September 22, 1927, I lost all my savings. Seems I inherited not only my daddy's hot blood, but also his bad luck at gambling. I bet on Jack Dempsey.

We all crowded around the radio Tully had put in the center of the bar, and listened to Graham McNamee describe what was called the Battle of the Ages. Dempsey had lost to Gene Tunney the year before but everybody, including and especially Tully, said it was a fluke. Dempsey was famous for this remark to his wife: "Honey, I forgot to duck." Everybody went around saying those words when anything went wrong. "I forgot to duck." Tully, who placed my bet for me and called it money in the bank, was confident Jack Dempsey would win this one by an early knockout.

Like Mr. McNamee said, the old "Iron Mike" plunged in recklessly and lashed a long wicked left to the jaw. Tunney toppled in the seventh round. Problem was, Dempsey stood over him like a buzzard instead of going off to his corner so the count could begin. Tully banged on the radio and hollered at the top of his lungs, "Go to your corner! Go to your corner, you damn fool!" We all joined in and yelled it again and again—"GO TO YOUR CORNER!"—until Dempsey finally took notice. But it was too late.

So there was the famous "long count" controversy and I lost close to a hundred dollars; the twenty-five I meant to send Momma on the first of the month with some extra for her to buy something nice for her birthday, my savings for Lhasa, and the rent money.

Gone. All of it gone.

After the fight was over Scat sat down at the piano and sang, "If I ever get my haaaaands on a dollar bill agiiiiiiiiiinnnn, I'll squeeze iiiittt till the eagllle grinnnnnsssss."

I could have cried. Oh Lord, I could have cried.

My rent was due on Monday, and Figgy was very particular about its timeliness. Once when I was a day late I was not allowed at the supper table. She would extend up to two days' grace on the roof over your head but if you didn't pay on time you didn't eat. And that was that.

So, after breakfast on the morning following the big fight, I politely asked Reverend Endicott if I could speak to him privately in the parlor. I told him flat out that I would be willing to play my horn at both the morning and evening services for a total of fifteen dollars.

"And what has caused this sudden change of heart?" he asked. "I thought you had other plans."

"I need the money," I told him honestly. "I need the money for my rent on Monday morning."

He thought that over. "So, you're talking about just this coming Sunday? Not future ones?"

"No, sir. If it works out you like my playing, which I have every reason to believe you will, I'd like to work for you on a regular basis."

"For your rent? Don't they pay you well at the . . . the restaurant?"

"They pay me very well but I have heavy financial obligations."

"Ahhh," he said, bringing the tips of his long fingers together. "Money answereth all things?"

The Reverend Endicott had no way of knowing he was dealing with a girl who had read Scripture through three times over, besides an extra helping of it every night after supper. I smiled and looked him dead in the eye.

"Ecclesiastes."

That tickled him. "All right, Cleo, we'll make it fifteen this time, as you have a genuine need, but in the future—if it works out, as you say—I will pay the ten dollars I offered previously. That is all my conscience will allow me to take from God's poor."

God's poor, my left foot! It was beyond my understanding how a smart girl like myself could be attracted to such a horse's behind. I agreed. I was up the creek and he had the paddle. "What time should I come?"

"You can walk over with me after breakfast. You'll need to speak with the pianist about the songs she has planned. There may be changes required."

"Not likely," I said. "I know them all."

He looked me up and down. I had on my newest flapper dress from the Lerner's shop. "Have you anything suitable to wear in the Lord's house?"

I sighed and thought about my pitiful old navy blue crepe crowded into the back of the closet by all the finery I had acquired over the summer, which excess was one of the reasons I was in this fix. "Yes," I said. "I have something suitable." I thanked him and went directly to my room to write a letter to Momma.

This is what I wrote:

> *Dear Momma:*
> *The money will be a little late this month and a little short. I have had some unforeseen expenses but nothing I can't handle. You will be pleased to know I play my horn at a church nearby where I also attend services. Also, I have learned from the Book of Knowledge which I study nightly that the Bible contains 1,189 chapters, 31,253 verses and 773,746 words. I thought you would find that interesting.*

I dated it the next day in order to make it the truth.

After I finished the letter, Rosemary and I went window shopping, which we usually did on Saturdays. Then she stood me to a grilled cheese sandwich at Kresses before we went to the public library to return our books and check out more. Rosemary, under my guidance, was now reading poetry in addition to her regular detective novels. I thought it was all this poetry reading that had affected her personality, making her softer and more vague than was her wont to be, but I was to learn different. After we got our books we went to the pond to feed the ducks and have a literary conversation before the three-o'clock matinee, which Rosemary got us into every Saturday for free.

The maples in the park were the color of fire, not yet dry, not yet ready to let go, and there was the smell of woodsmoke from some secret place. The pond sparkled in the sunlight. It was rumored to be bottomless; there was even a sign that said DANGER—DEEP WATER.

That's where I was—in deep water. It wasn't losing the money I felt so bad about. That's the chance you take, and like as not I'd be placing more bets once Tully got over his remorse about my losses. I didn't blame him one bit and told him so. In spite of his confidence in Jack Dempsey I knew going in that there was no such animal as a sure thing. What troubled me was my total lack of temperance, and inability to see up the road aways, to see you had to keep something back for emergencies—like food and shelter and bad luck. It was my tendency to go whole hog that bothered me.

I lay back on the grass and announced to Rosemary and the sky and the ducks and the leaves and the clouds, "I do hereby make a resolution."

She looked up from her book. "What's that, Cleo?"

"I do hereby resolve to live my life with more regard for the needs and possibilities of the future."

Rosemary nodded the way people do when they've got something else on their mind besides what you're saying. "Just listen to this," she said. And she read with expression from her new book of poems. "My love brings me honey; white, wild and sweet. / He takes my hand, he kneels at my feet. / I taste wild white honey on his tongue. / I hear wild white honey in his song. / I wonder. / Are there other lives? / he visits? / Are there other hives?" Then she let out a sigh like a death rattle. "The wild white honey . . . Oh Cleo . . ." Big tears stood in her eyes.

"What is it? What's the matter?"

"I'm in love."

Well. This was the first I'd heard of it. I raised up off the grass, truly shocked. "With who?"

She looked off into the distance. "Raymond, the new manager at the Rialto. Raymond Francis Malone."

The fact that I myself was in love—in pure love with one man and in dire physical attraction with another—should have caused me to be happy for her. It didn't. "Humph," I said. "Sounds Catholic." Me who wouldn't have known a Catholic if I stepped on him in short grass.

Rosemary gave me a puzzled look. I was puzzled myself; then I got the drift of what was taking place in my wretched spleen. It was pure and simple jealousy. I was afraid she would begin to spend her Saturdays with this Raymond person and I'd have to go by myself to the library and the picture show. No more long walks in the park, no more window shopping and grilled cheese sandwiches. Rosemary was the big sister I never had and now that I'd found her, I wanted to keep her all to myself.

"I never saw any white wild honey," I said, puffed up like a toad. "Wild honey is yellow, everybody knows that. It's a stupid poem."

"It depends on the color of the pollen, doesn't it? Maybe it isn't pure white but is a sort of white."

"White is white," I said. "It's a stupid poem."

Rosemary shrugged and closed the book. "Well, it's about time for the picture show."

I thought about how this Raymond, the new manager, would probably be there and would probably come down to sit with us and whisper his stupid white honey words in Rosemary's ear. And they would giggle and feel each other up and carry on so I wouldn't be able to keep track of what was happening between Charles Farrell and Janet Gaynor.

I threw the whole bag of scraps at the poor innocent ducks. "I guess I don't feel like a movie today," I said. "Anyhow, I've got to practice for tomorrow." More jealousy talking. And I knew it! I knew it and there was nothing I could do to stop myself. I was willful and selfish and mean as a snake, just like every other fifteen-year-old girl before and since.

Rosemary got to her feet. "Oh, come on, Cleo. You don't need to practice, you said so yourself. You said there isn't any church music written you can't play in your sleep. Come on, now." She leaned over and offered me her hand, and she smiled at me sideways like a somebody who's got all your numbers. "I want Raymond to meet you," she said. (Smart, see? Not I want *you* to meet Raymond.) "I said to Raymond, I said, 'I want you to meet Cleo, the best friend I have in this whole wide world.' "

So I met Raymond. If he was given to any wild honey words you couldn't have noticed—he was struck dumb as a bucket by Rosemary. But I could see he was a good sort. I've always had an eye for the quality of a person's heart. In a moment of generosity, I told Rosemary he was a keeper.

5

I<small>T DIDN'T LOOK LIKE A CHURCH. IT WAS A</small> simple white clapboard building, an old square house with its inside walls torn out and its roof held up with spit and amens. It had plain casement windows, and wooden benches instead of pews. Oh, but the flowers! I had never seen so many flowers outside a high meadow in early spring, and here it was October.

Two young women in long white dresses curtsied nice as you please to the Reverend, then went back to arranging bouquets at the foot of the altar and across the front rail. There was a knock on the side door and a woman poked her head in, holding out a big Mason jar of yellow mums. One of the young women sailed over to collect it.

The Reverend introduced me to Lila, the piano player, who also wore a white dress with long sleeves and a prissy high neck. The girls, like the dresses, were cut from the same pattern. The same pale brown hair was gathered into a skimpy bun at the nape of the neck, same eyes the color of a faded blue washrag. All three had the distinct odor of young calves.

After he made us all acquainted, the Reverend said he was going into the vestry to commune with God. Lila told me we would have a few minutes to go over the songs for the service. She pointed to a hymnal open on the piano and said she only played in the key of F. Well, Scat was doing his level best to teach me about keys and how to read music but it might just as well have been algebra. But when Lila started up on "Where Are the Nine," I played right along with her, no problem at all. I could tell right off that she wasn't much of a musician. When we finished I politely suggested maybe if we were going to do this on a regular basis, we could get together during the week and practice.

"I work nights," I said. "Anytime during the day that's convenient with you would be fine for me."

She looked as grave as a great horned owl. "I have no need to practice," she said. "The Lord Jesus guides my fingers."

I had about a half-dozen smart remarks on the tip of my tongue but I restrained myself and played along in the key of F, which I quickly discovered has no passion in it.

One of the flower girls motioned to Lila and floated up the aisle to open the front door. Lila turned to a page she had marked with a slip of paper and nodded at me to begin. We played "What a Friend We Have in Jesus" while the people filed in, a few family groups but mostly lone women past their prime. The girls came down the aisle in front of the faithful, strewing flowers in their path. It was a pretty goofy sight but it lent a certain drama to the proceedings. I figured the preacher had seen Aimee Semple McPherson work, and that's where he'd got his ideas. I hadn't seen her in person but I'd seen pictures in magazines and I'd heard her on the radio at Mam's. As I said before, Mam and Momma took a dim view of the fundamentalists, but they loved to listen to the singing, and they'd laugh and slap each other's knees when Aimee told the afflicted out there to put their hands on the radio and they'd be cured.

While people were getting settled, we played a couple choruses of "The Light of the World"; then Lila beckoned for me to sit down beside her on the piano bench. There was not a rustle or a cough as we waited. Finally, the Reverend came in from the vestry. In truth he *materialized* when he stepped up to the altar, which was suddenly flooded with slanted sunlight from the window behind him. It made a halo around his golden head, and shone brightly on his pristine white suit. His violet blue eyes shot fire into the congregation, which heaved and sighed as one. He moved his head slowly, like he was making personal contact with each and every person in the room; then he looked up toward the ceiling, lifted his arms, and said:

"I am a brother to dragons, and a companion to owls."

He let that sink in for a minute; then he closed his eyes and went on, "I cry unto thee, and thou dost not hear me; I stand up and thou regardest me not. Thou art become cruel to me with thy strong hand, thou opposest thyself against me. Thou liftest me up to the wind; thou causest me to ride upon it."

Very slowly he lowered his hands, palms up, cupped as if he held the burden of the world in them. At that moment he opened his eyes and looked straight at me where I sat stuck to the piano bench.

This is what he said:

"My bones are burned with heat. My harp also is turned to mourning and my organ into the voice of them that weep."

Well, I like to fainted. And so did every other female—nine to ninety—in that little clapboard house. I did not recognize these words as anything I had ever read in Scripture, and I did not comprehend their meaning. But oh Lord did I feel their power! I felt them slide into my ears, bypass my brain altogether, and slither and slink down my insides.

I looked out on the congregation. The women moaned and twisted their handkerchiefs and gnashed their teeth. I looked back at the Reverend and saw a little smile of satisfaction on his lips. I knew that what he was doing, he was doing on purpose.

He nodded at Lila and she played a few bars while everybody caught their breath. Then the Reverend lifted up the Bible and took a few steps away from the altar. In truth what he did was to follow the sunlight as it moved across the floor. The halo took its place around his head, and he spoke in a voice filled with sorrow.

"Every man, woman and child here today knows that same feeling of hopelessness . . . of despair . . . of loss of heart that ravaged Job when he cried out thus to God:

"I cry unto thee, and thou dost not hear me!"

Ah hah! That was why I hadn't recognized the passage. The Book of Job was a complete mystery to me, even though, like the rest, I'd read it through three times. It wasn't one of Momma's favorites so her finger seldom lit on anything from Job, as it tended to on Ecclesiastes and Proverbs and Isaiah. One time she told Mam that she understood perfectly why God was put out with Job, that the man was stiff-necked and proud to a fault, at which point Mam interrupted to say that if anybody could understand those particular failings it would be my momma. They took a little time out to assess each other's shortcomings, which always gave them pleasure. Then Momma said that God, who was trying to win a vital battle with Satan, got out of patience with Job for his lack of cooperation. She said that cooperation with God was the deep meaning in the Book of Job. Mam argued that it was about friendship. It was Job's friends that bothered Mam. She said that what Job needed during his long travail was better friends. Anyhow, Job was not one of my long suits.

When the preacher ran out of sunlight he came back to the altar. He was much more reserved than Brother Glover in Robina, who tended to wave his arms and jump up and down a lot. The Reverend Endicott never once took his handkerchief from his pocket to wipe his brow. Not a bead of sweat on him anywhere that I could see. But the way he used his eyes and his voice claimed more territory that morning than Brother Glover would cover in ten and a half years of Sundays. I suspected the congregation had no real notion of what he was talking about, but they shouted amen and hallelujah just the same every time his voice dropped.

"And that, dearly beloved, is what we're going to talk about this morning. We're going to talk about . . . *abandonment.* Not the abandonment of man by God, because we know from the Holy Word that God does not abandon man. Scripture tells us . . . 'He will not forsake thee.' Scripture tells us . . . 'When my mother and my father forsake me, then the Lord will take me up.' Scripture tells us . . . 'I will never leave thee, nor forsake thee . . .'

"And Jesus, the only son of the Lord God who said these things— he, Jesus, said also unto you . . . 'I will not leave you comfortless. I will come to you.'" He shook his head and clutched the Bible to his breast. "Noooooo. No, my friends, God does not abandon his children."

Then he raised his voice just a notch. "Do you believe?" he asked us. "Do you believe the word of God?"

Everybody shouted out "YES, YES, PRAISE THE LORD!"

"Would God lie to you?"

"NO! NO! AMEN!"

"Would Jesus who is the beloved son of God lie to you?"

"NO! NO! GLORY BE TO GOD!"

The Reverend shook his head and looked bewildered. He held out his hand with the Bible in it. "Then why? Why? Why has your harp turned to mourning? Why does your organ weep?" He bowed his head, his shoulders slumped in grief.

We all looked at each other like confused little children. We had clearly done something wrong but we couldn't quite recollect what it was. Grown men had tears rolling down their cheeks, and red-faced women fanned themselves and longed for grace.

Lila poked me and pointed to the hymnbook. She put a finger to her lips. We played softly, and then the flower girls came up front and sang:

> One offer of salvation
> To all the world make known;
> The only sure foundation
> Is Christ the Corner Stone.
> No other name is given
> No other way is known
> 'Tis Jesus Christ the First and Last
> He saves, and He alone.
> One only door of heaven
> Stands open wide today
> One sacrifice is given
> 'Tis Christ, the living way.

We kept on with the chorus and the girls hummed while the preacher commenced to talk about money. He said he was the incarnation of the Holy Ghost here on earth and he'd been sent by God personally to do His work. This work was to help the poor and the oppressed and the abandoned, and to do that sacred job he needed every nickel the congregation could spare. He needed it even if they couldn't spare it. Surely they wouldn't abandon God's servant and his holy work. There was only one door to Heaven and the name printed in big letters across that door was . . . Charity.

While the Reverend went on about Charity and Sacrifice, the girls took a couple plates from in front of the altar and went up and down the aisles. When they came back with the plates the preacher stared at the contents for a minute; then he looked out on the congregation as if he'd been struck by lightning. He nodded at Lila and she bore down on the keys, keeping a heavy foot on the pedal. I took out after her. The girls began to sing again, louder. "One only door of Heaven, stands open wide todayyyyyyyy. . . ."

When they started to hum again the preacher told about a child down on South Lewis that needed an operation for his poor little lame foot. This very child leaned on his homemade crutch in front of the door to Heaven, waiting to pass us through to the throne of God.

With great and obvious contempt, the preacher dumped out that first paltry offering onto the altar, put the empty plates in the girls' hands, and sent them out for a second go-round. The congregation dug deep into its billfolds and pocketbooks, and the sun began to shine again on Reverend Endicott.

The girls brought the plates back, overflowing with next week's grocery money. The Reverend gave thanks in the lame child's name, and in the name of all the poor and afflicted who were his own personal flock to be tended. Then he got down to the serious business of saving souls.

Lila and I played "Just as I Am" a dozen times at least and they still kept coming, weeping and wailing for all they were worth.

"Who wants to know Jesus?" the preacher called out again and again in his golden voice. There was a sea of hands, a sea of tears, a sea of prostrate bodies piled up around the altar. I'd never seen anything like it. At the end, he blessed everybody and ordered them to return that night for the prayer meeting, although where on earth they were going to get the price of admission between now and then was beyond me.

Figgy served Sunday dinner at 1:30 prompt. It was usually roast beef (the preacher's favorite) with potatoes and carrots and onions tucked around it on a big white platter. There'd be string beans or peas or squash, and biscuits and gravy. This was topped off with Figgy's delicious apple pie with cinnamon sauce.

Usually my mouth would begin to water like a dog's at the first clang of the dinner bell, but the preacher's sermon on abandonment had stolen away my appetite. Rosemary was off with Raymond for the afternoon, it being his day off, so of course I was feeling forsaken by my best friend. But mostly I was feeling bad about Momma. For the first time since I'd left home, I could see clearly that I had abandoned her. Without a word, a note even, I had snuck off in the middle of the night to make a journey to a far-off place nobody had ever heard of. I had left her short a pair of hands she relied on. I had been heartless and cruel and surely deserved whatever bad fortune befell me.

I was settling down to feel real sorry for myself when there came a knock on the door. Mildred poked her head in and said, "Cleo? Are you coming?"

"I don't think so." I was piled up in the middle of the bed, arms hugging my knees. "I don't feel hungry."

"That's unusual." She looked me over. "Are you ill?"

"Just tired," I said. "I played 'Just as I Am' maybe thirteen and a half times this morning."

"Humph." Mildred was immune to the preacher. Her first day he'd invited her to church and she told him no thank you she was Unitarian. He said we all serve the same master and she said, "I think not," her voice crisp as a lady apple. Then she asked me to pass her some more of that excellent butternut squash and got Figgy into a long serious discussion about baked beans. She said she would share her family recipe if Figgy had any interest in it.

I liked Mildred a lot, and we'd gotten pretty friendly in the month she'd been at the boardinghouse. Since I'd confided in her I hadn't finished high school she'd been at me to complete my education. She said I had native intelligence. She was a grass widow, no children, forty-three years old, and she had left Boston for some reason she was too refined to discuss. I figured it had something to do with the divorce. Whatever it was, I knew she was sad about it. I could tell from her eyes that Mildred understood abandonment.

"Would you like me to bring you something?"

"No, I don't think so." Then I thought some more. There was no supper served on Sundays, and Figgy did not allow anybody to raid her icebox. That, I had learned to my sorrow. "Well," I said, "maybe a little wedge of pie, if you don't mind."

"With cinnamon sauce?"

"Yes, ma'am, please. Extra. And maybe a little roast beef. And a potato . . ."

Mildred smiled, patted my arm, and said she'd be back later.

I stared out the window for a while and watched the shadows from the trees play across the bed. A breeze moved the thin white curtains in and out while a lone bird in the maple sang for all it was worth. I fancied its flock had flown south and left it behind, forsaken their brother to a cold, unforgiving winter. I was just about to give myself up to total melancholy but decided I would read a book instead. You could always find people in books that were worse off than you were. I picked up the *Decline and Fall of the Roman Empire* from my bedside table, and there underneath was Alexandra waiting patiently for me to get her to Lhasa.

I had left her and Yongden on the way to the villages of Po. Because they are traveling illegally, they must avoid the main road and Alexandra has to be very particular about her disguise. Every so often she touches up her hair with ink, and every morning she darkens her hands and face with soot from the cooking pot. She is in constant dread of discovery for which she could be put to death, so she must be cunning and watchful at all times. They have asked some herders about the best route to Po and have learned that only one pass is still open. Since Yongden is a holy man—a lama—the herders invite them to spend the night. Yongden leaves Alexandra, who is posing as his old mother, to rest while he, as is the custom for lamas, goes out to beg food from the villagers.

Alexandra pretends to sleep and one of the herdsmen wonders aloud what is in the packs the strangers carry. In truth there is a revolver and a small bag of gold. The herdsman creeps toward Alexandra, who wonders what trick she will use if the situation worsens. It does. He puts out his hand to feel the pack that she is using for a pillow.

"Lags, lags, Gelong lags," she says, imitating the voice of one who speaks in a trance. (What this means in English is Yes, yes, Reverend monk). And that's the trick. She sits up and says, "Is my son, the lama, not here? Oh, strange! I have just heard him telling me, Awake Mother! Awake quickly!"

The herdsman looks frightened and his wife offers Alexandra some tea to calm her. Then, lo and behold, Yongden enters the room.

The herdsman's wife has made a pot of broth, and Alexandra and Yongden are invited to share it. The woman dips a long iron hook into the pot and brings out the heart, lungs, and liver of a yak, together with its stomach and bowels. The woman then pours barley flour into the broth and in ten minutes time dinner is ready. Alexandra, whose feats of digestion are truly marvelous, drinks three bowls of this broth for she must be strong tomorrow if she is to climb the high pass that is the only route to Po. . . .

I laid the book on my stomach and thought about how much Alexandra and I had in common. We had both craved to go beyond the garden gate and explore the unknown. As a young girl she ran away to England to study Buddhism and become an opera singer. I ran away to Tulsa and began to study Life and became a professional trumpet player.

But I wondered. Oh, Lord! I wondered! I wondered if Alexandra ever missed her mother.

Mildred came in then with a tray, and I perked up some. She set it down on the table by the window. She'd brought two cups of coffee, which meant I would not have to eat alone. I put a marker in the book and left it on the bed.

"What are you reading?" Mildred asked.

"It's a new book, *My Journey to Lhasa*."

"Ah yes, Alexandra David-Neel. Remarkable woman. Come on, now, have this before it gets cold."

I sat down and Mildred handed me a napkin. "You mean you've heard of her?"

"The book is quite popular in Boston. I've not read it. Perhaps you'll loan me your copy when you've finished."

"You can take it now if you want. I'm reading it slow. I want it to last."

She laughed. "You could read it again, you know."

"Oh yes, I always do. I read everything at least three times, but you can only read something for the first time once."

Mildred nodded thoughtfully. "That's true, Cleo. The first time happens only once. Now, eat your dinner. You look wan and peaked."

While I ate, Mildred drank her coffee and told me about the Boston Common and how beautiful it was this time of year. I said that fall was my favorite season and told about the farm, and how from our kitchen window it was like looking across a yellow sea all the way to Kansas. It was clear we both suffered from homesickness, pure and simple.

Finally, I told her what was troubling me. She didn't ask, it would have been impolite and people from Boston are always proper, but she listened with her full attention, not like many folks who wait for you to take a breath so they can break in with their own woeful tale. I told her the Reverend had preached on abandonment that morning and it had made me think of how I had treated my momma.

"Does she live in town?"

"No, in Robina, some fifty-sixty miles from here. We've got a farm out in the country."

"Do you write to her?"

"I send postal orders to help out and sometimes a note saying I'm fine."

"That sounds very dutiful to me. Sending money."

"But I haven't told her my address."

"Oh? Why's that?"

"I'm afraid she'll send my brother to fetch me home."

Mildred shrugged. "Well, that's up to you, Cleo. He can't carry you off bodily. You're of age."

I squirmed at that and decided to wade a little deeper into the bottomless river of truth. "I'm not," I said. "I'll be sixteen next month, the same age as Alexandra when she ran away to England."

Mildred nodded. "I see."

"Momma'd have my hide if she knew I was working in a speakeasy. My daddy had a drinking problem that led him to gambling and . . . well, other excesses. She takes a hard view of anything that has to do with whiskey."

"Perhaps you wouldn't have to mention where you work. At first."

"I have to tell her something. She'll want to know where I get this money I send home."

Mildred thought on that for a minute; then she sighed. "I don't know what to tell you, Cleo. I'm sorry, I wish I could help." She stood up and began to stack the dishes onto the tray; then she put her hand on my arm. "Cleo, I don't think this estrangement with your mother is all that troubles you. I don't mean to interfere and this is none of my business but . . . well, you are so young. Whether you're sixteen or eighteen, you're still so young." She looked away, clearly embarrassed.

"I'm old for my age," I said. "Either way."

"Yes, I know. In many ways you are. But the world can be a dangerous place. You meet so few people in this life who have your best interests at heart." She looked me square in the eye. "Cleo, the Reverend Endicott is not one of those few, I hope you realize that."

"Yes, ma'am, I surely do."

"There are people born without scruples, in the same way a person is born with a missing finger. There is nothing to be done about it, that's just the way it is. I hope you will be prudent in your association with the Reverend."

I wanted to blurt it all out right then. I wanted to tell Mildred about my pure love for Mr. Shannon, and how at the same time I was drawn against my will to the preacher. I wanted to tell her about dragons and owls and how when the preacher fixed his blue eyes on me it was like the Frisco had just blasted through, vibrating the windows of my soul, causing a tremor in the very earth I stood on.

But I had already burdened her with my trouble about Momma, and I felt it was unfair to take further advantage of our friendship, newly born as it was. I knew it was all right to share good tidings, even with strangers, but big doses of fear and sorrow and moral failings had to be kept in reserve for friends of long standing—people who'd been tested on the worst that's in you.

So I laughed as if the preacher should be the furthermost concern from her mind. "Don't worry," I said, "he's soft. I could whup him if I had to."

"Oh, Cleo . . ." She shook her head and picked up the tray.

"You want to take the book?" I asked her.

"No, I have a stack of essays to go over. I'll borrow it another time."

I jumped up to open the door for her. "Thanks for bringing up my dinner, Mildred. I likely would have keeled over from starvation at the prayer meeting tonight."

She got a worried look again. "How will you get home?"

"On my two big feet."

"We could ask Amos to meet you there when the service is over. He could escort you."

"Oh Mildred, I don't need any escort. I been walking around in the dark by myself since I was a kid. I walked right through a pack of coyotes one time, yipping and howling like I was one of their own."

She lifted an eyebrow. "I wasn't thinking about coyotes, Cleo. I was thinking about a lone wolf."

I waved my hand and spoke with reassurance in my voice. "Figgy goes to Sunday prayer meeting and the preacher sees her home. I think that's how he pays his room and board."

"That man!"

I put my hand on her shoulder. I felt warm and protected and looked-after. "You're good to worry about me," I said. "I think you are one of those."

"Indeed? One of those what?"

"One of those people who has another person's best interests at heart."

She smiled and I watched her down the hall to the stairs, thinking how much easier my life would be if Momma had been more like Mildred, had read more of Jane Austen and less of the Old Testament.

6

THE RAINS CAME IN NOVEMBER, AND THEN the snow after the next cold, full moon. The closer it got to December 25th, the more I brooded about home. We always went to church on Christmas Eve and spent the night and Christmas Day at Mam's house, where we opened our packages and feasted until the sun went down. Mam had propane gas and an inside toilet. A million times at least she told Momma to come on back home where we'd all be more comfortable. She had two spare bedrooms and wanted Momma to use her own place as a rent house to generate a little income. But my momma was as stubborn as an Arkansas mule, and determined to make her own way.

Things were going just fine at the Gusher. I had progressed in my music lessons with Scat to the point where I could sight-read scales and a few simple tunes like "Row, Row, Row Your Boat." I didn't like it, made me stiff as an old pine board. My natural gift was my ear. It was like putting sheet music down in front of a yellow warbler and telling it to sing, but I kept at it. I didn't want to disappoint Scat, who was working me up to "The Flight of the Bumblebee." Mr. Shannon drove me home sometimes when Tully couldn't get away, but he never put a hand on me, not even to help me into the car, not even in friendliness.

I still played my horn at the morning service and the prayer meeting on Sundays. The Reverend Endicott kept his word. There'd be a ten-dollar bill under my plate at breakfast on Monday mornings. Every so often I'd catch him looking at me like I was something good to eat, but for the most part he kept his distance. He had other fish he was frying on a regular basis. Every Sunday morning after the service, either Lila or one of the "prayer partners," as he called the two flower girls, would go off with him to the vestry. To commune with God, Lila said.

I still spent my Saturdays with Rosemary, but it wasn't the same since the advent of Raymond. It was Raymond this and Raymond that and how they were going to save their money and get married and move to Bakersfield, California, where Raymond's uncle owned a hardware store and could use an extra hand. There was even talk of a partnership, as this particular uncle was childless. Rosemary stopped reading poetry and got herself a subscription to *Good Housekeeping* magazine, and we commenced to do our window shopping at furniture stores. Deep inside I think I had Rosemary's best interests at heart. It was just that I was bored silly by her company. People planning for their own future don't have interest in much else. To my shame I must admit I made snide remarks about Raymond and married bliss. Such as: "Is poor Raymond losing his hair?" "I hear Bakersfield is hotter than the Sahara Desert." I don't recall my comments on the state of marriage but I'm sure they were full of gloom. Rosemary just ignored me.

There was another reason for my bad humor. I was having bad dreams about Momma. I would hear her calling me and when I'd find her she was falling off a cliff, or going down for the third time, or leaning out the highest window of a burning building. My legs weighed about two hundred pounds apiece when I tried to get to her.

By early December I couldn't stand it anymore. I wrote and told her I'd be coming home for Christmas. I put my return address on the letter and on the envelope, and I waited. A week went by and no answer. I knew it only took a couple or three days for mail to get to Robina so I began to worry that my letter had got lost. After all, you can't trust your life to the United States Post Office. Then I began to think maybe there was such a thing as prophecy in dreams.

The next Saturday morning, a week or so before Christmas, the postman brought a large brown envelope. I hugged it to me and took the stairs to my room two at a time. I tore open the envelope and what fell out was a batch of postal orders.

This is what Momma's letter said:

> *Daughter:*
> *I think you meant well in sending this money. If the children had been taken sick or if we had been hungry, I suppose I would have forced myself to use it. There was no need. Ethan has a regular job over at the Warwicks where he is learning to repair farm machinery. The chickens are laying well. Also, Mr. Hawkins at the pharmacy is buying some of my curatives.*

I have been sorely troubled not knowing where this money came from or how it was earned. In your first letter you said it came honestly from your ability with your trumpet. But I know you, Daughter. You have always been a child to bend the truth to suit you. Just last month I learned the true source of this money. Somebody—I'll not mention any names—saw you playing your horn in a saloon, and now all of Robina is acquainted with the shame you have brought on this family. If you want to come home for Christmas I suppose I can't stop you. It's your home however much you have disgraced it. But I hope you don't. I hope you don't further shame us by showing your face where I try to hold up my head under the mean eyes of the Beulah Baptist Auxiliary. Their tongues have not stopped wagging about your black satin dress that's no more than a slip, and how you are naked under it. My cheeks burn as I write this. Mam says I'm making too much of it but then she always takes up for you. She says it's your daddy's Irish blood that causes your wildness. You can't help your genes—I know that—but that still doesn't make it acceptable. You wrote that you were playing your trumpet at a church and attending services there. I don't know whether to believe that or not. If it's true, Daughter, the two do not go together. You cannot dance in Satan's house during the week and be welcome in God's on Sunday morning. If you decide to come home for Christmas, I will take it to mean you come to stay and mend your ways. If you come with the idea of a visit and then returning to a life of iniquity, then you must realize that I will have nothing to say to you. And of course I cannot have you filling the children's ears with city notions. I have enough trouble keeping your brother on the straight and narrow.

I have just this moment prayed for guidance in this matter. I opened the Bible and the Lord caused my finger to come to rest on Genesis 3:5. Your eyes shall be opened, and ye shall be as gods, knowing good and evil.

You, Daughter, were raised up to know the difference.

There was a smudge at the bottom of the page, as if something had been rubbed out, as if she had put a signature there and then thought better of it. When you've written to your child and told her she is not welcome in the house where she was got and born, how then . . . oh, how then do you sign yourself?

I wasn't much in the mood but I went out window shopping with Rosemary anyhow. We'd been looking forward to today's picture show for weeks. The theater—as Raymond called it—had been wired for sound, and that afternoon was the opening performance of *The Jazz Singer* with Al Jolson. It was the first talking movie. Raymond, as Rosemary said, was a real go-getter, and had built a counter in the lobby where you could buy Coca-Cola and popcorn. Rosemary said Raymond had come to the attention of the owner, who had a string of "theaters" all across the country, and it was possible they wouldn't go to Bakersfield after all. Instead, Raymond might be sent to headquarters in Los Angeles to think up ideas. She said I could come with them. She said Hollywood would be a lot more fun than Lhasa.

I did my best to work up some enthusiasm for this possibility, but my heart wasn't in it. While Rosemary oohed and ahhed over divans and dining room suits, I found myself again thinking about the preacher's sermon on abandonment. *When my mother and my father forsake me, then the Lord will take me up.* When my mother and father forsake me . . . The words kept going around and around in my head, like a new song you can't get shed of until you've learned it note perfect.

Even the movie didn't get my attention. It wasn't the sort of thing a professional musician like myself could appreciate. I mean the sound was terrible! Whoever was responsible should have known better than to send that picture out before it was ready.

Afterward, Raymond clutched my shoulder and said, "You've seen history made here today." From the sappy look on his face you'd have thought he was talking about the Second Coming.

"How long is this piece of history going to run?" I asked. I was thinking longingly of Charlie Chaplin and Theda Bara and the man who usually played piano down front. This man was a crackerjack at his job. He looked at a movie four-five times when it came in, and figured out what music would go with the action. He was especially good at the *Perils of Pauline*. And now he was almost out of a job, all in the name of progress.

"For a full month," Raymond said proudly. "I had to turn at least a hundred people away this afternoon. Probably twice that for the shows tonight."

"You mean this is what'll be playing for the next four Saturdays?"

"That's right, Cleo, and there'll always be a seat for you." He said he had to go see to the popcorn machine and he and Rosemary kissed each other. They didn't really kiss—they rubbed lips like people about to celebrate their fifieth anniversary.

Figgy was off her feed that evening so there were make-them-yourself sandwiches out of cheese and baloney. That was okay by me. I didn't have any appetite anyway. Even a long soak in the tub didn't raise my spirits, or my new emerald green dress. Miss Ada had ordered my costume in four different colors, so now in addition to the black and the white, I had that same dress that so upset the Beulah Baptist Auxiliary in scarlet, emerald, ice blue, and purple.

Scat had a couple new tunes, and a friend of his from Kansas City sat in on the alto sax. That was really something. With a trumpet you can do the beginning and the end of the world, but for the everydayness of the middle you need a saxophone. Tully had to tell us to quiet down three times during the evening. It was good to have the music to take my mind off my troubles for a while. Tully was busy so Mr. Shannon drove me home and saw me politely up to the front door. Ordinarily that would have pleased me, but I had a full-blown case of the sulks and it showed.

"Is there something wrong, Cleo?"

"No. What could be wrong?"

"I don't know, that's why I'm asking. You're not your usual bouncy self."

"I've settled down," I said, in a cool, settled voice. "I'm older now."

He smiled. "Which makes you . . .?"

"Nineteen."

"You're going to stick with your story, huh?"

"I sure am. And while we're at it, you may as well know that I would appreciate it very much if you didn't interrupt when gentlemen come up to talk to me after Scat and I finish a set."

The porch light was shining on his big nose, and I could see from the baffled expression on his face that he was taken aback by my tone of voice. He put his hands in his pockets like he was not sure what to do with them.

"It is an embarrassment to me," I went on, "to be treated like some three-year-old you got to keep your eye on or she'll fall in the creek." I was getting wound up and it felt real good to be mean to somebody.

"Now, Cleo," he said, "there is a certain bad element inherent in a place like the Gusher . . ."

"You think I can't tell the difference between a good element and a bad element? They just want to *talk*. They just want to express their appreciation for my musical ability."

He looked up at the ceiling. "Cleo," he said, his voice low and earnest, "it is not just your musical ability that attracts some of these men. Now, please be reasonable."

I lifted my chin. "This is my reasonable side," I said.

He shook his head. "You are very good at bending the truth, Cleo."

I said, "I am very good at anything I put my mind to. That includes looking after myself. I am not your responsibility, Ed Shannon, not for one minute!"

He sauntered around the porch, his hands deep in his pockets, nodding as if he was talking to himself. Then he stopped short. "You're right, Cleo. You're absolutely right. It's none of my business." And he went off down the walk, whistling like he always did.

This was the good man who had bailed me out of jail, rescued my belongings from the hotel, given me a paying job, and found me a place to live. I could have kicked myself all the way to Main Street.

It was 11:15 and everybody was signed in except Rosemary and Amos. I stopped outside Mildred's door, but there was neither sound nor light in evidence. Sometimes when I came in, Mildred made cocoa on her hot plate and we talked for a while. I coughed a couple times, and scuffed my feet, hoping she might be lying there in the dark, thinking about the Boston Common and the Charles River, hoping I might hear the creak of bedsprings and bare feet padding toward the door. But the silence just got louder. Only sleep waited up for me.

I put on my nightdress and thought I might catch up to Alexandra and Yongden. It was no use. I couldn't concentrate on their passage into the villages of Po. Po was as far away as Jupiter and just about as important in my earthly scheme of things. So I turned off my light and pretty soon my loyal troubles lined up on the foot of the bedstead just like starlings on a telephone wire.

7

E VEN THE REVEREND ENDICOTT COULDN'T keep the sun from its appointed path across the heavens, so when it stopped slanting through the window on cue, he had it replaced with a pink spotlight. I couldn't swear to it but I suspected he brushed something into his hair to make it give off sparkles. I asked him about it once, asked him why his head looked like it had a halo around it. He said it was the dust of angels.

That morning he swirled out of the vestry—he'd taken to wearing a long white cape over his white suit—and up to the altar, at which moment Lila flipped a switch with her foot and the pink spot came on.

The Reverend held out his arms and said, "It is not possible that the blood of bulls and goats should take away sins."

Lila and I played a couple choruses of "Sun of My Soul" while the preacher locked eyes with each and every member of his congregation. Then he told us that what God wanted was not slaughtered goats and bulls but *living sacrifices.* He wanted the *living* hands and the *living* minds and the *living* hearts of his whole flock to be consecrated and dedicated to God's service.

"Your bodies," he said, "are only the poor vessels that hold your souls and spirits. In the great hereafter those of you who have kept your souls and spirits pure will receive new and finer bodies to house them in the perfect sight of God."

Big surprise! What he quickly worked up to was the money he saw wasted on the coverings for these poor vessels. "Fashion," he said, "is the work of the devil. A beautiful soul, a beautiful spirit, doesn't need to throw away money on a new dress or a new suit of clothes. God loves your rags—if your spirit is pure."

And then he had a whole lot to say about ladies' hats. God, he said, disapproved of feathers, flowers, veils, and other such frivolous adornments. In other words, the congregation, particularly the female element, was rendering unto Caesar and Mammon what was rightfully the Lord's. He allowed it was especially difficult this time of year what with the devil whispering in your ear to buy this and that and the other, but how could we think of pleasing ourselves with these trappings of the flesh, this worthless finery to be wrapped up in ribbons and placed under a tree in a heathen ceremony.

"Thy money," he said, in his deep golden voice, "perish with thee, because thou has thought that the gift of God may be purchased."

He told us to turn to First Timothy, wherein we would discover the kind of sacrifice the Lord required of us. He held out the Bible with his right hand and his cloak shimmered in the light.

"For we brought nothing into this world, and it is certain we can carry nothing out. Having food and raiment, let us be therewith content." He put down the Bible and leaned forward in a confidential way. "Let us speak about raiment for a moment," he said. "What is raiment? Nothing more, my friends, than a protective covering for the body . . . the body, that lowly vessel. Raiment protects the body from heat and cold and wind and storm." He lowered his eyes. "And from the lustful feelings that nakedness engenders in the son of man cast out of Eden. God tells you to supply yourself with food. Does God mean you are to indulge in gluttony when he says that? Of course not, my friends. Nor does he mean you are to be gluttonous with your raiment.

"Let us be therewith content. But . . ." He paused meaningfully. "They that will be rich fall into temptation, and a snare, and into many foolish and hurtful lusts, which drown men . . . *and women* . . . in destruction and perdition."

A couple ladies down front had removed their hats and were plucking them like just-dead chickens. The Reverend smiled his blessing upon them. But he wasn't through with them yet. He was just getting warmed up.

He said, "Do you believe that God spoke to the apostle Paul and guided his hand and heart when he wrote these words to his beloved son Timothy? Do you believe?"

A great "YES" resounded. Everybody believed; everybody except me. The Reverend had made a mistake about Timothy.

He picked up the Bible again and held it aloft. "Yea, this is the word of God, spoken to his servant Paul: 'For the love of money is the root of all evil, which while some coveted after, they have erred from the faith, and pierced themselves with many sorrows . . .'"

A woman on the aisle stood up and ripped a big cabbage rose off her hat, flung it to the floor, and stomped on it. The preacher rushed to her side. "Praise the Lord!" he cried out; then he picked up the rose between his thumb and forefinger. "Our sister has divested herself of the trappings of Satan." He put his hand on her shoulder and she looked up at him. Tears flowed down her cheeks. Then he guided her onto the bench, and returned to the altar, that cape floating out behind him like a zephyr.

"Let—us—be—therewith—content. Say it with me, dearly beloved. Let us be therewith content. Say it again, say it in your hearts. God charges you to trust not in uncertain riches, but in Him who giveth us richly of all things to enjoy."

He leaned forward and speared the congregation with beams of light from his eyes. I knew he had arrived at the meat and potatoes of his message.

"In the sixth chapter, verse eighteen, God charges you to *distribute*. To go forth in your old clothes . . . which he loves. To eat simple food which is pleasing in his sight. To distribute your mortal riches to the poor. I speak of the wretched poor who come to this blessed time of our savior's birth without even a crumb of bread on their tables.

"Say 'NO' to the heathen practice of the buying of gifts! Say 'NO' to the devil—my good sisters—when he speaks to you of fashion. Who worried about fashion and fine raiment? Who trusted in uncertain riches? I'll tell you who! Delilah! Jezebel! The fallen women of Bible times. Ah, but Mary. Mary wore her simple blue cloak, her everyday raiment to the blessed stable where she gave the greatest gift of all to the world."

He took a deep breath, shook his head, and wagged his finger. "I know what you're thinking," he said. "You're thinking of the three kings who brought gifts of frankincense and myrrh and gold to the baby Jesus. My friends, surely you can't believe the three kings went to the marketplace and *bought* these things? Oh no! The gold was laid by, waiting for a holy purpose, and the resins were gathered from the earth's forest which is the Lord's.

"Let us be therewith content. Be rich in good works . . . share your bounty with God's poor and unfortunate. I promise you, in this way you lay a good foundation against the dark time to come." He raised his arms to embrace them all. "You—lay—hold—of—eternal—life."

The Reverend didn't have to send the girls out twice that day. The collection plates ranneth over.

That night at the prayer meeting, he coasted like a man who had done a good day's work of which he was justly proud, and so deserving of rest. There sat the chastened flock in their rattiest old raiment, looking like sheep in need of shearing, each old ewe trying to outdo the other. But as the Good Book says. A live dog is better than a dead lion.

After the blessing and the hand-shaking out on the porch he came back inside and told me to wait up. "We'll get something to eat," he said. He snatched my horn and said he'd put it in the vestry for safe-keeping.

Figgy was still under the weather so there had been cold cuts for Sunday dinner, about which the Reverend Endicott had done considerable grumbling.

"Simple food is pleasing in God's sight," I had told him with my most vacant face.

At first he stiffened up and narrowed his eyes at me, but then he laughed and said, "Touché, little sister, touché."

Lila waved goodbye to the prayer partners and came down the aisle. She gathered up the music and put it inside the piano bench. I told her the Reverend and I were going to have a bite to eat and asked if she wanted to go with us.

"No, thank you," she said, in her prissy little voice. "I commune with Reverend Endicott every third Sunday after the morning service."

"Oh, Lila, for crying out loud. We're not going to *commune,* we're going to go get something to eat."

But she just shook her head and said she'd see me next Sunday. I watched her go. I knew I ought to walk out that door as fast as my feet would take me. I remembered how I once saw a young badger fooling around with a rattlesnake. An old badger knows a rattler is serious business and he worries the creature in an expert way, dashing in and out but never going over an invisible line. He's always out of range until the snake strikes and puts itself in a vulnerable position. Then the old badger grabs it before it has a chance to coil up again. A young badger, on the other hand, one that's inexperienced, thinks some kind of game is going on. He pays attention to the game instead of the invisible line. Which is why there is a high mortality rate among young badgers that mess with rattlesnakes.

I was thinking hard on young badgers when the preacher came out of the vestry. He'd loosened his tie and he carried his white coat hooked over his forefinger and thrown across one shoulder. He wore a vest over a shirt of the palest blue, the cuffs rolled a couple of turns to show off his arms, which were golden like the rest of him and covered with a down of fine blond hair. A forelock hung over one eye, making him look as dashing as Douglas Fairbanks preparing to fight the pirates. It was a crime against womanhood for any rattlesnake to look that good.

"Come on," he said, taking my arm, "let's go have ourselves a big thick steak. How 'bout that, Cleo?"

"Suits me," I said. "I'm starved." Which was never any news.

We walked over to Betty Anne's Diner, an all-night place in a converted railroad car just a couple blocks from the church. The night was crisp, but not cold. It was as if fall had forgotten something and come back in December to retrieve it. That's what they say about the weather in Oklahoma. If you don't like it just be patient a couple hours and it'll change.

The steaks were two inches thick and bleeding from the middle. They were covered with french-fried onion rings and there was a wedge of head lettuce on the side, all drizzled over with orange-colored salad dressing, which was okay as long as you didn't look at it. I looked at the Reverend. I watched him eat his steak. I never knew that a person chewing on a piece of meat could engender so many base feelings in the observer. He locked eyes with me and his lower jaw moved from one side to the other in a lazy kind of way—like a dog with a bone he knows for certain nobody is going to take away from him. His teeth gleamed, and every so often he groaned like a Roman at a three-day feast.

While I was still working on my ugly salad, he polished off his steak and ordered up another from Betty Anne, who was watching him from behind the counter. He took a napkin from the container on the table and patted his lips in that dainty, elegant way he had about him. Then he leaned back in the booth and gave a great sigh.

"I've been thinking about that steak since today's miserable cold cuts," he said. "I hope Mrs. Figgs will have recovered by dinnertime tomorrow."

"It's the flu," I said. "Mildred says she has the flu."

"No," he said, "it's not the flu. She's suffering from revenge. Mrs. Figgs has decided—no, she has determined that she will be the next Mrs. Endicott. These poorhouse meals we've been having represent one of her methods of persuasion. She's not a very bright woman. She actually believes her roast beef lies on the route to my heart."

I felt like I was listening in to gossip I had no right to hear, so of course I wanted to hear more of it. "You do flirt with her," I said, flirting just a tad myself.

He lit a cigarette and blew out the smoke with the same kind of pleasure he brought to chewing. "I flirt with all women," he said, "all sizes, shapes, colors and ages. It's my nature. Doesn't mean a thing . . ." He fixed his blue eyes on me. ". . . as a rule."

I began to search for the old badger's invisible line. "The next Mrs. Endicott? Does that mean there is a former Mrs. Endicott?"

He raised his eyes. "Gone to her reward."

"I'm sorry."

"No need to be. God knows I'm not."

I took in my breath. "Sometimes you sound very worldly for a preacher."

He leaned toward me. "I wouldn't say that to just anybody, Cleo. I feel like I can really talk to you, like I can be myself with you. I get so tired of not being able to be myself. We're apples out of the same barrel, Cleo."

"What barrel is that?"

He leaned closer. "The one that's full of ambition," he whispered, "and self-regard. When you wouldn't play your trumpet unless you got paid I knew I'd found what I was looking for."

"That so?"

He narrowed his eyes. "Can you sing?" I shook my head that I couldn't. "Are you sure? The voice doesn't matter as much as the heart, you know."

"I'm sure. At home, a man came through on a wagon once, teaching people to sing for ten days' board and room. Momma caught him with his hand on my rib cage—where you're suppose to breathe from, you know—and she kicked him out of the house. I mean really kicked him. When he got to the road he yelled back that her daughter couldn't sing even to call hogs."

The Reverend chuckled. "Well, that's too bad," he said. "We'll need a singer. Don't get me wrong, you play a mean horn, even with the decided disadvantage of Lila's accompaniment." He blew out another cloud of smoke and offered me a cigarette.

"No thanks," I said. "I need my breath for my trumpet."

He looked at me carefully. "You should have taken me up on the percentage deal, you know. Collections have doubled since you've been with me. Ah, but people like to hear the lyrics. You know what I mean?"

"You have the prayer partners."

He rolled his eyes. "Little choirboys whose voices haven't changed. That's what those girls are. I took them to a colored church in Greenwood one night. I said, "Now, that's the way to sing, girls, like you mean it, like the words come from your heart. No. They won't do, they just won't do."

Betty Anne brought his second steak and he lit into it with as much gusto as he'd spent on the first one. When he finished she took his plate and asked in a hushed voice if his supper was satisfactory.

"The best I've ever had," he told her. "You are certainly pleasing in my sight, Betty Anne."

She giggled and folded her arms across her chest. "The second steak is on the house."

He smiled up at her in great amazement. "The Lord will show his gratitude to you, that you so succor his humble servant."

I could see that Betty Anne didn't know "succor" from a hole in the ground, but that was the word that turned her into a pillar of salt. I had to tug three times on her white apron to get more coffee. She brought it, then backed away like she'd just served royalty. Him. Not me.

After she'd gone, the Reverend asked me my opinion of the morning's sermon.

I hemmed and hawed a bit, then said honestly, "I thought you were unduly harsh on the ladies about their hats."

"Nonsense, they loved it. Women love to be scolded, makes them feel like little girls again."

74

I thought that was debatable, but I let it pass. "And another thing," I said. "Timothy wasn't Paul's son, he was one of his converts. And Jezebel and Delilah were not fallen women, and they didn't have anything to do with fashion or Christmas presents. They just happened to be on the other side. They were warriors fighting for what they believed in."

He cocked his head in what appeared to be genuine interest. "Really?"

"Really." I felt a little silly instructing an expert, but I went on anyhow. "Delilah was a Canaanite," I said. "Samson was her enemy, an invader in her country. Sure she was going to cut off his hair if that was the only way to get rid of him. And Jezebel . . ."

"You're hired," he said, interrupting the lesson. "When you're not playing your trumpet you can do research for the sermons. How do you know so much about the Bible?"

"Raised on it," I said, as if it was a trifle, but I was pleased by his remark. "My momma knows it backwards and forwards." I gave him a sly look. "She does the same thing you do, interprets it to her own needs. I don't have any ax to grind, I just try to figure out what it says."

He stared at me like I'd just blasphemed. "You've got a brain in your pretty head, Cleo. I like that. Want some pie?"

I said I didn't, and watched while he wheedled a big piece of green apple pie à la mode out of Betty Anne—"on the house." Then I said, "You're not from around here, are you, Reverend?"

He smiled and held out his hand. "Christopher Robin Endicott. My friends call me Robby. I think we're going to be friends. Good friends."

I tried it out. "Robby. Robby." It felt soft and warm on my tongue.

"No," he said, "just passing through, following the sun, looking for my fortune. I'm from Philadelphia. My father is a minister there—a poor, honest, God-fearing Methodist minister."

"Oh, so he taught you . . ."

"He tried. Lord knows he tried. He tried to make me into a poor, honest, God-fearing Methodist minister. Fortunately, he failed." He took a bite of ice cream and let it melt some before he swallowed it. Then he winked at me. "There's money to be made in God's work. Look at Aimee, the old crook. She's rolling in it."

And so I heard the story of Robby Endicott's life. He was only twenty-six years old, which came as a surprise to me. I would have put him in his early thirties. Maybe living fast had aged him beyond his years. He'd left the Union Theological Seminary in New York to go on the stage, and soon after abandoned his acting career to marry a rich widow more than twice his age. It wasn't clear just how and when she went to her reward, but she left her considerable fortune to her children, so the bereaved widower had to go back to work.

"I played a Four Square preacher in a play in the Village and it was evident to me where my talents lie. With a voice like mine, which is a gift from God, you either become a Shakespearean actor or a man of the cloth."

"So you don't really have the calling?"

"I have the calling to be rich, Cleo, and I can make you rich, too."

"Ha!" I said. "I haven't gotten very rich on the amount you leave under my plate Monday mornings."

"Not *here,* little sister. Not in Tulsa, Oklahoma, the backwash of the world. By spring I'll have enough saved to buy a truck and a tent. We'll tour the farm towns between here and Los Angeles. Those little towns—it's like taking candy from a baby. In a couple of years, maybe sooner, we'll build a great tabernacle on a bluff overlooking the Pacific Ocean—a tabernacle with an organ and professional lighting and stained glass. California has the highest population of sinners in the world. Why should Aimee have them all?" He drummed his fingers on the table, clearly agitated. "She wasn't kidnapped, you know. That was a lot of baloney."

"I've heard that," I said, "that's what my grandmother says."

He narrowed his eyes and spoke in the same tone he'd used to criticize fancy raiment. "It's rumored she was with her lover."

I nodded. "My grandmother says that too."

"Thirty-seven days in the desert and not a hair out of place—not a sign of malnutrition."

"Maybe the Lord succored her," I said, my face as straight as a broomstick.

The Reverend started to chuckle; then he leaned back in the booth and just hee-hawed. "Cleo," he said, "oh, Cleo! What a joy you are, little goose. I could spend the rest of my life with you—just so I could be reminded from time to time of my own fatuousness—a mild case, of course." Then he frowned. "But we need singers. You can't make it in this business without singers."

"We?" I asked, and made a mental note to look up "fatuous" in my dictionary.

"What do you think I've been talking about? You and me and that splendid trumpet of yours." He made a marquee in the air. "Just imagine. Cleo and her trumpet from On High."

"Somebody once called me Miss Gabriel."

"Not bad, not bad at all, or perhaps Gabriella."

I looked down at my plate and thought about California. Then I thought about Lhasa and the villages of Po. The great unknown. Then I thought about the Gusher, where I felt at home and had kind friends. Of course, the Gusher was just a detour, but I wasn't quite ready for another unknown just yet. "No," I said. "I've got other plans at the moment."

He smirked. "Ed Shannon?" I couldn't speak for my surprise. I thought my feelings were safe since Noreen had gone off with the bootlegger. Robby waved his hand. "Nothing will come of that, Cleo, I can assure you. Edward Shannon is a born gentleman. He is certainly not going to mess with a virgin, and he isn't about to marry a farm girl with no family credentials. I know about these things. We have something in Philadelphia called the Main Line. That's what Ed Shannon is in spite of his occupation. Main Line—you're born there and you breed there."

I sat straight up on the booth. "Who says I'm a virgin," I said, sounding like a somebody who's been gravely insulted. Truth is, I didn't want to hear any more about this Main Line business, which made me feel skinny as an owl in broad daylight.

He reached across the table and clucked me under the chin. "I do," he said. "I have an eye for the stages of virtue. And a nose. A virgin has a certain look to her and a peculiar, unmistakable scent." He wiggled his nose and grinned. "You finished there? Shall we go?"

Walking back to the church to pick up my horn, Robby draped his arm over my shoulder like we were comrades, and he talked the whole way about the beaches and sunshine in California. I only listened with one ear. I was wondering about this peculiar smell I gave off, and if there was some way to disguise it.

At the side door of the church, Robby put his hand up under my hair and ran his long fingers over my neck. That got my full attention. We went inside and he guided me across the front and into the vestry. He switched on a lamp by the door that gave off a rosy glow but not much light. I thought I had wandered into the Arabian Nights. There was a small desk and a file cabinet against one wall but any resemblance to a church office ended right there. There were heavy drapes at the windows and between them an alcove filled with an oversized daybed, covered over with a shiny spread and maybe a dozen big pillows. The rug was the fuzzy kind that causes you to want to take off your shoes. And there were big vases of fresh flowers even though it was the dead of winter.

I said, "This is an unusual vestry."

He said, "I am an unusual man." He pointed to the daybed. "Make yourself comfortable." Then he got a bottle and two glasses from the file cabinet. "Drink?" he said.

"What is it?"

"Wine, little sister. A fine old port courtesy of the congregation."

I thought about it. I didn't drink alcohol because of my daddy. Momma said I probably had a built-in weakness for it and Lord knows I didn't need any more weaknesses. But port, of course, was different. I seemed to recall that Elizabeth Barrett Browning drank a glass of port every day for medicinal purposes. I nodded and took the glass he handed me.

Then he tended to some housekeeping. He moved my trumpet from the daybed to one of the side tables, rearranged the pillows, and turned on another lamp that began to rotate and send colored shadows around the room. I swear.

I took a sip of the port and thought about it being courtesy of the congregation. I thought about all those folks in their old clothes, about those women plucking the feathers from the only pretty things they owned, and I tossed off that port like some drunk, hell-bent on forgetfulness. He smiled and filled up my glass again and he sat down next to me. We sat there, thigh to thigh, sipping that fine old port, watching the colors go 'round and the temperature rise.

This time when my glass was empty he set it on the side table. He took his long forefinger and ran it over my nose, my lips, my neck, then spread out his hand over one of my wonders. I was familiar with that sort of thing because of my association with Willis Henderson, but I was not prepared for the lustful feelings that came over me when he started fooling with the elastic on my underpants. That was the time for me to wiggle away and get out my comb and say I'd have to go home now if he couldn't behave himself and keep his hands up above my waistline where they wouldn't wander into trouble. That's how I always threatened poor Willis. Poor Willis who spread enough seed on the ground to raise an army. I formed the words, I lined them up and prepared to march them out of my mouth like well-reared children.

He must have felt a wariness in the tender skin under his fingers. He whispered in my ear with the slippery tongue of a fallen angel. He said he loved me. He said he was bound for Paradise. He said he wanted to take me with him. I knew he wasn't talking about California.

I could say that I had too much wine and wasn't myself. I could say I was seduced by an expert in the field, but that wouldn't be the whole truth. The truth is this: I said to myself, I am going to commit this sin. And I am going to take joy in it. I refuse to be a casual bystander at such an important occasion as my own deflowering.

And so I started to help undo the buttons and other restraints on the both of us. I watched him kiss all my uncharted territory in that rainbow of lights. Then we were all arms and legs and sweaty sticky skin. A girl never had a sweeter introduction to the way of all flesh.

Afterwards, as I lay there contemplating my contentment, I suddenly thought about the locked door at the boardinghouse.

"What time is it?" I said, and sat bolt upright.

"Don't worry," he said, like some mind reader. "I have a key." He poured the rest of the wine, then got up and went to the file cabinet for another bottle. I watched him move around the room in his beautiful multicolored nakedness. For the first time I fully understood what King Solomon was getting at.

Momma said it had nothing to do with love between men and women. She said it was about the love between Christ and the Church. This had made no sense to me on two counts. Jesus wasn't even born yet, and there was no church in this world with pomegranate juice and foxes and beds of spices. The church had no lips like a thread of scarlet, or breasts like two young roes. Momma was mistaken. The Song of

Solomon was about two hot young bodies pleasuring each other.

I held out my arms and said, "Let him kiss me with the kisses of his mouth for thy love is better than wine."

He came back to bed in a hurry.

"Do I smell different?" I asked.

"Ah," he said, with a sly smile, "how much better the smell of thine ointments than all spices. Honey and milk are under thy tongue."

We laughed and clinked our glasses in congratulation, so full we were of ourselves and each other.

"Listen," I said. "My beloved is white and ruddy, and the chiefest among ten thousand. His belly is as bright ivory overlaid with sapphires. His legs are as pillars of marble, set upon sockets of fine gold. . . ."

I was showing off, of course, but why not? How many girls in my situation had the Song of Solomon committed to memory?

He snapped his fingers. "We could use this, Cleo. You could be the Church and I could be Christ. We'd have to do something about your accent—a voice coach, perhaps. We could use two altars, one on each side, and we could get you a long white robe like Aimee's. They'd love it in California. You could say . . . 'His countenance is as Lebanon, excellent as the cedars . . .' Then I say . . . 'The joints of thy thighs are like jewels and thy . . . Ummmm." He stared into his glass of port, then at my belly. "Ummmm, yes . . . Thy navel like a round goblet . . ."

And he anointed me all over with that fine port, beginning with my goblet, and then he retrieved every drop of it, his lips like lilies. He said I was a vineyard.

Then suddenly, to my amazement and astonishment, he rolled me over on my stomach and climbed on me like I was some dog. I tried to wiggle out from under him but his passion gave him the strength of ten.

"Be still, little sister, little goose," he whispered. "Be still and loving. I am entering the temple of joy."

I kept on squirming. "Not from that direction, you're not!"

"You don't understand. . . ."

"I understand all right—I was raised on a farm!"

"My tender grape," he whispered, "this is just another way for thy portal to receive the blessing."

I bunched myself up and gave a great buck like a mule. "You get your blessing away from my bottom," I yelled out. Then I sank my teeth into his hand. He yelped but he didn't get off. I bucked some more and felt him move a little to the side. Then I flailed around until my hand lit on cold metal. My trumpet! I got a good hold on it, pulled up enough to brace myself, and swung it around with all my might. It caught him full across the face. I heard a crack, then a groan, and he rolled off the daybed like a sack of feed.

I got into my clothes as fast as I could. Finally I got up the nerve to look at him. I could see that his eyes were closed. I inched closer and to my horror saw that his perfect nose was lying on its side. Blood was flowing from it, and even worse, from his mouth. I knew it was a bad sign when blood flowed from the mouth.

I shook him. "Wake up," I cried. "Oh, mercy! I didn't mean to hurt you, I was just trying to save myself. I swear it! Oh Lord, I swear it, please wake him up."

I sank to my knees and felt for a pulse. I put my ear to his chest. He was as still as the air just before a cyclone. "Oh Momma," I whimpered. "Oh, Momma, what'll I do?"

The lamp threw strips of color into the dark silent room. My teeth began to chatter and I started to shake all over. Then, all of a sudden, clear as day, there came my momma's voice. "You'll think of something, Daughter. You'll think of something."

I got up and paced the floor, thinking, driving out the wine that had clabbered my brains. It was 12:30 by the clock on the desk. That meant I was locked out. And hadn't signed in. Lila knew the preacher and I were going out to get a bite to eat. Betty Anne herself served us supper and could identify me. The police would have no trouble ascertaining that I was with the victim on the evening of his demise. Nobody was going to believe that he dragged me in here by the hair of my head and against my will.

"Momma?"

"Keep thinking."

I thought and paced some more. "I'll have to dispose of the body."

"Can you lift him?"

I tried. "He's too heavy. I could drag him, I guess."

"Where to?"

"Damn it, I don't know."

"Don't swear, Daughter. Think."

"I need some help. I need somebody to help me."

"Who?"

"Mr. Shannon?"

"Do you want him to know about this? Do you want him to see this bed? And these glasses of wine? And this naked dead man?"

"No. Never. Not in a million years."

"Your friend, Mildred?"

"She wouldn't break the law. She's a schoolteacher."

"Well?"

"Rosemary! She's little but she has a stout heart. Rosemary will help me. Oh mercy!"

"What now?"

"How'll I get in the house. It's after midnight. The door's locked."

"He said he had a key. Look in his pants pocket."

I found his pants on the back of the desk chair. "It's not here."

"Try his vest. Hurry, Daughter. It'll be dawn before you know it."

There was a key in his vest pocket. I held it tight in my hand and began to pray out loud it was the right one. Then I heard myself, wailing and moaning and carrying on. I had, if not broken, at least bent sideways most all of the Lord's commandments. I had not made any graven images that I could recall, but I was not in any position to be asking for favors.

I picked up my pocketbook and my trumpet and I hightailed it out of there. My trumpet—my poor innocent trumpet—a murder weapon. How could I ever play a love song on it again?

8

THE BOARDINGHOUSE WAS BLACK AS A NEW-
dug grave. I took off my shoes and crept up on the front porch,
slipped the key in the lock, and turned it this way and that. It wouldn't
budge. I was thinking I'd have to risk throwing a dirt clod at Rosemary's window when I remembered there were two locks on the door.
The key fit the second one, and the bolt slid open with a thud that
could wake the dead. I edged in and waited for Figgy to come barrel-
ing out of her room, demanding to know what I was doing with the
Reverend's key. When this didn't come to pass I started up the stairs,
thankful they were carpeted. Even so, every third one gave off a creak
like the place was haunted.

I felt my way along the second-floor landing, trying to remember the
exact location of Figgy's mangy Boston fern. At that moment I heard
the unmistakable flush of a toilet, and soon after a door opened at the
end of the hall. There was somebody with a flashlight. I was on the
men's floor so it had to be either Mr. Roads or Amos. I hoped it was
Mr. Roads, who was deaf as a post and shortsighted. My hand brushed
against the fern and I sank down beside it.

I watched the beam as it skittered along the hall. If he shined it in
my direction, how was I to explain what I was doing there? Oh hi
there, just checking to see if it needs water. Good evening. Did you
know there is a rare beetle found on ferns only after midnight? But the
beam went on past, and from the sluff and shuffle of the carpet slippers I knew it was Mr. Roads. A door opened and closed. Then there
was blackness again. I waited until the bedsprings stopped creaking.
Then I inched around the fern and started up the stairs to the third
floor.

When I got to the landing I stopped to catch my breath, and my
nerve, which was fast on its way to New Jersey. Then I opened the
door to Rosemary's room, eased in, and closed it behind me. I felt for
the light on her dresser—a ballerina with a little bulb in the skirt—
then I got to the bed and whispered in her ear so as not to alarm her.

"It's Cleo," I said. "It's Cleo, don't yell out."

She sat up. "What on earth . . ."

I got down on my knees and took her hand to calm her. "Just listen, Rosemary, just listen to me. I have something terrible to tell you."

And I told her the whole miserable, rotten story, sparing myself no shame. "And that's it," I said, when I ran low on the facts and had started to embroider. "That's just what happened."

"What are we going to do?" asked Rosemary, her eyes as wide as the Arkansas in a flood.

I could have wept with relief. *We* she said, not *you*. What are we going to do? "Well," I said, "I figure we've got to hide him somewhere."

"Shhhh," she said. "Keep your voice down, you'll wake Mildred." She slipped out of bed and went to her closet. Next thing I knew she was standing in front of me, all dressed in black like some thief from a detective story.

I had thought about it all the way from the church to the boarding-house. I'd conjured up Alexandra David-Neel, that most courageous of women, and tried to imagine what she would do in a case like this one, but I'd decided she was too smart to get herself in such a fix. When the tribesman tried to steal her belongings she pretended to be in a trance, and scared him away with holy words. *Lags, lags, Gelong lags.* She sure hadn't shot him dead on the spot, which she could have easily done with her hidden revolver. No. Alexandra had ingenuity and cunning. I had about as much cunning as a tree frog.

And that's when it came to me. I could hardly tolerate the plan my brain was hatching, so I said it out loud to get shed of it. I hoped Rosemary had a better idea.

"The duck pond," I whispered. "It is said to have no bottom to it."

Rosemary nodded. "That's what they say."

I thought about how dark it would be in the park. "You have a flashlight?"

"No. Don't you?"

I shook my head. "Mr. Roads does."

"Well, we can't exactly go ask to borrow it."

"Maybe there's one at the church. In the vestry."

Rosemary frowned and sat down on the bed. "We've got to take this step by step. We're going in too many directions at once." She held up a forefinger. It was hard to imagine those slender little hands holding up one end of a dead preacher. "Number one," she said, "we have to have something to weight him—uh, it—down with. A body comes to the surface no matter how deep the water if you don't have a weight on it."

I shivered. "Back to haunt you."

Rosemary patted the bed and motioned for me to sit beside her. "Maybe we should think about that part of it, Cleo. Maybe we should just go to the police and tell the truth about what happened."

"Who'd believe me? He's a preacher. I work in a speakeasy."

"He tried to take advantage of you." She put her hands on her hips. "He tried to bugger you!"

"Not to begin with. I was willing the first time."

She threw up her hands. "You don't have to tell them *that*. Oh, Cleo! How could you? You know the sort of man he is—uh, was."

I shook my head. I was as puzzled by myself as she was. "I don't know," I said. "My daddy's hot Irish blood, I guess, and all that nice port wine. While it was happening, I didn't think about anything else. I didn't think about consequences."

Rosemary took her breath in and grabbed my hand. "Oh Lord, Cleo, was he wearing anything on his . . .?"

"He wasn't wearing a thing except colored lights."

"Oh Lord, oh Lord, what if he made you pregnant."

I lifted my chin. "Let's not bother trouble, Rosemary. Let's get back to the question of the weights. There's rocks around the duck pond, big ones. We could tie a rope . . . you have any rope?"

"What would I have with rope, for heaven's sake?"

We were beginning to suffer the irritation that comes with hard choices.

"The clothesline," I said with sudden inspiration.

"It would be missed," Rosemary said firmly. "And if the Reverend was—well, you know, recovered, they might trace the clothesline to this house."

We sat in the longest, most desperate silence I had ever known. Then Rosemary squeezed my shoulder. "I know," she said. "We'll put rocks in all his pockets. Enough rocks will do the trick. I read that in one of the mysteries from the library."

I was suddenly very grateful I had had the foresight to introduce my friend to Mary Roberts Rinehart. Course I'd read those books, too, but my mind was simply not functioning at peak level.

We got down the stairs and out of the house with no trouble, no toilets flushing, and a minimum of creaks. Coming down the brick walk we both started to giggle in that uncontrollable relief that comes after a big fright. The dog next door set up a howl and we tore off down the street, carrying our shoes. We ran the length of the block then stopped under a light to check Rosemary's wristwatch. It was five after two, a mere hour and a half since I had sent a fellow human being into the next world by my own hand. I thought about what we aimed to do. "Oh, shit."

"What is it?"

"He hasn't got any clothes on . . . you know, no pockets."

"I didn't expect he would have." She pulled me along. "We'll just have to get him dressed, that's all. Come on now."

My hands were shaking so bad I could hardly find the knob to the side door of the church. We listened as we made our way across the room and stood in front of the vestry, hanging on to each other for dear life.

"I'll go first," said Rosemary, a quaver in her voice.

But it came to me that I was letting her play the big sister to an unfair degree. "No," I said, and stepped forward. "I must face the consequences. I am the cause of them." It was a piece of bravado, but it did prop up my spirits some.

The moment I opened the door I knew something was wrong. I had left one light on, but the vestry was pitch dark. I found the lamp by the door, switched it on, and peered into the shadows of gloom it cast, shadows that had danced on the belly of my white and ruddy beloved just a couple of hours before. The Reverend Endicott was not on the floor by the daybed where I had left him.

"He's gone," I said. I didn't recognize the hollow voice as my own.

"Maybe he came to and crawled off in a corner," said Rosemary.

We searched the room, including the closet. It was empty except for his cape, which hung there like a big white bird whose wings had been clipped.

"Do you suppose somebody took him?" Rosemary whispered.

"What for?"

She crossed over to the day bed. "There's an awful lot of blood here."

I couldn't look. "He didn't come home or we would have heard him."

"I don't see any clothes."

"No wineglasses either." I went to the file cabinet. There were the glasses—clean—and the empty wine bottle. The one that was half-full was gone.

Rosemary opened her arms wide and gave a great sigh. "You know what that means?"

"I sure don't."

"It means he's alive, Cleo. You didn't kill him. You just knocked him senseless, which he certainly deserved. Don't you see? You had his key, he couldn't come home. He's probably gone off somewhere to lick his wounds like the dirty dog he is."

She went on about his shortcomings while I stared at the bed. I saw something white, gleaming up at me from a wrinkle in the spread. I picked it up, and another one almost hidden by one of the pillows. I held them out to Rosemary.

"What is it?"

"The Reverend's front teeth," I said. I had a great feeling of sadness I couldn't account for. "Oh, Rosemary," I moaned, "I knocked out Robby's beautiful front teeth with my trumpet."

"Serves him right," she snapped, and chuckled like an old crone. "And you mashed his beautiful nose, you said. I don't think the Reverend Endicott will be showing that face around here very soon."

Then she got back into the spirit of Mary Roberts Rinehart and went all over the room wiping off fingerprints, including any that might be on the bottle and the glasses. She wiped the doorknobs as we left. We went right home and curled up like two kittens in her bed, asleep as soon as our heads hit the pillows.

The next morning while we dressed, Rosemary talked about how important it was that we act normal. I told her I would never be normal again. She said all the same we were to be surprised and concerned when we noticed the Reverend wasn't at the breakfast table. She said it would be smart for me to pretend some annoyance when I discovered my wages for Sunday were not under my plate. She said that would be the normal reaction of an employee.

When we couldn't put it off any longer we went down to breakfast, and found a whole crowd of people in the parlor. Figgy was lying on the davenport with a cloth on her forehead, and two men, one in a policeman's uniform, stood over her. Mildred took the cloth, dipped it in a bowl of water, wrung it out, and put it back on Figgy's head. Mr. Roads sat in a straight-backed chair by the piano, tapping his foot, and Amos stood near the doorway, hands jammed in his pants pockets.

Rosemary leaned over and whispered in my ear. "Remember now, act normal." Then she turned to Amos. "What's going on here?" she said, like she'd just arrived from the moon.

Amos shrugged and pointed toward the men. "The lieutenant says foul play."

"Gracious," I said. "What about?"

Amos shrugged again. "The preacher, I guess."

If you wanted the time of day from Amos you had to keep after him. He was not the sort to rattle on. "What about the preacher," I asked.

"He's gone."

"Gone where?"

"Don't know."

"What's wrong with Mrs. Figgs?"

"Fainted."

"Oh, Amos! What happened?"

"His bed wasn't slept in." He motioned toward the davenport. "She sent me down to the church to see if he was there."

"Well?"

"Well what?"

"Was he there?"

"Nope."

Rosemary nodded at the policemen. "Why do they suspect foul play, Amos?"

"Blood."

"What blood? Oh, Amos!"

"On the bed. On the floor."

"Go on," I said. "Tell us all of it."

He sighed. "I knocked on the vestry door like she told me. There was no answer. I went in." He raised his eyebrows and lowered his voice. "That's a pretty fancy office he's got there."

"What about the blood?"

"I told you. On the floor and some on the bedspread. I brought the bedspread back and showed it to Mrs. Figgs. She called the police. Then she fainted."

Mr. Roads came toward us. "You girls going to make the breakfast? I haven't had my breakfast."

"In a minute, Mr. Roads." He turned his good ear toward me. "In a minute," I repeated, louder, and the lieutenant looked up, then joined us. He had a notebook and a yellow pencil, which brought back a flock of migrating memories of my night in jail and the cold hard oatmeal and the blanket that looked like it was pox-infected. I gave him my polite attention.

He asked our names and wrote them down in the notebook. He nodded at Rosemary. "When did you last see the Reverend Endicott?"

"Sunday morning at breakfast," she said promptly.

He turned to me and I did my best to look concerned and surprised like Rosemary said. "After the evening service," I said. "We went to Betty Anne's Diner for a bite to eat, then I came on home. He said he had some work to do at the church."

"And that was the last you saw of him?"

I said it was; then I said what I thought a normal person with normal curiosity would say. "What's the trouble, sir?"

"The Reverend appears to be missing, and we suspect foul play in connection with his disappearance. When did you get home?" he asked Rosemary.

"Close to eleven. I don't remember the exact time. My boyfriend brought me. That's Raymond Francis Malone, the manager at the Rialto."

He wrote in his notebook. "And you?"

I pretended to search my mind. "I'm not positive. It was before midnight, that's when the door's locked."

"Did anybody see you?"

That made me feel like a suspect. I looked at the floor and wondered if a normal person would right away protest her innocence? Or would a normal person just figure the question was routine? "Well," I said, electing routine, "I stopped by Rosemary's room to say good-night—like always—then . . ." I broke off my story as I suddenly realized I had made the worst mistake of my life.

I had not signed in.

I could say that I'd forgot, everybody forgets to do something from time to time. But I had never forgotten to sign in in the whole nine months I'd been at the boardinghouse. How was I to get away from this policeman, out of the parlor, and into the hall so I could sign my name without anybody seeing me?

"Lieutenant?" It was the man in uniform. To my relief the lieutenant grunted and went back to the davenport. Mr. Roads started in again about breakfast and it occurred to me that would be a good excuse to get out of the room. I asked the lieutenant if I could go to the kitchen and fix something for Mr. Roads to eat, and maybe a nice cup of tea for poor Mrs. Figgs. He nodded and I whispered my plan to Rosemary, told her to keep everybody in the parlor.

She stared at me. "How?"

"Faint from the excitement," I said. Then I told Mr. Roads I would bring him something to hold him over. Amos started after me but Rosemary gave him a steely eye and told him to go stand by Mr. Roads. Unless a person was right in the doorway of the parlor, that person couldn't see the wall where the sign-in sheet was tacked up. The pencil hung from a string so it was just a question of a quick signature.

I picked up the pencil, looked at the list, and a chill went through me, bone deep. My name was there, written in what looked for all the world like my own hand.

I made toast and tea like some zombie and took it to the parlor on a tray. Mrs. Figgs was sitting up by then, still holding the cloth to her head. She called me "my dear"—first time ever—when I handed her the cup.

The lieutenant was looking at me closely. I opened my eyes wide and tried to look as harmless as Mary Pickford. He flipped the pages of his notebook. "So," he said, "apparently you were the last person to see the Reverend Endicott."

"I guess so."

"Did he seem upset about anything?"

"No, just like usual."

"What did he talk about at the diner?"

"Well, you know—God. He talked about his work for the Lord,

about how someday he'd like to take the gospel to California."

"California." He wrote that down.

"Yes, sir." I figured I'd hit on something and I went on with it. "He said there was a great need for his ministry in California. He said California has the highest population of sinners in the United States."

The lieutenant didn't even crack a smile at my little joke, which I'd thrown in to ease the tension. "Hmmm," he said. "And you say you got home sometime before midnight? So this conversation about California took place . . .?"

I knew when he talked to Betty Anne he'd learn what time we left the diner, so I thought it would be smart to mention that. I frowned like I was in deep thought. "Well, actually, we left the diner a little before eleven-thirty. Eleven-twenty-five, maybe. Maybe Betty Anne noticed the exact time. You could check with Betty Anne."

"And you came directly home?"

"Yes, sir."

"But you didn't notice the time?"

Mildred looked up in surprise. "I can help you with that, Lieutenant," she said, in her brisk, schoolteacher voice. "It was eleven-forty-five. I heard Cleo come in and thought I'd ask if she'd like a cup of chocolate. Then I looked at the clock and noticed how late it was." She smiled pleasantly. "Time for all of us to be in bed."

He wrote that down with all the other evidence he'd taken and snapped his book shut. He had the look of a man who liked things neat and tidy.

I tried to catch Mildred's eyes, but she was wringing out the washcloth again. Then, like a bolt of truth sliding into place, it came to me that none of this would ever be mentioned between us. None of it. Not the mystery of the sign-in sheet nor the phantom cup of cocoa. There was no question that in both Mildred and Rosemary, I had entertained angels unawares. Hebrews 13:2.

9

THE REVEREND ENDICOTT'S MYSTERIOUS disappearance never made it onto the front page of either the *World* or the *Tribune,* although he lingered inside both those newspapers for a couple weeks. Then he was gone, along with Christmas and New Year's Eve. Nineteen twenty-seven hobbled off into eternity, taking with it Lizzie Borden, Sacco and Vanzetti, Isadora Duncan, and sixty-nine people by tornado in St. Louis, Missouri. Nineteen twenty-eight came in bright blue and cold. My big resolution was to try and stay out of trouble.

On the morning of that first day of the year, I suffered the worst case of the monthlies I had ever endured. I came out of the bathroom yelling, "Rejoice! Rejoice!" That was the code word Rosemary and I had hit on. "I'm rejoicing!" I was to say, in case I fell off the roof in polite company. Then the Lord saw fit to remind me of my transgressions and sent a plague of cramps that dropped me to my knees right there in the hallway. I went to bed with a hot-water bottle and stayed there until almost suppertime. I thought I would surely die.

When I didn't, but instead recovered my full health, I turned mean. I wrote my momma a letter, because in my mind she was the one to blame for all this, the one responsible for my being in Tulsa instead of in my own home where a girl belonged at Christmastime.

This is the letter:

Momma,

I expect you noticed that I did not come home for Christmas. You made it clear that I was not welcome. I will not bother you any more with my natural desire to see you and the rest of my kin, especially during a family holiday. You know where I am if perchance your heart should soften up some. I want to say that I think it is unfair and unjust of you to put more stock in the gossip of the Beulah Baptist Auxiliary than in your own flesh and blood. I do honest work in a costume appropriate to my Art. A trumpet player tends to sweat, and would be hindered and uncomfortable in a high-necked, long sleeved outfit. I have done nothing to be ashamed of.

I chewed on the pencil, then amended the last line to read:

There is nothing about my work that I am ashamed of. Momma, I opened up my Bible just now, and my finger fell on Ephesians 6:4—Provoke not your children to wrath.

I was not my mother's daughter for nothing.

I also wrote a note to Ethan in care of the Warwicks where Momma had said he was working.

Dear Ethan,
Here is a United States Postal Order for fifty dollars. Cash it and give the money to Momma. Don't you dare tell her where it comes from or she won't take it. She is a stubborn woman. Tell her you got a bonus from Gideon. Do not—I repeat—do not spend any of this money on liquor or get into any poker games. I mean it, Ethan. I make a good wage and am saving up. I can help out again if the need arises. If you ever come to Tulsa please come see me at the address on this envelope. I miss all of you something fierce. Don't let on to Momma that I wrote to you. It would just upset her.

At Mildred's urging, I enrolled at Tulsa Central High School at midterm. I hadn't finished the eleventh grade in Robina, but I was given tests in which I excelled in all subjects except mathematics. I was pronounced a senior. A lot of boys asked me out, and I was invited to join a couple girls' social clubs that got together on Friday nights, and learned how to smoke cigarettes. But after my adventures and being on my own and all, those people seemed like little children to me. I didn't make any close friends. Polite but aloof, I kept to myself. I went to school every morning, paid attention to the teacher and my studies, and then came back to the boardinghouse and did my homework until suppertime. Mildred helped me with my algebra and was the sole reason I passed that subject. She was a stern tutor. She'd look over her glasses and say, "In mathematics, Cleo, we do not divine the answers."

I allowed myself few pleasures. There was no shopping or grilled cheese sandwiches. I went to a picture show with Rosemary only if I had conquered my algebra assignment. I even gave up my soaks in the tub. After supper I went to work at the Gusher, where I no longer flirted with the customers.

And that was what I did day in and day out. I just put one foot in front of the other and marched straight-arrow like some Girl Scout right through 1929. The United States won the Olympics that year. Herbert Hoover said if he was elected he'd put a chicken in every pot and a car in every garage. Amelia Earhart, at twenty-nine years old, flew the Atlantic from Boston to South Wales in twenty-two hours. And Thomas Hardy died at age eighty-seven. They put his ashes in Westminster Abbey but they buried his heart on Egden Heath. I checked out all his books from the library and brought him back to life.

They didn't have a ceremony for people who graduated in the middle of the school year. You were expected to come back in the spring if you wanted to parade down the aisle to "Pomp and Circumstance." But they gave me the piece of paper and I knew my momma would be proud—if only she would allow herself that indulgence. I had it framed and Mildred helped me wrap it so it would travel safely. Then I sent it home. She didn't acknowledge its receipt. But she didn't send it back, either.

Ed Shannon gave a big surprise party for me at the Gusher on a Sunday afternoon when it was closed to the public. The gang from the boardinghouse came. Even poor sad Mrs. Figgs, who still watched out the parlor window for the Reverend Endicott to show up. She gave me a nice card and the three volumes of the Book of Knowledge from t e bookcase in my room. Miss Ada brought a big box, a little something she had ordered for the occasion. It was a black satin cap and gown. A trumpet case from Scat was to replace my gunnysack, he said. There was a fountain pen from Tully, and a string of real cultured pearls from Mildred and Rosemary. Amos and Mr. Roads brought roses, dear in January. I was so touched I bawled.

Ed Shannon gave me a wristwatch, a fourteen-carat-gold Lady Hamilton. I tried to talk myself into some double meaning behind the brand, but it wasn't easy. He had himself yet another new girlfriend and she was there too, beaming on me like some fond auntie. His girl-friends, except for Noreen, never even had the grace to resent me. This one was blond and expensive-looking like Constance Bennett, and she drank seltzer water neat. I figured it was the real thing.

But I thought, Oh, what the hell! I held out my wrist so Ed could put the watch on it, then I put my arms around his neck and kissed him full on the mouth. He laughed and turned red. Then he looked into my eyes like I was a somebody he had never seen before.

While we stood there gawking at each other, I realized with a great pang of loss that I was no different from any other female coming to flower. Oh, sure, I thought about going to California with Rosemary and Raymond, and sure, I still had my dream about Lhasa. But, the truth is, more than anything else I wanted to be Mrs. Edward Hamilton Shannon, and live in a house with a backyard big enough to grow some tomatoes, and enough bedrooms for three or four kids. Enough room so nobody had to sleep on a cot out on the porch or in an add-on of many uses. Enough money so everybody had their own shoes and ate cornbread and clabber for supper only out of choice.

All this was going through my mind when Constance Bennett swept Ed away to the kitchen to check on the feast she had helped him order. She stuck close to him for the rest of the celebration.

That night I lay on my bed and contemplated the mysteries of the flesh. I thought about the Reverend Robby Endicott, and in spite of everything that had happened, lustful feelings rose up in me as if they'd been summoned. No more than that. Just lust. Lust in my privates. No houses or tomatoes or the two of us with grey hair and wrinkles, holding hands and being kind to each other.

No babies. Not a sign of a baby.

Then I conjured up Ed Shannon, and stood the two men next to each other. There was the Reverend—a brother to dragons, a companion to owls—so beautiful as to make your heart stop. And there was Ed Shannon, homely and gaunt as Abraham Lincoln.

Ah, but what did the Reverend have chasing after him? Veal calves, the Prayer Partners and Lila, and poor old Figgy. Whereas Ed Shannon, with his plain face and his arms and legs that were too long for the rest of him, attracted women of standing and substance—excepting Noreen, of course. At least she had spirit. You can tell a whole lot about a man just from the kind of women who want him.

As I lay there pondering the riddle of love and sex, I suddenly heard the sharp bark of a fox from my distant past.

Daddy found it wobbling on its haunches in front of a den down by the creek. Just inside were four more pups, all dead. This one was on its last legs, but even so it growled and tried to back off. Daddy figured it was orphaned so he brought it on home to my momma, who could fix most anything that was still breathing. This was a bitch, Momma said, maybe five-six weeks old. She was sound except starved, a condition my momma soon remedied.

We called her Fox. Just as we had called the hawk Hawk, the raccoon Raccoon, the possum Possum. It was the same with all the other creatures God sent to Momma for rehabilitation. She kept them just until they were able to be on their own. She said there was no point in giving a name to something unless it came to stay. Wild animals, she said, came to pass. And Momma was the sole caretaker of these foundlings and accidents. She said animals were not put here for children to learn doctoring on. We could watch and listen but we could not handle. Which was probably one of the reasons for Momma's high rate of success.

Fox had the run of the place, although Momma took her in at night. The two of them came to an early understanding about the chickens. Fox never bothered them, but she was a champion mouser, and we benefited from her presence. When she'd been with us for about a year she began to have suitors. Handsome young dog-foxes started hanging around out by the fence—one at a time like they'd made reservations. A couple of them were bold enough to come into the dooryard and show themselves off up close. Fox would go out and frisk around with them. She'd touch noses and lick muzzles, but she kept her abundant tail pressed flat against her haunches, and she'd shortly come trotting back to the house. Momma began to worry she was tamed down too much.

Then one day just about the sorriest-looking specimen I'd ever seen showed up. He had big nicks in both ears and an ugly scar across his muzzle. Still, he was proud and self-assured. He pranced and preened for Fox like some Prince Charming. She fell in love with him on the spot and they went off together that very day.

I asked Momma why Fox chose him when she'd had her pick of all those handsome fellows that paid her court. Momma said it was because Fox was a fox, and not a cougar or a bobcat or some other solitary creature that raised her young on her own. If a daddy was just around for the mating, then the female didn't have to be choosy about his character. If he was to help raise her litter—as was the way with foxes—he had to be strong and reliable. She said a vixen looked for a good provider, a somebody who knew his way around the swamp.

Momma folded her arms and looked off toward Kansas. She said I would be wise to remember that.

In the late summer of 1929 Ed Shannon and I began going around together. I was the one who started it. One night at the Gusher I walked right up to him and told him that in two short months I would be eighteen years old—*truly*.

He looked me up and down, from head to foot, and said he believed me. He asked me to have dinner with him the next Sunday evening at the country club. People of quality had dinner at night, not supper, unless it was a little cold supper after the theater as in Henry James and Edith Wharton.

As in the old days, Rosemary and I went shopping on Saturday morning. My wardrobe was suited to the speakeasy and the high school. Neither one of us had the vaguest notion of what a girl should wear to a country club. With no enlightenment, we looked in a lot of shop windows. We confessed our ignorance to Miss Ada.

Her eyes lit up and she put me into something silk and beige, with a skirt that went past my knees, and a jacket that hung on me like an old feed sack and completely obscured my wonders. I examined myself in the mirror and said I looked like a somebody that didn't give one hoot about what she looked like. Miss Ada patted me on the head and said that was the general idea. She said I was to remove the jacket when we sat down to dinner at the club and I was to hang it over my chair so the French label would show in case anybody came by to say hello. She said men didn't know anything about labels but their women did, and would pass around the information that Mr. Shannon's new girlfriend was a person of taste and discernment.

She told me to go next door and buy a pair of simple beige pumps and a bag to match. And to wear my cultured pearls for jewelry—nothing else. "Don't wear those earrings, Cleo, they look like they came from Kresses." They had. Then she pointed her finger at me and said it was absolutely *vital* that this dress not look new, not like something I'd gone out and bought for the occasion. She told us how to fix that.

So I paid her almost as much as I'd spent on all six of my costumes put together. Then Rosemary and I took the dress home and spread it out on a sheet in the parlor. We put on clean white socks and walked on it for over an hour, back and forth, forth and back, as Miss Ada had directed.

First Mr. Roads and then Amos stopped in the doorway to watch. Amos, who wouldn't spit out a question even if it burned his tongue, stood there gaping, but Mr. Roads said, "What are you girls doing there?"

Rosemary and I, who had been taking this job dead serious, looked at each other and burst out laughing. I laughed until my sides ached. Then, Rosemary scooped up the jacket on her toe and swung it around.

"Mr. Roads," she said. "What we're doing here is preparing Miss Cleo for her entrance into Tulsa society. If you and Amos have some clean white socks you can help."

Mr. Roads wagged his head. "You're crazy."

I grinned. "Like a fox," I said.

10

OURS WAS A PROPER COURTSHIP, THOUGH not through any fault of mine. The one time he took me to his apartment I did my level best to get the Murphy bed out of the wall and him into it, but he was a man of stern principle and unmovable resolve. Naturally I was embarrassed, having made clear my intentions and being turned down flat.

I said, "I suppose you're going to tell me you haven't been to bed with all those other women you've been running around with. I suppose you're going to tell me you take them to Hot Springs just to see the horses run."

He said, "No, I'm not going to tell you that. I'm not going to discuss it. It has nothing to do with you."

I picked up my pocketbook and headed for the door. He stopped me, put his arms around me, and said he was sorry, said what he'd meant to say was that it had nothing to do with *us*. "Cleo," he said, "I've never been serious about anyone before. This is different. I want it to be right."

A born gentleman, the Reverend had called him. So, we went back to kissing and heavy breathing.

The first Sunday in October he asked me to marry him. This is what he said:

"Cleo, would you do me the great honor of becoming my wife?" Just like in books.

We were at the country club and I was wearing a grey dress that was a first cousin to the mousy beige thing. The orchestra was playing "Thou Swell" and the waiter had just brought champagne. It was all obviously prearranged. I felt like I was living in the last paragraph of a fairy tale. I took his hand and kissed his fingers one by one, right there in public. I would have kissed his feet if they had been handy. The Reverend had been only half right. Ed Shannon wouldn't mess with a virgin, but he would marry a farm girl with no credentials. I was so choked up with emotion all I could do was nod my head.

From his coat pocket, he brought out a little velvet box, opened it, and set it down in front of me. It was a diamond big as a pear, with an opal—my birthstone—on each side. He took it and slipped it on my finger, and we looked deep into each other's eyes while the vocalist went on about how swell and witty and grand we were.

Our engagement did not accelerate our lovemaking. He wanted us to be married over the Christmas holidays, which seemed to me to be in the next century. He wouldn't hear of an elopement. He wanted to "do it right." He wanted me to make up with Momma and "clear up this unfortunate estrangement," so my family could be at the wedding.

"From what you say, Cleo, it sounds to me like all you need to do is apologize."

"I'm the one due the apology." I could've tripped over my lower lip.

He shook his head. "That's the kind of thinking that built the Great Wall of China."

The wedding was to be at the Episcopal church, which Ed attended on Sunday mornings without fail. The reception would be at the country club. The mere thought of the long white dress, the bridesmaids, the flowers, the organ music, all that high church ritual, brought me to the cliff edge of a nervous breakdown. Even though I was outgoing and friendly by nature, I still felt like a peasant immigrant in Ed Shannon's Main Line world. I hadn't even accustomed myself to walking up and down on my new dresses.

And I was impatient.

I'd had the sweet taste of pomegranates, and even though they'd gone sour I was prepared to visit that garden on a regular basis. All pretty poetry aside, I was a cat in serious heat. He was a tom raised on chivalry.

"But we're engaged," I argued.

"We're not married," he answered.

It was beyond me how I'd gotten in such a backward situation. "Where on earth did you get such old-fashioned ideas? This is 1929, not the middle ages."

He said he wanted what I wanted. I slid my hand down the inside of his thigh. He took in his breath, and moved my hand back to my own lap. I swear, I think by then it had gotten to be some tug of power, rather than a moral question of doing things right.

I'd written Momma half a dozen letters and torn them all up. I sailed right through the part about how his mother had been a Hamilton from Roanoke, Virginia, and his father a famous judge from Chicago. And how Himself, a lawyer graduated from Northwestern University, had come to Tulsa to work with the police department at the personal request of the lieutenant governor. Then I'd get to the speakeasy part and there was just no way I could make it presentable.

After a while I didn't try anymore. I was so wound up in myself and my future I forgot all about it. Like any other child I thought about my momma when I was in trouble. Robina County, like Jupiter, was a million miles away.

Ed gave in. We were married on a Wednesday afternoon at the courthouse, with Rosemary, Mildred, Tully, and Scat standing up for us. We had our reception at the Gusher. At my request, Scat played "Thou Swell" about every fifteen minutes. He played it straight. He played it jazz. He played it Dixie. He even played it country. I went up and played it with him. Just for fun, I played "The Battle Hymn of the Republic." Oh, the glories! Oh, the hallelujahs!

We went home early to the apartment. For all my bold and shameless pursuit, I suddenly turned shy and demure as a twelve-and-a-half-year-old virgin with no brothers. I worried some to begin with that he might be able to tell it wasn't my first time, although I thought I had taken care of that during our courtship when I told how I rode the mule to town, and I'd even invented some spirited rides on one of Gideon Warwick's Arabians for good measure. There'd been a moment when I'd almost told him—not about the preacher, but I'd thought to substitute Willis Henderson with the excuse that he was my steady.

Mostly I wanted to tell him because I understood the mean streak in my nature. I was afraid I might get mad at him some day over some trifle and decide then and there that I owed him the whole miserable truth for his own good. Mam always said when a person starts to tell you something for your own good, get behind a nearest boulder as fast as your feet will take you there. I didn't tell him. I kept it all to myself and hoped for the best.

When it came right down to it, I could see some virtue in all that waiting. It put a marker on the day. We could say, this is when we were joined, in the sight of God and of each other. The Bible word is "coupling." We coupled our bodies and our minds and spirits. We didn't just become husband and wife, we became relatives in the finest sense of the word. That's all I can say about my wedding night. Ed Shannon was a private man and I respect that.

We were just about out the door to drive to Shadowlake in Missouri for our honeymoon when the telephone rang. It was Ed's stockbroker in Chicago. We didn't go to Shadowlake. We hung around the apartment for a while listening to the radio and chewing our fingernails. Ed talked a lot on the phone to Chicago.

My practical understanding of mathematics improved that day and in the days to come. This is what happened: Ed Shannon lost money he didn't even have, money that had been invested on something called "the margin." His broker was an old friend of the family and had done well by them, especially in General Electric and American Telephone and Telegraph, so when Ed inherited the money he also inherited the broker. He didn't pay much attention to what happened in the stock market, except to deposit in the National Bank of Tulsa the dividend checks that came every month in the mail. He relied on his father's friend, as his father had before him, for investment decisions. One of those decisions had been to buy stock with nothing more than a ten-percent cash downpayment. The broker himself supplied the other ninety percent on paper. This is called speculation, and it is an old honored American custom.

When the market collapsed, the loans were called home to roost, and it was legal. All those beautiful blue chips that were falling like big rocks were sold to cover the loan—the margin—and by the end of the day the considerable Shannon fortune amounted to one hundred shares of something called Art Metal Construction selling at twenty-six dollars and four bits. G.E. and A.T.&T. went back up in the afternoon, but Ed's shares had all been sacrificed by then.

The broker shot himself and missed. I pointed out that it wasn't easy to shoot yourself in the head and do a poor job of it, and that should tell us a lot about the man's capabilities. But Ed didn't put blame on the broker. He blamed himself for not paying attention to his own affairs.

Ed had arranged to close the Gusher and have it spruced up while we were away, but when we realized just how bad things were we went down and stopped work on the kitchen. Ed paid everybody off. Then the two of us put things back together as best we could and commenced to paint the walls. He'd already bought the paint and there was no point in wasting it. It gave us something to do with our hands besides wring them.

We spent our honeymoon working every day until we were ready to drop, then dragging ourselves home and crawling into bed without even taking our clothes off. We didn't even put the Murphy back up in the wall. There wasn't much coupling going on, that's for sure, but we snuggled close and tried to keep each other's spirits up.

The following Wednesday we reopened like our sign in the window said we would. The restaurant did about fifteen percent of its usual business, and only the old regulars showed up at the speakeasy. Wall Street was a thousand miles from Oklahoma, but still people were scared. Ed's Tulsa banker said his money there was safe, but there wasn't enough of this safe money to cover expenses. Both Scat and Tully said they'd wait it out and take just what he could pay them. The other help, including Amos, couldn't afford that kind of loyalty, so besides playing my trumpet, I cashiered, waitressed, and washed dishes. Ed learned how to cook in a hurry.

Business began to pick up in mid-December but not enough to pay the bootleggers who dealt only in cash. My diamond ring and gold watch went back to the jeweler, and my Lhasa savings, which survived the crash in a hatbox on the top shelf of the closet, went to help pay for our last delivery of booze; scotch, bourbon, and rye. We decided to make the gin ourselves and do without rum. Tully told the customers rum was going out of fashion.

On New Year's Eve we closed the doors for the last time. Tully stayed on with the new owner, who had bought the business for next to nothing. Scat went to New Orleans. And I went to work as a waitress at the Red Lion, where the owner was a personal friend of Ed's. Himself got a job in the district attorney's office. It was several steps down from the one the lieutenant governor had given him, but he was grateful to have it and said so.

And that pretty much took care of 1929, the year of the Big Crash. It was also the year I lost Rosemary. The man who owned the Rialto— which was part of a chain of theaters—started making movies out in California. He hired Raymond to be a director. I couldn't believe it. Raymond Francis Malone, whose big contribution to the industry was hot buttered popcorn. He and Rosemary got married and moved to Hollywood. I saw them off at the train station with a heavy heart. Rosemary, my angel unawares. I watched the train until it was out of sight, tears running down my cheeks. You don't make many friends in this life who'd be willing to help you dispose of a dead preacher in a duck pond.

Ed and I spent 1930 working our tails off. We were lucky. Four million people were without jobs, and by wintertime it seemed that most of them lived in Tulsa, Oklahoma. Tulsa had only one industry, oil, the price of which went up and down according to those mysterious forces that govern such things. When it was up, people worked. When it was down, they didn't. That winter, because of the new fields that opened up in Seminole and Oklahoma City, it went down to a penny a barrel, and the streets were suddenly filled with men and women selling apples or oranges or rags. Some plain begged.

It got worse as the months went by. By 1932 the rate of unemployment had risen to thirty-eight percent. Those were not just cold hard figures lined up in a column. They were people lined up for soup or a place to spend the night. They were men with their hats in their hands, offering to rake leaves or shovel coal or do any kind of work at all, in exchange for a couple potatoes or whatever leftovers you could spare for the kids.

By comparison, Ed Shannon and I were millionaires and I didn't feel right about it. I looked across the table one morning where we sat with our *Tulsa World* and our big breakfast of toast and eggs and coffee. I said, "God is not just."

Ed put on his lawyer look. "Are you bringing formal charges?"

I shoved the front page under his nose and pointed at the headline which declared that 11,675 Tulsans were out of work. There was a picture of a crowd of men in front of the unemployment office. You could tell from the set of their shoulders that they were new to despair, that they hadn't buckled under yet. It about broke my heart.

"I'm not going to church with you anymore," I said. "I've made up my mind. I feel like a hypocrite praising the Lord when he allows all this misfortune."

Only part of this was righteous indignation. The other part was that the Episcopal service put me to sleep. I had told Ed that what his bloodless church needed was a little glory and hallelujah. "Bloodless?" he said. He said Henry VIII had shed enough blood in the name of the Church to last it forever. This sent me to the library on the track of English kings, and I welcomed the distraction. In spite of my nasty remarks about Mayor Watkins and President Hoover, I wasn't much better than the worst of them. I hadn't done anything to help. I wouldn't even open the door to hand out a bowl of soup to one of God's unfortunates. I was afraid for myself, and if there was anything in this world I couldn't tolerate it was a coward. I couldn't help it. I was six months pregnant and Nature had laid her hand on me and said I was to behave in a cautious manner. This pregnancy was not on purpose. This was not a child planned for and welcomed—certainly not by its mother—but a failure of what is known in English novels as French letters.

Ed was just as happy about the situation as if he had unlimited funds with which to raise this restless creature that moved itself each time I finally got comfortable, and which was making me truly ugly in both body and soul.

Ed said we'd have to rent a house with proper bedrooms. No Murphy beds for a family man. In order to pay for this extravagance he had applied for a weekend job at the country club, where he could no longer afford to be a member.

We had a big fight about that. We had just finished supper and were sitting on the couch, fanning ourselves and having ice tea. I said, "I will not have you shaming yourself. You can't work as a coolie in a place where you used to play golf with the bigwigs."

"Coolie?" he said, absolutely dumbfounded. "I'm going to be the weekend host—a job for which I have a lot of experience. I'm perfect for it. I know everybody at the club."

"That's the point. That's what I just said."

"I'm missing something here."

"You *know* everybody."

"It pays a hundred dollars a month. That's the point."

"They'll look down on you."

"Why?"

I instructed him in human failings. "Because you lost your money, that's why. They don't want to be reminded that one of their own lost a fortune. They may be next."

"That's unfair, Cleo. Really unfair. My friends at the club have been kind and helpful to us and you know it."

"Well, they can keep their kindness," I snapped. That was my momma talking. *We don't take charity here.*

Ed Shannon was not a lawyer for nothing. He said, "Does Mildred look down on you because you're poor?"

"That's different."

"How? In what way?"

"I've always been poor. It's not the same thing."

"How is it different." He put his arm around me. "Explain it to me."

I pulled myself up off the couch—a real athletic feat—and determined to walk away from this no-win argument; then I threw up my hands and said what was on my mind. "Why don't we just move away from here. Why don't we just move to someplace where nobody knows us."

He folded his arms and studied the roses in the rug. When he looked up I could tell I had hurt his feelings, which had not been my intention. I thought I was trying to save him from humiliation.

"I think," he said slowly, "that you are the one who will feel ashamed if I take this job."

He had struck the truth right between the eyes but I wasn't about to admit it. We were a long haul from where I had imagined we would be. I'd married Edward Hamilton Shannon of the Chicago Shannons and the Hamiltons of Virginia. I had not married a somebody who showed folks to their tables and told them how good the pork roast was tonight. A fox that knew his way around the swamp hadn't ought to get in such a fix. Not only that but it was his fault that I was in trouble. He'd said it wasn't called trouble if the woman was married and I said, HA! that he wasn't the one big as a barn. I felt like the fat lady at the carnival. My back ached, and my ankles and my perfect wonders were swollen up twice their normal size. In my mind, this man who'd turned out to be as ordinary as oatmeal had infected me with a dread disease—pregnancy—right up there with chronic arthritis and beriberi. Now I was destined to be ordinary too and have a houseful of ordinary kids probably homely like their father. I would never get to Lhasa. I would never make my journey to the unknown.

He went back to studying the roses. The way his shoulders gave just a hint of a droop put me in mind of the men in the newspaper who were about to have the pride knocked out of them. I felt like the meanest woman on the face of the earth.

"Of course I wouldn't be ashamed," I said, in a tight little voice. "Don't be foolish."

But Ed Shannon was not one to allow the Great Wall of China to be built in his own living room. He came over and took my hand. "Cleo," he said. "I assure you my friends are not going to think less of me because I want my wife to have a nice place to raise our children." He bent over and looked me in the eye. "And her tomatoes. Let's see a smile, huh? How about a walk around the block, it's cooling off now, you'll feel better. You've been cooped up here all day, that's the problem. Okay? And I want you to see the doctor about this sudden weight gain. No wonder you're so miserable."

"We can't afford it," I muttered.

For just a fraction of a second, his eyes turned hard. "Call the doctor tomorrow."

I sighed and said I would.

He smiled, kissed me, and smoothed my hair back. "Cleo," he said, "I do not sit a white horse well."

I hadn't fooled him. Not for a minute.

Ed Shannon was two men. Maybe that's the nature of the beast. He was soft-spoken and easy with me, and with his friends, even on those rare occasions when his eyes went hard. Sometimes, though, I would hear him on the telephone with his office about somebody who'd performed some dire criminal act, and you could tell from the tone of his voice he'd as soon send that person to the guillotine as look at him. That other Ed Shannon gave me chills. From time to time there were pieces in the paper about some case and there'd be references to the "icy" or "deadly" cross-examination by the assistant prosecutor. Just as before, I learned more about Ed from the newspaper than I did from Himself. I resolved to go down to the courthouse during one of those trials and get to know my husband better.

But that had to wait until I was shed of the creature that so burdened my days.

11

AFTER TWENTY-SIX HOURS OF HARD labor, Edward Hamilton Shannon, Jr., was born at Morningside Hospital in Tulsa on August 15, surely the hottest day of 1933. Once he was laid, squalling and furious, on my belly I completely forgot all the grief he had caused me. The sight of him, red and wet and wearing my grandmother's face, caused my heart to sing and hurt at the same moment.

I stayed in the hospital one full week, six days of that against my will. My feet were not allowed to touch the floor. That was the rule. Breast feeding was discouraged and held in low regard, but I made a fuss. I refused all medication because I was afraid they'd give me something to dry up my milk. The doctor tried to explain to me that babies needed to be on a strict schedule so they'd grow up disciplined, but I'd been around too many farm animals to pay any mind to such foolishness. I said, "Doctor, try to imagine a Guernsey trotting off from her calf because it isn't six o'clock yet."

Once Ed took us home we were just fine. Eddy knew exactly how to be a baby. He let out a howl when he was hungry and ate and burped and slept and pooped the right color and then howled again for any or all of the right reasons. I knew exactly how to be a mother, which was a great relief to me after my sorry performance as a mother-to-be.

Another relief was the knowledge that I didn't have to worry about getting pregnant again as long as I was nursing the baby. In those days contraception was a dirty word and against the law except for the rhythm method. There's an old joke about that:

Question: What do you call folks who use rhythm?

Answer: Parents. Har-dee-har.

It is my contention that there are women with aggressive eggs. These eggs have got eyes in the back of their little round heads and they never sleep. They sit poised on the shore and wait for sperm to swim upstream. Without so much as a by-your-leave they call out,

"Over here, honeybunch . . . this way, sugarplum," and they set out to populate the planet. There's an old joke about that too: "All he has to do is put his house shoes under my side of the bed."

So four months after Eddy was born, one of my fine aggressive eggs caught herself another sperm. (So much for the nursing theory.) The difference this time was my attitude. I had the hang of it. When I got to the uncomfortable stage, I hired a girl to come in a couple days and help with the housework, and be there to tend Eddy in case I took a notion to go to the library or a matinee or visit with Mildred. The secret of an easy pregnancy is total surrender and a husband with a steady job.

We named her Emily for his mother, Frances for mine. And now that we had a "boy for you, a girl for me" we kept my eggs in check again with drugstore products. We rented another house, a two-story with three bedrooms on Pierce Avenue, just a block from the Sixth Street park. Ed got a promotion and a raise and I persuaded him to stop working at the country club so he could be home with his family on weekends. It was "My Blue Heaven," right smack dab in the middle of the Great Depression.

I had sent a printed announcement to Momma when Eddy was born. She sent a white suit with a lot of handwork on it, and her curative for colic. No letter. No note. I sent another printed announcement after Em. I underlined Frances, then fretted that it stood out as a second name. A pink dress arrived with stitches and smocking that could have caused blindness. More curative, but no note.

Ed said he had never heard of two more stubborn women in his whole life. "This is what we'll do," he said. "Next Sunday we'll take the babies and drive over to Robina to see your mother."

"Not till she asks us," I said, putting my foot square on the neck of his good intentions.

"All right, then, I'll write her a letter. I'll introduce myself and invite her to visit."

I gave him my mean-eyed look. "You'll do no such thing. It's none of your business."

The counselor didn't give up easy. He presented Momma's side of the case so well that one Sunday we got as far as Wagoner before I made him turn around. He didn't speak to me on the drive home, and for the rest of the day there was a heavy frost all over the house.

"I'm disappointed in you, Cleo," he said, after the chill wore off some.

"I'm disappointed in myself," I told him, "but I can't seem to do anything about it."

And I couldn't. Too much time had passed. Too many hard words had been recalled and imagined. In my mind I had played the scene of being turned away at the door so many times I felt it had already happened. I let go of my past and looked to my future.

Eddy started to kindergarten at Longfellow Elementary. Then Em. One day was like the next, and the one before. I delighted in this sameness, was comforted by this ordinariness that had so offended me while I carried Eddy. It was Monday, then Tuesday, then Monday again. Spring, then ripe tomatoes, then winter before you knew it. It was as if life knew just exactly where it was going. Life was the Arkansas River, flowing sure and steady, and high on its banks.

There were no days to put markers on. You put markers on events that change your life forever, events both good and bad. My markers were Miss Hawkins, Daddy's death, Alexandra's book, leaving home, the letter from Momma that broke my heart, my passion for the Reverend Endicott, my pure love for Ed Shannon, the wedding, the Crash, then Eddy, and Em. A marker can be a celebration or a tombstone. A marker can be something you're obliged to pay back.

It's early spring. I'm awake every morning before the alarm goes off. I get up, wash my face, brush my teeth, pull my hair back with a satin ribbon, put on a pretty housecoat, and come downstairs to make coffee. I light the oven, squeeze the orange juice, and sit at the kitchen table, where I have half a cup of coffee while I listen to the familiar noises my house makes of a morning. The pipes shudder when Ed gets in the shower. The floorboards squeak overhead. Em's been to the bathroom, now she's crawling back in bed. Eddy is over by the window feeding his goldfish. I strike a match and light the fire under the griddle, then turn it down low. I go to the foot of the stairs.

"Eddy, you dressed? Emily . . . Emmmmmaleee . . . get up now. You hear?"

Ed walks down the hall to their rooms. Groans. Laughter. Bliss.

They come down one at a time, Ed first. He opens the front door, then the screen. I hear him mutter something about oiling those hinges this weekend. He has said that every morning for the past month. He goes out on the porch, down the steps, then comes back, slapping the newspaper against his palm. He says he wishes we had a paperboy who could throw straight. He and Eddy come into the kitchen. They sit down in the breakfast nook. Eddy asks for the funnies. Ed hands them over. Then he laughs.

"Here I am again," he says.

I flip the hotcakes. "What did you do now?"

He leans forward. "Caught a big one."

"Is that what it says?"

"Says Edward Shannon is Crime's Number One Enemy." He laughs again. He gets a kick out of reading about himself in the paper.

Em comes in, rubbing her eyes. She is a night child. Her blouse is wrong side out. Sunlight hits the blackberry jelly in the pressed glass bowl I got with boxtops. I stack the hotcakes on a big platter we won at the picture show. I serve something different every morning. I take pride in it. Hotcakes this morning, bacon and eggs tomorrow, oatmeal and cinnamon sticky buns the next day. Always the orange juice, vitamin C for my family, fresh squeezed with the pulp floating on top, pulp that makes a mustache on Eddy's upper lip.

I smile. I hardly ever think about Lhasa anymore.

I pack the children's lunch buckets. I bake muffins with silly notes in them. "Little Red Riding Hood Was a Dope." "Major Bowes Wants YOU on His Show." "The Brothers Grimm Made This Muffin."

Ed leaves first. Kisses all around. I dash upstairs and change so I can walk the kids to school. Not all the way, that would embarrass Eddy, who is in second grade now. Just through the park and to the cross-walk on Sixth. I tell Eddy I'm walking his little sister. He grins and allows me that lie. He's a smart kid.

I come home and do my housework. Make the beds, clean the kitchen, pick up the towels in the bathroom, use the feather duster on the pretty doodads I've collected, sweep the front porch. I lean on the broom and gaze out over my yard. I never get over the wonder of it—a house with a lawn and six rooms and an inside toilet.

Then I take the bus to the university, where I study music. I play first trumpet with the orchestra, the first woman to sit in that seat in the history of the university. I am twenty-eight years old, the oldest member. Once a month we try out for first chair. I worry about losing my lip. I am a wife and a mother; I don't have enough time to practice. I don't understand second chair. I am Creek Indian on my mother's side. I am descended from royalty. I close my eyes and hug myself because I'm so happy. I read in a book that happiness is the absence of pain.

One morning we all get up late. Ed will drive the kids to school. No time for the waffles, just toast and orange juice. He bustles the children out the door—frowns at the screen. They hurry down the walk. Em yawns and waves; she carries her shoes. Eddy runs back to the porch and tells me he forgot to feed Moby.

"Don't worry," I say. "I'll take care of the goldfish."

I watch them get into the car then hurry back to the kitchen to see if I've turned the fire out under the coffee.

There is a great explosion out front. I run to the door. Neighbors spill out of their houses and into the street. Somebody yells about the fire department, screams for the police. In front of the house, where our car was parked, there is a heap of torn metal with smoke and flames pouring from it. I start toward it and someone grabs me and pulls me back. There is another explosion. We are thrown to the ground. I sit up, shake my head and crawl toward the street. Then I see my daughter's shoe, one of her black patent Mary Janes, on the lawn under the pepper tree.

Someone must have asked me if there was anyone to call and I must have given them Mildred's number because she came and took me to her apartment where I stayed for almost three weeks. For some time I had no memory of going there or of what happened—only what Mildred told me. She said she found me in the living room, sitting on the floor in the corner, hugging the fishbowl.

Mildred made all the arrangements, the funeral, the bank, the insurance. She put papers in front of me and guided my hand when I signed them. She talked to the police, kept the reporters away. She sold the furniture, packed up the things she thought I would want to keep, and put them in her garage. She told me I hated her because she made me eat, poked spoons of soup and Jell-O into my mouth and made me swallow.

She said that one morning I got up, stripped the bed, and said I was ready to go home.

"To Robina?"

I nodded.

She asked what I wanted to take with me.

"What I came with. My satchel, my trumpet, my Lhasa book . . ." I looked over at the windowsill. "The goldfish."

She arranged with a friend to drive me home that Saturday morning. They let me out at the turnoff so I could walk the rest of the way. Her friend didn't want to do that, but Mildred understood.

Momma was out front in the vegetable garden. She straightened up when she heard the gate open, leaned on the hoe, and watched me come toward her.

I stopped, set my belongings down on the ground. I said, "God has punished me beyond all understanding. You have got to let me come home."

Her face softened, but she didn't move.

I said, "My husband and my babies are dead."

She reeled like she'd been struck, then dropped the hoe and came and took me in her arms.

"What am I to do with myself, Momma? What'll I do?"

She held me tighter and began to sway. She rocked me back and forth, back and forth. "Grieve, daughter," she said. "And work with your hands."

PART II

My soul is weary of my life.
—JOB 10:1

12

THE MULE AND I WENT OUT SIX MORNINGS
a week at dawn and worked the fields until I felt sorry for both of us. I
did it for the single reason that most things get done: there was nobody
else to do it. My brother, Ethan, was in the state prison at McAlester
for bootlegging. Sarah was married and living in Fort Worth. (Momma
herself held the shotgun, so to speak.) And Baby Fidelity had disappeared in the middle of the night the year before I came home.

"With the egg money. Just like her big sister," Momma said after
she stopped tiptoeing around me, and became her normal nettlesome
self again.

I was watching her one day after my grief had let up some, after I
began to see what I was looking at. She was struggling up and down
the rows behind the plough, an old undershirt that had belonged to
my daddy plastered to her back, her long grey hair stringing out of the
twisted braid on her neck.

I walked out to the field and took the reins from her. "I'll do it," I
said. "I'm sorry, I didn't notice."

She looked relieved for a bare second, then took the reins back and
pointed her chin at me. "This is my job," she said. "Yours is the
garden."

We wrestled over the reins for a time, the mule showing us the
whites of his eyes over his withers; then the last time she snatched
them away I let her keep them.

"Momma," I said, "what makes you so stubborn anyhow? This is
no job for an old woman. Out here in hundred-degree heat. And what
makes you think you can grow anything here but dinosaur bones? It's
clay, Momma." I reached down and scooped up a handful of the stuff,
then shoved it under her nose. "Look at it. It's clay! And rocks! Just
look at all those rocks!"

She drew herself up and clucked at the mule. "Whatsoever a man
soweth, that shall he also reap. I am sowing corn. I shall harvest corn."

"Then let's hire it done." I was trailing along beside her, tripping over the damn rocks. "I've got the insurance money."

"You keep that money in the bank," she said sharply. "Hard times are not over yet, not by a long shot. And only a fool pays a stranger to raise his crop for him."

I threw up my hands and went on back to the house, slammed the screen door, near knocked it off its hinges, and then I realized that for the first time in three months I felt something besides sorrow and loss. I was thankful.

Momma came in about an hour later, bright pink as a stalk of rhubarb, and slumped down at the kitchen table. She looked up at me like I was a somebody come to collect the rent. Then she blew out her breath and asked me to please get her a dipper of cool water. "You're right," she said. "I'm an old woman. I hadn't noticed till you so kindly pointed it out." She took the dipper and pressed it against her forehead. "I have been young and now am old. Lord Almighty it's hot out there. Not a breeze in sight, not a leaf stirring between here and Colorado. What's the rest of it? See, even my memory's going. First the eyes, then the back and then the memory. And now am old . . .?" She closed her eyes and sipped the water. "Ah yes, I have been young and now am old. Yet have I not seen the righteous forsaken. Psalms 37:25. Thank you, Daughter. You're a good girl, not a righteous girl but a good one in your own way. I swear I think I have sunstroke. Yes, I would welcome your help with that field. I've ploughed it up three times. Taken out as many big rocks as I can lift. One more ploughing, a good manuring, a good raking and it's ready to sow. You can't reap if you don't sow." She drained the dipper and held it out to me. "Please get me some of that lemonade out of the cold house. I've sweat so much my blood's gone thick."

I brought in two crops, summer and fall, then packed up my satchel, my trumpet, and the goldfish and went over the way to tend to my grandmother, who had decided she would die momentarily. Every so often Mam would decide to die, usually when she'd had a long spell of feeling poorly, or had misplaced something and thought her mind was going. She said she didn't have to worry about getting senile or losing control of her bodily functions. She had the gift. Like her mother before her. She could, she said, just up and stop breathing of her own will. She was ninety-seven now, so I didn't take this latest pronouncement to heart. I knew she would live forever just like she'd always done, but I humored her anyway.

I was more comfortable at Mam's house; I could be myself there. Even though Momma had told me to grieve, she didn't know how to handle it when I did. My weeping would send her off on sudden shirttail errands out to the barn or the vegetable garden or down to the creek. So even before I moved to Mam's house to look after her, I'd done my grieving there where tears were regarded as the normal fellow-travelers of sadness, and treated with kind words, pats on the shoulder, and hickory tea sometimes laced with peach brandy.

One day in mid-December she wanted to talk about the music for her send-off. " 'La Golandrina,' " she said. She was sitting in her rocker by the kitchen stove, looking like some old frozen Eskimo, a shawl over her shoulders, a blanket wrapped around her knees. "You know that one, Cleo?"

I hummed a couple-three bars. "Da daa da daaaa . . . da da da dee da dummmmmmmm . . ."

"That's it. That's the one. That's what I want all right. You play it on your trumpet and get somebody to strum the guitar along with you. No piano, you hear? It's a Spanish song, needs a Spanish guitar with the big neck."

"Aren't there any Indian songs you'd like to have?"

She frowned and shook her head. "Creek songs all go whump whump whump—not a musical tribe." She patted herself on the chest. "I want to fly out of this old house. I want to soar. You pay attention now, I can't trust Frances with my wishes, you know how she is. After the regular church service, I want the Creek burial and the Spanish song. You got that?"

"But what will all your Presbyterian friends think? Heathen rites and foreign music?" I spoke in a grave tone like a lawyer trying to cover all the possibilities. Mam wasn't fooled, she had my measure down to the allspice. She winked at me and grinned. She still had all her front teeth except the one behind the eyetooth on the left, so her grins—out of vanity, truth be known—were one-sided. She'd been to the dentist in Muskogee about a bridge, but then decided she was going on soon and wouldn't be needing it.

"Well," she said, "I just don't care what they think. It's my funeral.

They don't like it they can stay home. It's fine to be a live Presbyterian but I don't want to be a dead one. Too complicated. Too many rules and regulations. You got to wait around for Judgment Day before you can soar." She brought her fist down smartly on the chair arm. "The Creek burial and the Spanish song." Then she leaned back and stared out the kitchen window, a little smile on her face. "My fourth husband was Spanish. You know that?"

"I've seen his picture. Handsome man."

"A fine man. I miss him."

"And my grandfather? He was a fine man, too?"

"They were all fine men, Cleo." She motioned toward the table and I took the sack of Bull Durham and rolled her a cigarette. "All fine men," she repeated, wagging her head. "I was blessed."

I lit the cigarette and handed it to her. "What kind of blessing is it to bury four husbands?"

She gave the question some deep smoky thought. "God's will," she said finally.

Ah yes, God's will. That bottomless repository for the faithful's disappointments. I didn't say that. I said, "God must be partial to widows."

She gave me her shrewd look, knowing which widow I referred to. "Your man loved trouble. They all do."

"It was his job."

"You mean he was forced into his line of work? Had no say-so?"

"He was sent to Tulsa because of the riots. He was sent as a negotiator—a peacemaker, Mam—by the attorney general because he'd done such a good job in Chicago."

"Oh, I see. No trouble. Just civilized conversation."

"It started out that way. He was making progress until the Klan got into it and Ed's deputy turned up dead. They got off and Ed was so disgusted he resigned."

"Resigned from the law?"

"Opened a speakeasy."

"I bet that was peaceful work."

"He didn't stay with it. He went back to the department."

She smiled and leaned back in her chair, satisfied. "That's what I said. He loved trouble. Was trouble killed him. But he didn't mean for his trouble to kill his babies." She fixed me with her shrewd look again. "And he didn't mean for you to come back here and look after two cranky old women for the rest of your life either. That's not what he'd want for your future."

My future. My future had been blown to smithereens on a bright sunny morning in early spring, leaving behind only my little boy's goldfish, whose vital signs I checked first thing on rising.

In less than a year I'd gone from numbness to grief to pure red rage and then into some strange condition I could only call heedlessness. I mean I took chances any time they presented themselves, even began seeking them out. I'd done everything from going outside in the freezing cold with a wet head to crossing the swinging bridge over Swenson's Gulch with my eyes shut, and it with no side ropes—a hundred-foot drop straight to Hell. I went to Cushman's Cave, which everybody knew was due to collapse on itself any minute and which had a sign posted—DANGER UNSAFE ENTER AT YOUR OWN PERIL. I did. I could not get enough of peril. I went deep into Cushman's Cave and cried out at the top of my lungs, daring God, provoking him. Called him everything but a white man. All I did was disturb the dust and the poor bats trying to rest up. God, as was his habit, had business in the next county.

After the heedless phase passed, one of restlessness came over me, which condition I was in at the time of this conversation with Mam, and which was—to my bewilderment and shame—accompanied by vivid dreams of a carnal nature.

Mam was surely right. A man with a heart the size of Ed Shannon's would not want me to hole up here and let my body and soul wither. Oh, but surely it was too soon. Surely such dreams were unnatural and wicked. Surely I was plagued with my daddy's hot Irish blood.

"Your man have a brother?" asked Mam, who could read minds like they were recipes. "In the old days a man took his brother's widow for a wife."

"That was the Jews, Mam, in ancient times."

"Creeks too."

"Doesn't matter. Ed Shannon was an only child."

"A year is long enough for mourning, lest you get in the habit of it. I married Juan eleven months after Emil passed. You have to get yourself back to the city, Cleo, no fit prospects around here. All the young people's gone off to California."

"It hasn't been a year," I said sharply. "Let's get back to these arrangements you're in such a hurry about. Who do you want to do this Creek ceremony?"

She was gazing out the window again. "Juan showed up in the doorway one day looking for work. Stayed out in the hayloft. I'd hear him play that guitar of an evening and every morning when I woke up my heart was a little lighter." She leaned toward me and lowered her voice. "He was younger than me, by almost fifteen years. Your momma came prissy-footing around when she heard from the Auxiliary ladies about him moving into the house. Told him to pack his belongings and git before sundown. I said, 'Frances, this man is my lawful husband and I'll thank you to mind your own business.' She had a snit-fit right there on the front porch. Said I was going senile and how she'd see a lawyer about putting me away up at the insane asylum in Vinita. Oh Lord! How I wanted to pinch a piece out of your momma.

"She didn't show her face again till after Juan got hisself drowned running a trout line. Couldn't swim a lick, Juan couldn't, but he wanted me to have fresh fish for my birthday. Five years with that sweet man. Five long years of that guitar and not having to listen to Frances quote the Bible at me. Best five years of my life. You keep your eyes open for a good man, you hear?"

"I had a good man. And a family and a good life. I don't want to do that again. Don't want to risk it." I got up and put more wood in the firebox, wondering how to get her off this painful subject. I said, "I plan to travel when the time's right. Maybe I'll take lovers." But when I looked over to see if I'd shocked her, her eyes were closed and she'd dropped off, as she tended to do sometimes in the midst of a long conversation. Gone off somewhere with Juan and his guitar. Or with one of the others, maybe even my grandfather. Mam had a lot of memories to choose from.

I had my first setback at Christmastime, not unexpected, not unprepared for, but a setback all the same. As was natural I was visited by the ghosts of Christmas past.

There's light fluffy snow, the kind that catches in your eyelashes and squeaks underfoot. We get bundled up and Ed drives us over to Tulsa's south side, where the rich people live, and we gawk at the lights and decorations. We come home and have eggnog and black-currant scones while we put up our tree. We put on the lights, then the popcorn and cranberries we strung that afternoon. We open the Christmas trunk and find that our angel has suffered a broken wing, and a lot of the balls have mysteriously lost their hangers. Ed says—just like he does every year—"This trunk eats hangers." Em's eyes well up over the angel but her daddy tells her not to worry, says he's had special training in the mending of angel wings. He sets the wing and I make hangers out of hairpins. All is well.

Eddy reads "The Night Before Christmas"—doesn't miss a word—and I play "O Holy Night" on my trumpet. The kids write notes to Santa describing their good deeds and intentions, and leave him a glass of eggnog and a buttered scone on the hearth. Em takes some straw from the manger scene for the hungry reindeer. They go up to bed and come to the head of the stairs every few minutes to ask if it's morning yet. Ed says they'll have nothing but a bunch of old sticks in their stockings if they don't get to sleep. Eddy smiles and hoods his eyes. Last year his note read: "I know who you are but I won't tell Emily."

Ed goes to the basement to put the finishing touches on a toy box he's built for Eddy. I fill the stockings, put a big navel orange on top. We sit on the couch holding hands, admiring our work. We put a jigger of rum in Santa's eggnog and drink it, eat the scone, and go off to bed. We make love in a tired, friendly way and drift off toward morning. Nothing special about it. An ordinary Christmas Eve. No black wings beating at the mind. No small voice that says this will never come again . . . store this up . . . protect it . . . remember it. Thank God the small voice knows when to keep its mouth shut.

I went with Mam and Momma to the Christmas Eve service at the Presbyterian church, but declined the invitation to bring my horn and play some carols. I hadn't meant to go at all but Mam said it wasn't good for me to be alone in my sad state of mind, and Momma said she couldn't see to manage the wagon at night anymore. Since I'd called her an old woman over the ploughing, she'd found more and more tasks that were beyond her competence.

I sat between them in the pew and did my best to concentrate on Reverend Shoemaker's familiar sermon about the star in the east and the hope of the world. But my mind kept circling back to Mary. Never before had I felt so close to that poor woman. Now we had a loss in common.

The next day Momma did a roast duck with all the fixings and when we'd eaten everything in sight I cleared the table, poured more coffee, and we exchanged our gifts. Momma had knit me a sweater, a cheerful red one of the difficult braided cable pattern, and Mam gave me a new ten-dollar bill.

"Buy yourself something real pretty," she said. "When you get to the city."

Momma glowered at her. "Who said anything about her going to the city?"

"I did." She craned her neck and searched the room. "You see anybody here 'sides us?"

"I guess you forgot what the city did for her last time."

"Today's bread is to bake. Yesterday's is eaten."

But Mam was no match for Momma in the pith department. She swatted that one down like it was some pesky fly. "Woe be to the bloody city! It is full of lies and robbery."

"I didn't mean she should stay there, Frances. I plan to leave my land to Cleo. I want her to find herself a good man and bring him back here to farm it for her. Girl's working too hard, don't you see that?"

"Your land should go to Ethan. By rights."

"Might as well leave it to the wind."

"Not so. He's learned his lesson in the penitentiary. He'll come home and settle down. You'll see."

"Like a blind man sees."

"He was young. When I was a child I spake as a child . . ."

"Wasn't childishness sent Ethan to McAlester. Was greed. A grown-up sin."

"He's the firstborn boy, the one to inherit by rights."

"Not Creek rights."

"God's rights."

"Wasn't the boy out there tending your crop last summer."

"The smell of my son is as the smell of a field which the Lord hath blessed."

"Dammit, Frances! Will you quit that! I'm about out of patience with your Bible-thumping."

124

"I'm talking about what's right."

"I'm talking about what's fair."

I tapped my water glass with my spoon. "Merry Christmas, ladies," I said. I put their packages in front of them and called for a temporary halt to the hostilities.

Mam loved anything wrapped in pretty paper and done up with ribbons, didn't matter what was inside. She picked uncertainly at the bow and streamers then asked me to untie it—careful so it didn't break. Then she took the paper off and folded it neatly. She hunched her shoulders and grinned so big she showed her empty space.

"What is it, Cleo?" she whispered.

"The Hope diamond."

"The what?"

"Open it for heaven sakes," said Momma. "Don't take all day." She had one hand on her own package and was drumming her fingers on it.

Mam opened the box and peered inside. She blinked and looked up. I lifted out a cigarette machine and put it in front of her, along with a half dozen packages of Bugler tobacco.

"What on earth . . . ?"

"Here see, you put one of these little papers here, fill it with tobacco—not too full—then roll this thing over and you've got a cigarette. Don't have to twist the ends."

"Well, I declare. If that isn't something." She poked at it like it might bite. "It's a far cry from Garrett & Honest Snuff. What'll they think of next? You lean over here, darlin' baby, and let your old Mam give you a big kiss."

Momma was frowning. "She'll just smoke more. That thing will make it easier for her."

I nodded. "Probably kill her."

We laughed. Even Momma.

"Your turn," I said. "Open up your package."

Her face lit up with pure pleasure when she saw what was inside. I'd written to Miss Ada at my favorite dress shop in Tulsa and asked her to pick out something for my momma that would knock the socks off the Beulah Baptist Auxiliary. She eased the dress out of the box. It was a beaut. Blue-grey wool with pleats on the bodice and little pearl buttons all down the front. She smoothed her hand over it and looked bewildered. "I've never seen anything so beautiful. So fine. Just feel this cloth, Mam. Oh just look at this work! French seams!" Then the pleasure faded. "Did you take your insurance money out of the bank?"

"Hush," I said. "Look underneath. There's more." She pulled out a pair of stockings and held them up. "It's called nylon," I said. "Something new, Miss Ada says. They need silk for the war in Europe. Aren't they pretty?"

She put the stockings back in the box, folded the dress, and covered it with tissue paper. "And just where am I to wear all this finery? You think the chickens will take notice?" Her voice was rough with embarrassment, but I could tell she had gone back to being pleased.

"Walk up and down Main Street in it," said Mam. "You might catch yourself a fella."

"A fella?" Momma snorted. "At my age? You think I'm foolish?"

"Know it for a fact . . ."

And they were off again. A pair of evenly matched India cobras, spitting at each other across the table, loving every minute of it.

13

IT WAS SURELY THE COLDEST JANUARY ON record. Freeze the balls off a brass monkey, as my daddy used to say. I was saddling Mam's horse to go into town to the library and grocery when it occurred to me I could buy myself an automobile. I had nearly five thousand dollars' insurance money in the Farmer's Bank of Robina. No good reason I should ride around in inclement weather on a mule, or a grey mare almost as old as I was. Since I'd gone into that money the thought of it was not quite so troublesome. That day—the day I went to draw some out for Momma's Christmas dress—it just lay there on the counter, me staring at it and making no move to pick it up.

"Cleo?" That was Neddy Wadkins. His father owned the bank and Neddy worked there as a teller. "You all right, Cleo?"

Everybody in town knew of my tragedy and I was subject to a great deal of kindness because of it. I just kept staring at those bills. Seemed to me they had blood all over them. "I don't know if I can do this," I said, close on tears.

Neddy looked at me with sad, concerned eyes; then he brightened. "I could write you a bank draft. Just a piece of paper. Would that be better? Want to try that, Cleo?"

I did and it was. You don't have to be very clever to put one over on yourself.

So, that cold January morning while I saddled the horse I was thinking I could find a car and have Neddy write me another bank draft to pay for it. I was thinking I could get shed of that full five thousand dollars without ever having to lay hands on it.

I went to the lending library to return the books I'd got the week before, find some new ones, and thaw out in front of Miss Hawkins' stove. She hadn't changed much in the years I was gone from Robina. She was a little greyer maybe, a new wrinkle here and there, but still as keen on literary matters as she'd ever been.

We were having some difficulty finding novels for me that didn't make me sad. Good books are always full of reminders of your own life, as if the author had sneaked into your mind and stolen away your thoughts. Sometimes a book would fall right out of my hands from the sheer amazement of it. "Now, how on earth did you know that?" I'd ask the book in question. I said this lots of times, to writers both alive and long dead, some of them even men, who you wouldn't expect to know the secret places in the female heart.

The week before, I'd checked out *The Yearling,* for which Marjorie Kinnan Rawlings won a prize, but I couldn't finish it. As soon as I caught on there was no way for Miss Rawlings to let that deer live without ruining her book, I put it aside.

Miss Hawkins smiled at me when I came in and said I looked like I could use a cup of hot tea. I said that'd be real nice, and put *The Yearling* and whatever detective books I had down on her desk.

"I have a new one for you." She reached back to the shelf behind her and pulled out *Rebecca* by Daphne du Maurier. "It's a good tale," she said, "but gothic, nothing you need to take seriously, just good entertainment." She picked up *The Yearling.* "You get through this one?" I said that I hadn't. "Didn't think you would," she sighed, "but it was worth a try. Get out of your things now and pour yourself some tea. How's Jessie coming along? She looked right perky on Sunday."

"She's fine," I said. "Her arthritis is bad in this weather, but she's over her cold. She's decided not to go on just yet."

Miss Hawkins chuckled. "She's a treasure, your grandmother. I love to hear her stories about the old days. You should write them down, Cleo. When she passes a whole era goes with her."

"I'm not so sure she doesn't make them up as she goes along."

"So? What do you think the historians do? I've always been sorry I didn't write my grandmother's life. Or at least pay closer attention when she talked about it. When Charles Dickens came to America for his big tour she was secretary to him and Mrs. Dickens—made arrangements—that sort of thing—went all over the country with them. The tales she could tell! And I didn't write down a word of it, sat by and let her adventures die with her."

"Gee," I said. "Charles Dickens."

"He was the most popular writer in the world then, and not even thirty years old. Gramma said the poor man's clothes were almost torn off him what with people just wanting to touch him. Can you imagine?" She frowned, looked up, and went over to the bookshelves. "You read this?" She handed me something called *Our Mutual Friend*.

I shook my head. "Never heard of it."

"He wrote it after he left his poor wife," she said, and I could tell she disapproved of the author's behavior in real life, not of the book.

"Never heard that either. I didn't think people got divorced in those days."

"They didn't, usually. It was frightfully complicated. They just lived apart and continued on with their own lives. That's what Charles Dickens did." She leaned toward me and lowered her voice. "Took up with an actress twenty-seven years his junior. Is that something? And after Mrs. Dickens had given him ten children and the best years of her life. Course she did let herself go, poor soul, weighed over two hundred pounds when he left her."

I pointed to the book. "Is it good?"

"Melodrama. It'll be fine for you." She put my name on the card, filed it away. "You think about that, Cleo, about writing down your grandmother's life. I've always thought it would be nice to have a little historical society here in Robina." She pointed toward the back wall. "I could make a special section for diaries and journals of local pioneers. Your grandmother's story would be very important to the collection."

I shook my head. "I'm awful busy. Working both farms."

She lifted her eyebrows. "Can't plant anything in January, Cleo. You think about it."

I finished my tea and went back to the pharmacy window to ask Mr. Hawkins if he knew anybody who had a car to sell.

"No one I know of. But you'd be wise to go into Tulsa to a dealership if you want to buy a car."

"I don't want a brand new one. Costs too much."

"False economy, my dear. You buy an old car and who'll fix it when it breaks down? No mechanics in town since . . ." He stopped short and got busy with some vials and powders. No mechanics in town since Ethan got sent up—that's what he started to say.

"Well, if you hear of anything let me know. I'm having a telephone put in out at Mam's place. One at Momma's too, if she'll let me."

"Gracious sakes!" Miss Hawkins came around the bank of shelves. "What's this? An automobile? A telephone? What next?"

"Some farm machinery," I said. "I plan to introduce Mam and Momma to the twentieth century."

Miss Hawkins frowned. "Don't know you'll be doing them any favors. This war . . ."

Her brother interrupted. "We'll stay neutral," he said. "Roosevelt will see to that."

"Neutral! He got that amendment through Congress in short order. We're selling them planes and guns, trading them ships for bases. Wilson did the same thing and you know where that got us."

"Now, Emma. We can't just sit here on our hands while that little lunatic sets fire to Europe."

"I'd rather fight a war from my front porch than send our young boys overseas."

"You might just do that, madam. The Atlantic isn't as wide as it used to be. The other night Kaltenborn . . ."

I slipped out unnoticed while they hashed over the world situation, in which I had little interest. Oh, I listened to the news. Mam turned it on every evening and banged on the radio when events were not to her liking. But somehow what was going on in Europe, scary as it was, just went in one ear and out the other without making much impression in between.

That night I cooked pork and cabbage, which Mam had requested. After I did the chores we settled down for our nightly game of poker—nightly except when Momma was over and we played Books or Old Maid, sedate and innocent as a couple of nuns, not a chip in sight. I'd brought a new deck from town, having accused Mam of marking the cards. She won anyhow. Said I was a sore loser and a worse poker player. "Cleo," she said, "how many times do I have to tell you—don't stay with a measly pair of nines."

"But you do," I whined.

"Only when I'm playing with the likes of you. Add it up. Let's hear the damage."

At that point I owed her about fourteen thousand dollars and some odd cents.

After she went to bed I sat by the fire with one of my new books. It was engaging enough; wasn't Daphne du Maurier's fault that I was so restless and inattentive. I put it down after the first chapter, got up and poked the fire, then paced the floor for a while.

Mam came to the doorway and wanted to know what I was doing prowling around in the middle of the night. Her hair was down—came all the way to her bottom—and the waves from her undone braids shone like new-mined coal in the firelight. I stared at her and wondered what she was doing walking around in a young woman's hair. To what use?

When I was in sixth grade I read in a magazine that American Indians seldom go bald or grey. It also said they don't have color blindness for red or green, and have arches instead of whorls in their fingerprints. I borrowed a stamp pad from my teacher and took all our fingerprints. It was true what the article said. Mam had arches instead of whorls like the rest of us. Mam was special.

I took her fingerprints to school and showed them all around. Ruby Leighton said that only proved my grandmother was full-blood heathen instead of just part, like me. This was the first time I'd heard anything disparaging in regard to my maternal ancestry. I got Ruby Leighton, who was a full head taller than me, down on the ground and pinched her till she took it all back. And I spent the rest of the day in the corner of the schoolroom, too prideful to tell the teacher the reason for the fracas.

I told Mam I couldn't sleep. That's why I was prowling around in the middle of the night.

"Make yourself some warm milk," she said. "Then go get in the bed so sleep will know where to find you."

That was the problem. Sleep would find me, all right. Sleep and dreams.

I heated the milk, put a little peach brandy in it, and prowled some more. When I heard Mam's stick pound the floorboards in her room, I sat down at the table and shuffled the cards. I didn't whip old Sol either.

I kept telling myself that dreams were not reality. But in truth, my dreams were as real as an ash-hopper. It seemed my head had no sooner hit the pillow than the Reverend Robin Endicott would come sit on the side of my bed. He would take my hand and press it to his lips. I am a brother to dragons, he'd say. A companion to owls. He'd say he'd come to take me to Paradise. Every morning I'd tell myself a person had no control over dreams, but then he began coming to me when I was awake. Daydreams a person has to answer for.

I bowed my head and asked God's pardon for the names I'd called him in Cushman's Cave. I asked him if there was no end to his punishment? No resting place? No wide clear contented plain? No way out of the Wilderness of Sin?

I listened. I listened *hard*. There was no answer to my questions, no sound at all except for the crackling of sap in the fire and the wind scratching at the back door like some old tomcat finished with his rounds.

This time I heated up the peach brandy—put a little milk in it. It would be sunup soon, and me with no difficult task to put a hand to. If only there was some hard labor to claim my full attention. But Miss Hawkins was right. You can't plant in January.

And then it came to me, a thought borne on the angel wings of saving grace. The way to contain the itch in the privates was to cultivate the itch in the brain. The brain had no winter dormancy, no seasons for sowing and reaping. The brain was a field in constant harvest. Like Miss Hawkins said, I could write down Mam's history to be placed in the library for posterity. With a mind fully engaged in good works, I could direct my feet on the narrow, slippery path of righteousness. Surely, goodness and mercy must be out there somewhere.

14

I DON'T KNOW WHAT YOU WANT ME TO SAY."

"Yes, you do. Whatever you remember, whatever comes to mind. Just talk about the old days like you always do and I'll break in from time to time to ask you a question like what the date was or somebody's name. Like that. The only difference is you need to talk a little slower than usual."

"Ask me a question to get me started. I'm old. I forget things."

Mam, in her whole life, had not forgotten so much as a loaf of bread left to rise in the warming oven. "Well," I said, "how was it in the olden days? When did your folks come to the Territory? What did you have to eat?"

"That's three."

"Pick one."

"I don't like this."

"What's wrong?"

"You sitting there like some fresh kid from a newspaper fixing to write up my obituary. I can't talk if you're going to put down what I say."

"But that's the whole idea, Mam. That's the point of it. We've been over this. Miss Hawkins is starting up a historical society and I told her I'd write up your history. All the pioneers' journals and diaries will be in a special section. And she'll frame some old pictures and put them up, with brass plates telling the year. It'll be nice, Mam. Children will be able to go to the library and learn about their roots."

"What do I care about that? Let the little boogers find out about their roots from their own folks. You go make that pie for supper now and leave me be. And you need to roll me some cigarettes. That last batch is almost used up."

I leaned back in my chair and crossed my legs, not going anywhere. "I'll make the pie and I'll roll those cigarettes after you tell me a story. Just one."

"Bribery is a sin, Cleo."

"So is pride, Mam."

She stared down at her hands, two old brown claws fingering the fringe on her lap blanket. I felt mean for keeping at her, but the way I saw it my salvation was at stake, and besides I'd promised Miss Hawkins. "Mam?"

She sighed. "Only if you put away the pen and paper. I'll not open my mouth as long as you perch there like some buzzard waiting to swoop down on my life and carry it off."

"Then I'll have to write it down later. As best as I can remember."

"Suits me."

"But what if I get it wrong?"

"That's your problem."

This standoff had been going on for two weeks. Mam would start on some tale and as soon as I reached for the pad I'd gotten especially for this purpose, she'd clam up and go poker-stiff. Sometimes she would stomp off to her room and stay there in a huff until she got hungry.

Miss Hawkins was delighted with the prospect of a historical society and a written history of Robina's early days. Since Mam was our oldest resident she was to be the cornerstone of this project. A big bake sale was planned and other fund-raising events to get the money to have Mam's recollections printed and put in a binding with photographs and illustrations. I'd told her it would be no problem, that I could work on it full time until good weather set in. So far all I had was starts and stops, mostly the latter.

Now Mam gave me her slow, cagey look, like some auctioneer judging livestock. "I could tell you something about Benjamin Franklin. That's something you can write down."

I perked up. "Your people knew Benjamin Franklin? Personally?"

"You might say that. My great-grandmother committed some of his words to memory and passed them down. All the children had to learn the words by rote as soon as they could talk."

"In English? Your great-grandmother understood English?"

"And French."

"So what did he say?" I had my pen poised over the pad ready to record some precious, little-known utterance from one of the Great White Fathers.

"Said the government should extirpate—that's e-x-t-i-r-p-a-t-e. Got that?"

134

"Got it."

"Know what it means?"

"Not exactly."

"Means to get shed of. Wipe out. Destroy. Said the government should extirpate these savages in order to make room for the cultivators of the earth."

My jaw dropped. "I never heard of him saying anything like that."

"They don't teach it in school, likely."

"Oh." I shifted in my chair and told Mam I didn't think that was the sort of recollection Miss Hawkins had in mind.

"Too bad about Emma," she said, lofty as the Queen of England. "I guess the little children won't get their roots lesson." She was laughing behind her eyes, like when she got the best of Momma.

I retrenched and came at her from another direction. "Your great-grandmother. She really understood English?"

"And spoke it. English and French. And Creek, three dialects."

I readied my pen. "Now, that would be something interesting to know about."

"I'm tired now. Time for my nap." There was no use arguing with her. She'd just close her eyes and take a snooze on the spot. I moved to help her up and into her room but she waved me away. "Put in more lemon juice this time," she said. "Those Jonathans are not tart enough."

It was a bad bargain. In exchange for one apple pie I'd got this useless statement from Ben Franklin, who ought to have known better.

I'd just dropped on the top crust and was fluting the edges when I heard a car coming up the road.

"Who's that coming?" Mam called from the bedroom.

I looked out the window. "Looks like the Bell Telephone truck. Yes, that's what it is. Man's coming to put in the telephone."

Like some ghost, she materialized at my elbow. "I've changed my mind," she said.

I thought she was talking about the history. "Just let me get this in the oven and I'll get my pen."

"I think it should go in the parlor instead of out here where we decided. A body might want some quiet when they talk on the telephone."

So because we had a brass band and a troop of Russian dancers in the kitchen at all times, I told the man to run the wire into the parlor—which we kept closed off in the wintertime. This meant I'd have to build fires in there. Mam showed him where to put it, down low on the wall so she wouldn't have to stand up when she talked on it. Then he showed her how to work it. She grinned so wide I knew she'd forgot all about her missing tooth.

He said, "You just take the receiver off the hook and crank this arm here. That'll get you the operator. You tell her who you want to talk to and she'll put you through. Now then, if you should pick up the receiver and hear somebody talking . . . watch this." He demonstrated by putting the receiver to his ear and pretending shock and amazement. "You hang up immediately because somebody on your party line is using the telephone. Always listen before you turn the crank."

Mam reached out and grabbed the receiver. "I want to call somebody and try it out. Who'll we call, Cleo?"

"Let's wait till he finishes with the instructions." I took the receiver and put it back in place.

The man smiled at me gratefully. I could see that he was a somebody who loved his work, enjoyed explaining the deep mysteries of this wondrous instrument.

"About the incoming calls," he said. Then he moved across the room and stared out the window as if he was just passing the time of day. "Suddenly you hear two shorts and a long!" His eyes got wide and he raised his forefinger. "Ding . . . ding . . . dinnnnnngggggg." He dashed over and picked up the receiver. "That's it, ladies. Two shorts and a long."

He asked if we had any questions. Mam was looking at him like she was measuring him for a suit. She said, "What's your name, fella?"

"Norman."

"You a married man, Norman?" She shot a meaningful glance in my direction.

He allowed he was, laughed nervously, and said, "The old ball and chain." He smoothed his hair back and slipped on his cap. "Two shorts and a long," he repeated, then told Mam what a treat it was to put in a telephone for somebody who took so much pleasure in it. He said, "I put one in a while ago for a lady just down the road. When I left she was still looking at it like it was something the cat drug in."

"That would be my momma," I told him, as I saw him to the door. "She was somewhat reluctant." I had finally convinced her because of the possible need to reach her quickly. "Mam might need one of your curatives," I'd told her, grave as a Methodist deacon. "You wouldn't want her to die for lack of proper medication, would you? By the time I got over to the house and brought you over here to look at her and you decided what was wrong and we went back . . ."

"Shush your nattering, Daughter. Put in the telephone."

The telephone man—Norman—lingered on the front porch, saying quite a bit about nothing in particular, looking me over and liking what he saw. Who could blame him? I'd been offered up like a plate of hot chicken livers. I watched him ponder the problem of how far his chain might stretch, then thanked him for his fine service and went back inside to have some pointed words with Mam.

She was flitting around the parlor like a demented towhee. "I'll call up Frances," she announced. Then she directed me to put another log on the fire and brew a pot of hickory tea. "Move that easy chair over by the wall under our telephone, Cleo, so I can be comfortable while I visit with your momma. And bring me my lap blanket, would you please. And move that little table over here by the chair for my tea and get me my cigarettes from the kitchen."

When the lowly handmaiden had finished her duties, she was told to close the door when she left, thank you. "For privacy."

She and Momma were on that telephone for as long as it took my pie to bake. The selfsame telephone Momma had sworn she wouldn't touch except in dire emergency. I put my ear to the door and got snatches of the conversation. At one point I knew I figured in the topic because I heard a lot of cackling interspersed with the words "historical society" and "roots" and "Benjamin Franklin."

The next day after breakfast she took herself off to the parlor again. She didn't close the door this time, probably so she could more easily summon the handmaiden for provisions in between calls. She talked on her new gadget all morning and had long-winded conversations with women she wouldn't give the time of day at church. Then I heard her say in her most indignant voice that she had paid good money for this telephone and she'd get off it when she'd finished and not a minute before.

In a few days the novelty wore off, or rather, Mam discovered that listening in was more fun than talking. I didn't make any progress on her ancestors that week, but I did get an earful of the Dooley baby's high fever, Mrs. Finewater's trip to Louisville, and the Anshaws' recent marital problems, among other items of local interest. Loreen Dooley was instructed to rub her baby all over with hog lard and dose her with slippery elm tea. (Mix one teaspoon powdered slippery elm with cold water. Add boiling water gradually. Watch for lumps. Season with cinnamon or nutmeg.) Mrs. Finewater was counseled on the inconsideration of paying a visit to her daughter so soon after the honeymoon, and Laney Marie Anshaw told to go out and buy a length of lawn cotton and some lace and make herself a sleeveless nightdress—low-cut.

Not long after, I heard from the lady at the telephone office. She said there had been several complaints and threatened me mildly with a private line, three times the price. I, in turn, threatened Mam with the removal of the blessed thing if she did not use it more graciously. One of the few times I could get close to it, I called Miss Hawkins and told her of my poor progress on Mam's history.

Then one day late in February Mam came all the way out to the barn, leaning on her stick and looking glum as an old bloodhound.

"You shouldn't be out here, Mam. The dampness will make your hands gnarl up."

"It's awful, just awful! Oh I need to set myself down, my knees are leaving me."

I covered a bale with a horse blanket and guided her onto it. She sank down and closed her eyes, caught her breath.

"Just awful what I heard on my telephone. I can't believe it. Emma Hawkins . . ." She pinched the bridge of her nose and took deep breaths through her mouth. "And I always thought that woman had good sense . . ."

"What's wrong?"

"Emma Hawkins plans to print up Elsie Bullard's recollections, put Elsie's words in a leather binding with gold letters. Plans a cake sale to raise money for it."

"I told you about that, Mam. You weren't interested. You turned down the honor."

"But I didn't think . . . I didn't know . . . Now, listen to me, Cleo, you know it for God's truth that I have not got one jealous bone in my body. You know that."

"Yes'm."

"That has nothing to do with anything."

"Course not."

"Thing is, Elsie . . . well, poor soul . . . it wouldn't be the sort of thing we'd want in our library."

"Wouldn't be the sort of thing we'd want our little boogers to read?"

"That's right." (Smooth as a mouse's lips, my gramma.) "Elsie Bullard—now, I don't have a thing against her, but Cleo, the woman is feebleminded, dim as five o'clock in the morning. I mean, what could she possibly recollect?"

I shrugged like a helpless bystander. "I guess Miss Hawkins was desperate."

"And worse—oh, child, so much worse—Elsie's people didn't set foot in the Territory till after the Civil War. They weren't pioneers, Cleo. The Bullards were carpetbaggers!"

And that's how if finally came to pass that I began to make headway on Mam's history.

Thank you, Bell Telephone.

15

The NEXT MORNING MAM SAID I COULD
have an appointment when I'd finished with the wash. "Appointment" was the word she used. Then she put it off until after she'd had her noon meal because her memory was weak on an empty stomach. After that she told me to go make myself useful outdoors until she was ready for me, and about an hour later yoo-hooed out the kitchen window for me to come on in. To use the parlor door. And to knock, Cleo, if you please.

All gussied up in her best church outfit, she had on every piece of jewelry—good and otherwise—she owned, and carried her Spanish fan with the scarlet roses decorated with dewdrops made of rhinestones. She smiled her crooked company smile and gave me her haven't-we-met-somewhere-before arch of the eyebrow. Her tea service, polished so bright you'd think we had regular help, sat on the lowboy. Beside it was a silver platter of cookies, not one of which would have made a decent mouthful.

"Miz Shannon?" she inquired, inclining her head in a distant but polite way, like I was some uninvited ambassador just arrived from Uranus. "Won't you take a seat."

She agreed it was a nice day, fine and crisp, then eased into her chair by the telephone. She touched her hair, which in spite of her arthritis she had managed to wind into a queenly bun high on her head.

"We could use some rain," she confided. "Clouded up some yesterday but nothing came of it. Please help yourself to tea, Miz Shannon. It's Lipton's. Store-bought. And do try one of my mother's sherry-almond cakes. Her mother's receipt."

"And may I pour you a cup?"

"If you please. Just lemon."

We never used that stuff. The tea service, the china, the bud vase, the silver spoons had all sat in her glass-doored cabinet waiting for Judgment Day as long as I could remember.

"Now," she said, folding her white-gloved hands in her lap. "Just what did you want to see me about?"

I got my pad handy and took a pencil from behind my ear. Scoop Shannon on the job. "As you may have heard, the Hawkins' Memorial Lending Library and Pharmacy of Robina is planning to install a special historical section. I've been sent to write down some of your early recollections." She nodded her royal approval. "Perhaps we could start with your birth?"

"I recall little of that happy event."

"But you do recall the date?"

She looked at me sharply. "Well, of course I recall the date, Cleo. You think you're talking to some feebleminded Elsie Bullard?"

"No, ma'am. That never once entered my mind. Sorry. You were born in eighteen . . . ?"

"Forty-three," she snapped. "Right here in Indian Territory, not off somewhere in New Jersey like Elsie. You sure this will be in a leather binding? And gold letters?"

I sighed. "If we ever finish it. And you were born here in Robina?"

She narrowed her eyes. "You testing my faculties, Cleo? You know I wasn't born in Robina."

"Oh, Mam! Miss Hawkins gave me this list of questions to ask you. You know, statistics and so on. Couldn't you just pretend? Like with the 'nice day' business. Pretend I'm a reporter and don't know squat about you. That way I'll get the details right instead of putting down hearsay. What good is a fine leather binding if what's inside isn't true?"

She rearranged her long skirt, fingered the cameo at her neck, then plunged in—a veritable entry into some encyclopedia. "I was born in 1843 on the Verdigris River near Fort Gibson in eastern Indian Territory which territory became the state of Oklahoma on November 16, 1907—forty-sixth state. I was the first child of four that lived, all born on my father's plantation which was established in the late spring of 1829, as much like the one in Alabama as he could make it." She leaned toward me. "Is that the kind of thing you want me to say?"

I was scribbling as fast as I could. Verdigris (two *i*s?), Fort Gibson, 1829, Alabama, plantation . . . *plantation?*

"And by plantation," I said, "you mean the family had a little farm?"

"I suppose you could call it that. Compared with the one in Alabama. Almost three hundred acres under fence and cultivation. Grew cotton, tobacco, upland rice, and naturally corn and vegetables. Had poultry and livestock—dairy cattle, horses, mules, hogs. Nine slaves besides the house Negroes, three of those, and the little ones. I have pictures of the house. Maybe Emma would like some to frame. With the brass plates under?"

I sat there with my mouth open. Most of what I knew about the Indians coming to the Territory I had learned in a course called Oklahoma History. That course had presented a picture of the poor, wretched Redman being escorted by kindly soldiers from abject poverty in the South to a new life on the Frontier. One that abounded with the riches of nature—yes—but there was no mention of plantations and house slaves.

Sure I'd heard Mam's stories while I was growing up, but I'd left home at fifteen on my own journey to the unknown, so most of what I heard, I heard either as a child—a captive, fidgety, toe-tapping audience at the supper table, thinking about being excused so I could go tend to vital matters up at the neighbors', or—later—about what time and where I would rendezvous with Willis Henderson.

It was just as Miss Hawkins said about her grandmother and Charles Dickens. We don't pay any attention to our old people. Then one day they're gone, taking all their adventures with them. Then we take a notion to find out How It Was in the Olden Days or which relation came over on the Mayflower or which back-pocket kin fought in the battle of Bunker Hill. We pore over old letters and diaries, the writing so faint as to cause blindness. Maybe even cut out advertisements from the back of magazines—YOUR FAMILY CREST—FILL OUT ENCLOSED QUESTIONNAIRE—SEND ONE DOLLAR. Thanks to Miss Hawkins that would not be the case here.

I told Mam, most respectfully, that I would surely like to see those pictures of the plantation. She directed me to bring the black album from the top drawer of her chiffonier. "Under my dainties," she said.

I fetched it and looked over her shoulder while she slowly turned the pages. She pointed to a picture of a three-story house, fronted by a tall fence almost hidden by rosebushes in full bloom. "It was yellow," she said. "Wood frame with clapboard siding painted yellow. Over here on this side big French doors went out to Mother's garden. She had maybe two dozen varieties of roses—European and native. People came from all over just to smell them. A woman came from Boston once, all the way from Boston, Massachusetts, to talk to Mother about her hybrid of an Alba and a native climber."

I stared at the photograph. The house was a long rectangle with four gables, and chimneys at both ends. Six great white columns with ivy winding around them held up the wide front porch. No, it was much too grand to be called a porch—a veranda, a gallery, a portico maybe.

I was stunned. "You lived there?"

"You expected a wigwam?"

"Where'd he get the money to build such a house? This is a rich man's house."

Mam opened her Spanish fan and hid behind it like some tango dancer. There's nothing like illustrious forebears to cause uppityness in offspring. "He was a planter," she said, "like his father before him. He brought his fortune with him." She closed the fan and pulled off her gloves. "Light me up a Bugler, Cleo. That's all I can divulge about my father's financial circumstances. There are certain matters one does not want written down in books and put in libraries for all and sundry to prattle over."

She took the cigarette and settled back in her chair, tickled as she could be over the slack-jawed astonishment she had produced in the raw reporter. "I grew up there," she said, and blew a thin stream of blue smoke through her nose. "It was called Rose Hill, for reasons I've explained and you can plainly see for yourself. I lived at Rose Hill until I was sixteen, except for the years at the Methodist School for girls in New Orleans. Then I married Harlan McQueen." She looked me squarely in the eye. "I recall that date, too—the date of my marriage. June 3, 1859. It took place in the garden at Rose Hill and was attended by everybody who was anybody for miles around. A three-pig event it was. You turn the page there and you'll see a picture of me and Harlan on our wedding day. Photographer came all the way from Fayetteville."

"But Mam . . . ?"

"Don't interrupt me or I'll lose my train of thought. Then Harlan and I came to Robina—wasn't called Robina then, wasn't called anything 'cept the McQueen place, nearbout a section of land the McQueen family had claimed. It was all tribal land then. You didn't really own it but a body could claim as much as he could fence and improve. Harlan's daddy parceled off eighty acres to us. We built a double log cabin with a gallery between and a separate kitchen house. There's a picture there. 'First House, 1859' written under it. You think that would be of interest to the library? And we put in a crop of cotton that same year. Didn't take us long. Harlan's brothers helped and Father sent us some slaves on loan."

"But, Mam . . . ?"

She held up her hand. "In a minute. I want to finish this part. That was just two years before the War Between the States, which my Harlan went off to fight in, leaving me flat, a bride with one baby and another on the way. Didn't I tell you, Cleo? Didn't I tell you men love trouble? Ever time they hear a buffalo snort, they're off and running, thinking it's a new war starting. Can't get enough of it. Now, what did you want to say?"

"So your first husband—this Harlan—he wasn't Creek?"

"Who says?"

"McQueen is a Scotch name if I'm not mistaken."

"Doesn't matter what the daddy is. If the momma's Creek, the child is Creek. Names have nothing to do with tribe—blood either. Creeks are full of Scotch blood, and English and French and Spanish and you name it. Anybody's that can build a big boat. Creeks started intermarrying almost the day old de Soto came ashore. We are known for our hospitality. Why do you think we're called civilized?"

"I thought it had something to do with reading and writing."

Mam reached for her tea, held the saucer in one hand dainty and steady as you please, and took a sip, her pinkie curled like some lady of the manor. "It had to do," she said slowly, spacing the words out so they didn't touch each other, "with aping our betters." She paused, pulled her lips into a thin line, then went on, her voice clipped and hard at the edges. "White man married us, gave us his European names, dressed us up in European clothes, taught us to use European spinning wheels and make white European bread, raise European cows and chickens. And you know what? You know what, Cleo?"

"No ma'am. I don't."

"We liked it. Sure a lot easier to go out in the yard, pick up a silly European chicken, and wring its silly neck than go out and hunt the wild, smart turkey. Lot easier to stick a penned hog than prowl around in the woods looking for deer. That right, Cleo?"

"I see what you mean."

"The Creek, Cherokee, Chickasaw, Seminole, and Choctaw were known as the civilized tribes. The others, those that had no interest in spinning wheels and white bread, they were called the wild Indians." She sniffed and narrowed her eyes. "I'm sure a bright girl like yourself can see the logic in that kind of reasoning."

I shifted in my chair and wondered where I'd gone wrong in my line of questioning. "Why are you riled at me, Mam?"

" 'Cause you're so dumb. You think it takes a brilliant scholar to learn the English language? You think it's some sacred, holy tongue? You think the Lord God himself speaks it? Way back in the early seventeen hundreds one of my ancestors married a Frenchman, a military man of high standing. They sent their children to school over in Paris, where they learned Greek and Latin. And how to translate it into French and by-the-way Creek and by-the-way English. How's that for education?"

I looked up from my mess of notes. "You mentioned something like that before. That's something we could put in the introduction. You have a date on that somewhere, and the names? The name of this French military . . . "

She stopped me midstride with a look that would have grown icicles in a tropical forest. "One of those children came back from France so full of goodwill he became a teacher, and he made the local civilized white trash so mad because of his fine talk and fine manners, somebody shot him dead."

I thought to myself that I needed a meeting with Miss Hawkins to determine just how much in depth Mam's book should be. "Is that factual, Mam?" I asked uncertainly. "Are you sure . . . ?"

"My own grandmother told it. A lie never crossed that woman's lips."

I decided to veer off in another direction until I had my meeting with Miss Hawkins. "So what this all means is that you're not pure Creek either. Remember your fingerprints? Remember when I was little and took your fingerprints? How they were arches instead of whorls?"

She grunted. "I guess I had enough pure Creek blood stored in my hands to make those arches for you. So you could show them off to your classmates. Got you in a pile of trouble, those fingerprints—if memory serves."

She put her hands on her knees and cackled long and loud, the anger that had risen up like a cyclone brewing all gone. I was relieved and disappointed at the same time. I wanted to know more about that young man cut down in his prime because of his good education. But with Mam you didn't cross over Swenson's Gulch with your eyes shut.

"Cleo," she said, still cackling, "don't believe everything you read, child. Arches and whorls! Lot of the lower Creeks were mixed . . . called *mélis*." She pointed to my pad and sliced the air with her forefinger. "That has a hoo-dinky over the *e*. But we *mélis* are just as Creek as the next ones. Now the upper Creeks, they weren't so hospitable, weren't so much for consorting, kept to themselves more. But we're all of us Creek. And lower has nothing to do with standing or character, just refers to the location of the towns. Upper Creeks lived in the Appalachian highlands, lower Creeks in the flatlands. You got that down? That's important."

She began to rub her chin in that distracted way she had and I thought she might drift off any minute. We'd been at this for long over an hour, what with looking at the album and time out for a Bugler.

"Harlan," she said with a long sigh. "Sweet Harlan . . ." I positioned my pencil. "He'd gone into North Fork for supplies at the mercantile. There were some agents there from the Confederacy trying to sign up soldiers for the cause. Harlan comes home all wild-eyed, poor old mules all lathered up, forgot half of what was on my list, Harlan did, and before he even unloads he's going on about the war and how he has to get in it. 'Jessie,' he says, his face so grave. 'Jessie, I got to go serve my country.'"

"Well, that was just about the most foolish thing I'd ever heard and I told him so. This was the early summertime of '61. I can place it because we had started thinning the cotton. Did it by hand. No skinner machines in those days. This war had been going on since the spring. We'd heard all about it, read about it in the St. Louis papers Father sent over when he finished with them.

"I said to Harlan, 'Harlan,' I say, 'this war is taking place in the state of Virginia. Has nothing to do with us.' I go on about how I'm expecting this new baby and we have this cotton crop to bring in and how Father's slaves have run off to Kansas so it's just us, him and me. I tell him we need to make our own way. Tell him we can't sponge off our folks like we were children. Shamed him into staying, that's what I did.

146

Harlan was raised on responsibility. Those are the easiest to shame.

"Then one day not long after, sometime in July, one of the Mc-Intosh boys comes by. He's been to a big meeting of the tribe in North Fork. The chiefs signed a paper. About half the Creeks, mostly upper, were to fight for the Yankees—they'd be called the Loyal Creeks, and the other half signed up with the Confederacy—they'd be the Southern Creeks. Just like they were organizing for a game of stickball.

"The McIntosh boy thought Harlan would want to know, thought he wouldn't want to be left out. Damn fool says, 'Knew you wouldn't want to miss it, Harlan!'

"I stand there on the porch listening to them blather on about the Enemy, one hand on the head of the baby hanging on my skirt, the other on the beating heart of the one not born, and I like to cried.

"I didn't ask the McIntosh boy to stay to supper, didn't offer him so much as a dipper full of cool water and it maybe ninety degrees that day. After a while he went off and Harlan comes on in the house. I'm nursing our baby boy, probably giving off sour milk I'm so distraught, fanning the blackflies off both of us like they were the problem. My sweet Harlan stands in front of me, holding his hat in both hands, sliding it around between his fingers. You know how they are when they're fixing to do something they know you won't like but they're going to do it anyway.

"Well, Cleo, I've always been one to know when I'm whipped. I never laid so much as a finger on a dead horse. Get it from Father. He saw there was no way he could get the best of the United States Government in that rigged poker game they were playing, so he took what they offered while he still had some chips left. He wasn't chased and burned and marched out of Alabama like so many were. Father negotiated. Don't write that down, Cleo. About Father. You hear?"

"Why not?"

"Because I revere his memory. Too many folks around who don't understand poker playing. I think I'm tired now, time for my nap."

"Just finish about Harlan. He went?"

"There was no stopping him. But I negotiated. I knew why he had to go. The knowing, Cleo, that's almost as good as a pat hand. Had nothing to do with serving his country, or the rights of states. We didn't even have a state then. Or with keeping slaves. We didn't have those either except to borrow sometimes. Had nothing to do with any of that. My poor sweet dumb stupid husband had to prove his manhood, that's all. Had to prove he was brave as the next one, had to prove he was a warrior. Nothing new. I understood this about him.

"I get up and put my baby boy in his crib, then I come back where Harlan's still standing there, fingering his hat. I come toward him looking as fragile and helpless as I can, given my nature, and I say, 'Harlan, I know you have to do this and I'm not going to try to stop you.' Well, he heaves a big sigh and puts his arms around me and breathes into my hair. 'Thank you,' he says, 'thank you, Jessie.'

"And I say, 'But you got to promise me something.' This was not idly asked and would not be idly answered. A promise from a McQueen was near as important as his manhood. I counted on that. He pulled back and looked down on me. I was a little thing even then and he was close on six foot—you saw in the picture. And he says, 'What's the promise, Jessie?'

"We lock eyes and I say, 'I want you to promise not to get killed.'

"Now, Cleo, this may seem to you like something a man has no control over, a soldier in the heat of battle, Fate and all that, but you just think for a minute. A child is going out berry picking and you say, 'Watch for snakes!' Well, that child, even though he thinks he's immortal like they all do, he watches where he puts his feet. Can't help it. There's this soft voice in his head that keeps whispering Snakes—Snakes—Snakes. That's what I was trying to do, plant that soft voice in Harlan's head. I promised—I promised—I promised.

"He looks at me for a long time and I do not once drop my eyes or even blink. Finally, he gives in. He says, and he says it like it's an oath: 'Jessie Iris McQueen, I promise you I will not get killed.'

"It was no guarantee, but it helped the odds some. It was the best I could do. That's all I'm going to say just now, Cleo. I need to stretch out and close my eyes. Lucy Finewater's going to call her daughter in Louisville at five o'clock sharp and I want to be rested up for it."

16

I KEPT MYSELF COMPLETELY OCCUPIED, KEPT a two-handed rein on my thoughts and made sure I was dead tired when my head hit the pillow at night. I worked on Mam's history, visited the neighbors to inspect their farm machinery and receive expert advice, ordered in a load of topsoil for Momma's place, and studied up on fish biology at the library.

I was astounded by what I learned about the longevity of goldfish. Moby could, in theory, live to the ripe old age of twenty-eight years. I also learned that He was a She, having made that transformation when he/she was two years old. The Lord doth move in mysterious ways.

Mr. Krause at the hardware store ordered me a fish tank, with all the necessaries for healthy fish keeping. He noted it was a lot of fancy equipment for one lone goldfish and suggested I get Moby some company. But I was afraid strangers might come bearing ill will or gill rot, so Moby swam in splendid isolation in her watery kingdom, decorated with pretty rocks from the creek, a sunken Spanish galleon, a treasure chest that glittered with rubies and emeralds and one perfect pearl, and a deep-sea diver that bubbled cheerful messages to the surface.

I told myself that by the time she lived out her allotted years I would be able to tolerate her passing, and would behave like a normal person going through the loss of a twenty-eight-year-old goldfish. I considered making provisions in my will. Truth is, I didn't even like her.

I also studied up on automobiles, read the advertisements in the papers, rode the bus to Wagoner to look at a 1932 Dodge straight-8 that took my fancy because of the wording of the ad—ONE OWNER, DRIVEN TO PARADISE WITHOUT INCIDENT. Later I looked up Paradise. It's in California, north of Sacramento. I had figured it for a much longer trip. I didn't buy the car even though it was clean and fairly priced, and had hydraulic brakes and a four-speed gearbox. It was a shade of green that turned my skin sallow. But I surely enjoyed the bus ride as I talked nonstop to the other passengers, and made them glassy-eyed with my enthusiasm for the scenery and current events.

I never mentioned a date, or acknowledged one mentioned to me. It was "I'll be there next Tuesday," or "I'll take care of that on Friday afternoon." I never so much as glanced at a calendar.

Because of this clever subterfuge, which put my mind at desperate odds with itself, on the first anniversary of my tragedy, I suffered another setback—a mighty one this time. I backslid past restlessness, past heedlessness, past rage, into a grief so profound I could not so much as stir from my bed. I started to get up and clean forgot that's what I meant to do. I tried again, got my feet over the side, but then they just dangled there, couldn't find the floor. It came to me that I was watching this happen. Part of me stood at the other end of the room, arms crossed on chest, and watched this other person crawl back under the quilt and bring her knees up to her chin. For a time I thought the me that lay in the bed was paralyzed. I said: I can't get up, I'm not able to move. The other one said: You have to get up. You have duties.

That was true. One of us had to help our grandmother on with her clothes, tie her shoes. She wouldn't wear a robe or house slippers in the daylight, said it was a sign of sloth. As soon as the kitchen got warm and her bones limbered up some she could tend herself, but she needed help rising. The one across the room with her arms folded kept telling me this. Told me in a nasty tone that I'd already done this once, didn't need to repeat it. That was true. Mildred said I hadn't spoken a word for seventeen straight days or have one sign of expression on my face. She said she had to put Murine in my eyes because they got so dry from my not blinking. That happens to people in the county home, people who've outlived their loved ones and stare at their remembered faces on blank walls and windowpanes. Not even thirty years old and I had outlived my loved ones.

I heard Mam's stick pound the floor. I heard her call my name. It was that other one's name too. Why didn't she do something? Just stood there like some cigar-store Indian. No help at all. I tried again, pushed the covers off and took my paralyzed legs, first one and then the other, and set them on the floor. I looked down at my feet, whose simple chore was to get me into Mam's room. But they were not my feet. They were two strange little dead animals, each with one eye rolled up showing the whites. I told the person across the room that it was no use, told her I wasn't able. I said, Don't you see? I would if I could but I can't!

She shook her head and looked someplace between wounded and disgusted, my momma's look when I had disappointed her in one of the five million ways I was so good at. But I couldn't help it. I pulled my legs back onto the bed, pushed myself up on my hands and knees and crawled under the covers all the way to the depths of Cushman's Cave and curled up there with the bats hanging all around me. ENTER AT YOUR OWN PERIL. It was my duty to warn them. I explained to the bats that the cave was long overdue to collapse on itself. They didn't mind. They'd heard that before. So we all went to sleep and waited for darkness, or the first rock to fall, whichever came first.

The next thing I heard was the sound of voices, hollow, indistinct, like they came from far away. I pulled myself up. I was at the head of my own bed. The late-afternoon sun took up the foot, making a leafy pattern on familiar old coats and overalls and wore-out dresses.

Not a little fearfully, I looked at the spot where the grim, unhelpful person had stood with her arms crossed. She was gone. Nobody in the room but me. I took a deep breath, lifted the quilt with both hands, and peeked down at my feet. They were just feet, two ordinary, calloused, bare feet—each with a corn plaster on the baby toe.

"Hello, feet," I said. I could have kissed them.

The voices were louder now. It was Mam and my momma in the kitchen. They were arguing. More evidence of normality. I slipped out of bed and weaved to the doorway, leaned on it for support. They were sitting at opposite ends of the kitchen table, their usual battle stations, and Mam had her finger cocked at Momma like a threat ready to go off.

Mam said, "I mean it, Frances, if she doesn't come around soon, I'm going to get on my telephone to Doc Hodges. This is not a head cold we got here, or skin boils or simple runs. What we got here is brain sickness."

I couldn't see Momma's face from where I stood, but I could read it in the set of her shoulders. Blank as a sheet just brought in off the line. She said calmly and reasonably that Mam could call the doctor after I woke up, but not before. Momma said my mind was not sick. She said it was weary of trying to defend itself and would be fine once it had rested. Her concern was that Doc Hodges might give me something to bring it back before it was ready. That, she said, could be fatal.

Coffee cups and a pan of sticky buns sat between them on the table. I stared at the buns and felt my mouth water, felt a little trickle of drool that didn't even faze me. I could not remember ever being so hungry. Without so much as a howdy-do, I lurched to the table, grabbed a bun, and popped it in my mouth—whole.

There was general loud celebration over my homecoming. Momma even kissed my cheeks and hugged me hard. She sat me down at the table, put her shawl on my shoulders, and clucked over my bare feet. Then she bustled to the sink counter and came back with a tiny glass of yellow water that looked for all the world like it had skinny little worms in it. She fished out the worms and handed me the glass.

"What is it?" I asked.

"Good for you," she answered, which was the selfsame name of every medication she dispensed, and stood over me until I drank it.

"I'd like another sticky bun, please."

"Not now. I'm making you some broth to start with. Go on back to bed and I'll bring it to you on a tray. Shouldn't be up until you get more of your strength back. Go sit with her, Mam, while I fix this."

I cast a long look at the buns, all covered with brown sugar syrup and black walnuts and raisins and a powdered sugar glaze, and sitting in a moat of butter that had dripped down the sides. "Just one more, Momma?" I begged. "I don't understand why I'm so starved. I feel like I haven't eaten for a week."

"Three days," said Mam. "Here, take my stick."

"Three and a half," Momma corrected her.

I felt my heart start to pound. Three and a half days in Cushman's Cave. What about my duties? A cold hand clutched at my chest as I looked over at the aquarium. The precious jewels gleamed their usual, and the diver bubbled away, but where was Moby?

"Moby?" I croaked.

Mam pointed. "There she is, coming around the hull. See? I took good care of little Eddy's goldfish. Fed her just like the directions said. You having a spell of weakness, Cleo? You're turning pale."

"Get her to bed, Mam. I got my decoction coming to a boil."

"Lean on me, child. You better now?"

"I'm all right. When I didn't see her—oh I don't know—it's crazy—but I thought about that yellow medicine. . . ."

Mam laughed. "You hear that, Frances? Cleo thought you fed her the goldfish."

Momma punched her fist in on her hips but she was smiling. "Was made of frog's eyes," she said. "And spider eggs, and the spit of an unborn salamander. Now get back to bed, I'm tired of this foolishness."

Mam tucked me in and said she'd be back after she used the telephone. Miss Hawkins, among others, was anxious about my condition and would be happy to hear Lazarus had come forth with such a good appetite. Shortly after, Momma brought a bowl of Good-For-You, and when I'd finished that, poached eggs and dry toast.

"That's all for now," she said, when I'd gobbled it up and held the bowl out for more. "Don't want to overtax your bowels. You can have more broth at suppertime."

She took my tray away and I heard her call to Mam to get off that telephone, that we were ready now. Man came in and said Miss Hawkins would stop by tomorrow with some new novels. Then Momma came in lugging two straight-backed chairs from the kitchen. She lined them up at the foot of the bed and she and Mam sat in them like Sunday visitors.

Mam said, "Tell her, Frances."

"No, you," said Momma.

"No, you," said Mam. "She's your daughter."

Momma looked at me then down at her hands folded in her lap. "I don't know where to begin."

"Just tell her straight out."

Momma glared at Mam and said, "Don't rush me." She turned to me again and sighed. "You know, Daughter, how I've been against you going back to the city. The Lord tells us the city is a place of corruption and violence . . ."

"Get on with it, Frances!"

Again Momma sighed. "We've been talking it over while your mind has been away resting, and I think Mam may be right about this one."

"Right about what?"

"That you need to go back to the city."

I couldn't believe what I was hearing. "To find a man?" I asked. "That's what Mam wants me to do. Is that what you mean?"

"No, of course not. That isn't what I mean at all. It's just that . . . well. You see, your mind shut itself off the other morning because you haven't owned up to certain . . . haven't allowed yourself to accept . . ." Her voice trailed off and she threw up her hands. "You tell her, Mam, it's your notion. You explain it to her."

Mam came and sat on the side of the bed. She took my hand. "Cleo," she said, "you must go to Tulsa and visit the graves." I tried to pull away but she held on. "If you don't, every year when this time rolls around, you'll get sick."

I pushed myself further back into the pillows. "I went to the cemetery after the funeral. I don't need to go again."

"But you said you didn't remember it, didn't remember anything after the . . . after the explosion."

"That's enough to remember. I don't want to remember anything more. I think I'll get up now, I'm feeling much improved. Time to shut up the chickens."

"That's what we're saying. That's what made you sick. Not remembering."

Now Momma came to sit on the other side of the bed. They loomed over me, their faces so full of pity I could hardly stand to look at them.

"You see, Daughter," said Momma, "there's a part of your mind that remembers the service and the cemetery and the time you spent at your friend's place. You have these two parts of your mind, one that remembers and one that forgets. The one part wants to grieve and the other wants to make out it never happened. So they battle over it, and the part that's pretending finally has to shut itself off for protection. Makes you sick. It can shut itself off forever, Daughter. It can take you away and never let you come back."

I felt a wide streak of meanness move down my back. I lifted my chin at Momma and said, "What do you know about grieving? You didn't shed one tear—not even one—at Daddy's funeral."

Mam squeezed my hand. "Don't you talk like that to your mother."

Momma drew back, and after a moment said, "That's all right, Mam." She looked at me for a long time, never once blinked. Then she said, "I remember the date, Daughter. I don't let it go by without marking it. I turn the calendar page over to August and I say, Well there you are again, this is the month and there's the day. I say, Frances, you're going to feel bad for a time and this is the reason. I say, Frances, there's no way to get to September without passing through August.

"You want grief? I remember them bringing him home with two big holes in his chest. I remember dressing him in his blue suit, the one he wore when he played his horn at roadhouses and saloons. I remember sitting up with him all night. I remember him lowered into the grave and giving you children each a handful of dust to sprinkle on his coffin. 'Say goodbye,' I said. 'Say goodbye to your daddy.' And I remember the preacher's words. *'He that is dead is freed from sin.'*

"You want tears? I didn't cry at the graveside because I had used up every tear I owned. I had wept all my tears over that man coming home smelling of whiskey on one end and a woman on the other. That night, the night I sat up with him, him with two holes in his chest, even then he smelled of a woman. The card game was only part of it. That was one bullet hole, the woman was the other. I have a lot to remember and I haven't forgotten any of it."

She lowered her eyes and began to pick at little pieces of lint on her skirt. "I know my memories make me spiteful, and I regret that, but they don't steal away my mind."

This was the closest I had ever heard her come to an explanation or an apology or an admission of moral weakness. I said, "I'm sorry, Momma." She nodded and the three of us sat there in the quiet for a while, trying to breathe the heavy air.

Mam cleared her throat. "Back to what we were talking about. I've taken the liberty of calling your friend Mildred on the telephone. We found her address on the back of the Christmas card envelope. I gave the name and address to the operator and the next thing I knew I was having this conversation with this person all the way in Tulsa, a stranger to me. I hope you don't mind my confiding in her."

"No," I said. "I don't mind."

"She says she can come get you any time. You can stay at her place and when you're up to it, she'll take you out to the cemetery." She put her hands on her knees and got to her feet. "This is something you have to settle before another spring comes around. You think on it. Now then, Frances, why don't you get your daughter another bowl of that broth."

*

Late that night I put a jacket over my nightdress and wobbled out on the back porch. The moon was full. You could see all the way to Canada. In a silence too great to tolerate on such a night I heard the coyotes yip-yip-yipping down in the creek bottom. They were on to something, crossing back and forth, then backtracking. As I listened I felt my heart quicken; then I heard that high-pitched jabbering chorus that meant they'd caught what they were after. I threw back my head and rejoiced with them. It was a sign. They were calling me. But to what purpose?

Momma came over every morning until I was square on my feet, did the chores and cooked a pot of soup or a casserole for me and Mam to have later on. I felt fine as long as I was piled up in the bed, but I didn't last long in a vertical position. Almost a week of being waited on and catered to. Not once did she complain or even quote the Bible. It came to me that we had embarked on the road to a new understanding and appreciation for each other. I certainly felt more kindly toward her since she'd talked about her troubles with my daddy.

Oh, I knew about Daddy. In a small town like Robina it's no secret who the players and strayers are. But Momma was not one to show her feelings and I hadn't understood how deeply he had wounded her. I hadn't had that kind of experience with a man. Willis Henderson was so smitten he was cross-eyed and couldn't see there were other girls who would let themselves be more cooperative than I was. And Ed Shannon was the sort who would suffer the boils of Job before he'd break a promise. Never having been down that path, how could I judge my own momma?

Every afternoon after Momma had gone home to her own chores, Mam would come in and keep the patient company. We started out working on her history. Then I ended up the one being interviewed. She wanted to know about Mildred, where I'd met her and how we became such good friends.

I just blurted it out. I said, "I met Mildred at the boardinghouse where I went to live after I got out of jail."

Mam didn't blink an eyelid. "Why were you in jail, Cleo?"

"Panhandling. That's what the policeman said, and possible prostitution."

Mam said I should back up about a mile or two and start at the beginning. I took Alexandra's book from my bedside table, handed it over and said, "This is the person who started it all." I told Mam that Tulsa was to be the first leg of my journey to Lhasa, and over the next few days I spun out my tale. Not all of it. Even though Mam had gone through four husbands and was broad-minded regarding matters of the flesh, there were certain facts and fancies I felt should not be included in my narrative. Even so, my last afternoon as an invalid I heard myself working up to the Reverend Endicott. I looked up to see that I had put Mam into a doze, which was just as well considering the direction my story had taken.

Mildred came to fetch me that weekend. Mam had told me to invite her for some cobbler and tea. Momma said to Mam, "Well, don't expect me to be here. You'll probably get out your china and linen and put on airs."

Mam said, "We'll miss your jolly company, Frances."

In truth, Mam served Mildred at the kitchen table on everyday dishes. Mam said, "Cleo tells me you are her teacher."

"Ah," said Mildred. "I understood that you are her teacher, and a Miss Hawkins."

Mam laughed. "I been trying to teach her how to sit through a poker game and not lose her shirt. I hope you had more success than I am."

Mildred nodded. "Cleo was an apt student. She completed two years of study in only one. That's not an easy task for a girl who works full time in a saloon. . . ." She put her hand to her mouth and looked over at me.

"It's okay," I said. "Mam knows about the Gusher."

Mildred looked relieved. She said, "The only problem was algebra. I had to keep reminding her that in mathematics we do not divine the answers."

They laughed easily, like people long and well acquainted, and after we finished the cobbler Mam offered Mildred a Bugler, which to my amazement she took, lit, and smoked like a veteran of the French Foreign Legion.

I watched them and listened and thought about how lucky I was. A person can never have too many good teachers.

It was a fine day for a drive, sunny and crisp and full of wildflowers along the side of the road. Mildred and I had corresponded frequently but I hadn't seen her since the day she and her friend let me off at the crossroads close to the house. She had retired from her position at the high school. I'd told her in a letter that she wasn't old enough for retirement. She wrote back that's exactly why she did it, that she had a legacy from an aunt in Boston, her pension, and the rare opportunity to do whatever pleased her while she was still active enough to enjoy it.

She had bought a small house near the university and this new car she was driving, a 1940 Chrysler. I showed off and told her it had eight cylinders and a hypoid rear axle. She said that was nice but she'd had enough trouble learning to operate the thing and didn't plan to acquire any knowledge of its working parts.

She had taken up golf, worked as a volunteer at the Gilcrease Institute, and read to children in a nursery school every Friday morning. She said she didn't want to teach high-school students anymore, especially the boys.

She said, "I look at them with their fuzzy faces and their long young legs stretched out in the aisle, and I think, why in God's name am I telling you about Gilgamesh? I look at them and wonder which ones will go, which ones will come back."

"Mr. Hawkins says Roosevelt will keep us out of it."

She glanced over at me, then quickly back at the road. "Would take a miracle, Cleo. A miracle."

Mildred didn't bring up the purpose of my visit. I did, in a vague, roundabout way. I said, "This is my grandmother's idea, and my momma's, and I may not go through with it. Truth is, I'm not sure why I've come, but I feel myself drawn somehow."

"That's fine with me, Cleo. We'll have ourselves a nice visit. I'm glad of your company and I have plenty of room, plenty of time. You stay as long as you like. Do what you like. It's entirely your decision."

*

Mildred was true to her word. She never once mentioned the cemetery. Every morning she cooked a big breakfast. Then we'd go for a walk, or a drive, or out to Philbrook Art Center or some other cultural place. We'd have lunch at Crocker's Cafeteria or a White Knight, and maybe do some window shopping, or stop in and have a chat with Miss Ada at the dress shop. Every afternoon while Mildred rested her eyes, I walked up to the Glencliff on Eleventh Street and had a double chocolate malt to hold me over until supper. Mildred kidded me about my hollow leg.

I had forced myself to take money out of the bank for my trip. It was real cash money, not a draft, but Mildred wouldn't let me use it. I was her guest, she said, and furthermore the legacy was considerable and hers to do with as pleased her.

We talked a lot but not about anything pertinent to my visit. I could see that Mildred was there and ready for me, but she put a lot of slack in her line. After almost a week I began to tire of all our high living, and Mildred was about worn to a nub, although she didn't complain, just had to rest her eyes more often.

Then, Friday morning in the grey just before dawn, I sat bolt upright in bed. I knew, in a sudden blaze of understanding, why I had come to Tulsa. It had nothing to do with going to the cemetery. I wasn't ready for that until I settled this other matter my cleverness had kept hidden from me. The insurance money that so burdened me was a *legacy,* mine to do with as I saw fit. Sure, I could buy telephones and farm machinery and even an automobile, but there was a better way to spend it, a way that would afford me great and lasting satisfaction and keep me out of Cushman's Cave forever.

I turned off the light and laid my head on the pillow. That's what the coyotes had been trying to tell me. That was the sign. I had been hiding with the prey when I should be running with the predator. I didn't need to visit the graves. I needed to avenge them. I fell into a deep sleep. I dreamed of a winepress. The great winepress of the wrath of God. Revelation 14:19.

17

THE DISTRICT ATTORNEY STOOD UP WHEN I was shown into his office. He smiled, held out his arms, came around his desk and gave me a big smack on the cheek like we were old buddies. "My dear," he said. "Oh, my dear!"

I knew Wally Foreman from the department Christmas parties, from the annual picnic at Mohawk Park, and I knew him especially from deadly little dinners, first at their house and then, when I couldn't put it off any longer, at ours. The invitations had been exchanged like duty calls on new neighbors, and I thought they'd end after the first round. They didn't. Sylvia asked us again right away, which meant I had to ask them again. That's how it works. I bet there are folks who've packed up and moved to Boise, Idaho, just to avoid reciprocation.

I'd wait longer and longer before calling to set a date, then I'd have a nervous twitch for the whole week before the big event. I kept my feelings from Ed. I understood that entertaining the boss was a fact of life.

Sylvia had, as she said, taken me under her wing. She gave me pointers in gracious living. While she was nibbling away on a thigh, she said she'd give me her recipe for Chicken Parisienne. It was more suitable for company since you ate it with a knife and fork. And she brought me some candles and holders, two ceramic rabbits with holes in their heads. She said it was chic to dine by candlelight. I told her, with this smile plastered on my face, that it was the wise person who knew what he was eating. The last night they came, she said when *their* children were small and she and Wally had dinner guests, she fed the children early and sent them to their rooms to read or listen to the radio or play quiet games. Wally broke in to say they each got a dime if they didn't fight. Then they laughed and poked each other, real tickled they had managed to outwit a couple of little kids. Sylvia offered this backhanded piece of advice while my Em was passing around a plate of crackers topped with some chic something I'd got out of the *Family*

Circle magazine. There they were, my beautiful children, all scrubbed and in their best bib and behavior, and the Foremans didn't have better manners than to be rude to them.

After they left, Ed gets this look in his eye, the one the newspapers would comment on from time to time. And he says, "If it's all right with you, Cleo, I'd just as soon not see the Foremans socially."

And I say, "Suits me fine. But what'll I tell Sylvia when she calls?"

"Tell her the truth. What's that thing you say?" He frowned and scratched his head. "Oh, yes. Tell her she was born in a barn."

So, I didn't come calling on Wallace Foreman as a friend. It was strictly business. I sat in the chair he offered me and asked him straight out how the case was coming along.

He looked blank. "The case?"

"The investigation into the murder of my family." I said the word "murder" with all parts of my mind in attendance.

He shoved his hands in his pockets and drifted back to the other side of the desk, where I suppose he felt more in charge. "I wrote you that the case was closed."

"I didn't get any letter." I probably had. That part of my mind Momma worried about, the part that pretended, had probably opened the letter, read it, thrown it in the stove and forgot about it as soon as possible.

Wally buzzed his secretary and told her to bring in the Shannon file. He leaned back in his chair, laced his fingers behind his head, and undertook polite conversation while we waited. How had I been getting along? What was I doing with myself? How was my mother? I was living with my mother, wasn't I? He'd heard that from my friend, Mildred Ashcroft. That's how he knew where to send the letter. Did I have plans to return to Tulsa?

I gave one-word answers, rapid fire—"Fine." "Farming." "Grandmother." "No." Then I said, "How can you close a case when you've not found the person who committed the crime?"

Before he could answer, his secretary came in with the file, not nearly as thick as it should have been to my way of thinking. He said that would be all and started leafing through it. "Here it is, dated November 18th, last year. 'Dear Mrs. Shannon . . .' " He leaned toward me. "I didn't mean to sound formal, you understand, it's just that in official correspondence . . . Let's see now, where are we? Ah yes. 'Dear

Mrs. Shannon: It is with great regret . . . da ta da ta da . . . here we are. Due to lack of sufficient evidence, we are forced to discontinue the investigation into the unfortunate deaths of Shannon: Edward Hamilton Sr., Jr., and Emily Frances. Rest assured, madam, if pertinent information comes to light, we will reopen the case immediately. Again I extend to you the heartfelt sympathy of this department, and of myself personally for the enormous . . . da ta da ta da . . .' "

"May I see the file, please?"

"I'm sorry, my dear, that's privileged material."

"Seems to me I should be one of the privileged."

"Yes, it probably does seem that way, but, I'm sorry, that's not the way it is. Policy."

"You didn't find anything? No clues? Aren't there any clues at all? The car?"

"Cleo, the automobile in question was . . . well, it was for all practical purposes demolished. No evidence of the method, the type of explosive. That sort of thing will often lead us to suspect certain . . . Cleo, I'm sure you don't want to hear this. This must be unbearably painful for you."

"Go on."

"The main problem is that Ed was so good at his job. He made a lot of enemies, I mean, my dear, they were legion. No question he was brilliant but he had a habit of stepping on the wrong toes, as they say."

"But that was the nature of his work. Seems to me you would want to avenge the death of such a valuable man, a man who was such a credit to the department?"

"Well of course we *want* to, but . . . Oh my dear, these matters are often very complex."

"Did you investigate any of those wrong toes he stepped on?"

He gave me a sharp look. "As I said, these matters are often complex."

"Then it wasn't your decision to close the case?"

"Of course it was my decision." He closed the folder and moved his hand toward the buzzer.

"Please, Wally," I said quickly. "What about the case he was prosecuting when it happened?"

"With a fine-toothed comb, Cleo, and the Butler case before it. We

162

did a thorough—I assure you, thorough—investigation of every case where Ed Shannon got a conviction."

"What about the ones where he didn't? Sometimes people get real upset over the humiliation."

"I can assure you . . ."

"What about the woman who was tried for extortion? The one in the tiger coat."

"This isn't the—ah, method—a woman would use."

"Why not? We can be just as mean as men. She spit on him, remember that?"

He fumbled with the file. "I'm sure we . . ."

"And the couple accused of kidnapping? The man swore right there in the courtroom he'd get even."

Wally pulled his hand away from the buzzer, leaned back in his chair, and gave me a calculating look. "You followed your husband's work very closely."

"In the papers," I said. "And sometimes I came to the trials. He wouldn't talk about any of it at home."

"I don't remember that specific case—the kidnapping. When was it?"

"Soon after he came back to work for the department."

"My dear! That's ancient history."

"So. There are people who hold on to grudges just so they'll have a reason to get up in the morning. That man said he'd get Ed Shannon if it was the last thing he ever did. That's a threat, isn't it?"

Wally looked down at the file, fingered the edge of it. "Can't do it," he said finally. "Don't have the staff for that kind of thing, anyway there's no evidence to warrant . . ." He stood up and came around the desk, leaned over me, and took my hand. "Now, I know you're distressed over all this. Who wouldn't be? Who could blame you? You've suffered a terrible blow and I can understand how you'd grasp at these straws. Oh but they are straws in the wind, my dear. If there was anything I could do I would do it, I assure you. But I can't reopen an investigation without sufficient cause. I can't justify it, do you understand?"

I nodded and pulled my hand away. "Yes," I said. "I understand." I understood that it had to do with budgets and elections and wrong toes.

"Now, are you in town for long? Maybe you could come for dinner one night while you're here. I know Sylvia would love to see you, yes indeed."

I stared at him and shook my head in wonderment. "Thank you, Wally, but this is a short visit."

"Then do give us a call the next time you come to town. Will you do that? Old friends are the best, you know."

I nodded. Oh, Lord, how I wanted to bash him up the side of the head with my pocketbook.

He stepped back and clasped his hands together like a man who had just settled a thorny problem. The gesture was also a dismissal. I got to my feet. "You'll call me if anything comes up? If you uncover any new evidence?"

"Of course I will." He took my arm and aimed me toward the door. "Cleo," he said, "it's time you got on with your life. Mustn't dwell in the past, you know. You're a young woman, and if I may say so, a very attractive young woman. You have your whole future ahead of you. Yes, yes of course, leave your number with my secretary, but Cleo, don't get your hopes up, don't count on it. I've been in this business for a long time and I have a kind of sixth sense about these things. This case is deep, like Ed Shannon himself, like so many of life's mysteries. Try to forget the past."

I sighed and bobbed my head. Momma told me I had to remember and this pissant said I had to forget.

I stopped in the lobby to use the pay phone. Tully was still at the Gusher and said I should come right over. The old neon sign, the one I'd mistaken for God's pillar of fire, was gone, but the place was still called the Gusher. There was a new door next to the old double doors to the restaurant. It was dull black and had the words PRIVATE CLUB written across it. It was still illegal to sell liquor in Oklahoma but matters had progressed to where you didn't have to walk through the kitchen and down the back stairs to get to the bar. I tried the door. It was locked. I knocked, and told the woman who opened it that Tully was expecting me.

"Mrs. Shannon?" I nodded. "He's in the bar."

He saw me coming. By the time I wound around through the tables there was a Coca-Cola with a lot of ice and a maraschino cherry waiting for me.

"How's my girl?" he said, and reached over and squeezed my shoulder.

I wanted to hug him but Tully had never been one for physical expression. This squeeze on the shoulder was a first, and his way of saying how sorry he was. I said, "Good to see you, Tully."

He picked up a glass from the sink and started wiping it. "Bring your horn?" I laughed and shook my head. "We got a piano player and a bass man nights. Maybe we could scare you up a trumpet and you could sit in."

"Wouldn't be the same without Scat. Anyhow, I don't have any costumes anymore. Remember my tramp outfit?"

He set the glass down and cocked his head. "The blue dress was worse, the one with the big white collar, looked like you'd just come from Sunday school. Terrible for business. Terrible! Customers all ordered soda water. Sobered everybody up."

"And the shoes? The brown brogans? Remember how you'd look at them and pretend to faint?"

"Who says I was pretending?"

The waitress came up with an order and Tully moved to the other end of the bar. I sipped my Coca-Cola and looked around. Except for the new staircase the place hadn't changed to speak of. Piano was in the same place. Same piano.

Tully came back and said he'd got somebody to watch the bar; then he took my arm and escorted me to a corner booth. He said Scat had been in a couple of months before on his way to Chicago.

"He's got a combo now, bass and sax. Said if I ever saw you, I should say he could always use a good trumpet man."

I nodded and sipped my Coca-Cola, working on my courage. Tully lit a cigarette and stared off into the distance, into those walls and windowpanes where the past carries on a life of its own. He chuckled. "Remember the first time you wore that black satin dress? That waitress? What was her name? Eileen? Darleen?"

"Noreen," I said.

"Yeah, Noreen. Boy did her eyes pop. She'd thought you were just a kid up to then. First time you'd shown off your . . ." He held his hands out in front of his chest.

I laughed. "I used to call them my wonders."

"Remember the Tunney-Dempsey fight? The second one?"

"I sure do. I lost all my savings for my trip to Lhasa. And the rent. You told me Dempsey was money in the bank."

He turned up his palms. "I didn't think the boss would ever get over that. Me placing a bet for . . ." He let the sentence trail off, then put his hand over mine. You couldn't rattle on forever about the good old days at the Gusher without bumping square up against the boss.

Tully cleared his throat. "What did you want to see me about, Cleo?"

So I told him how I'd been to see the district attorney, and how he said the case was closed for lack of evidence. Tully shook his head and said what a shame that was, how it wasn't fair, how they'd thrown away the mold after they made Ed Shannon.

I said, "I thought you might know some private investigator I could hire."

He shook his head. "You're talking a lot of money. Those guys don't come cheap."

"I have the insurance money. I can't think of any better way to use it."

He thought for a minute. "Yeah, I know somebody."

"Could you call him for me?"

"Yeah, I can do that. Where can I get in touch with you?"

"I mean now. Right now. I'd like to see him today. As soon as possible."

He gave me a steady look. "You sure you want to do that? Means going through the whole thing again."

"I know. I'm sure."

He disappeared behind a curtain at the far end of the bar, and was back in a few minutes with a slip of paper in his hand.

"Two o'clock at his office. Name's Ahern, Michael Ahern. He knew Ed, did some work for him. Here, it's all written down. You want another coke, Cleo? How 'bout a sandwich?"

My knees did not fully cooperate when I slid out of the booth and stood up, but for the first time in two weeks I wasn't hungry. I thanked him and said I thought I'd just walk around for a while, get my thoughts together so I could answer Mr. Ahern's questions. Ahern, I thought, Michael Ahern. Probably Irish, likely a drinker. But the Irish were generally brave, and they understood revenge.

I walked south on Main, taking my time, trying to concentrate on what I'd tell him. Pertinent information, that's what Wally said. Rest assured if any pertinent information comes to light . . . da ta da ta da. I got mad all over again. District attorney! The man was about as much use as ten dead flies.

I passed by Kresses, stopped and went back, lingered in front of the window. It brought Rosemary to mind, and all those grilled cheese sandwiches and shared confidences. She was living in a place called Glendale, now, in California. Raymond hadn't lasted long in the movie business. He had a good job in the advertising department at Western Auto. They had two fine boys, and they'd bought a house with a Spanish tile roof. In every letter there was an invitation to come visit. Rosemary said there was plenty of room. She said Glendale had a fine library. I'd thought about it. One could get to Lhasa by way of California. But that was in the future. Just now I had a full plate.

I turned west on Fifth and stopped in the lobby of the Mayo Hotel to call Mildred and let her know my plans and whereabouts. Mr. Ahern's building was close by. I was early, but figured I'd look at magazines till he could see me. Number 307 had one of those crinkly glass panes in the door, with MICHAEL S. AHERN, PRIVATE INVESTIGATOR written on it in gold letters. I stood there and went through all the Irish S's I could bring to mind. Sean, Shamus, Sullivan, Shane . . . Then a shadow loomed on the other side and the door swung open. The biggest man I'd ever laid eyes on told me to come on in. He wasn't fat, just big. Way over six feet, with shoulders that almost filled the doorway. He had rusty-colored hair and those blue eyes that are all shallows, no depth to them, the kind that don't give away any secrets. I liked the looks of him. I figured he could get Wally's full attention.

"I'm early," I said.

He stuck out his hand. "That's okay, so am I."

I followed him through the small reception room (no magazines) into his office. I expected it to be a mess like they always are in detective stories, but it was clean and spare. Two file cabinets in the corner, a large desk with a telephone, penholder, blotter with nothing doodled on it, a typewriter on a stand, two straight-backed chairs. No pictures on the walls, not even a calendar. I sat on the edge of one of the chairs and thanked him for seeing me on such short notice.

He sat down, got a yellow pad from his top desk drawer, took one of the pens from the holder, and fixed me with his shallow blue eyes. "I'll do what I can," he said flatly. "I admired your husband."

"The district attorney says the big problem is that Ed had so many enemies."

He rolled his eyes. "The big problem is that Wally Foreman is a certifiable asshole. Pardon my French, Mrs. Shannon." He rolled the pen between his fingers. "Tell me what you can remember about that morning. Anything different. Anything unusual."

I shook my head. "The only thing unusual was that he was going to drive the kids to school. I usually went with them to the crosswalk." I looked down at my hands clasped in my lap. "I got up late."

"I see. So you think you're at fault."

"Yes and no. Not exactly. Ed was in a dangerous line of work. Like my grandmother says, he loved trouble. I always knew it was possible that someday somebody might kill him. I was prepared for that. No, I wasn't. But I meant to be."

"So, it's the children."

"That's right. It was my responsibility to see them safely to school. I understand that whoever did this may not have expected innocent children to be in the car, but that doesn't soften my attitude any." I took a deep breath. "Mr. Ahern, I have almost five thousand dollars in the bank and I'm willing to spend every penny of it on this."

"The money is not a problem."

"I don't want you to take this job just because you admired Ed Shannon. I know from my own experience that people work better if they're fairly paid. I want you to find the person or persons who did this and I want you to find the kind of evidence that will cause that person or persons to be punished. I should tell you this. What I'd really like is burial up to the neck in a red-ant hill. If it's not red-ant season and the guilty party is a man, which Wally seems to think it is because of the nature of the crime, then I'd like his testicles cut off one at a time and scrambled with some eggs and served up to him for supper. Just one at a time. I'd like him to hold the hope he'd get to keep one."

There was a glint in the shallows of Mr. Ahern's eyes. "Mrs. Shannon, I am a private investigator. Not Attila the Hun."

"I just want you to understand how strongly I feel about this."

"I think I've got the picture."

"Wally said he needed pertinent information before he could re-open the case. I'd like you to find it. Then if he still won't do anything, I'll need some names from you."

"Names?" He tilted his head to one side with the expression of a man who didn't like what he was hearing.

"I've read a lot of detective novels and I know a man in your business has certain contacts . . ."

He started to laugh, then quickly rearranged his face and said gravely, "I don't know one soul who deals in anthills. Or scrambled testicles."

He looked at me for a long moment, then picked up the telephone and rescheduled his appointments. I told him everything I knew about Ed Shannon, including what I'd learned about his work in the twenties as a special investigator. I told him about phone conversations I'd overheard, about the extortion woman, the kidnap people, a case involving bootleggers out of Chicago, a stockbroker he'd had a run-in with, even those wrong toes Wally had spoken of. I told him everything I could bring to mind.

Around five o'clock, when he had maybe a dozen pages of notes, Michael—he was Michael by then and I was Cleo—got out a bottle of whiskey and two shot glasses. We sealed our bargain; then he said I should go home and go about my business, because he had a lot of digging to do and it would take time. He said I was not to be impatient. Then he called me a taxi and I went back to Mildred's.

Over supper I told her about the meeting—not the red ants part—but I covered the essentials and said I had confidence in Michael Ahern.

I said, "If we can just find the truth and settle up with who's responsible, then I can put this part of my life behind me."

Mildred was unusually quiet, but I figured she was done in after the week's activities.

Early the next morning she drove me home. There was no mention of the cemetery, not much mention of anything. We did not ride in a comfortable silence. I asked her in for a cup of tea but she had some cataloguing to do at the institute. She said she'd be pleased to visit another time.

I got my satchel from the trunk and came around to the driver's side. I laid my hand against her cheek and said, "There is no way in this world I can ever thank you for your kindness to me."

She covered my hand and squeezed it. I stepped back. She started the car, attempted a smile, then a look of great pain grew in her eyes and settled over her face. She leaned toward me and said, "I hope and pray Mr. Ahern will be able to find the truth for you. But I hope you won't expect miracles of it."

"I don't know what you mean?"

"Oh Cleo, I have lived long enough to know that we can't put large pieces of our lives behind us and expect them to disappear. Those pieces are always attached to what went before and what comes after. The truth doesn't change that. At best, the truth may let us move with grace and purpose through the ruins."

18

MAM SAT AT THE KITCHEN TABLE, A STACK of paper in front of her and a pen in her hand. She didn't look up. "That you, Cleo? Miss Ashcroft with you?"

"Yes, it's me. No, Mildred had to get back. Said she'd be pleased to come another time."

"Good. I like that woman, she's got good sense." She pointed with her pen toward the tank. "Moby's fine, been looking for you."

"Goldfish don't recognize people." I set my satchel by the door and got a cup from the shelf.

"Sure they do. Every creature knows the hand that feeds it. Pour me one while you're at it."

I poured the coffee and sat down across from her. "I didn't go to the cemetery." I wanted to get that out of the way.

"Didn't expect you would, not this time. There's some mistakes here, Cleo. I marked some of it out and put checks by the parts we need to talk about."

I looked down at the table. The stack of paper was that part of the history which, before I got sick, I had so painstakingly typed with two fingers on Miss Hawkins' Smith-Corona.

"Harlan started as a lieutenant, you got that right, but he ended a captain, youngest captain in the Indian brigade. You need to put that in."

"I'm way behind in the work around here. Why don't we make an appointment for next week."

"No, let's do it now. I may go on next week." She looked at me slyly. "What good is a leather binding and gold letters if the facts aren't right?"

I got my pad. I was hardly in the mood for history. I was still puzzling on Mildred's words about truth and ruins. "So, Harlan was a captain," I sighed. "Okay, I got that."

She pointed to one of her many checkmarks. "You got your dates wrong here. You say the war was over in April."

"That date's correct. I looked it up at the library."

"That's when Lee handed over his sword, but General Watie didn't surrender his Creek regiments until two months later."

"Mam," I said impatiently, "this is not a textbook. The war was officially over in April."

"That's not what I'm getting at. You say here, 'The last shot was fired on April 9, 1865, and Harlan McQueen came home to his wife and children.' They don't stop shooting 'cause some general hands over his sword, but that's not the point, the point is Harlan came home a full year before it was over."

"You didn't tell me that."

"You didn't ask me."

"Why did he come home early? Was he wounded?"

She looked away, then down at the papers. "Maybe you're right. Maybe we should just leave it be."

I waited.

"Yes," she said, finally. "He was wounded. Harlan sustained two wounds to his body and three to his soul."

I waited again, lit a Bugler, and passed it over to her.

"Soon after he joined up, just a while after he was made lieutenant, he was in the battle at Elk Creek. Wasn't a real battle, Harlan said, not planned—a skirmish, he called it. They ran into these Yankee boys when they were getting set to camp. So they square off and shoot at each other. This Yankee tumbles down off the bank and Harlan gets a good look at him. It's his cousin. He'd grown up with him, they'd gone to school together at the Arkansas College. My Harlan thought he'd be fighting Upper Creeks and Cherokees. They'd always fought, nothing new about that. He didn't expect to be shooting at his own kind, his own relations.

"He was just over twenty years old, just a boy. This other boy, Harlan's cousin, he lands on a sandbar, doesn't move. Harlan sinks down in the bushes. He's never felt so bad in his life. Up to now he's been having a good time, whooping around on his horse, shooting off his Mexican gun, sneaking up on people, setting fire to everything in sight. But it hadn't been personal.

"After a while the Yankees fall back. It's getting dark and come morning, Harlan's bunch'll go out and count how many they killed, they'll take the uniforms, what items they can use . . . shoes especially.

Harlan said it was sometimes hard to tell who was on what side from the uniforms. He hears his own men regrouping on the woods behind him, but he stays put, hidden in the bushes. When it's real dark he wades over to the sandbar. His cousin's dead, big hole behind his ear. Harlan sits there beside him and thinks about how sorry he is and how he hopes it wasn't his own bullet that did it. He thinks about how he doesn't want anybody taking his cousin's clothes come morning. He wonders what a Lower Creek is doing fighting for the Loyalists. He wishes he and his cousin could have a long talk about the reasons for this war.

"Then he digs a grave in the sand close to the bank where there's overhanging bushes, where it won't be noticed. He regrets a burial so close to fresh water but there's no help for it. He rolls his cousin into the grave and covers him over. He wonders what he'll say to his aunt when he gets home. If he gets home. This is the first time he's thought about dying. Then he remembers his promise to me and he wades back across the creek, quiet as he can.

"Not long after, his captain was shot and Harlan was given the job. One day he and his men come on some Yankee haymakers, Negro soldiers cutting and putting up hay for use at Fort Gibson. Harlan orders a cannon shot into the ricks and everybody scatters. That's the sort of work they did mostly at that time, burn hay so Yankee horses would starve come winter. Harlan said he never meant to make war on horses. He orders what's left of the ricks set fire to. Then one of his men spies a Negro in the weeds, and shoots him. Some other Negroes spring up from hiding places with their hands in the air. Harlan's yelling for his men to cease fire. They claim later they didn't hear him. They claim one of the Negroes drew his weapon.

"It was Harlan's policy to take these men prisoner, these men minding supplies and hayricks and the like. He said they were like civilians, sometimes didn't even have firearms. Just men out in the fields cutting hay to feed the animals. Harlan thought maybe that was what set it off, that his men didn't get to do as much killing as they'd signed up for. He felt that was why they disobeyed.

"It was his own actions that mystified him. Somebody found a white man hiding in the pond, just his nose sticking out. They brought him to Harlan and wanted to know what to do with him. They're all laughing now, drunk on it, drunk on the power of it. Harlan looks away and puts his thumb down like he's a Roman emperor. They shoot the man, him begging for his life. Then 'cause there's nothing else left to shoot, they shoot the mules.

"Harlan never got over the shame of it. That was the deepest wound. He told his colonel he wanted to resign his commission. Instead he got a commendation. The colonel said Harlan had come to the attention of General Waite and he and his men would be getting special assignments instead of wandering around looking for supply trains and hayricks.

"Come a time he was sent to burn down a house where it was suspected Union high-ups met to make plans with Loyalist Creeks and Cherokees. Rumor was there was an underground passage that came from the river, and people could come and go unnoticed. That house turned out to be Rose Hill. Harlan didn't know it till he got there. What he had was a map with an X on it. He couldn't believe it. My father was Lower Creek. Almost all the Lower Creeks were for the Confederacy or neutral. Harlan tells his men there's been some mistake. He says to his lieutenant, 'This house belongs to my wife's father. We got the wrong house.' He writes in his report that the target was misidentified, that the house was the home of a neutral Lower Creek.

"Maybe a week later the colonel sent another raiding party in the middle of the night. Rose Hill was burned to the ground, Mother and Father and my three little sisters with it. Harlan shot himself in the hand, his gun hand, the hand with the killer thumb on it. And he came home.

"We stayed out of it best we could. Soldiers from both sides thieved from our cornfield and garden—they called it foraging—but other than that nobody bothered us. Then it was over. General Watie surrendered his Creek regiments on June 25th. I don't know why in this world it took him so long.

"My sweet Harlan, he couldn't seem to do anything with hisself, got worse and worse. We went over to Rose Hill. Nothing left. Not even one of my mother's native climbers. We poked around, tried to find something to bury, to say words over. That was my idea, I thought it might help him, and we searched for an underground passage. That was my idea too, even though I knew in my heart there wasn't one. I knew every inch of every acre, but I hoped we'd find it. I prayed we'd find it. I'd of gladly seen my father a traitor if it would help poor Harlan.

"I told him over and over it wasn't his fault, not any of it. He'd shake his head, go out to the field, and try to work, try to strip cotton, try to plough the ground. Then he'd give up—go into town and get drunk. Only thing that helped. I tried to take him to myself at night, but his manhood was gone. So I put him to my breast like a child and he'd finally sleep.

"Then one morning I heard a gunshot from the direction of the orchard. I picked up my skirts and ran as fast as I could, knowing what I'd find when I got there. But I hadn't guessed all of it. He'd dug a grave—deep and narrow—crawled in it and shot himself in the head. He left this neat mound of dirt, and the shovel leaning against a tree nearby. Didn't want to put me to any trouble. My sweet Harlan had two body wounds, one of them mortal, but it wasn't the body wounds that killed him."

She took a deep breath and blew it out slowly, then leaned on her elbows, cradled her head in one hand, and began to trace the grain in the pine table with the other. I took a Bugler from the jar and struck a match, but she shook her head. We sat there like that for maybe a half hour in absolute silence, a silence so full of death even the birds wouldn't risk disturbing it.

I followed her finger's progress over the table. It would move along a path to a knothole, circle it, back up, and start again, like an ant that encounters an obstacle then patiently, finally, finds a way around it. It came to me that her fingers were even older than the table. Old brown fossil hands that had once been young and firm and gainless. Kindly fingers that had tried their best to smooth and tickle and rub some desire into Harlan's manhood.

I couldn't feature it. Mam had been wrinkled and gnarled and hunched since I could remember. Always old—like all grandmothers were old. I could not bring my mind's eye to see her in the act of love. I could not see her thighs spread—not even to bring the dead back to life.

Her finger settled on a long-necked bird with a hooked beak. I had eaten at this table, had done homework here, had been punished here for sass and lies and irreverence—told to sit here until I was good and sorry. Odd that I had never noticed this strange collection of creatures in the grain and knotholes. The bird had a single horn growing out of the top of its head. An alligator waited for a meal to fall off a fork . . . a peacock feather here . . . owl eyes there . . . a wolf's tooth . . . half a gander. Boards carefully chosen for their flaws.

Mam roused herself. "You won't say anything about Harlan's personal loss, and just write he had an accident while he was cleaning his gun. You go look up at the library how that kind of accident can happen."

I patted her hand. "After all this time how can the truth hurt anybody?"

"You don't know?"

"I guess I don't," I said carefully. I felt a need to be very careful. There were things all around me easily broken.

"This will be in the library with the other books?"

"That's right, in a special section."

"You don't know what happens in libraries in the nighttime?" I admitted I didn't know, and she said, "The pages open up, that's what, and all the restless spirits come out and go visiting. The men sit on each other's porches and drink home brew and swap tales and compare brave deeds. That's how they are. It's their nature. I wouldn't want to put my sweet Harlan at any disadvantage. You understand what I'm saying?"

"Yes'm, I do."

"You make him a hero, you hear?"

I gave a passing thought to my responsibilities in this matter; then I nodded. She nodded back and we shook hands in a solemn, formal way. Conspirators. Queens of foreign nations. Historians. Allpowerful.

I lit her up a Bugler and on second thought took one for myself, puffed on it, coughed, worried a bit about my breath for my trumpet; then we settled back and filled the room with blue smoke—a ceremony. After a while, I got up and poured us some hot coffee. I said, "Tell me something, Mam."

"I'm tired, Cleo. You make an appointment?"

"Not for the history. For me. I have a question."

"I hope it doesn't need hard thought."

I phrased it first in my mind, carefully again. There were still all these breakables lying around. "After it happened," I said, "did you ever want to get back at them? For all the grief they caused?"

"Them? They?"

I shrugged. "The colonel that gave the order? General Watie? President Lincoln? Somebody . . . ?"

"Oh, I can't remember, Cleo. I suppose I did in the beginning but there was no time to dwell on it. I had two babies to raise, farm to run, nobody to help me. After a decent time for mourning I started looking around for a husband. One that was a churchgoer, knew how to grow cotton, only drank whiskey on a Saturday night. Today's bread is to bake, Cleo." She looked at me wearily over the rim of her cup. "You fixing to get back at somebody? You fixing to waste your valuable time?"

I realized I had erred in thinking Mam would cheer me on. I said, "I don't see it as time wasted." I folded my arms on my chest and clamped my mouth shut to give the clear impression that my mind was made up and I didn't mean to discuss the matter further.

She made a great show of putting on her spectacles. She adjusted them, took them off and cleaned them on her apron, put them on again and squinted at me. "Um hum," she said, "sure is. Your mother's daughter all right." Then she took off the glasses and rubbed her eyes. "I can't talk any more, Cleo. I'm too tired. Why should I tax my energies to give you advice anyway? You pay about as much attention as a grasshopper." She sighed and reached for her stick. "Let's have a nice potato soup for supper. With a little middlin' meat fried up crisp, and some cornbread. Lord, lord, I am so tired."

She rose up, one hand on her stick, the other on the small of her back—stiff and queen-regal—and made for her room. When she got to the door she turned back and looked at me. "You don't have any notion, do you, Cleo? No notion at all?" She lifted her stick and brought it down like a thunderclap. "Listen to me! God is the only one got the time and the stomach for vengeance. It spoils the rest of us. Trying to keep track of all the eyes and teeth of a lifetime." Another clap of thunder struck the floor. "I am nearbout a century old. But it was just the other morning that me and Harlan put in that first cotton field. *Just the other morning.* Do you have any idea what I'm saying?"

I stared at her, kept one wary eye on the stick, half afraid she might try to whomp some sense into me with it. Then her shoulders sagged and she shook her head as if to say there was no help for such a sorry specimen as myself.

"Just the other morning," she said again. "Oh Cleo, dear child, try not to waste your chips."

19

EVERY FRIDAY AFTERNOON I CALLED MIchael Ahern to check on his progress. He told me not to waste my money, he'd call when he had something to say. Mam and I—by virtue of that unspoken agreement that occurs between blood relations—did not discuss the nature of these calls.

Because I had no idea how much money Michael was going to cost me, I did not invest in farm machinery as I had intended. But I did ask Gideon Warwick to kindly, at his convenience, come over and consult about what I might grow as a cash crop on Mam and Momma's worthless land.

We walked around the fields, him taller than God and longer-legged, and me, the budding agriculturist, scampering along after him with my notebook. He'd stop from time to time, narrow his eyes, kick at a rock with one of his big dusty shoes, push back his hat, scratch his head, give a little shudder, then move off again like a Red Cross official appraising the scene after a disaster.

As Abraham was to the Israelites, so also was Gideon Warwick to the people of Robina. Rumor had it Gideon once took on a tornado single-handed, met it outside town, straddled the road, shook his fist, and told the wind it was approaching sacred ground. Rumor had it that funnel stopped dead in its tracks, did a one-eighty, and went back to Kansas.

And during the worst part of the Great Depression, it was Gideon Warwick who led the faithful right past the gaping doors of the poorhouse. There was not a soul in the county that didn't have enough to eat and a warm place to rest his head. Gideon accomplished this by means of socialism, although that word was not included in his polite vocabulary.

Like Abraham, Gideon was childless until late in life, although not as late as Abraham by any means. Adam, a change-of-life miracle, the joy and comfort of Gideon's middle age, was taken from him twenty-five years later on the sharp hooves of his favorite blooded mare.

Rumor is Gideon wept only twice in his lifetime—when he buried Adam, and again that night when he put a bullet in the Arabian's skull.

But what sent me to Gideon for help was no mere rumor. Everyone for four counties around knew it for God's truth that Gideon had a genius as regards the fruits of the earth, and that he had dominion over them. He planted seeds, admonished them to flourish, and they obliged like well-mannered children. So I trailed along after him that afternoon with the sureness of heart that he could will fertility into our rocks and clay.

It felt like we walked off about sixty acres. It was warm for May. I had sweat in my eyes, and shoes full of grit, but Gideon showed no signs of discomfort. He didn't even take off his suit coat. We were almost back to the house, where he'd been invited for coffee and apple cobbler, but so far no advice was forthcoming—just grunts, clicks, and shudders. Then he stopped short, turned back, and spread his arms as if to embrace the fields. There was a smile buried in his great white beard.

"Strewberries," he said.

"Sir?"

"Strewberries. That'll do it."

"Never heard of them."

"People call them strawberries in error. Real name is strewberries. Because they strew, grow by sending out runners, strewing themselves. Not a berry either. Belong to the rose family."

I couldn't believe it. I'd wasted a whole afternoon for such as this. "We've grown strawberries—*strew*berries in the garden, only place there's decent soil, but it's not big enough. . . ."

"No," he said, and waved his arm. "I'm talking about the fields out there. And your momma's too. What the Lord has given you, Cleo, is one big rock pile. All you have to do is find a use for it."

"I had hoped you would find it for me."

"I have. Just told you. Strewberries. You hitch up your mule and plough yourself some rows. Mound them up. That's the first job. Then you go down those rows and every foot or so you give those rocks a big whack with a dull ax. Then push the rocks aside to make a triangular hole. Drop in some topsoil and set your plant. Lot of work. You want a fall harvest you'll need to hire yourself some help."

"I can't do that, sir."

"I don't see why not. It's no secret you've got a tidy sum in the Farmers' and Merchants'."

"That money is put by to a special purpose."

"You could borrow some of it. Borrow from yourself and pay yourself interest when your crop come in. I have found that to be a sound business practice."

"If," I said with a snort. "If my crop come in."

"Strewberries are money in the bank."

"Somebody once told me that same thing about Jack Dempsey."

He laughed and kicked at a pile of rocks.

"What's the cost of the plants?" I said. "Roughly."

"I have enough to get you started and I can poke around and come up with maybe two or three acres worth. That's more than enough if you won't get yourself some help. I'd give them to you if it wasn't for Frances. She'd see it as charity. But I can advance them and you can pay me when your crop comes in."

"If," I reminded him.

"I don't advance on 'ifs', Cleo. Shows what kind of faith I have in strewberries."

I gazed off into the fields, trying to get a glimpse of the sure thing he saw out there. "Is that all I do? Just beat up on those rocks and set the plants in topsoil?"

"Water them. Get yourself about a dozen pails. Krause'll give them to you on credit when you tell him I advanced you the plants. You need a narrow base cart, I'll loan you one. Hitch the mule to the cart and fill your pails with water. Load up your topsoil and the plants then go up and down the rows like I said. Whack your rocks with your ax . . . put in a handful of topsoil . . . set your plant crown even with the soil and give it a dipperful of water, maybe more, depends on the weather."

"That's it?"

"That's how you begin."

"Then what?"

"Wouldn't hurt to ask a blessing on them. That's probably what went wrong with Jack Dempsey."

Mam called to us out the screen door. "You all coming in? My cobbler's getting cold." She had on one of her Sunday dresses and carried her Spanish fan with the dewdrops—in honor of that rare bird, a Gentleman Visitor. She held the door for us. "Take his hat, Cleo. You sit wherever you want, Gideon. Coffee all right or you rather have tea? I got a new batch of hickory or some Lipton's from the grocery. What's your pleasure?"

Gideon said a cup of coffee would really hit the spot; then he settled down to obligatory niceties. "How's Frances these days?"

"Oh, she's fine," said Mam. "Mean as ever. How's Evelina?"

"Fine. Just fine. Had a touch of the flu last week but that seems to be cleared up now."

"And Adam's girls, how they?"

"Oh well, you know, fight all the time, probably kill each other before they grow up."

They both laughed, but I had seen those little girls perform around town and thought such an outcome was a clear possibility.

"You know how it is," said Mam, and she passed Gideon the pitcher of heavy cream. They nodded agreement about how it was—just another one of life's astonishments.

Mam said, "So what's the verdict out there?"

"Strewberries," I said.

"Never heard of them."

Gideon went through his recitation about the proper name for these berries that were, in truth, roses.

"Roses!" said Mam, clearly charmed. "My mother had a rose garden on the home place. It was called Rose Hill. Did you know that, Gideon?"

"Yes, I seem to recall I've heard that, Jessie."

"But Cleo was hoping for some kind of cash crop."

And Gideon explained to her about all the money we were going to make thrashing rocks.

"So you'll loan us the starters?"

"If it won't upset Frances."

"We just won't tell her. What she doesn't know won't get her long nose out of joint." She put her hand out for Gideon's empty bowl. "Another helping?"

"Don't mind if I do, thank you."

"So we just tend them the usual way?" Mam asked, the Royal We speaking.

Gideon leaned back and folded his hands over his vest. "Not exactly," he said. "I'd recommend you sacrifice the daughters."

I perked up my ears. Sounded like something Abraham might say. Abraham who went childless for almost a hundred years then begat eight sons in great spurts of fertility. No girls we know of, but that's how it was in Old Testament days. Girls weren't begot. They just showed up, full-grown and sun-ripened for men to lay with.

"Thing is," Gideon was saying, "any fool can raise strewberries, even in a little backyard in the city. What our Cleo needs to do is raise special strewberries." He leaned toward Mam, like he was about to impart secret information. "There are three ways to approach strewberries. You leave the daughters alone, you train them, or you sacrifice them. Last year was the first time I tried sacrificing." He made a circle of his thumb and forefinger. "Whoppers, and just as sweet as honey from a hive."

"You pinched off the runners?" Mam asked in amazement. "Why, Gideon, that's just wasteful—just pure waste."

"You don't throw them out, Jessie, you keep them for the next planting. It's the only way to go in this situation. The daughters will do their level best to strew, but the good soil is all in these little holes you've made. You leave them be and they'll wander off and die, or they'll turn back and try to crowd out the mother. You could train them but that means more runs with your cart, and you don't get these big whoppers I'm talking about. That's the whole idea. Special strewberries. Now, you water and weed the usual way. Watch for mites and root weevil. Don't plant them all at once or they'll come ripe all at once and you'll be busier than a sinner on his first trip to New Orleans."

I said, "And what am I to do with these special strewberries after I harvest them?"

"Ah-hah!" he said, and gave his knee a swat. "You'll sell some to Julius at the grocery and you'll have folks pounding on your door day and night once they hear where these special strewberries come from. But that's peanuts. What's going to make you ladies rich is your Suspension!"

Mam and I looked at each other.

"I brought in my first pickings to Evelina last summer and she took one look and said, 'Gideon, these berries are too beautiful for jam.' Then Pepper said, 'We can suspend them.' And by golly, that's what they did. I took a few jars into this company in Tulsa and they said

they'd take all we could put up." (The Royal We again. Gideon Warwick never so much as hard-boiled an egg.) "But Evelina doesn't want
to fool with it this year, so the job is yours. You get the receipt from
Evelina."

Mam and I gave each other another look.

"Now then," Gideon went on, "you want to order yourself some
pretty jars from Krause. Then you have some labels made. He has a
book of samples you can choose from. Flowers on them, or a girl in a
sunbonnet, that sort of thing. And you can have whatever you want
printed on the label. Something catchy. CLEO'S SWEET STREW-
BERRIES or . . ." He winked. ". . . SWEET CLEO'S STREW-
BERRIES. Just be sure you call them strewberries, city people will
think it's a new discovery."

He slipped his gold watch out of his vest pocket, looked at it, and
got to his feet. "Thank you for the cobbler, Jessie. Mighty fine. Probably ruined my supper."

"Any time, Gideon. You're welcome any time. And we are certainly
beholden to you for your good advice."

I could see these last words were offered more in company manners
than enthusiasm. I got Gideon's hat from the hook and showed him
out.

"You get those mounds in, Cleo, then come on over for the cart and
the starters. You need to get on this project day before yesterday."

I watched him stride out to his shiny black Buick sedan, a man
uplifted by his own good deeds, then I sank back down at the table
and stared at the kitchen counter. I saw it covered with pretty little
jars. There were catchy little labels stuck on every one of them. Trouble was, those pretty little jars were all empty. How could a man as
smart as Gideon Warwick be so dense about the female nature. No
self-respecting woman in Robina county—not even a saint like
Evelina—was about to share her special receipts.

"Maybe you could ask her for it," I said. "Maybe you could plead
hardship."

"You know what she'd say." Mam imitated Evelina's lilting North
Carolina soprano that was responsible for so many Baptist converts.
" 'Jessie, hon, I don't have that old thing written down. I never do it
twice the same way. You know how you do . . . little of this . . . little of
that . . .' "

184

"Maybe we could ask Gideon to get it."

"Child, I will not face my Maker with a divorce on my conscience. It is beyond me, Cleo, how a man can live with a woman day after day, night after night, year after year, and not know the first thing about her. My poor, sweet Juan, getting himself drowned trying to catch me a fish. I don't even like fish."

"Does Suspension sound French to you? Miss Hawkins has a French cookbook in the library. I mean I know it refers to holding up a man's pants, or the back end of an automobile, but what on earth does it have to do with canning?"

"Lord, I don't know. Puts me in mind of that green Jell-O salad the Auxiliary ladies bring to the Fourth of July picnic. With the little pieces of marshmallow trapped in it? But you can't put up Jell-O, not that I ever heard of. It was Pepper's idea, wasn't it? Isn't that what Gideon said? That Pepper said they should suspend them? So maybe it's a Creole receipt, that's part French. Wouldn't hurt to have a gander at that cookbook. But don't tell anybody what you're trying to find, you hear? Everybody in the county'll be suspending their fruit."

My mind's eye gazed over at all our empty jars, lined up like baby birds with their beaks open.

"Strewberries," Mam said.

"Strewberries," I echoed.

We said it together. "Strewberries." A sorrowful Greek chorus of two.

20

Miss Hawkins lined up a printing press in Muskogee that would do Mam's book for a reasonable amount. Volunteer labor was available for the new shelves in the library, and every day there appeared on her desk another diary or journal or family album from the local pioneers. The grand celebration was scheduled for late September.

I lagged behind in my contribution. Trouble was, I met myself coming and going. I had very little daylight to spare from my strewberry operation, and Mam said she was too tired of an evening to think about anything as complicated as her life. So, I had a mess of notes I'd scribbled on the run or at mealtimes, and hoped to put into order to meet the printer's deadline.

I was sacrificing strewberry daughters early one August morning when I glanced up and saw Willis coming toward me. Willis Henderson! The last time I laid eyes on him we were in the backseat of his automobile having our usual difference of opinion about my underpants.

I knew he'd married Ruby Leighton and moved to California three or four years after I'd left home. Then Mam heard from his mother that they'd divorced and he hired out on a banana boat that went back and forth to Central America. Fancy that. Down-home boy takes journey to the unknown. And now here he was, grinning down on me like a beam of strong light.

He had on a white Stetson that looked new, a checked short-sleeved shirt, the sleeves rolled a couple turns to show off his considerable muscles, Saturday night cowboy boots, and jeans that left little to ponder about the state of his manhood. Mercy! Here he was—his eyes green and dangerous, his teeth gleaming in the shadow from his hat, his dark curly hair falling across his forehead—Mr. Unfinished Business himself.

He didn't say a word, just took my hand, lifted me up off my knees and we went at a dead run to the sandbar at the creek, me clutching sacrificed strewberries like some bridal bouquet. The sandbar was one of our trysting places from the old days, when Willis was a handsome hot-eyed boy and I was an innocent maiden under the impression if you went all the way with a somebody, you were obliged to marry him.

We caught our breath then took ourselves out of our clothes, slow and easy, our eyes bold as brass, taking note of every inch of sweet sweaty skin as it revealed itself. The creek water fairly sizzled when we waded in. Then, on the brightest, clearest day of the twentieth century, the sky darkened and was rent with great rolls of thunder and spears of lightning, turning that placid little creek into a veritable whirlpool. And me and Willis came together like it was preordained. When the waters finally settled down we scrambled up onto the sandbar and came together again.

We still hadn't spoken a word—just groaned and grunted like a couple of happy primitives. When I found my power of speech I said, "Well! Well, finally!" And I laughed because I thought that was the most comical thing I'd ever heard. I kept on laughing, and I'm sprawled out there on the sand like some French courtesean, Willis's fingers playing in a lazy way across my wonders, shafts of sunlight keeping my privates warm and interested.

"What is it, hon? What's so funny?"

"Nothing. Everything." And I snuggled under his chin, ran my hand down the long leanness of him, already wanting him again. Wanting him for each and every time I had denied myself this fine animal pleasure.

He raised up on his elbow and looked at me. "I never stopped thinking about you, you know that, hon? It broke my heart when you ran off to Tulsa."

I lowered my eyes. "I hear it didn't stay broken for long," I said, flirting, hoping he'd go on some more about my unforgettability.

"Rebound," he said. "They were lined up waiting to console me. How come you left, hon? Went off in the middle of the night without telling me. Did I do something wrong?"

"Oh no, Willis, you didn't do anything wrong. It was just that we were headed for the altar in a dead heat, and I couldn't see that we had interests in common, except for being set on fire by each other. You know what I mean? Then I read something in this book I got from the library. . . ."

He frowned. "You were always one for reading books, even books that weren't homework. I thought you might go off, but I figured it would be to college."

"I went to college," I said proudly. "After I was married I studied music at T.U."

"You still play your horn?"

"Not so much anymore. I try to practice at least once a week so I won't lose my lip."

He smiled and ran his fingers across my mouth. "So far, so good," he said; then his face went soft and serious. "Cleo?"

"Yes, Willis."

"I'm so sorry about your trouble."

"Thank you, Willis. I'm better now. I'm sorry about your trouble too."

"Divorce isn't like . . ."

". . . It's a loss all the same."

He nodded. "Ruby and me didn't have any kids. Just ourselves to get broken up."

"You didn't want any?"

"Oh yes I did, I sure did! I wanted a big family, a big noisy family around the supper table. I meant to sire presidents and opera singers—loud people. There was just me and my brother at home, you know, and we were both quiet boys, not much fun for one another."

"Ruby didn't want them?"

"In the worst way." He looked out across the creek, then down at his hands. "Don't let on. I wouldn't want to cause Ruby any embarrassment. It turned out she was, well, you know, barren."

"I'm real sorry about that, Willis. That's a terrible shame."

"Things between us went downhill after the doctor told her. She said she didn't feel like a woman anymore. Said it wasn't worth the effort to make love. Like we were just breeding stock or something. Like that was the only thing there was to it."

I felt so sorry for him I didn't know what else to do but take him in my arms and hold him like you would a despairing child. There is no creature on this earth more pitiful than a grown man who's been wounded in his ego. I was sorry for Ruby too, even though I'd never forgiven her for calling Mam a heathen. But this was mighty retribution—even for a bigot. I sighed over the strangeness of life, hugged

Willis to me, and we lay there for the longest time just listening to the creek flow to the river and the birds complain about the heat.

I must have drifted off because when I opened my eyes Willis was dressed and skipping stones on the water. "You hungry?" I asked him.

He grinned. " 'Bout starved, but we better get some work done first. That's what I told your gramma, told her I'd come to help you. She said when we finish I should come on in and have a bite to eat." He picked up another stone, inspected it, rubbed it between his fingers, then skipped it in six perfect jumps to the bank on the other side. "That's what I meant to do, Cleo, honest. But the sight of you . . ." He pulled on his ear and smiled like a boy. "Mr. Boone here just took over my good intentions. I hope you don't feel I've taken advantage."

I sat up and pulled on my jeans. "I'd say we're fairly matched, Willis. Now, what is it you're going to help me do?"

"You know. Weed, hoe, prune the runners. Gideon said you were doing all the work yourself, said there was too much work for one person."

I buttoned my shirt and looked around for my hat. "I can't afford to hire anybody."

"I know that, hon. Gideon told me. I don't need the money, I want to help you for old times' sake."

As I laced up my shoes I wondered what else Gideon had told him, wondered if he'd mentioned my tidy sum in the Farmers' and Merchants'. I said, "I never knew of anybody in Robina County that couldn't use money."

"I'm all set, Cleo. Home on hardship leave from the Merchant Marine, trying to get my mom's place in some kind of shape."

I stared at him. "Why?"

" 'Cause it's gone all to hell since Dad passed on."

"No, I mean why did you join the Merchant Marine?"

He laughed and said, "Where you been, hon? I didn't want to get drafted in the army. There's about to be a war, a big war."

I got to my feet and put on my hat. "I guess I haven't been paying much attention to world affairs."

"Come on," he said, "let's get at those runners."

"Daughters," I said. "We call them daughters."

We worked until the sun had passed overhead. Willis was a steady quiet worker like me, stopping only to stretch or have a drink every so often. He'd drink a dipperful and pour another one over his head. His face and hair glistened, causing me to think about the sun dappling through the leaves onto the eddies and wakes we made in the creek.

I put that picture out of my mind, stood up, and gazed back on the rows. I told Willis I was surely gratified by how much we'd accomplished. He gave me his hot-eyed look and said it had indeed been quite a morning.

On the way to the house he talked about how good it was to feel the earth in his hands again, and I told him I couldn't feature a farm boy out in the middle of some ocean. He opened the screen door for me and took off his hat. "Fact is," he said, "I don't want to shoot anybody up close. Fact is, I never killed anything bigger than a jackrabbit. I'd like to have some distance between me and the enemy. Anyway, I'm a good swimmer."

Mam called out from over by the sink. "What's that? A good what?"

"Swimmer," I told her. "Willis has gone into the Merchant Marine."

Her shoulders drooped and she scowled at us. I knew she'd watched from the kitchen window as we walked arm and arm toward the house. She'd probably hummed a few bars of Mendelssohn and given hard thought to what she'd wear on the happy occasion. "Well," she said, "he better have himself a good meal first. Sit over there, Willis. Help me get this on, Cleo."

It looked like she'd been cooking for him to move in. There was the ham we'd been saving for the Labor Day picnic, and from our garden, new potatoes and peas, tomatoes, squash and green onions. And the watermelon pickles I'd put up, and wild berry cobbler with heavy cream. A feast for my caller—culinary entrapment. She was still scowling and I could almost hear the thoughts rattling around in her head. *After all my hard work this fine prospect is going off to fight a war—just like they all do.*

But he didn't disappoint her as to his appetite. In truth, Willis approached the dinner table in much the same way he approached matters of a carnal nature. No words wasted. When Mam asked him to say grace, he bowed his head and said, "Thank you Lord for the multitude of blessings before us. Amen." Then he took a slice of ham, cut off a chunk, and popped it into his mouth. He closed his eyes and chewed.

And chewed and chewed. He chewed, he savored, he smacked his lips, then opened his eyes long enough to fill his plate with vegetables. Every once in a while he'd let out a little moan, but there were no words of appreciation until he'd finished off the last tomato.

I thought about the Reverend Robby Endicott, and how he'd savored a rare steak at Betty Anne's diner before we went back to the vestry. Seemed to me that I was drawn to men with large hungers.

"Tomatoes," Willis said, like he was just making their acquaintance. "Real tomatoes. I haven't had a tomato all the time I been gone."

"They don't grow them in California?" Mam asked.

He shook his head. "They grow something they call a tomato. It's the right size and the right color and it grows on a tomato vine, but it ain't a tomato and anybody who'd ever had themselves a real tomato would spot it for an imposter right off. Got so I wouldn't eat them anymore, couldn't bear the disappointment."

Mam said, "Why that's the saddest thing I ever heard. Cleo, you slice this boy up a couple more."

I reached for the plate and Willis quickly took a biscuit and sopped up the juice. I had never seen a happier man.

"Now, wait a minute," he said. "That's not quite true. One time Ruby's folks came out to visit us in San Jose. How'd I forget that? The old lady Leighton brought a whole lug of tomatoes with her—a whole lug! I tell you I could have kissed that woman's feet. Pardon me, ma'am, no disrespect intended."

"None taken. Where was that? Sounds Spanish."

"San Jose? Little town just down the road from San Francisco—lot of Spanish names in California. San Jose's not really little, but it feels small. You know, friendly. Ruby had a second cousin that ran a coffee shop out there, told us there was a lot of work. That's why we went. I sure couldn't make no living in Robina. Ruby and me got married one day and it seemed like the Depression jumped on us with both feet the next."

I set the plate of tomatoes down in front of him and he didn't look up or say one word until they were all gone. When he finished he let out a big sigh, tipped back in his chair, and asked Mam if it was okay if he had himself a smoke. Mam pointed to her Buglers, but he brought out a pack of Chesterfields from his shirt pocket, leaned across the table, and offered her one. While I cleared the dishes and got coffee and dessert, the two of them sat in a friendly silence and smoked their cigarettes. Willis closed his eyes when he blew out the smoke, just like he closed his eyes when he chewed, just like he closed his eyes when we made love at the creek. No hurry. All the time in the world. Willis Henderson was clearly a man who brought his full attention to the moment at hand, and I could see there was a certain virtue in that quality.

He snubbed out his cigarette, ate his berry cobbler, then went on with his story. "I got me a job at a Texaco station," he said. "Made manager before I left. Ruby worked the late shift at the coffee shop and went to secretarial school in the daytime. Ruby's a hard worker. And good with money. She saw to it we saved up and got us a nice house."

"She still there?" I asked.

"In San Francisco, has herself an apartment in a ten-story building. Marble floors in the lobby, gold mailboxes, ferns all over—real nice. She's private secretary to the president of a big company. Gets all dressed up to go to work. Goes to the beauty shop once a week. Looks real nice." He nodded thoughtfully. "Yessir. Ruby knows what she wants."

I couldn't remember ever hearing a man speak so respectfully about his ex. The customers at the Gusher always talked about their former wives like they were lower than egg-eating snakes. And here was Willis going on about Ruby like she was Miss Perfect Herself. Made me feel uncomfortable, like maybe they weren't finished with each other, like maybe I was poaching on posted land.

Willis said, "Well, I guess I better get on home now. Lot of fence to mend." He bobbed his head at Mam. "I surely do thank you for that fine dinner." Then he asked me what time I wanted to start in the morning.

I gave him a smile, measured and sly. "The strewberries, you mean?"

He glanced over at Mam, blushed, nodded and got up from the table.

I said, "I start at sunup, but I'll welcome your spare time whenever you've got any. I don't want to keep you from your own chores."

"That's right, Willis," said Mam. "You're welcome any time, any time at all."

She was taking it all in, I knew that. Mam and God knew the life history of every leaf that fell. I could hear her thoughts rattling around again. *Maybe all is not lost after all. Maybe it'll be a short war. Maybe he'll promise not to get killed. Snake. Snake. Snake.*

I walked to the car with him. "Nineteen thirty-five Pontiac Silver Streak," I said, showing off again. "Independent front suspension, all steel body." Willis looked suitably impressed Then he took my hand and said he'd like to see me that evening but he'd promised to visit the Leightons.

"That's fine," I said. "I need to get to bed early. Sunup comes before I hardly get the kinks out from the day before."

He put my hand to his lips like some gallant cavalier, kissed it, and looked me dead in the eye. "Maybe we could work real hard in the morning then have a picnic, and cool off down at the creek? I got an ice chest. I could bring some beer and sandwiches."

"I could bring a couple dozen tomatoes," I said gravely.

He put his arms around me, then stiffened, stepped back, and glanced toward the house.

"That's Mam," I said, with some impatience. "Not Momma. Mam likes you. You heard what she said—you're welcome any time. She means it, Willis. She's back there right now going through her chif-forobe trying to decide what she'll wear to the wedding."

He didn't laugh at my little joke. Just sighed and said, "I sure was glad when Gideon told me you were staying over here. Your momma'd soon as take a horsewhip to me as look at me." He shook his head in wonderment. "I never did understand what she had against me."

"It's nothing personal, Willis, it's just that you're a man, and good-looking to boot. My momma doesn't trust good-looking men."

He was still shaking his head. "I was just a raw boy when she put that cornbread muffin in your lunch bucket. About the whorish woman? I mean, Cleo, that's an unnatural thing for a mother to do."

Then I told Willis about what Momma had said. About not having any tears left for Daddy at the funeral. How he always came home smelling of whiskey on one end and a woman on the other. How Mam said Momma had spent too much time trying to bring her husband to God and not enough enjoying what he was good at.

Willis smacked his forehead with the palm of his hand. "Ah, Cleo! Christ, Cleo! That's so sad. Why do people have to hurt each other like they do?"

We put our arms around each other and protected each other while we pondered that difficult question. After a while Willis said, "Maybe this Saturday we could go into Wagoner? Have supper at a café and go to the picture show?"

I looked up at him. "You asking me for a date?"

"If it isn't unseemly. I know you're a widow and all, but it's been a year."

"More than a year," I said. "Mam says a year is long enough for mourning, or else you'll make a habit of it."

"I don't think you'd do that, hon, you got too much life in you for that."

I said, "I'd like that very much, Willis. I haven't seen a movie since I left Tulsa."

He fooled with the handle on the car door. I could see he was reluctant to leave, and as a matter of truth I didn't want him to go. I wanted us to sit down under the maple tree in the side yard and talk for about a week. I wanted to explain about Alexandra David-Neel and what had drawn me to Lhasa. I wanted to tell him about my life in Tulsa, wanted to spill it all out, wanted to tell him about my night in jail, tell about the boardinghouse and my best friends, Mildred and Rosemary, and how Tully couldn't tolerate affection and how patiently Scat had taught me to read music.

And like a burden lifting, I found I wanted to tell him what a sweet soft child my Em was, and how Eddy took a radio apart and put it back together when he was only six years old. How Ed Shannon had so much respect for his family he was willing to snub his boss and risk his job. I wanted him to know these people I loved. All of them. The quick and the dead.

But it was too soon. It appeared that Willis Henderson had grown up to be a kind, thoughtful man—yes—but he was no priest, or doctor to the soul. I knew in my heart that something besides fence mending weighed heavy on his mind.

21

*L*ET A BEAR ROBBED OF HER WHELPS MEET *a man! Not a fool in his folly!*

"Left his poor wife alone and destitute in a strange city. Went off awhoring to Mexico. That the kind of man you want to take up with? The kind of man you want to be seen with in a public place?"

I was hardly inside her back door when Momma spat out these words at me. "Where did you hear that? Where on earth did you hear such a thing?"

She lifted her chin and arched one eyebrow. "I have my sources." Momma had a way of pointing her nose at you, then making it quiver ever so slightly.

I said, "Well, you can just tell your sources that they're full of baloney. Willis didn't leave Ruby in a strange city. He left her in San Jose, California. For that matter—and you be sure to tell your sources—he didn't leave her, not in the way you mean. They left each other and on friendly terms. She's got family out there—cousins. She's not alone. And destitute? She works in San Francisco as secretary to the president of a big company and lives in an apartment building that's got marble floors. I wouldn't call that destitute!"

Momma sniffed, quivered her nose again, and pulled down the corners of her mouth. She was turning into a witch in front of my very eyes. "That's what he says," she hissed. "The wicked is snared by the transgression of his lips. The poison of asps is under his tongue."

"Miss Hawkins said so too. You suppose Emma Hawkins has asps under her tongue?"

She leaned toward me and wagged her finger. "An old woman is easily fooled by a comely young man. Favor is deceitful and beauty is vain."

I knew better than to get into a Bible contest with the world expert but I couldn't resist the one good shot I had handy. I wagged my finger back at her and said, "From the sole of his foot even to the crown of his head there was no blemish in him."

It was an unfortunate choice of quotations. She clasped one hand to her breast and held on to the kitchen table with the other. "I knew it," she gasped. "I knew it!" She lowered herself into a chair, still clutching her chest like she was holding her heart in place. "You've seen him naked!"

"I haven't seen any such thing," I said, with the moral outrage I sometimes brought to necessary lies. I waited until she caught her breath and then I touched her shoulder—easy—the way you touch a nervous horse. "Listen, Momma. Willis didn't run off to Mexico. He worked on a banana boat. It was hard honest labor. Now he's in the Merchant Marine."

She looked up at me. "Sinners cross over borders like thieves in the night."

I sighed and shook my head. "I don't know why I try to reason with you. It's just a waste of words. Momma, don't look away, look at me. Look at me! In October I will be thirty years old. It's not up to you who I'm seen with in a public place, or anywhere else. I'm a grown-up, Momma."

She slumped lower in her chair and began to fan herself with a folded newspaper. "The dogs will eat Jezebel," she moaned. "There will be none to bury her. Oh Lord, Oh Lord! So much shame has been visited on this poor family. I don't know . . . I just don't know . . ."

She took two envelopes from the table and handed them to me. "This one last Friday, this one today. God knows what next week will bring."

I sat down and opened the letters. One was from my sister Sarah. The other was from the chaplain at the penitentiary. Ethan, the chaplain said, had tried to escape and had shot and wounded a guard. Ethan himself was shot, not killed, but shot bad in the leg and lower arm. His sentence would be extended, said the chaplain, for which he was truly sorry because Ethan had been doing well and on his way to becoming a master mechanic. He'd got mixed up with hardened criminals who used him because of his access to the prison vehicles. Ten more years on top of the five he had left to serve. Ethan was fortunate in that he was a poor shot.

Sarah's husband had gone off, left a note saying he never did think the kid was his anyhow and why should he break his back to support some other guy's bastard. He'd been laid off two months before and couldn't find work. Sarah was down to her last can of spaghetti and last box of cereal. She needed bus fare to get home.

I looked over at Momma. Her face was hidden in her hands. I put the letters down, one at a time. Here was the man who'd gone off to Mexico and left his wife destitute. Or maybe Nebraska or Tampa, Florida. Awhoring after a new life without old baggage. And here— ah, yes—*here*—was the comely young man who could fool old women.

"Did you send the money?"

She nodded. "Went into town on Monday."

"Would you like to go down to McAlester?"

She lowered her hands from her face. Her eyes were red but there was no sign of a tear. "What for?"

"To visit Ethan. He's in the infirmary. Maybe they'll let you see him. I'll call up and find out, if you want me to."

She shook her head. "I don't want to see him. Don't care if I ever lay eyes on him again. A foolish son is a bitterness to her that bare him."

I knew she didn't mean that. Children always know which one of them is favored. Ethan was my momma's joy, her sorrow too, but she'd walk barefoot to Caanan just to bring him a cool drink of water. I said, "I'll talk to the chaplain, in case you change your mind."

She shrugged. "No point in that. How would I get there? Even if I wanted to go?"

I scratched my head and pretended to give that question some hard thought. I didn't figure this was the time to suggest Willis and I drive her over on a Sunday. "Don't worry about that," I said. "We'll find a way if you want to go."

She picked up the letter and studied it. "He does say Ethan's doing fine. He does say that. I suppose if he had a setback, if I really needed to go, I could get there on the bus."

"Yes," I said. "You could do that."

"You suppose it goes right up to the prison?"

"Probably not. There's probably a special bus from town."

"I'd have to get off the one bus and get on another one?"

"I would imagine so. I can find out."

She let the letter slide out of her hands, picked up the newspaper, and commenced fanning herself again. "You think maybe you could come with me, Daughter? If he took a bad turn, I mean. If I had to go for one reason or another?"

By one reason or another, she meant if Ethan was to ask for her. I wondered what there was about Momma that would let her call me Jezebel in one breath and ask me to oblige her in the next. I wondered what there was about myself that let me go along with it. "Sure," I said, "I'd come with you." I knew that barring a deathbed request, this bus trip was not likely to transpire. To my knowledge Momma had been on a bus only once, when she and Mam went to Muskogee to see a specialist about Mam's tooth. Mam said Momma was white-faced the whole trip, said she was like a rabbit surrounded by coyotes in an open field. Took her Bible with her, clutched to her breast for comfort that was not forthcoming. Told Mam she would never leave Robina again—not until she made her final journey to the foot of the throne of God.

"I'll talk to the chaplain," I repeated. "We'll see. Do we know when Sarah will get here?"

Momma sighed. "I sent a letter with the money, told her to call on the telephone at the grocery and I'd come and fetch her in the wagon. I told her if she saw anybody in town she was to say she was home for a visit."

"They," I said.

Momma frowned. "They?"

"Errol," I said.

She clucked and shook her head. "Errol," she said with grave disapproval. "No wonder I can't remember I have a grandbaby. What kind of world is it where people name their babies after movie stars. That's what Sarah did, named her own innocent child after somebody in the pictures. How does she expect him to get on Heaven's Roll with such a name? Bad as your daddy naming you after an Egyptian that worshiped housecats and lay with her own brother. That poor little soul will be almost five years old now, he'll need to go to school soon, probably need some clothes. The treadle on my machine is acting up. I wonder what I did with Ethan's old cot. Oh Daughter! I'm too old and tired to raise any more babies. I've been alone so long that's all I know how to be. I swear! Your kids go off and you never hear a word. Then they get in trouble and first thing you know here they are in the dooryard bringing trouble with them. I swear! Sarah has not put pencil to paper since last Christmas. I haven't heard from Fidelity in nearly three years. She could be dead and gone for all I know. Errol! Er-rol! What kind of name is that for a Christian?"

"They can come to Mam's," I said. "There's more room there. And I can use Sarah's help with the strewberries."

"Ha!" Momma snorted. "Help? Sarah? That girl doesn't lift a finger except to comb her hair and paint her face."

"She's older now, Momma."

"Ethan's older now. Didn't help him any." She picked up Sarah's letter again, read it through, nodding her head slowly. "Yes," she said, "if it suits Mam, it'd be better if they stay over at her place. Like you say, there's more room. That way I can come over and see them when I feel like it and come on home when I get tired. A five-year-old can sure take the stuffing out of a person. I'll see what I can do about that treadle, maybe it just needs a little Three-in-One."

That afternoon I got on the telephone to the prison. The chaplain said Ethan would not be allowed any visitors—not even family—for a while so there was no point in our coming, but he would tell Ethan we had inquired about that possibility and it would no doubt raise his spirits. I called up Momma and gave her the news. I also told her Ethan was coming along just fine and had asked to be remembered in his mother's prayers. I figured a little embroidery couldn't do any harm. I could tell she was relieved to have that bus ride off her mind. Later on, Momma called me, said Sarah had called from Sherman, Texas, where she had stopped off to see a friend who used to live in the apartment next to hers. She'd be in on the Saturday bus. "Just like it was some pleasure trip," said Momma. Then I called Julius at the grocery to check on the bus schedule, called Willis at his momma's to ask if he could drive us, called Momma back and said I could pick up Sarah and little Errol. I didn't say how. Momma didn't ask. She said that suited her just fine, and that she'd fry up a chicken and bring it to Mam's for supper.

I don't know how we managed our busy lives before I put in those telephones.

22

WILLIS CAME BEFORE SUNUP ON SATURday so we could get a good morning's work done before we went into town. The strewberries, which were flourishing beyond all expectations, had begun to put a dent into our creek time. Willis had developed a case of the sulks as a result. He said if Boone didn't have it regular—he always called sex "it"—then they couldn't seem to concentrate on other aspects of life. I was just as interested in "it" as he was, but I didn't regard it as a vital, daily, bodily function. And those strewberries called to me like a moral duty.

It had been over a month since I looked up to see him striding across the horizon in his new white Stetson. He came six mornings a week to help me in the field; then we'd go churn up the creek for an hour or so. Saturday nights we went into Wagoner. That first Saturday we saw Carole Lombard and James Stewart in *Made For Each Other*. Willis leaned over and whispered it was a pretty mushy picture, but he ran his hand along my thigh every time Carole and Jimmy went into a clinch. The picture show changed every other week, so every other Saturday we went dancing at the roadhouse outside town. There was a cowboy band and what they lacked in talent they made up for in enthusiasm. Ed and I had gone dancing, but only at the country club and the Mayo Hotel Ballroom, where you were in no danger of working up a sweat.

On the way home from Wagoner, Willis would pull off on some lonely road and we'd make love, somewhat hindered in its free expression by the gearshift and the steering wheel. There was no backseat in the Silver Streak. Afterward, he would smoke a cigarette, then we'd talk, or rather Willis would talk, mostly about his life with Ruby in California. I was developing a dwindling interest in that subject.

Then one day when I said I couldn't go to the creek because I had to go see Mr. Krause about the jars for the Suspension, Willis got his back up and said I was just like Ruby. I always had to have my own way.

I said that wasn't fair, which it wasn't, and he said he was sick and damn tired of strewberries, and I said who needed him, and he narrowed his dangerous green eyes and said he wished me luck, then he stalked off and didn't show up the next morning. Or the next. That first day I told myself it was good riddance, but by the next afternoon I was down at the creek waiting for him, just like some old sow in a wheelbarrow. I thought about poor Bette Davis in *The Old Maid,* growing old and tight and sour, and how Miriam Hopkins said it was every woman's right to have a home and children and a good man who cherished her. She didn't say anything about having that right more than once.

The next morning Willis showed up at the door bright and early, turning his hat in his hands, saying how sorry he was. I told him we needed to talk but he just hustled me right past the strewberry field and down to the sandbar.

When he first came home, that first day in early August, I'd told him I couldn't afford to hire any help, but I was beginning to feel like I was paying for his labor with the oldest form of currency there is.

The bus pulled up in front of Julius' Grocery just a few minutes after we got there. A couple people got off and the driver hurried back onto the bus. I groaned and told Willis it would be just like Sarah to miss her ride or come on the wrong day. Then, here came the driver again, carrying a suitcase tied with a cord, and a big stuffed teddy bear. A few seconds later, Sarah appeared on the top step. She smiled down on the welcoming party and posed there in the doorway like she was waiting for an armload of roses. She was wearing a gauzy print dress that showed a lot of lacy slip under it, a big picture hat with a red feather, and Miss America's own smile for the judges. If she was broken up by her situation, you sure couldn't tell by looking.

The driver offered his hand and she floated down to the next step. Little Errol peeked out from behind her. He was the image of his momma and his granddaddy. He had the same fine, fair hair, same even features, same surprised hazel eyes.

I moved forward and Sarah and I hugged each other. The driver called Errol "my little man" and swung him down, then stood there panting at Sarah like some faithful hound waiting for the next command.

Sarah touched his arm. "I have two cardboard boxes, sir. I surely would appreciate it if you would put them in our wagon."

"No need for that," said Willis.

"Willis brought his car," I explained.

"Why, Willis," said Sarah. "Willis Henderson! I didn't even recognize you. I thought you were some oil man or something like that."

I looked over at Willis in his checkered shirt and Saturday night cowboy boots and tried to figure where she'd got that impression. Willis shrugged and went off with the driver to get the boxes. I crouched down in front of Errol. "So you're Errol," I said.

He stuck his thumb in his mouth and moved closer to his mother.

"You go by your Aunt Cleo, honeyboy. Aunt Cleo has a trumpet, maybe she'll teach you to play it. He's very musical, probably gets it from his grampa. I've changed his name to Flynn, it goes so nice with Fletcher. Flynn Fletcher. Now, don't that sound like somebody who's really a somebody?" She reached down to smooth his hair out of his eyes. "Flynn Fletcher is my little somebody, ain't you? Come on now, honeyboy, show your Aunt Cleo what fine manners we have, say I'm pleased to meet you, Aunt Cleo."

Flynn inched forward and said, "I'm pleased to meet you, Aunt Cleo," and then he offered me his hand. For just a moment I saw in his face how close we were, saw the same blood run in this child as had run in my own. In *The Old Maid,* somebody said memories have a way of inviting themselves to the family feast. I took his hand and shook it solemnly.

Willis loaded up Sarah's belongings. It turned out the teddy bear was hers, not Flynn's; she'd won it at a carnival. The five of us crowded into the car. I sat in the middle, straddling the gearshift and holding the bear. Flynn was on his mother's lap.

Right off, I settled the matter of where they'd stay. "There's the spare bedroom at Mam's," I said.

Sarah waved her hand. "Whatever," she said, in that breezy, vague way that so irritated our momma. Then she hugged Flynn tighter and kissed the top of his head. "We'll be just fine, won't we honeyboy. We're just as grateful as we can be to have a roof over our poor heads. I can't imagine what got into that man, running off like that. I mean, he never said a cross word to me, or to honeyboy, never a cross word. I never had any idea he was so upset. I kept telling him he'd find hisself a job tomorrow, that I just knew in my heart he would. Ever morning I sent him out with a smile and my confidence in him. Then to just go off without a word? Except that mean nasty note he left. Men are surely a mystery, aren't they, Cleo. I mean, you never have the slightest notion of what's going on in their heads. Not a notion in this world."

Willis nudged me but I didn't look at him. I had told him Sarah was here on a visit, as I dutifully spread the story my momma wanted the town to hear.

I said, "Sarah, Momma wants you to say you're just visiting. You know how she is."

She widened her eyes and put her hand to her mouth. "Oh, I forgot about that, it just slipped my mind. I'm sorry, Cleo. Willis, you just forget I said all that, will you?"

Willis nodded and said he was not in the habit of spreading gossip. Then he leaned forward so he could see around the bear and told Sarah he was sorry she was in such difficulty.

Sarah smiled and widened her eyes again. "I ain't in any difficulty. Well, maybe I am, but it's only temporary. You see the way I look at it, life is full of ups and downs. Well, you can't appreciate the ups without the downs. I mean how are you going to know the difference? I tell honeyboy life is like the weather. One day it just clouds up and rains. It rains and rains, you think it will never stop. Then you wake up one morning and there it is. A rainbow! And the sun shining in a bright, blue sky." She pointed out the window with one of her long, red fingernails. "See? There it is now. See that old sun hanging in the sky, honeyboy? Means everything is going to be just fine. Oh, what a good time you'll have here on the farm. Your Aunt Cleo will show you how to feed the chickens and gather eggs and play the trumpet and your great grannie'll tell you stories about cowboys and Indians and there's a mule you can ride and a creek to go swimming in. Won't that be fun, honeyboy?"

Willis nudged me again and shot me a quick look that said in no uncertain terms he didn't plan to share the creek. I looked over at Sarah, who was just as tickled as she could be with the thought of all these wholesome country activities that would occupy her little boy's time. Sarah, one more person around the place, hard at work on my life story.

"I'll teach him how to pick strewberries," I said firmly, and I explained how we planned to get rich putting up fancy French preserves. I said, "You've come at just the right time."

"Me?" said Sarah, with a stricken look. She held out one hand and considered her nails. "Pick them?"

"It's the only way I know to gather strewberries."

She sighed and pushed back her cuticles with her thumbs. "I have myself a fingernail kit," she said, like she was confessing a small sin. "Saved up for it out of my household money. It has orange sticks and files and a buffer and little tiny scissors and a precious oil you heat up for a weekly treatment. I have fourteen different shades of polish. I can go for two weeks and never wear the same color twice." She looked over at my hands and shuddered. "I just don't know how I'll live my life without my pretty fingernails."

Willis nudged me again. I could feel his shoulder moving in a silent chuckle. I frowned and poked him back. Sarah's husband had gone off and left her flat and her big philosophical comment on the situation was that men are mysterious. Now, the thought of the loss of a few fingernails—a renewable resource if there ever was one—had brought tears to her eyes. Sarah had always been a silly little thing. But she was my sister and I would not have Willis laughing at her.

She sniffed and said, "I suppose I can grow them back again when this is all over," making "this" sound like the east wind that brought the locust.

I put my arm around her shoulders. "That's right, Sarah," I said. "Fingernails are just another one of life's ups and downs—just as mysterious as a rainbow, as reliable as the sun in a bright blue sky."

Mam was on the back porch when we drove up, waving for us to hurry. Momma's mule was tied to the fence by the horse trough.

Gloom descended upon Willis. "I guess I hadn't ought to come in."

Mam pointed her cane at us. "Willis!" she shouted.

He glanced around, looking for more signs of my momma, then we all piled out. He got Sarah's things and moved cautiously, like a scout in enemy territory, toward the porch.

Mam banged the railing with her stick. "Willis, you get yourself over here. I got something to tell you. Don't make me raise my voice. It taxes my strength."

What Mam had to tell him was that he was to get himself home as fast as he could. "Your mother called on the telephone. Her sister's been in an accident and your mother wants you to drive her up to Wichita."

"Aunt Vi?"

"I don't know. How many aunts you got in Wichita?"

"Just Aunt Vi."

"Well then, I guess she's the one."

"What happened?"

"I don't know. Your momma couldn't take the time to discuss it, had to get herself ready to go." She flapped her apron like she was shooing chickens. "You go on now, you hear? Oh, wait! Wait right there." She went inside and came back with a basket. "I fixed a picnic lunch so you won't have to stop on the road. Now, git!"

Willis thanked her then nodded at Sarah. "You really will have to help your sister," he said gravely. "She's really going to need you . . ."

"Willis!"

"I'm going, I'm going."

I ran back to the car with him. He looked all around, then gave me a quick peck on the cheek. He slipped behind the wheel, started the car, and said he would call as soon as he got to Wichita. I leaned in and kissed him on the mouth, thinking how sorry I was that he was going off carrying our unsettled differences with him. I wasn't sure what those differences were, but I knew they were there, floating around like fall pollen, the worst kind.

He backed up to turn around, then stopped and motioned to me. "Cleo," he said, "I know you don't want to spend any of that money you've got in the bank, I know you feel strongly about it. I don't know why and I guess it's none of my business, but I think you better reconsider and hire yourself a couple pickers. Those first rows may come ripe before I can get back."

I felt like I'd been socked in the stomach, like I'd been run over by a team of draft horses, but I nodded, smiled, and waved him on.

I watched until the car disappeared in its own dust, then walked slowly toward the house. As a matter of truth I had not thought about that money in the Farmers' and Merchants' since early August. I had not called Michael Ahern in over a month. I'd been so busy on my knees and on my back, I'd clean forgot my mission in life. Burning for burning, wound for wound, stripe for stripe. For all my brave talk of vengeance, my children and their father were as good as buried in unmarked graves.

23

THE MORNING SARAH AND FLYNN AND I brought in the first pickings, Willis had been gone exactly one week. He didn't know when he'd be home. His Aunt Vi had fallen from the haymow, broken both legs and all her ribs on the left side. The doctor was worried about pneumonia. Willis's uncle Herndon was in a terrible state; his wife was in the haymow forking down hay while he was off fishing with his buddies. Willis said he had to stay and look after the place because Uncle Herndon just sat by her bedside day and night, stroking her hand and saying the same words over and over: "She was doing my job. She was doing my job."

I swear. There is nothing like a big dose of guilt to incapacitate a person.

Miss Hawkins had put off the opening of the Pioneer section at the library until the Christmas holidays. She said it would be a more appropriate time anyhow. She could call it her gift to the community. I estimated we'd be suspending strewberries until late October when the first frost was predicted, and after that I could devote my full energies to Mam's history. Then I could get back to my mission. Maybe Uncle Herndon could take the time to beat himself up over his moral shortcomings, but I couldn't.

Those first pickings were indeed whoppers—the biggest, most perfectly formed, most beautiful strewberries I'd ever put in my mouth—and sweet as honey from a hive just like Gideon said. He was surely right about the daughter business. I had parceled out the labor; me and Sarah and Flynn in the fields and Mam and Momma in charge of the Suspension Problem. I figured with at least 150 years of culinary experience between them they'd come up with the solution.

Momma tied on her apron and dipped into her big wooden box of receipts. "We'll use the Sunshine Method," she announced. "That'll make a syrup thick enough to suspend them and they won't cook long enough to explode. That's what we got to watch out for—explosion."

"That'll take too long," said Mam. "Sunshine berries got to set in the sun two-three days before you put them up."

"But it's foolproof," said Momma. "Won't waste time on failures."

Mam shook her head and scooped sugar into the kettle on the stove. "No," she said, "you want to fool around with sunshine berries you do it in your kitchen."

Momma huffed and went for her apron strings.

I said, "This is not the time for you two to get in a fight."

"We're not fighting," said Mam. "We're discussing. Let's just try a little batch the usual way, Frances, keep them on a low boil and be careful when we stir them. If we don't disturb them too much they ought to stay whole."

Momma thought for a minute, then retied her apron strings. "Have it your way," she said with a sniff, "but I can tell you right now it won't work."

So we crept around and spoke in low voices so as not to disturb that first kettle of berries. They fell apart anyhow, disintegrated, turned into ordinary everyday jam. Mam swore. Momma didn't even scold her. She didn't say a word, just pulled a skinny smile and hooded her eyes.

I got out the French cookbook I'd borrowed from the library. "Says here not to wash them. Says if you have to wash them you should pat them dry."

Momma looked out toward the field. "We'd be patting strawberries till next Easter."

"Says here to bring them to a boil then take them off the fire. Let them set overnight."

"No. If you don't cook them long enough they ferment. I always boil my berries twenty minutes at least."

Mam sided with Momma. "Frances is right. We're not making strewberry beer. Twenty minutes at least."

"That's not the way the French do it. Says here the French have been cultivating strawberries since the fourteenth century. They ought to know what they're talking about."

"The French," said Mam, rolling her eyes. "One wonders how they had the time."

"Says here," I went on in my most patient voice, "after you bring them to a boil and let them set overnight, you bring them to a boil again and pack in hot jars." I held out the book. "Look at that picture.

See? That's what we're after. It's that twenty minutes of boiling makes them fall apart." I thumped the book with my forefinger, and said I thought we ought to give it a try.

Momma shook her head. "We're not even sure Pepper used a French receipt."

I let out a deep sigh and looked out the window. I could almost hear those strewberries calling to me. We're getting close, they sang out. We're almost ripe now. Cleo! Oh, Cleo! We are fast approaching our prime. I looked over at my staff of pickers sitting idle at the kitchen table. Sarah was buffing her nails; Flynn, with his chin on his folded arms, watched the action, or rather the lack of it.

"That's the advantage of my Sunshine Method," Momma was saying. "You bring the berries to a quick boil then spread them out on platters and let them cook quietly in the sun." Her nose quivered. "But who listens to me."

"Tell you what," I said. "Let's do both. Do one batch like it says here and another batch Momma's way."

Mam and Momma watched each other; then finally they nodded, a single nod from each head at precisely the same moment—a mode of compromise they had perfected over the years. I crooked my finger at Flynn and touched Sarah on the shoulder. I said, "Let's get back to work before it gets too hot."

With the French receipt a lot of the fruit stayed intact, but it didn't suspend—just floated around in the pretty little jars making it appear we were shorting the customer. Momma smiled at me, insincerely. "Since the fourteenth century, you say?"

"We need a heavier syrup," said Mam. "Most of these berries look pretty good, we can fish out the bad ones."

"No," Momma said firmly. "There'll be the debris from the exploded berries. They all got to stay whole or your syrup won't be clear."

So we experimented to no avail the rest of the afternoon and into the evening. Every so often Momma announced with great ceremony, "Well, I guess I better go check my platters." It was *your* syrup and *my* platters. That night we had a late supper of biscuits and fresh butter and several versions of failed Strewberry Suspension. They were sweet and would have taken every prize at the fair, no question, but they weren't suspended and as Momma gleefully pointed out, they suffered from ugly debris.

The following morning was overcast. It threatened rain all day long. The next two days were cloudy and unseasonably chilly, which was a disaster for Momma's sunshine berries, but a blessing too because it slowed the ripening in the fields. Then the sun came out, bright and hot. Those berries turned even as we watched them, even some rows I hadn't expected to come ripe for another week. Mam and Momma tried glazes and gelatins and even tapioca. Nothing worked.

In the French cookbook I found something called agar-agar, which came from seaweed. The book said it was used in fine jelly making, and also in bacteriology, which seemed an odd mix to me. Julius didn't have any at the grocery—never heard of it—but Mr. Hawkins had it at the pharmacy. He said it was his understanding there was some Chinese bird that regurgitated the seaweed to build its nest, and then these nests were gathered up, stolen right out from under the hapless bird, and made into agar-agar. I shook my head, thanked him, and had just turned to leave when he mentioned that Evelina Warwick bought it from time to time. He had no idea what she used it for. I said I'd take all he had. I figured I didn't need to confess to my associates that we were dealing with bird vomit.

The agar-agar didn't come with any directions and we couldn't seem to get the hang of it. It turned our syrup as hard as Oklahoma bedrock. Momma was more testy than usual and Mam, my stalwart, began to lose heart. In a desperate move I called Pepper and asked her flat out how she made her Suspension. She said she'd never heard of Suspension. I asked to speak to Evelina, who, of course, hadn't the least notion what I was talking about.

"I'm talking about your Strewberry Suspension. Gideon said you and Pepper made some last year."

"Cleo, hon, we just make strawberry preserves like everybody else, nothing unusual about them. I can't imagine him saying that. You sure you didn't misunderstand?"

I said, "Evelina, I owe your husband for my starters and I can't pay him unless I learn how to make this Suspension for that company in Tulsa."

There was a long silence on the other end of the line. Actually, there were at least three silences besides the one on the Warwick telephone. Now our plight would be all over town.

I said, "Mr. Hawkins told me you bought some agar-agar. Could you just tell me the proportions you use?"

She turned prim and cool, said she used agar-agar for a recurring rash if I must know. I thanked her kindly and hung up. Evelina Warwick and Pepper Hawley—two God-fearing Christian women were lying like yellow dogs.

Everywhere we turned there were strewberries. They covered every flat surface in the house, waiting impatiently for their glorious transformation. I called up Julius again and he said he'd take some if they weren't overripe. I loaded up the narrow base cart and sent Sarah to town with them, which pleased her as her supply of movie magazines was dog-eared. I jury-rigged a sign and had her put it up at the crossroads on her way. FRESH STREWBERRIES—ONE MILE. Then I set about to wring my hands some more.

Mam and Momma went on with their experiments in a grim, silent way, demonstrating the advantage of stubbornness in the bloodline. The berries either floated to the top, sank to the bottom, or fell apart—sometimes all three at once.

We were two weeks into the season when Momma dipped into her box of receipts and came up with a slip of paper that had Prick With A Needle written on it.

"Prick what with a needle?"

"Well, I don't know, Daughter, but I seem to remember it had something to do with strawberries."

"Is that all it says?"

Momma lifted her glasses and brought the paper close to her eyes. "Says I-r-i-n-a. That's what it looks like. Irina? It's not my writing."

"Irina," said Mam. "That's the foreign woman that rented the Walker place way back. Talked funny. Had an accent. From Russia or someplace like that."

"They have strawberries in Russia?"

Mam shrugged. "Who knows? I didn't know they had them in France." She put her hands on her hips and gazed around the kitchen. "We sure got them in Oklahoma, I know that, and they're multiplying like range rabbits. We tried everything else, Frances, won't hurt to poke a few and see what happens." She got her pincushion from her sewing basket and handed Momma a needle.

Momma said, "Where should I prick it?"

Mam looked over at Flynn, who was lying on the floor with his coloring book. "I'd like to tell you," she said, "but there's innocent ears present."

The pricking worked a miracle. Even at a rolling boil our strewberries kept their perfect shape.

But they still did not suspend.

By this time people were showing up on our doorstep to buy strewberries—just as Gideon had predicted. Mam began to complain about having to answer the door every time she turned around. She said she wasn't about to become a grocery clerk at her advanced age. So I nailed a few boards together and set up a stand at the crossroads. I put Sarah in charge. She could read her movie magazines and file her nails between customers. But I kept Flynn with me.

"You're my vice-president," I told him. I had never known a child with such powers of concentration. In the beginning I thought I needed to fool him into thinking it was a game. I said dumb things like "Let's go play in the strawberry field." He'd give me a sideways glance and follow along behind. Finally, he shoved his hands deep into his overalls pockets, scowled, and said, "Aunt Cleo, this ain't really a game, is it?"

"Isn't," I said. "No, Flynn, it sure isn't a game. It's hard work and you're good at it. I beg your pardon."

He grinned and I felt a big crack go right down the center of my heart. It was my Eddy all over again, forgiving me a harmless lie.

In late September I shaded my eyes and looked down that endless row we were working. I saw the truth in all its fierce reality spread out before me.

I told Flynn, "We need some help here."

He went right on picking. "Mom can help us."

"We need her at the stand. She's good with the customers. We need to hire ourselves some pickers, maybe a couple of town boys can come out early of a morning."

I confided in him that I figured our Suspension business was at a dead end but maybe we could salvage something by putting up another stand on the highway at the edge of town. "And another thing," I said. "I been thinking I could take our berries into Wagoner and sell them to the grocery stores there—maybe even on the street corner. We can get a pretty umbrella and put it on the narrow base cart. Maybe that way I can make enough to honor my debt to Gideon for the starters and Mr. Krause for the jars and labels . . ."

Flynn interrupted and asked the meaning of honor. I told him it depended on how you used the word. I said, "In this case it means I owe them money. We'll put it on our list to look up."

Around noontime, on the way to the house, my spirits suddenly sank right into my shoes. I could see myself scrambling around, setting up roadside stands, hawking berries from the cart like some fishmonger, going from house to house with my baskets, having doors slammed in my face. Flynn took my hand and asked me why I was sad. I figured it was good policy to keep up appearances in the presence of one's vice-president. I said, "I'm not sad, Flynn, I'm thinking."

As we approached the back stoop we heard a rare sound—laughter. Inside we found both Mam and Momma in a fit of giggles. On the kitchen table sat a dozen half-pints of strewberries. There was another dozen on the windowsill over the sink. I couldn't believe my eyes. Those jars looked like a painting by one of the masters. Big, beautiful berries, all separate from each other like the picture in the French cookbook. I took one of the jars and turned it around and around in my hands. Each berry gleamed and glittered from its appointed place, suspended—SUSPENDED—in a clear, rosy pink. . . .

"What is it?" I said. "How'd you do it?"

They went on laughing like they'd gone daft, like candidates for Vinita; then I caught Momma winking at Mam. "How did you do it?" I repeated, louder, with a hard edge on my voice. "Come on, now. We're partners, remember?"

Mam quieted to a chuckle. "It was Frances. Got down on her knees in front of that stove. Oh! How she carried on. Asked the good Lord to see if he couldn't find His way clear to bless this undertaking. Finally got a little cross with Him, she did."

"I did no such thing," said Momma, her shoulders still shaking.

That's when it came to me that they weren't going to tell me, that they'd go to their graves with the secret of the Strewberry Suspension. I sank into a chair at the table and stared at the pretty little jars. I said, "I see. So this is God's receipt. Kind of like Evelina's? A little of this, a little of that?"

Mam patted me on the head. "Don't get your bowels in an uproar. We're just joshing, having a little fun. Can't you take a joke, child?"

"Not today," I said sharply. "Today I faced right up to failure and it broke my funny bone."

"I did pray," said Momma. "I was not cross."

It was then I noticed the jelly bags hanging from the rafter and dripping rosy pink into the big kettles on the back of the stove. "Jelly," I breathed. "It's just plain jelly!"

"Oh no! Not just and not plain . . ."

"A very fine jelly . . ."

"On the delicate side, wouldn't you say, Frances?"

"It is. It is that . . ."

"Ah, but the secret . . ."

"The secret!" Momma winked at Mam again and lowered her voice. "The secret is in adding those berries at just the right moment."

"And I suppose that's where the good Lord comes in. A great white light shines down on those kettles and a deep voice says, 'Add your berries now, Frances' . . ."

Momma drew herself up and her face got grim. "Don't blaspheme, Daughter."

Mam said, "Now, Cleo . . ."

Flynn said, "What's blaspheme?"

I decided then and there that my vice-president and I were entitled to an afternoon off. I flounced out with him in tow, making clear my displeasure, and we went into town on the mule, leaving the Lord and his handmaidens to celebrate on their own.

24

I DIDN'T HAVE TO HIRE ANY TOWN BOYS BE-
cause Willis came back from Wichita and took up the slack. We
picked and put up strewberries until October 20, at which time the
first frost covered the ground I was born to thirty years before.

Thirty years old. A hard number to face up to if you're afloat in your
life. It causes you to give serious consideration to what you'll do with
the rest of your allotted time. You say, Just ten years ago I was twenty
and in my bloom. In just ten more I'll be forty and almost old. You say,
How did I get here? Where is it? You say, Will I ever make my journey
to Lhasa?

That day, the day of my thirtieth birthday, it seemed I'd probably
spend the rest of my allotted time sticking labels on pretty little jars.
Earlier in the week, Momma had thrown up her hands and allowed
she was finished with strewberries. She had done her part. She was
going to stay home and tend to her own affairs. She quivered her nose
at Sarah and said she might just sew up some decent clothes for her
poor ragged little grandbaby.

We had an assembly line—Flynn, me, Sarah, Mam, and Willis.
Flynn brought the jars to the table as they were needed. I dampened a
gummed label on a wet dishrag, plunked it on a jar, and slid it down to
Sarah, who positioned the label neatly and smoothed it with a clean,
dry cloth. Then Mam checked the seal and Willis put the jars in cardboard boxes, which he stacked out on the front porch.

We had the loan of Gideon's pickup and were scheduled to drive
into Tulsa the next day. Gideon, as he promised, had taken samples to
the canning company and they had contracted for our full crop—
nearly eight hundred jars.

I'd told Mam that Willis and I would visit Mildred after we finished
with our business. In truth, we planned to stay overnight at the Mayo
Hotel and celebrate in style on some of the profits. Willis was reluctant
at first, said he'd never taken money from a woman, but I convinced
him it was company money and lacked gender.

I heard Momma before I saw her. She called out, "I brought you a birthday cake, Daughter." I jumped straight up. "Chocolate," she said, as she came through the door. "With an almond cream filling." She blinked at Willis, which was her standard greeting for him, and he inclined his head politely as he taped another box.

I went on and on about the cake, took it from her and set it on the counter, then aimed her back toward the door. I told her she had done enough work and that we had matters well in hand.

"What's that?" she said, looking over her shoulder.

"We're just finishing up, just putting on the final touches. Nothing for you to bother about."

"What's that on the jelly jars?"

"Labels, Frances," said Mam. "Our company labels."

Oh, Lord.

Momma pushed by me and went to the table, where she plucked a jar out of Sarah's hands. "Who's that woman?"

"Nobody," I said. "Just decoration."

"Fruit of the Gods," Momma read. "Fruit of the Gods?"

"That's the name of our company," said Sarah. "Isn't that the prettiest label you ever saw? Looks like it came from New York or someplace."

Mam said, "Hand over that jar, Frances. You're disturbing our rhythm."

"Fruit of the *Gods?*" The jar hit the table with a thud, then Momma jerked her hands back and wiped them on her skirt. She said, "I know that woman. That's Cleopatra, the one that lay with her own brother and burned incense to housecats." She was still wiping her hands up and down on her skirt, as if they would not come clean.

"Now, Frances . . ."

Momma stepped back, spread one hand on her breast, and lifted the forefinger of the other like a torch. "Against all the gods of Egypt I will execute judgment. Thou shalt not bow down to their gods, nor serve them . . ."

"Frances, this is business," Mam said dryly. "Has nothing to do with religion . . ."

"Ye provoke me unto wrath with the works of your hands."

Flynn, unlike the rest of us who had nervous eyes trained on Momma, went on with his job, lining up unlabeled jars at the end of

216

the table. Suddenly, Momma grabbed two of them out of his hands and lifted them high over her head.

"Ye shall not go after other gods lest the anger of the Lord be kindled against thee!"

And she dashed a jar right up against the far wall, barely missing Willis, who dove under the table, followed in short order by Sarah and Flynn.

"If thou walk after other gods and serve them and worship them I testify against you this day that ye shall surely perish."

And she threw the other one, which made a bull's-eye of Mam's favorite picture, a still life of a harmless bowl of fruit. Glass flew all over and strewberries splattered to the floor. She snatched up one jar after another, reared back and began to throw them like speedballs.

"The houses . . . of the gods . . . of the Egyptians . . . shall He burn with fire!"

Mam was yelling at her to stop. "Frances! Frances, you quit that! You quit that this minute!"

I was struggling to get my arms around her from the rear, but she had the strength of madness. "Willis!" I screamed. "Willis, come help me!"

Willis stayed where he was, under the table with Flynn and Sarah. I swear! How was a man to face the bullets of war if he couldn't deal with a 130-pound woman armed with jelly jars?

Finally I bumped the back of her knees and got her off balance. I wrestled her up against the wall and pinned her against it with the legs of a chair—like some lion tamer. I was still yelling at Willis to help me, and she was wiggling and shouting, "Burn the Egyptians! Burn the Egyptians!" Then she went limp and began to whimper like a whipped dog. After I was sure the fight was gone out of her I set the chair down and guided her onto it. Slowly, Willis's head appeared over the edge of the table, then Sarah's, then Flynn's. All of us, except Momma, stared openmouthed at the damage.

Streaks of rosy pink Suspension dribbled down the far wall of Mam's kitchen. The floor on that side was covered with big whoppers and shattered glass. I could see there was no great loss. She'd executed judgment on less than a dozen jars, and it would take only an hour or so to clean up the mess, but the sight surely did put a damper on my sense of industry.

Momma was shaking her head and scrubbing her hands with that gummy old dishrag. "The first time," she moaned. "The first time!" I touched her shoulder but she shrugged me off. "In all my life," she said, "I have never prayed a frivolous prayer. The first time. All the things I could have asked for and didn't." She looked up at me with hard eyes. "I prayed a frivolous prayer for you, Daughter, and you have soiled it. You have soiled my prayer with strange gods and the likeness of a whore."

She took a firm grip on her knees and rose to her feet. I kept myself between her and the counter, protecting our investment. She moved slowly toward the back door, then stopped and glanced at the cake. She looked over at me, her eyes still hard. With one hand she swept my birthday cake off onto the floor.

Nobody said anything for the longest time after she left. Then I got the broom and wrapped a rag around it. I glanced over at Willis. "You sure weren't much help," I said. "Get the dustpan, Sarah, and a pail."

Willis said, "I don't fight with women."

"I wasn't fighting her. I was trying to restrain her."

Sarah said, "I wish she hadn't of ruined the cake. You think we might slice some pieces off the top?"

"No," Willis said in a firm voice. "Probably has glass slivers in it."

I misunderstood him. Funny how your mind works. "Glass slippers?" I said.

"Slivers, Cleo. Glass slivers, for chrissake. There's probably slivers all over. Don't anybody go barefoot. You hear, Flynn?"

"Oh," I said. So General Willis Henderson was coming out from headquarters to take command of the trenches.

Mam said, "We better get this mess cleaned up and back to our labeling. Don't want to miss your appointment at the jelly company."

I sighed and leaned on the broom. "I just wanted our jars to look professional. You think she'll get over it?"

Mam shook her head. "I told you she wouldn't like those labels. I warned you, Cleo. You know how she is."

I swept up a pile of glass and motioned to Sarah for the dustpan. "We always say that."

"Say what?"

"About Momma. We always say, 'You know how she is.' Truth is, I don't think we know how she is at all. I don't think anybody knows the first thing about her."

Mam sighed and rubbed her forehead. "She was always stiff-necked, even as a youngster. Maybe because she was a change-of-life child—all the others grown and gone. I thought it was a good thing that she read the Bible every day. I didn't see any harm in piety, thought it would keep her out of trouble. Maybe the Old Testament lessons are too harsh to grow up on. I don't know. All I know is Frances has always howled at the moon, even when it's not shining."

Sarah bent down with the dustpan. "We don't even know any Egyptians," she said. "They might be nice people." Flynn, who was hanging on to her skirt, began making little mewing sounds and I realized that in the commotion we hadn't paid him much mind. Sarah dropped the dustpan and took him in her arms. "Poor little honeyboy, now don't you fret, don't you be scared. It's all right now, everything's all right. Your gramma just had a little thunderstorm in her heart—it'll pass over in no time."

I looked at Willis, expecting to see him smirk or roll his eyes like he usually did when Sarah made one of her blue-sky pronouncements, but he had his head tipped thoughtfully to one side and a sweet smile of indulgence on his face. He crouched down in front of Flynn and asked if he'd like to go for a little joyride in the Silver Streak while the womenfolk cleaned up the slivers.

We were loading the boxes into the pickup the next morning when I heard the telephone. Right after, Mam came out on the porch and crooked her finger at me.

"Is it Momma?" I asked, hanging back.

"That man in Tulsa," she said with a sniff, and went back in the house.

"What man in Tulsa?" Willis asked.

I shrugged. "Just some business."

Michael Ahern said he had some information for me, but I interrupted to tell him I'd rather not discuss it over the telephone. My business with a private detective was not something I wanted divulged on a Robina party line. I told Michael it just so happened I'd be in Tulsa that very day and if it was convenient I could come by his office in the late afternoon. He said fine, to make it 4:30, and I hung up, my hand trembling so I missed the hook and banged the receiver against the mouthpiece, no doubt causing deafness in our good neighbors.

I borrowed one of Sarah's nice dresses for the trip, and her fingertip white coat and a hat and high heels and some ear bobs. Willis whistled when he saw me. I whistled back. He'd gone home and changed into a double-breasted suit, a white shirt, and a blue and white striped tie. His Stetson was brushed and his boots polished to where they reflected the sunshine. Mam, Sarah, and Flynn came out to the yard to see us off, waving and smiling like we were some honeymoon couple driving into the happy ever after.

We delivered the strewberries to the president of the jelly company. He opened a few boxes, admired our work, took random samples, and said he looked forward to more business with the Fruit of the Gods folks next season. He gave us a check and we went directly to the Mayo Hotel. Our agreement was that Willis would pay for the trip, then be reimbursed for the room—the room only—after I deposited the check in the Farmers' and Merchants'. He said I was not to mention our financial arrangement to a living soul, said he wouldn't want anybody to think of him as a kept man.

The bellboy brought up our bags. Inside the room Willis peeled off some bills and whispered in his ear. He nodded and came back a few minutes later with a fifth of Jim Beam in a paper sack. Meanwhile Willis called up room service for ice and 7-Up.

Willis took off his coat, rolled his cuffs a couple turns, and loosened his tie. He looked like some newspaperman in the movies fixing to write the story of the year. He grinned and me and said, "Take off your hat and stay awhile." There was a knock on the door. "That'll be the setups."

I took off my hat, eased down on the edge of the bed, and looked around. There were gold brocade drapes at the windows, the bed covered with a spread of the same material. Blue Boy, in a heavy gilt frame, smiled down on me from one wall, Pinkie from another, and red roses bloomed in a crystal vase on a table between two easy chairs. The Mayo justly advertised itself as the finest hotel between the Mississippi and the West Coast. I should have felt delighted and privileged to be there—after all, it was my idea. As a matter of truth, I didn't.

220

I moved from the bed to one of the easy chairs. It was one thing to make love at the creek where all of nature celebrated with you and the water sang out your name as it flowed by, or even in the Pontiac where you could laugh over the cramped quarters. A hotel room was another matter. Even one done up in elegant gold brocade fairly reeked with past sins. It was a wonder little Blue Boy and Pinkie still had their eyes open after all they'd witnessed.

My discomfort had begun to set in when Willis signed the register Mr. and Mrs. Willis B. Henderson. As I watched him write down that lie in bold black letters, I half expected a bolt of lightning to crash through the lobby striking us dead, along with any unlucky Egyptians that happened to be there.

On the way up in the elevator I gave myself a good talking to, told myself I was being silly, that my nervousness had to do with my meeting with Michael Ahern. I told myself it was only natural. But I kept picturing Willis hunkered down under the kitchen table while I did my poor best to subdue my crazy momma. Anybody you're close to, anybody you care about, is bound to let you down from time to time, but I was beginning to count my disappointments in Willis Henderson on both hands.

Willis peeled off more money for the room service boy, then shoved his hands in his pants pockets and waltzed around like he owned the place. He pulled open the drapes, gazed down on Cheyenne Avenue, and spread his arms wide.

"This is the way to live," he said, and began to shed his clothes. When he got to his sock-feet he sat down on the bed, bounced up and down, and leered at me. I was still glued to the easy chair, trying to sort out my ambivalences.

He tossed his socks into the corner, got up, and ambled toward me in his altogether, Mr. Boone leading the way. He said, "You're over-dressed for the occasion, hon," and then he went to the dresser and mixed a couple of drinks, handed me mine, and started in on my buttons. I said I didn't think I better have anything until after my appointment.

He frowned and looked at his watch. "You've got two whole hours and it's just across the street."

I said, "I know, but I'll need my wits about me."

He nodded, took the glass, and set it on the table. "You may change your mind," he said, and went back to my buttons. "It's not your wits I'm after, hon."

I pulled back. "Willis . . ."

He glared at me. "Honest to Christ, Cleo, you're as stubborn as a hard-mouthed horse."

"I'd like to talk, Willis. I need to talk to somebody about this meeting."

"We're not paying twenty-five dollars a day for that fine bed in order to have a conversation."

"Willis . . . ?"

He shook his head, sighed, and slumped into the other chair; then he lit a cigarette and addressed the ceiling. "Why is it, Lord, that women always want to talk before they do it? For that matter, Lord, why do they always want to talk after they do it? Lord, why can't women do their talking while they're having supper in a fine hotel restaurant? Why can't women talk during a long ride home in the car? Lord? What say, Lord?" He inclined his head, nodded, then looked over and met my eyes straight on. "He says He doesn't know either."

I laughed. I couldn't help it. Then I composed myself and said earnestly, "It's a matter of life and death, Willis."

He looked down at his lap. "So's this," he said mournfully. "Poor Boone's about to breathe his last."

He turned his dangerous green eyes on me and commenced to trail his fingers up and down the inside of my thighs. I shivered and he slipped out of his chair, bent over, and began to nibble on my ear. First thing I knew he'd munched his way down past my collarbone and I was visited by a flood of disorderly pleasures.

It was true what I'd told Willis that day back in early August. We didn't have many interests in common except for being set on fire by each other.

No small thing, that.

Willis handed me my glass of whiskey and 7-Up, and with great ceremony clinked it against his own.

"To the fruit of the gods," he whispered.

25

I WAS ASHAMED, DISHEVELED, AND DRUNK AS nine hundred dollars when I showed up twenty-five minutes late for my appointment with Michael Ahern.

He sniffed. "Whew!"

I lowered my eyes. "I been celebrating."

"Good fortune? Here, have a chair."

"Fortune has nothing to do with it. Stoop labor . . . sweat . . . persistence . . . tenacity." I held up a finger with which to instruct him further. "Willfulness." And I launched into the saga of the Strewberry Suspension.

After a polite interval Michael interrupted my long-winded tale and asked if I wanted to hear his news.

"No," I told him. Bottled honesty talking.

"Why not?"

I hemmed and hawed. He smiled encouragement. Finally, I took a deep breath and told the truth as I understood it. I said, "I had misjudged my character when I came to see you before. I just can't feature myself killing anybody—well, actually I can, but not premeditated, not by proxy."

He glanced at his watch and reached into his desk drawer. "Five o'clock," he said. "One for you?"

"You go on. I already caught up." I could feel the silly grin on my face, the slackness of it in my cheeks. I said, "Is it Philip Marlowe keeps his in the safe? There's one of 'em keeps it in the bookcase—I don't recollect which one—behind a copy of *The Merchant of Venice* . . ."

He sighed. "Cleo, as I recall, that was an alternative that came to you in great anger. The hired gun and the red ants and that sort of thing." He smiled. "I won't hold you to it."

I shook my head. A big mistake. I had to steady it with both hands. "No," I said, "if you tell me who did it and if ole asshole Wally won't send him to the electric chair . . . Do we have an electric chair in Oklahoma? Or do we still hang folks? No, don't tell me. If Wally won't do his job then I'll be obliged to keep my word. It's a matter of honor."

He took a dainty sip from his shot glass.

I turned suspicious. "You don't drink like an Irishman."

"That's probably to my credit. I'd like to tell you what I've found out."

"No, you just give me the bill. I'll send you a money order, I'll go to the Farmers' and Merchants' first thing. What do I owe you? I made some money on my strewberries, should've brought you a jar. Got the receipt from on high, no less, divine intervention due to my devout, demented momma. Did you know that in the old days in Europe the women picked strewberries of an early morning and put them in pottles. Don't ask me what a pottle is. And they carried them on their heads, up to forty pounds' worth! Five miles to market! Just shows you what a burden strewberries can be."

Michael Ahern was a patient man. He waited until my mouth quit running off, and said, "You owe me for a few long-distance calls, a trip to Texas, and maybe a hundred dollars' worth of my time."

I whistled. "Philip Marlowe would've been more dear."

"Philip Marlowe wouldn't have been able to get one of Wally's flunkies to do most of the work. No charge for that."

I stood up, wobbled, and had to grab for the chair arm. "You just send me a bill when you get it figured up."

"You could have said that on the phone."

"I guess you never had a party line. Anyhow, I hadn't made up my mind. I have in the meantime. Oh, it's been a mean time, Michael. My momma took leave of her senses and made a mess of my grandmother's kitchen. Strewberries like life's own blood all over the wall. And my birthday cake. And her carrying on about judgment and destruction and how we'd perish because of the labels. Wrath. Wrath! My poor momma has kept herself alive on wrath ever since I can remember. I don't want to live like that. My grandmother says only God's got the stomach for vengeance."

"Sit down, Cleo." He indicated the chair with an outstretched hand and a face full of kindness. "I think you should hear what I have to say. I think it can make a difference in your life."

Maybe my curiosity got the better of me, or maybe I wanted to believe him, or maybe I was so weak and weary I was willing to rest on any milestone. I sat down.

"Just a minute," he said, and opened a door to what looked like a closet, disappeared inside, and came back with a cup of coffee.

"I take cream and sugar, if you please."

"It's better black under the circumstances. You have an Irishman's word for it." He sat at his desk and opened the file folder in front of him. "Now then," he said, "I checked out every case Ed Shannon worked on, convictions, aquittals, hung juries, arraignments. Everything."

"That sounds very thorough," I said approvingly. "I told Wally . . ."

"Cleo, please. Just listen. I also checked his personal life. He was law-abiding and true blue. No women on the side, no gambling, no bribes. As you know, there was the speakeasy but no money or favors ever changed hands." He smiled. "Even your bail was on the up and up."

"I could've told you that. Ed Shannon, he . . . Sorry."

"I'm just giving you general background here. I want you to understand the scope of the investigation. It all checked out. Big stuff. Little stuff. Everybody was clean."

I waited while he shuffled some papers.

"But there was one peculiar thing that happened after . . ." He paused and frowned. "After the explosion. I have no proof, nothing I could go to Wally with. You understand?"

"I understand." I understood that we were back where I didn't want to be. With honor.

"The story was in the *Tribune* that night. Early the next morning a man committed suicide. Shot himself in the head with a Colt .45. Open-and-shut suicide."

"So?"

"This suicide was one of two brothers Ed Shannon arrested after the race riots. . . ."

"I know. That was before I met him but I read about it in some old newspapers. Ed was certain they'd killed his deputy. They got off twice. Not enough evidence, the paper said."

"That's right."

"You're saying the man who shot himself had something to do with blowing up the car?"

"I'm certain of it."

"But that was so long ago. Why would anyone wait . . . ?"

"Ed—oh, shit!—Ed never let go of it. He never stopped bird-dogging them. Talk about revenge! It's all here. Charges dropped for reckless driving. Charges dropped for insurance fraud. Charges dropped for doing business without a license. There's a list here as long as my arm, most of it nuisance stuff. All trumped up, all dropped. Ed Shannon meting out his own justice. Just kept nipping at their heels until they . . ."

"But if they planted a bomb, surely they knew what would happen? Surely they knew . . ."

He licked his lips and looked uncomfortable. "It's the way you called it. They didn't expect the kids to be . . ."

I interrupted him with a dry, sober laugh. "You saying they don't harm little children?"

"Not white, Protestant children. Not this man. Father of four, Sunday-school teacher, scout leader. He left a note for his wife, said there was innocent blood on his hands, said he couldn't live with it."

"He didn't say whose blood?"

"I told you I have no proof." He leaned forward. "But I have no doubts."

"Was that all? In the note?"

"He hoped God would forgive him."

"And the other one? The brother?"

"A bachelor, quite a bit older, no family of his own. They were very close. In business together, a dry cleaner's and laundry in East Tulsa. Did everything together, worked, went hunting, fishing, holidays . . ."

"And burned crosses."

He didn't say anything, just looked at me.

I said, "Where is he?"

"Galveston. Sold the business, gave his brother's widow everything."

"What does he do in Galveston?"

"Nothing much. Lives in a trailer park near the beach, cries in his beer at the local bar. No friends. Doesn't wash very often."

"You've seen him. That was the trip to Texas."

"I've seen him. I'll take you to see him if you want to go."

"No. No, I don't want to do that."

"The important thing, Cleo, is there's no reason for you to concern

226

yourself with honor, or wrath or vengeance. You got what you wanted without lifting a hand."

I shook my head. "I don't understand?"

Michael reached across the desk and put his hand over mine. He said, "Like I say, I've been there, I've seen him. I can assure you, Cleo, that man is buried up to his neck in a red-ant hill."

I took a cab to Mildred's. She didn't seem in the least surprised to see me. When I told her I needed to use the telephone, she said to help myself while she brewed some tea.

I told Willis I wouldn't be coming back to the hotel, that I had something I had to tend to and it might take a couple days. I said he should go on home without me. I said I'd still pay for the hotel room.

"Well," he drawled, "if it isn't Miss Lady Bountiful herself." Then he said if I didn't get myself back there on the double he'd call up room service and have them send him a woman.

"I can't help that, Willis. This is something I've got to do. I wish you'd try to understand."

There was a long silence. Finally, he said, "You can do it tomorrow, hon." I could hear him forcing some sweetness and reason into his voice. "Whatever it is, we'll do it tomorrow, together. You come on back now and we'll talk about it."

"I appreciate that, Willis, but . . ."

"Cleo, I thought we had an understanding?"

I wasn't sure I'd heard right. "A what?"

"An understanding, a future together."

"We've never said anything about . . ."

"For chrissake, Cleo, we're as good as engaged."

I took the phone away from my ear and just looked at it for a moment. Then I said, "Willis, I don't know where you got that idea. We haven't said one word about . . ."

"Actions speak louder than words. I'm not the kind of man who plays fast and loose. I don't take physical intimacy lightly."

"I don't know what to say. I mean, Willis, we didn't talk about marriage. I'm flattered, I really am, and honored. But it's too soon. I'm not ready yet."

Again, the long silence. Then he said, "You've used me. You don't care about me. It's Boone."

If I hadn't been so dumbfounded I would have laughed. I said, "You're kidding."

Then he said, "I'll give you one more chance. You get yourself back here. I made us reservations for supper. I expect you in a half hour, you hear?" And he slammed down the phone with a thwack that made my head swim.

I stared at the telephone for a couple minutes, then slipped out of Sarah's high-heeled shoes and went in my stocking feet to the kitchen.

Mildred had gotten out her tea service, and some thin, white cups. She said, "Let's have this in the parlor, and you can tell me about it." She smiled. "If you'd like to."

I didn't mention the part about Willis, but I told her everything else from beginning to end. She squeezed her eyes shut and took quick, shallow breaths when I got to Em and Eddy.

"I always walked them to school," I said. "Always. I don't remember any other morning when I didn't walk them to school. It was my responsibility to see them safely to school." To myself, I added, And safely home. And safely grown-up, to see their elders safely to their graves.

For the longest time the only sound in the room was the clink of a cup when it was placed in a saucer. Then Mildred got up, gathered the tea things, and said, "I'll heat some soup."

I nodded, amazed that I was hungry.

Early the next morning Mildred drove me to the cemetery, drove directly to the grave site without checking in the office for the location. It was a large plot with a low chain that went all the way around it. There was a great white stone in the center with a smaller one on each side. My name was on the large one next to Ed's. My name, then the words WIFE—MOTHER—BORN 1912.' Then a big blank space. I felt an awful weakness come over me and had to lean on Mildred for support.

"You wanted it that way," she said.

When I got my legs back I straightened up and moved closer to the chain. "Is that holly?"

"Yes."

"Did I ask for holly? Holly is for foresight."

She put her arm around my shoulder. "You asked that the graves be tended. You said it was a shame to the living if the dead lacked flowers."

I broke off a sprig and held it against my cheek. "That was my momma talking. About shame, I mean."

Mildred nodded. "Yes, I know. Sometimes my mother speaks through me. Says things I would never dream of saying. Is it all right? The holly?"

"It's real nice, Mildred. Thank you for going to the trouble."

"No trouble. I spent my childhood in a small town outside Boston. Twice a year, spring and fall, we went to the cemetery to tend the graves. We all went, the whole village—men, women, children, the family dogs. We raked and mowed and weeded. And we planted. All the graves, not just those of our own people. Those of the dead who had no one left to look after them. When we finished with our work we had a picnic right there in the cemetery. The living and the spirits. I wonder if people do that anymore? I think it was very good for the children. It made death seem like a normal condition. How can there be anything frightening about a graveyard if it's a place where you eat egg salad sandwiches and throw sticks for the dogs?"

I said, "When I come in the spring, will they let us do that? Plant flowers and have a picnic?"

"I don't see why not." She held out her hands to take in the chain, the plot, the holly, the stones. "You own the property."

I only meant to get my Webster's Unabridged so Flynn and I could look up words without having to go into town, but I got into those cartons and kept finding items I wanted to have with me. I understood the photograph albums, and baby clothes, and the pressed glass bowl we got with boxtops. I understood my black satin costume and the angel with the mended wing. I even understood—in an odd way—the Reverend Endicott's broken teeth in a little velvet box. But whatever did I want with my algebra book from Tulsa Central High School or old movie programs from the Rialto or three odd volumnes of the Book of Knowledge?

I opened the Webster's to the H's. *Honor*—a slippery snake of a word that took up about a half column on the page and covered every-thing from chastity to the ace of spades. With such a language to work with, it's a wonder we ever make ourselves understood. I flipped to the P's. A pottle, it turned out, was a measure equal to two quarts. A plain, simple, no-two-ways-about-it word. You could search out a pottle, you could hold it in your hand, fill it up, empty it out. And you could define it to a five-year-old without stepping all over your own big feet or falling into past grief.

I packed and repacked for three days, then in the end took every-thing, a half-dozen cardboard boxes full. You can't leave pieces of your life stored in somebody else's garage forever.

I wouldn't let Mildred drive me home this time. It came to me that she was getting older, and a little worn. I also realized that each time I showed up on her doorstep I brought trouble with me, and her not even kin. She took me to the bus station where they were none too happy about my load of boxes.

I knew I didn't dare ask Willis for the favor of transportation, so I called home from Krause's to tell Sarah to come get me in the wagon. I figured I'd have plenty of time to do my banking and visit with Miss Hawkins about the progress of Mam's history to which I now planned to devote all my waking hours.

Mam said the wagon had a broken wheel.

I said, "She can bring the cart. I've got a whole load of boxes."

There was a long pause. Then Mam said the cart wasn't there. "Gid-eon picked it up," she said. She said I'd best see if I could scare up a ride from somebody in town.

Mr. Krause said he could spare his son for an hour or so in return for a couple jars of our Strewberry Suspension, which had become world famous in my absence.

George helped me stack the boxes on the front porch and I got him some Suspension from the fruit cellar. As he was leaving I noticed the narrow base cart sitting out by the henhouse right where I'd left it. I scratched my head and went to the barn. There was the wagon, all four wheels in perfect condition. After I closed the barn door I looked up and saw Mam watching me from the kitchen window.

As I neared the porch, I nodded toward the henhouse. "There's the cart," I called out, then pointed to the barn. "Nothing wrong with those wheels."

230

She held the door for me.

"What's going on, Mam?"

"Come on in and set down. I didn't want to tell bad news on the telephone."

"Momma? Is it Momma?"

"Frances is fine. Moby's fine. Everybody's fine. Set down." She brought the coffeepot to the table, poured two cups, and sat opposite me. "I don't know what went on in Tulsa . . ." she began.

"I told Willis to tell you I had business to tend to."

"That's what he said, and you could of roasted a pullet on the fire in his eyes."

"We had a disagreement."

"I guess you sure did. Anyhow, he's gone."

"Gone where?"

"Back to California."

I stirred my coffee and tried to decide how I felt about that. As far as I could determine I wasn't surprised. Or angry. Or my feelings hurt. As far as I could tell I didn't feel much of anything, except a kind of sad relief; the way you feel when an old animal dies, one that's been sick and you hadn't the sureness of heart to send it on.

Mam was staring hard at the tabletop, like she expected to find some answers there. "Cleo," she said finally.

"Yes?"

"Sarah went with him."

Well, that got me right in the pit of my femaleness, turned me bright green all over.

"They aim to get married."

"Sarah's already married."

"They aim for her to get a divorce on the way to California. Willis told her she could get a divorce in Reno. Easy, he said. Reno, you know, where they gamble?"

I looked around the room. "Flynn?"

"Willis says he needs a daddy. Says Sarah and Flynn need somebody to look after them. Willis says Sarah's not tough like you."

"Oh." I wondered if I should take that as a compliment. "And how'll he look after them if he's off in the Merchant Marine?"

"Ruby's going to put them up at her place."

"Ruby?"

"Said he called her on the telephone about it. Said he and Ruby had a deep abiding friendship."

"Ruby?"

"Just till the war blows over he says, then he's taking them to San Jose. Says San Jose is a good place to raise children."

"And did you approve of all this?"

Mam laughed. "That man wasn't asking for my approval, he was telling me what's what."

I looked down at my hands, bunched into fists in my lap. "I'll miss Flynn," I said, and I was struck by the deep truth of my words, of how attached I'd become to my vice president, of how I'd looked forward to making him a present of my Webster's Unabridged.

"You were good with him," Mam said. "You're a good mother, Cleo. You need your own child, not one that's ready-made. You need a husband."

We didn't say anything for a while. We just sipped our coffee and trailed our fingers around the beasts in the table. Then I said, "I saw that man in Tulsa."

"The one that was to help you get even?"

"I told him what you said about all those eyes and teeth being God's business."

She waited.

"I visited the graves."

"Good."

"Mam, I'm so ashamed. I'd had my name carved on the tombstone, and a blank place for when the time comes. When I first saw it, all I could think about was myself. I didn't feel the proper grief for my babies and my husband. I just thought about my own wretched self."

I looked up expecting to see horror and disgust on Mam's face, but she was just smiling and nodding. Smiling and nodding the way she did when you'd done something right.

26

At the farmers' and merchants' I transferred the insurance money and the strewberry proceeds from my savings into a checking account. It was, as Mildred said, mine to do with as I saw fit. I saw fit to pay Momma for her part in the Suspension success but every time I called to talk to her about it she hung up on me, and Neddy Wadkins said I couldn't make a deposit into Momma's account without her knowledge and consent.

I also saw fit to get an automobile. I took the bus to Muskogee, where I found a 1936 Lincoln Zephyr. It had its original whitewalls, a synchromesh gearbox, and 523 miles on the odometer. The headlights were faired into the front wings, producing the look of a wild animal running into the wind. I bought it.

I just barely beat a blizzard home. The snow was coming slantways out of the north when I pulled in, and it was all I could do to shut up the chickens and get the stock and my new car into the barn. It took all my strength just to close the doors against the wind. This was a storm that got written up in newspapers across the country. Mam said she'd seen worse.

I couldn't get the house warm, so I had to close off the parlor and the bedrooms and move Mam's bed into the kitchen next to the stove. Even so, her teeth chattered and her joints stiffened up. I brought in my mattress and made a pallet on the floor. The woodpile wasn't two dozen steps from the back door, but every morning I had to shovel a good half hour to get there and back. Not to mention the path I had to make to the henhouse. Chickens can withstand freezing cold but they're stupid when it comes to conserving food. But the worst was getting to the barn. I'd read where people in Montana got lost forever just trying to get out to the barn to tend their animals.

Mam fretted about Momma. The telephone lines went down the first night so we had no way of knowing how she fared. I got all bundled up and tried to make my way through the drifts over to her house but I soon gave up, figuring I was no good to anybody frozen stiff in a snowbank. I again humbled myself, and asked forgiveness for the sin of blasphemy, if indeed in His eyes I had committed that sin, and delivered Momma's welfare into His hands.

For more than a week we were marooned there. We did a little work on Mam's history, but mostly we just huddled around the fire and played poker. I had to put blankets over the windows, not just to help keep the place warm, but because the whiteness hurt Mam's eyes. The wind would let up every so often and it would be deathly quiet for an hour or so. So quiet you could hear each little sliver of wood hiss when the fire took it. You could hear your own breath sliding in and out, and your skin crackle when you scratched it. You could hear your eyelids blink.

Then the sky would suddenly turn dark and the wind would come roaring out of the Dakotas, across Nebraska and Kansas, and drop a new load of snow on us. The henhouse completely disappeared in a great drift. I tied one end of a length of rope around my waist and the other to the porch railing. Then I shoveled a path before the drift could freeze over. I gave the chickens all the feed there was in the henhouse and told them they were on their own. I didn't even have the heart to bring one in for our supper; I figured we were all in this together.

The pipes had frozen that first night. I kept the sink filled with snow for cooking and drinking water, so that was no problem, but of course the pipes to Mam's flush toilet were frozen too. She couldn't get her old haunches down on a slop jar even with me helping, so I sawed a hole in one of the kitchen chairs and nailed a couple runners across the bottom so I could slide the jar in and out. I'd empty the jars as quick as the weather would allow, but in a few days that small, closed-in kitchen began to reek of our bodily smells. We were fortunate, in a way, that our bowels soon froze up just like everything else.

The fourth or fifth day of this—I don't know, I lost track of time—Mam started calling me Frances. At first she'd catch herself. She'd *tsk* and shake her head and mutter, "Cleo, you're Cleo." Then she'd call me Frances again and not notice. I didn't think too much about it until she started asking when Juan would be home. Then she wanted to go over to Rose Hill and visit with her momma. She wanted a bouquet of white Albas. She commenced having long conversations with Harlan, as if he were sitting right there at the kitchen table. She'd ask him a question or make some comment, then incline her head and wait for a response. From what I could gather, they talked mostly about their cotton crop. I didn't know what to make of it. I'd never known Mam's mind to wander so far from the present. I really began to worry when she lost her appetite and stopped smoking her Buglers.

The third time I won with a pair of nines she looked over at me very calmly, her eyes not glazed over like they'd been all that day—and she said, "Cleo, I think I'll go on now."

I stared at her, my heart bumping around in my chest like it had slipped its moorings. I told myself I'd never paid any attention to such talk before, why should I now? But I didn't dispute her. I didn't try to jolly her along. Not at first.

She said, "I'll sit over there in the rocker while you move my bed back in my room."

"It's cold in there, Mam."

"It's cold in the grave, Cleo."

"Oh, Mam . . ."

"Cold for a little while. When I soar it'll be into the warm arms of my sweet Juan." She rose up stiffly from her chair and I helped her to the rocker. She closed her eyes and leaned back. "It's warm where he's waiting for me," she whispered. "Probably getting set to fry me up a mess of fresh fish. Never got it through his head . . . You move my bed now, Cleo."

"Let's leave the door open a while first. Take the chill off." I reached for a Bugler from the jelly glass, lit it, and wedged it between her thumb and forefinger. "I'll make a nice pot of hickory tea," I said, my voice light and nursely. "You can't go on just yet, Mam, we're not finished with the history."

"I am," she said firmly. "I'm finished with my history. Your history is over and done with when you can't wipe your own behind."

"When the storm lets up . . ."

"There's just one thing bothers me, Cleo." She frowned and blew out two long streams of blue smoke through her nose.

"When the storm lets up," I repeated, "I'll go out to the fruit cellar and get some berries for a pie."

She wagged her finger impatiently. "Listen," she said. "You think the Lord will make me choose?"

"Choose what, Mam?"

"I don't think old Jehovah minds if you got more than one husband, but what if God is a Christian like the Reverend Shoemaker says he is?"

I put a handful of snow in the teakettle and set it on the fire. "Well, I don't know, Mam. It isn't like you were divorced or something. I think that's what they object to—divorce. You're allowed to remarry if you're a widow."

"That's not what I mean. I'm not worried about us being accepted, but what do you do when you get there and find all these dearly beloveds from your lifetime on earth? Surely you can't have four husbands in Heaven, surely they won't allow that? So, how do you choose? Or does the Lord choose for you?"

I grinned, cheered that she was sounding like her old self again. "Maybe they play a hand of high card to see who gets you."

She hunched her shoulders and picked at the fuzz on the lap blanket. "I wish I could talk to Frances about what the Bible says in this regard."

I thought for a minute, searched my mind for a soothing verse. "Proverbs," I said. "In Proverbs it says to rejoice with the wife of thy youth."

Mam smiled. "Sweet Harlan."

The kettle whistled and I poured the water over the hickory tea and set it on the table to steep. "I knew a preacher in Tulsa," I said. "The Reverend Robby Endicott, and it was his contention there's no marriage in Heaven. He said there are no problems in Heaven, and even the best of marriages has its problems. The congregation got a big chuckle over that. When he wasn't all tensed up over the collection plate he had a real sense of humor."

Mam shook her head. "That doesn't sound right to me. No marriage."

"Just think about it. The vows say till death do us part. There's nothing about the contract being valid in the hereafter. In Heaven we're all probably just good friends."

She shook her head harder. "No, I want to have a husband there. I miss having a husband, somebody to do for, somebody to warm my bones at night, somebody's arm to take on the street and sit next to at the Sunday service." She sighed and began to pick at the fuzz again.

"Thing is," she said sadly, "thing is, good men as they were, there isn't a one of them I'd want to spend eternity with."

I nodded. "It's a long time, eternity." I thought if I could just keep her talking she'd regain her interest in this world and forget about the next one.

"Yes," she said, like it was settled. "Yes, I'd like to believe there's marriage there, but I'd like to think it's as it is here, on a kind of rotation basis." She frowned and motioned toward the Buglers. A good sign. Maybe I'd get a bowl of soup into her.

"Oh my!"

"What is it?"

"I wonder if we'll all be young again? I wouldn't want to live with Harlan in my present state and him only twenty-two years old."

I poured the tea. "It's sure a mystery. As soon as the storm lets up I'll go fetch Momma. She's a crackerjack on Revelation."

Mam didn't say anything for a while, just followed me with her eyes while I set the kettle on the back of the stove, sliced some carrots into the soup, then settled myself at the table and began to shuffle the cards.

She cleared her throat. "You won't forget about the ceremony, the Creek burial. The Presbyterians would have you in that cold ground till Judgment Day. I don't want to wait that long to soar."

"How about those Creeks?" I said, pretending surprise and inspiration. "What do they think about marriage in the Hereafter?"

"Oh, I don't know. I didn't learn about that. My people lost their gods a long time ago, lost them in Alabama when they started wearing trousers and raising chickens."

"Then why do you want the ceremony? Maybe it's not a wise thing to aim for a Christian Heaven with a Creek send-off."

"I want them both," she said stubbornly. "We have birthrights. We have deathrights."

I put on a sage look. "Well, I can see we need to discuss this with some knowledgeable Creek. When the storm lets up . . ."

She sipped her tea, holding the cup with both hands, staring into it, blinking. Then she looked up at me. She said, "You can move my bed now."

"But Mam, we haven't worked out this Heaven problem."

She sighed. "I'll have to take my chances."

"But Mam . . ."

"Don't argue with me. Please. I have to do this while my mind is clear. The gift is no good to me unless my mind is clear. Ever so often now it starts to leave me. It might leave me and wander around out there and not find its way back."

"But if you just wait till I can go get Momma. Momma has a mind medicine . . ."

"Cleo, move the bed now. I want to go on from my own room, from my own bed, at a time of my own choosing. I'm at your mercy."

I did like she said, thinking to crawl in with her and keep her warm, but she wouldn't have it, told me to close the door and leave her be. I slipped in every few minutes and checked to see that the covers were still moving up and down. I slipped in and out for over an hour. Then the last time, as I watched, she turned herself toward the window where the bright light off the snow hovered and fell across her own bed, covered with a Cross and Crown quilt made by her own hand seventy years before. I eased closer. Her eyes grew wide as if to let in more light and she used her gift, owning that moment like she'd owned her first shed blood.

27

REVEREND SHOEMAKER SAID WE COULDN'T
have the Creek ceremony.

I thought maybe I'd misunderstood him. Or he'd misunderstood
me. I repeated myself, slowly and clearly. "Mam wanted the regular
service too. What I'm talking about is after. It's what she wanted."

He shifted in his chair and tapped the desk with the eraser end of
his pencil. "It isn't written down," he said. "It isn't a written request."

"You think I'd lie about this? She told me what she wanted more
than once. She told me again the day she died."

"I'm sorry, Cleo, but that's not enough. It has to be written down.
And signed."

"Oh, good Lord!" At that moment it seemed to me there was always some man sitting on the other side of some desk telling me what
could and couldn't be done. I pulled my chair closer and rallied my
arguments. I said, "Reverend Shoemaker, I can understand how some
members of the congregation might object to the Creek ceremony, but
I think if you explain to them how important it was to Mam—" I
broke off, wondering what good it would do if he did change his mind.

I sighed and confided in him the difficulty I was having in this regard. "I can't find anybody to do it. I can't find anybody that knows
what to do. All this land—" I spread my arms wide to take in the eastern part of the county. "All this land once belonged to the Creeks.
This very church sits on tribal lands. Now you couldn't find a full-
blood if your life depended on it. Where've they all gone? They were
still here before I went to Tulsa. Do I have time to go down to Muskogee and rustle up somebody? Can we put off the service a couple
days? Reverend, I was expecting you'd help me carry out Mam's
wishes. I need help. I can't even find a guitar player. We got banjo
players and harmonica players and fiddlers till the cows come home,
but there's not a soul from here to Wagoner that knows Spanish
guitar. . . ."

He waved his arms for silence. "Cleo," he said patiently, "you've not been listening to me. There will be no Creek burial. There will be no Spanish song."

I slumped back in my chair. "Whatever is wrong with the song? It's a beautiful song."

He removed his little half glasses and pinched the bridge of his nose. "It isn't liturgical," he said wearily.

I stared at him. I couldn't believe what I was hearing. I'd always thought of him as a reasonable man. Course he wasn't one of us. I mean, he'd come from Milwaukee, but he'd been the preacher at the First Presbyterian Church of Robina for over twenty-five years. That was long enough to learn what's what. I felt ire rising in my chest. "Sir," I said, forcing myself to be calm, "we're talking here about something holy, a person's wishes for going on. My grandmother's wishes! Surely for such a woman as my grandmother you could bend the rules a little."

"If it were liturgical I could argue with her about it. I'd have grounds."

"Grounds for what? Argue with who?"

"Well your mother, of course. I have no objection to the ceremony. I have no objection to 'La Golandrina.' It's a lovely song. One of my favorites. If it were up to me . . ."

"What does Momma have to say about it?"

"She next of kin, the only surviving child. If there's nothing in the will about arrangements then it's the responsibility of the next of kin."

"I'm next of kin, too."

"But not as next as Frances, as close I mean. You're one more step removed, so to speak."

"Oh, good Lord!"

"You talk to your mother about it, Cleo. This is something you have to settle between yourselves. My hands are tied."

I set my elbows on the corner of the desk and put my head in my hands. Retribution. My momma's wrath again. "I can't talk to her," I muttered, embarrassed to make that admission. "She's not speaking to me."

He got up, came around the desk, and touched my shoulder. "Of course she'll speak to you," he said. "At a time like this family members are drawn together, regardless of differences and misunderstandings and . . ." I looked up. His face was troubled. "That business with

240

the perserves," he went on. "Frances talked to me about it. Of course I'd already heard. She came because of her concern that she had committed a grave sin. I told her that in commerce one often uses symbols, and that it didn't mean that one is necessarily involved in the worship of idols." He cleared his throat and looked even more uncomfortable. "Your mother is, I think, unduly influenced by her interpretation of the Old Testament. I explained to her that Christ loves even the heathen."

"I appreciate your efforts, Reverend, but it's not the labels. It's the will. Mam left her land to me—that's written down. Momma thought it ought to go to Ethan. She's getting even, that's what she's doing. And not just with me. She's getting even with Mam by not honoring her wishes. She knows exactly what Mam wanted."

"Oh now Cleo, you mustn't think such harsh thoughts about your own mother."

I looked him straight in the eye. "It's the truth, or may God strike me dead right here where I'm sitting."

He sucked in his breath and hopped back. Just in case a bolt of lightning came crashing through the ceiling. Then he said, "If that is so, Cleo, then you must forgive her. Jesus says forgive and ye shall be forgiven. Jesus says, to whom little is forgiven, the same loveth little."

"Momma says Jesus was too softhearted for his own good."

He clasped his hands and closed his eyes, probably wondering for the millionth time why he'd ever left Milwaukee. I felt a little sorry for him. Not an easy job shepherding a stiff-necked flock over the hills and valleys of life.

"I'll call her," he said, glancing at his watch. "I'll pay her a visit."

I got to my feet. "Can we put off the service for a couple days? Is that possible? Give me a little time?"

"Yes, I think I can find a necessary reason for that. I'll call you after I talk to Frances." With a wave of his hand he went back to his desk, leaving me to see myself out. As I closed the door I heard him humming in a distracted way. "Da daa de daaa, small swallow free and haaaaaaapy. Take back the daaaa da of a heart forlornnnn . . ."

He couldn't carry a tune in a big water pail but all the same I was heartened.

*

I phoned Tully at the Gusher and told him to find me a somebody who owned a Spanish guitar and could back a trumpet on "La Golondrina." I said money was no object. Then I called Mildred and asked if she could find a Creek elder or shaman or medicine man or whatever they called themselves through Gilcrease where she volunteered. A somebody, I said, who could rattle gourds or dance in a circle or mumble incantations. Mildred was taken aback by this show of irreverence and I told her I hadn't singled out the Creek religion, that I was fed up with all of them. I told her all I wanted to do was see Mam safely on her way, then I planned a trip of my own. There was nothing to keep me in Robina now, nothing to keep me from resuming my journey to Lhasa, my journey to the unknown.

Nothing but that damn goldfish.

Mildred said she loved me dearly and would do almost anything for me, but she could not take on the responsibility of Eddy's goldfish.

I talked to Miss Hawkins about it. She suggested that I get a caretaker in return for reduced rent. She said Sonny and Agnes Mary Tipton, who had eloped in the wake of a lot of raised eyebrows, were living with Agnes Mary's mother in her one-room house.

Sonny reached out for my offer like a drowning man. He wanted them to move in that very afternoon.

"Saturday," I told him. "After Mam's service."

I had them come over to receive their instructions about the place and about Moby. I said as long as Moby was alive and well they could live in Mam's house rent free. Agnes Mary was poking in the cabinets and running her hands over the furniture. "Three bedrooms," she kept saying. "Three bedrooms."

Sonny crossed his arms on his chest and surveyed his new castle. "Maybe we could buy it from you, Cleo, on down the road when we got something put by."

I shrugged. "That's not out of the question." Actually, it was, but I figured they'd treat the place with higher regard if they thought it could be theirs one day.

I turned to Agnes Mary and told her that only two of the bedrooms were available. "I'll be storing some things in one of them, but other than that you're welcome to use what's here." I thought Agnes Mary might faint from joy.

I gave them the fish book to take home and study. I was very firm.

"Moby is accustomed to living by herself, so you're not to put any other fish in there with her. I know it's a big tank, but she's growing into it."

When I showed them to the door I reminded them that Miss Hawkins would be stopping by ever so often at her convenience to check on Moby's well-being. I gave them a steely eye and pointed to the fish book. "Watch for gill rot."

Miss Hawkins asked if I couldn't see my way clear to stay around until I finished Mam's history. I could've kicked myself all the way to Nebraska for getting so wound up in strewberries and Willis Henderson. If I'd finished the history in September when I said I would, when I promised I would, then Mam would have had the pleasure of seeing her life in a leather binding with gold letters, would've gotten all gussied up and carried her dewdrop fan to the celebration. I could just see her with her braid twisted into a shiny crown on top of her head, her holding that fan under her eyes and flirting shamelessly with Gideon Warwick.

I told Miss Hawkins I just didn't have the heart for it right now, and she said she understood. I wrote down Rosemary's address in California and said I could be contacted there if anything came up I should know about. I said I'd be there until I could make arrangements for my trip to Lhasa.

She said, "I don't know that this is a good time to contemplate a visit to Asia."

I said, "At least I'll be two thousand miles closer to my destination."

Reverend Shoemaker talked to Momma like he said he would. She told him if he wasn't prepared to do the service the way she wanted, she'd have it in the chapel at the funeral home with a minister over from Wagoner. She also told him I was to sit with her in the mourner's pew—for appearance' sake only.

"I think we better do it the way she wants," he said, shaking his head. "Frances is obviously beset by grief. She's not herself."

I bit down hard on my tongue, didn't tell him that Momma was herself all right. Just more so.

It was a plain and joyless service she arranged, stiff and formal as a linen tablecloth. As far as I could see none of it had anything to do with my grandmother. Momma looked me square in the face only once. This was after I sifted my handful of dust onto the casket and turned to step back in place beside her. She pointed her chin at me and pulled her mouth into a tight little smile, the one she saved for use when she'd got the best of a situation. I lowered my eyes, and let my shoulders slump like a somebody who'd given in.

Then, as the preacher was working up to the Resurrection and the Life—the very words Mam didn't want, the ones about having to wait until the last day to rise—Momma leaned over and put her mouth next to my ear. Her breath was hot and mean on my cheek. She whispered, "It was just failed jelly."

"What?" I whispered back.

"Your precious Suspension," she hissed. "Your fruit of the gods. It was nothing but *failed* jelly!"

The Tiptons moved in with their pitiful little mess of possessions while I packed up the Zephyr. Agnes Mary said, "Why don't you spend the night, Cleo? No good reason to start off on your trip in the dark. That right, Sonny?"

Sonny looked hard at his shoes. "Sure. Sure thing," he mumbled. I could see he wanted me out of there and on my way, didn't want me to hang around and maybe change my mind.

I said I liked driving at night, then I went over to the tank and tapped on it. Moby swam up, kissed my finger, and did her little food dance. I fed her, leaned my forehead against the glass. "Eddy," I whispered. "As regards this goldfish, I believe I've done all that could be required of any human being—even a mother."

There was nothing more to do or say so I got in my car and headed for Wagoner.

They were waiting for me, as planned, in the all-night diner, and they were easy to spot. One was clearly an Indian and the other had his feet propped up on a guitar case. I introduced myself and said we'd need to take one of their cars because mine was full up.

The Indian—his name was Seth Mackenzie—said he'd hitched a

ride. The guitar player, Billy Rule, said he had a pickup and that'd be five bucks extra if you please.

I told him he didn't look Spanish.

"Who said I was? Don't have to be a spic to play spic music." He stood up and reached for his case.

I gave him a dark look. "You watch your mouth. My grandmother would find your language offensive."

He shrugged and said, "How come this service is so late in the night?"

I turned to the Indian, who had a new haircut and was wearing a dark suit with a clean white shirt and a string tie. I said, "I trust you're Creek."

He smiled. "Eighty-seven and a half percent."

I looked them over again, hoping I'd done the right thing, hoping it would all work out. I nodded at Seth Mackenzie's coffee cup. "You about finished there?" He reached in his pocket and put some change on the counter.

"The money up front," said Billy Rule. "That's what you told me on the phone."

I opened my pocketbook and brought out two white envelopes. Tully had told me I was nuts. Fifty apiece was like a fortune. Billy tore into his envelope and counted out the money, but Seth Mackenzie just slid his, unopened, into his inside pocket like a gentleman.

Billy held out his hand. "And the extra five for the use of my pickup."

I gave it to him and motioned for them to follow me. I got my horn, locked the car, and we loaded into Billy's pickup and took off down the road toward Robina.

I had explained to both of them on the telephone that this was a graveside service. I had not mentioned that we would be the only people present, and that we'd be sneaking into the cemetery like thieves in the night. For one thing, I didn't want them to think I was some kind of crazy woman, and for another I didn't want them to get the notion they could get into trouble. Which was a possibility if anybody saw us and told my momma. I wouldn't have put it past her to have the sheriff throw us in jail for desecration.

I took a deep breath. I owed them at least a brief explanation. I said,

"My grandmother's funeral was this afternoon." I turned to Seth. "Like I told you, she was Creek and wanted a Creek burial. For reasons that don't make any sense, she wasn't allowed her wishes. So, this isn't official. I'm doing this on my own." I looked over at Billy, who was hunched over the wheel, concentrating on the road. "The same," I said, "goes for the music."

He gave me a quick look, then peered back at the road, his heavy chin thrust forward. "Don't matter none to me," he said. "For fifty bucks I'd play 'The Star-Spangled Banner' on a street corner in Berlin, Germany."

Seth motioned to my trumpet case on the floor at my feet. "Not exactly a quiet instrument."

"The cemetery is a ways from town. No houses close by. Unless somebody's driving that way on purpose they won't even know we're there."

Billy lit a cigarette and we rode in silence. I thought about what I'd just said, about nobody knowing we'd be there. I thought about the money I had in my pocketbook, from closing out my account at the bank to finance these two journeys—mine and Mam's. Here I was, a rich woman, on the way to a dark lonely cemetery with two men I didn't know from Tucker's hat.

I asked Seth what he did at Gilcrease.

"Gardener," he said. "I take night classes at T.U."

That eased my mind some. A college man. "I went to T.U.," I said. "I studied music there."

"I'm taking philosophy."

Billy snorted. "I bet there's a whole lot of work for Indians in the philosophy business."

Seth leaned forward and spoke without a sign of rancor. "I also study botany for my gardening. Don't care about graduating, I just like to go to school. Been going to night school at T.U. for almost ten years now. On and off."

I said, "You're sure not what I expected. How come you know about burial ceremonies?"

He smiled, and his white teeth gleamed in the light from the dashboard. "My grandmother had a funeral too."

I felt easier. Not about Billy, but I thought I could count on Seth Mackenzie if it came to trouble. We talked about what we would do, got ourselves a program. Seth said he'd say a few words first, then when he signaled Billy he was to play some nice background music, like the organist did in church, except Spanish. Then he'd speak some more and perform some rituals, then we'd end up with "La Golandrina."

"In E-flat," I told Billy, and he nodded. It all sounded pretty good to me. I thought Mam would approve. I said, "Take a right at the crossroads." He swore like an expert as we bumped and scraped over the five miles of dirt road to the cemetery.

Most of the snow had melted but there were patches of it piled up against the headstones, and it glinted silver when the moon shined through the clouds. Billy, who'd been so fearless about the Germans, shuddered and said, "Let's get this over with." I figured he'd never thrown sticks for dogs or had egg salad sandwiches in a graveyard.

I led them to our family plot, which was of a good size. It accommodated Mam's children and her husbands, excepting Harlan, and my daddy because he had nowhere else to go. And Mam, waiting for me to keep my word.

Seth stood at the foot of the grave. Billy and I faced each other on either side. To my amazement, Seth took out a Bible and a flashlight and commenced to read from Ecclesiastes about the seasons. He switched the verses around so he ended up with "A time to be born, and a time to die." Then he bowed his head and motioned to Billy. "Softly," he said, "as soft as the owl's wings."

Billy played a few minor chords then broke into something that sounded classical. I didn't recognize it but it was surely magical. He may have had a bad mouth but he knew how to make a guitar sing.

I moved over and touched Seth on the arm. It seemed I could not make myself understood by men of the cloth. I said, "We already had a Christian service. You're supposed to do something Creek."

He nodded and bowed his head again. Billy went on strumming, and after a while Seth began to speak in a low voice. He talked about a big beautiful bug that hatched out of one of the leaves of an old table, a table made of apple-tree wood that had sat in kitchens in Connecticut and Massachusetts for more than sixty years. That bug, he said, had hatched from an egg laid decades before, when the table was a living tree. He held out his hands. "Who does not feel his faith in a resurrection and immortality strengthened by hearing of this?"

I shook my head in despair. I had wasted my money. I'd let Mam down!

He held the Bible to his breast and looked down on Mam's grave. He said, "You will now enjoy your perfect life. . . ." He put his hand on my shoulder. "What is your grandmother's given name?"

"Jessie," I said.

"Awake, Jessie! Awake, Sister! There is more day to dawn. Awake! The sun is but a morning star."

I poked him in the ribs. "Henry David Thoreau was not Creek," I said dryly.

Seth looked surprised. "Ah, but in his soul he was. Shhh now, shhh."

He switched off the light and began to call on God by all the names I'd ever heard of and some I hadn't. He asked for blessings and intercessions from everybody from Muhammad to the tooth fairy—well, not really the tooth fairy, but it was sure an assorted bunch. And then—I swear—right there in the big middle of a Protestant cemetery, he crossed himself!

I reached over and snatched the flashlight out of his hands, turned it on, and shined it full in his face. I said, "What is this? Some kind of religious lottery? Pick a faith? Any faith?"

Billy laughed and hit the guitar strings with the flat of his hand.

Seth Mackenzie's eyes were closed against the light. His cheeks were wet. He said, "They're all the same. It's the believing, not the belief, that matters. I'm trying to summon as many powerful spirits as possible, to lead Jessie on her way."

He took the flashlight from me, motioned to Billy for more music, then reached in his pocket and pulled out a paper bag. "Hold out your hand," he said, and filled it with corn, which he told me to scatter on the grave. When I finished, he waved an eagle feather over it. Then he spread his arms wide and he called on the trees and the flowers and the beasts of the field and the buffalo and the birds of the air and wild tigers and whales and great elephants and even honeybees and the fallen sparrow. He admonished them to come sit at his feet and he greeted them one by one.

Behind me, I heard the stamping and snorting of a hoofed animal.

Seth sank down on his haunches. "Your steed is here, Jessie. A winged white horse to carry you home." He pointed to me and to

Billy. "And your sacred swallow, your beloved bird, your fellow-pilgrim, to show you the way."

Billy and I played softly, sweetly, played it through twice. Then Seth waved the eagle feather again and a mist rose off the grave, gathered, and soared skyward. There was the sound of a galloping horse in the distance. The three of us stood there, still as the tombstones.

No one said a word all the way back to Wagoner. When Billy pulled up beside my car, he told Seth he'd be pleased and honored to give him a ride home—no charge. Seth hopped out of the truck and offered me his hand. I took it and climbed down. I couldn't seem to find the words to thank him with. Then it occurred to me I didn't need to, that he could hear what wasn't spoken.

I said, "I'm on my way to Lhasa, Seth Mackenzie. I could use a good holy man."

He smiled. "Wish I could take you up on it. I'll ask for mighty spirits to accompany you."

We shook hands. I waved at Billy Rule; then, fourteen years after I had begun it, I resumed my journey to the unknown. That was in the dark, early-morning hours of December 7, 1941.

PART III

Let us run with patience the race that is set before us.
—HEBREWS 12:1

28

On saturday afternoons i usually
went with the Malones on some kind of outing. We took the Red Car
to the beach in Santa Monica, or the bus to Hollywood for a first-run
matinee, or we'd squander our gas coupons and drive over to Griffith
Park or up to Indian Springs for a picnic. But this particular Saturday
in late June, Rosemary and I were in the den, with the shades drawn,
listening to the Happy Hills Radio Theater and drinking rum and
Coca-Cola. We were goofing off in front of the big Motorola because
Raymond was at an all-day sales meeting at Western Auto, and the
boys, R.J. and Jody, were away at the YMCA summer camp.

Since my arrival in Glendale, three and a half years before, I'd lived
in the Malones' garage apartment, but I was accepted as one of the
family so I spent a lot of time in the front house.

The commercial was coming on and I was on my way to the kitchen
for more cheese and crackers when Rosemary called out. "It's him!
Cleo, get back here this minute. It's him!" I hurried back and found
her bent over the radio, frowning and cupping one ear. She said, "It is
him, isn't it?"

I closed my eyes and listened. "He sounds older," I said.

"Well, what do you expect? It's been . . . What's it been?"

"Seventeen years," I said, without a moment's hesitation. "And a
half."

Rosemary said, "He must've got his teeth fixed."

I shushed her and squeezed my eyes shut even tighter. It was his
voice all right, that voice that caused the females in his congregation to
twist their handkerchiefs and fan themselves. Now, in that most
golden of all voices, the Reverend Robin Endicott was selling used automobiles.

"My friends," he was saying, "if cars could get divorces, a lot of
them would. It's true. They would file for divorce because their owners don't appreciate them anymore."

There was a brief pause for that to sink in. I could just see him flash a sideways smile. Probably he gave his head a little toss and a lock of hair fell forward, making him look boyish and harmless. I hardened my heart as he went on about neglect and cruelty and desertion.

"You've begun to take your car for granted," he said, "so you forget to have her washed and . . ." He cleared his throat. ". . . serviced regularly."

"Oh for Pete's sake," Rosemary sniffed. "That man! That nasty man!"

I waved at her to be quiet.

". . . bring her little baubles like new filters and hoses, like you did when she was newer and shinier. If that's what it's come to, perhaps it's time to trade her in on a newer model. Perhaps that's the best thing for both of you."

"Imagine! Just imagine! A preacher advocating divorce!" Rosemary shook her finger at the radio. "Shame on you, Reverend Endicott!"

". . . can drive home in a 1939 Packard Eight Touring Car, formerly the property of a famous Hollywood star now serving with our brave forces in the Pacific. Too expensive, you say? Can't afford it, you say?" He sounded amazed and dumbfounded at that possibility. "Oh my friends, surely you deserve a few small pleasures in this life, in return for all your sacrifice and hard labor."

"Listen to him! Taking food out of the mouths of babes."

I poked Rosemary and moved closer to the radio.

"Here at Happy Hills Motors we have our own financing. You don't have to get involved with a . . ." He put a little sneer in his voice. ". . . a bank and all that paperwork and investigation into your private life." He made going to the bank sound like a trip to the stockyards.

Rosemary flounced down on the davenport and crossed her arms. "He's just as devious as he ever was," she said, and added grudgingly, "and just as sexy."

I didn't say anything. I was listening for the address of this car company that handled divorces.

On Sunday, after a troubled night, I called up Happy Hills Motors and asked the price of the '39 Packard they'd advertised on the radio the day before. A salesman came on and told me cheerfully that they didn't give quotes over the telephone. He said a whole lot depended on the condition of my trade-in and my financial situation. He told me to come on over and he'd fix me up.

I asked if the announcer worked there at the car lot. The man said Mr. Endicott owned the car lot; then he chuckled and said the boss wasn't for sale.

I hung up, feeling like a damn fool, and resolved to forget all about Robby. What did I need with him anyhow? The animal part of my brain had a quick and ready answer, but I ignored it. I reminded myself I had a couple gentlemen friends who took me out to supper and the picture show, and there was the interesting new piano man at the Sundowner, where I played my trumpet three nights a week, and a half-dozen nice boys I'd met at the USO and who I corresponded with regularly. Rosemary kept at me to find a husband. She had Raymond drag home any and all eligibles he came across, and on those occasions would ask me to cook up a mess of my famous fried chicken for bait. She was as devoted in that respect as Mam had been.

"You can't fool around forever," she'd say. "You're getting up there, Cleo. First thing you know you'll lose your fertility and have nothing to show for it."

I was edging up on thirty-four—true—but I didn't feel "up there." My shiny black hair still didn't require any help from a bottle. My teeth were sound, not a filling in my head, and my eyes were strong as a chicken hawk's. Gravity was working away on my wonders but so far we were ahead. So, I still had my looks and my health and with the women in our line the change came on late. I told Rosemary there was plenty of time, and besides I hadn't met anybody I wanted to go down to the creek with—so to speak—much less have babies.

For the past six months Rosemary and I had been employed at a cannery off San Fernando Road, one of the several defense jobs we'd had since I arrived. So, Monday morning we went to work and I put Robby Endicott right out of my mind. I put him out of my mind again on Tuesday, and Wednesday. I didn't log any extra cans that week, but Robby was not entirely at fault.

This was the second week of tomato season. To get to our station we had to take a footbridge, under which ran a red stream of tomato leavings. We were told they were tomato leavings but I suspected they were destined to be juice. When we'd complain about the mess, or the worms, or the awful smell that clung to your nose hairs, our supervisor, Mrs. Thornton, would point to the posters on the walls and remind us we were soldiers without guns, that we were freeing up fighting men, that if it wasn't for us our nation would starve to death both at home and abroad.

Our station was about halfway up the line. We'd started at the bottom due to lack of experience but we progressed to the middle in no time and were still moving up. At least we were moving until the advent of tomato season.

The way it worked: The conveyor belt brought the tomatoes down from the great vats where they'd been steamed. We were doing the solid packs, the premium stuff. We'd remove the stems, slip off the skins, and pack the fruit whole in cans, which we pulled down from an overhead dispenser. An automatic counter kept track of how many cans you pulled down, and that's how your quota and bonus were determined. The girls at the front of the line had the first shot, so of course they scooped up the best fruit. They worked quicker and made bigger bonuses because they didn't have to mess with stubborn skins or bruises or blemishes . . . or worms. There is no creature in this world as ugly and fat and juicy as a steamed tomato worm.

On Friday while we were having our break in the lunchroom, the supervisor came over and asked me if I was sick or something.

I shrugged and said I was okay.

She said, "I've just checked your production sheet for the week and I must tell you, Shannon, you are way behind your quota—*way* behind."

I straightened in my chair and said I was sorry. I truly was. It was not in my nature to fail.

"I wouldn't want to be forced to demote you, Shannon, put you back with the new girls."

"Oh, I wouldn't want that either, Mrs. Thornton." The end of the line. Worms wrapped in tomato skins.

She frowned and narrowed her eyes. "Or over in Puree and Sauce."

"Cleo's had a bad pain in her shoulder," Rosemary broke in quickly. "Came to work anyhow, yes she did, said it was her duty. We'll dose it good with Ben-Gay over the weekend. She'll be fine on Monday. Arm just needs a little rest."

Mrs. Thornton gave us a tight little smile and told me she'd be keeping an eye on my sheet next week. She suggested that for the rest of the day I make good use of my other arm.

I went back to work determined to clear my head of everything except my automatic counter. I succeeded for a time but then my mind let down its defenses, and a crowd of renegade thoughts and desires disguised as premium Romas came riding down that conveyor belt and they all got off at my station. One of them doffs his hat and says, TOMORROW IS SATURDAY. I snatch him up and plop him in a can, juice flying everywhere. And the next smart-mouth, and the next, them laughing at me and crying out, SATURDAY SATURDAY SATURDAY. One big steamy fella slithers out of my grasp, rears up, and looks me dead in the eye. I AM A BROTHER TO DRAGONS, he says, A COMPANION TO OWLS. I press a knuckle to my mouth and watch as he tumbles on down the line, him laughing like a fool until somebody catches him.

I reach for another can and I see myself stuck to the piano bench in that little clapboard church in Tulsa, listening to Robby go on and on about poor, pitiful old Job. MY BONES ARE BURNED WITH HEAT . . . MY HARP IS TURNED TO MOURNING . . . AND MY ORGAN . . .

Another Roma gives me the eye. THOU CAUSEST ME TO RIDE UPON THE WIND.

The rotating lamp sends colored shadows around the vestry. HONEY AND MILK ARE UNDER THY TONGUE. THE JOINTS OF THY THIGHS ARE LIKE JEWELS. THY NAVEL A ROUND GOBLET. His lips are like lilies. He says I am a vineyard.

"Cleo? Cleo!"

I shook my head to clear it. Rosemary was punching my theoretically sore shoulder. "For heaven's sake, Cleo! You've put four empty cans on that belt. Come on now, wake up. You hear? Mrs. Thornton isn't talking just to hear her head rattle. She means it. She'd as soon put you over there in Puree and Sauce as look at you. Come on now, get busy. Here. I'll help you."

For the rest of the afternoon Rosemary alternated cans from her dispenser and mine. Every time I slowed down or gazed off into the distance of Saturday afternoon, she gave me a smart jab with her elbow. It was my rib cage, not my shoulder, that required Ben-Gay that night. I made my quota, for all that it mattered.

Saturday was nippy and overcast, so the Malones decided on the movie at Grauman's Chinese and a hot-fudge sundae at Brown's. I said I thought I'd stay home and catch up on my correspondence. Rosemary raised an eyebrow but she didn't say anything. I went back to my garage apartment and got out my stationery. It was a whole two hours until the Happy Hills Radio Theater, and I owed letters to both Mildred and Miss Hawkins, plus V-Mail to my sweet USO boys. I told myself I might get so involved in my letter-writing I'd forget all about the radio program. Fat chance, said the old animal brain.

Mildred's letter was on top. It was postmarked Boston and was short and to the point. She had moved back East and was living with her sister with whom she had "come to an understanding." She said she had hired "that nice young man I found for your grandmother's funeral service," to tend the graves over the summer and do the planting in the fall. "Seth MacKenzie, you remember?" She enclosed his address and spoke highly of his reliability. "You should contact him," she wrote, "regarding future arrangements. At my age, life is uncertain."

I was struck by the words "come to an understanding." I took that to mean there had been some sort of estrangement in the past. I knew that Mildred had moved to Tulsa because of some falling-out with her family, but she had never spoken of the details. I also knew she was married, or had been, because her mail at the boardinghouse came addressed to Mrs. Mildred Ashcroft. When I was impolite enough to ask her about it, she admitted she was divorced. A divorcée was rare in that day and time, especially one from Boston. I had always puzzled over Mildred. It's strange and wondrous how you can know a somebody for years and years, how they can save your life and tend your graves and still keep large pieces of themselves hidden away.

As I stared at the envelope, it was suddenly revealed to me what had happened. The understanding Mildred and her sister had come to was in regard to Mr. Ashcroft. The transgression Mildred had forgiven her sister was that of adultery. The sister and the husband had run off to the south of France—no, to the Florida Keys—and poor Mildred couldn't bear to face her family and friends. She got out a map, closed her eyes, and brought her finger down on a spot—Tulsa, Oklahoma.

Meanwhile the husband—the scoundrel—leaves the sister for a night-club singer in Key West. The sister goes back to Boston where she enters a convent and prays and practices self-flagellation. Years later Mildred wakes up one morning to find the hurt and humiliation gone. She writes to her sister and says, "We are but flesh, a wind that passeth away." So, they get an apartment together, near the Boston Common, and on the mild spring days they walk in grace and purpose along the banks of the Charles River. Mr. Ashcroft—the scoundrel—was run over and squashed flat by a 1939 Packard Eight Touring Car.

With this satisfying turn of events I realized that in my divining I'd got the husband mixed up with Willis Henderson and the sister with Sarah, and maybe Mildred herself with my momma. Not to mention that Packard Touring Car. This sort of confusion is one of the dangers of divining.

Miss Hawkins' letter was, by contrast, long and eventful. We corresponded on a regular basis—once a month or so—and she'd always make mention of Momma's activities.

. . . "Frances took three blues for her jelly and an Honorable Mention for her peach chutney. She was peeved about the latter."

. . . "Your mother is teaching the Sunday-school class. As you can imagine, all the little Presbyterian children now abound with godliness."

. . . "We celebrated your mother's 70th last Saturday with a surprise potluck at the Community House. Frances was truly surprised and pleased! She thought she was coming to roll bandages."

. . . "Sarah and Willis have another new baby. Eight pounds two ounces. Another boy."

. . . "Your sister Fidelity was here, looking prosperous and bearing gifts. A kitchen stove and a big Servel refrigerator. I gave her your address so maybe you'll hear from her. She's just as pretty as a picture, Cleo, the very image of you."

She would always end her letters with something like, "And how is Jessie's history progressing?" My response was usually about how I had to do more research on the Creek Indians, or how busy I was with the war effort.

In my letters to Miss Hawkins I tended to put myself in a good light. I knew this apprisal of activities worked both ways, so I wrote Miss Hawkins what I wanted Momma to hear. I had written only one letter direct, shortly after I arrived in California. There was no answer and I hadn't expected one, but I remembered what Rosemary said so many years before about folks feeling easier as regards their children if they could locate them on a map. In this case the map was a problem. I knew the people in Robina, Oklahoma, would figure the whole Japanese navy was lined up along the west coast, ready to come ashore any minute and perform unspeakable deeds on the female population. I wanted to dispel that notion, so I described to Momma how Glendale was miles and miles inland, and protected by high mountains and the National Guard.

Just because she wasn't speaking to me didn't mean she wouldn't worry.

Robina, like everyplace else in the country, had sent most of her sound young men to war, including my caretaker, Sonny Tipton. Sonny's wife, Agnes Mary, who was about eight months along at the time, moved back with her mother, and Miss Hawkins took it upon herself to make arrangements for the goldfish. Moby's tank now sat on a special stand in the library, where she did her food dance for patrons and tripled in size. Miss Hawkins wrote, "I declare, this fish is trying to grow into her name." Sonny was wounded in the eight-day siege of Bastogne. When he got home he wrote me about the farm. It was a thoughtful letter. He told how he'd seen so much of God's good land blackened and laid waste, and how he wanted to have a hand in the earth's renewal. He said he planned to take some agricultural courses over at Tahlequah. I couldn't imagine what he thought he'd raise. Gideon himself said it was only fit for strewberries. I slept on it for a couple nights, then wrote back to say he and Agnes Mary were welcome to live there. They could have all the profits on whatever crop he could get to grow, and pay me whatever rent he thought was fair. I said I was truly sorry but I could not bring myself to sell it, that it wasn't mine to sell. I told him the land belonged rightfully to my grandmother's people, and I was just holding it in trust.

When I looked up from my woolgathering, it was ten till. I had a choice. I could get busy and answer my mail—and stay out of trouble. I could fix a sandwich and settle down in front of the Motorola in the Malones' den. Or I could shower and get all gussied up and take myself in person over to Hollywood. The choice was mine.

29

I PARKED ACROSS THE STREET FROM THE radio station, marched in the front door, and told the receptionist I was from Happy Hills Motors and had a message for Mr. Endicott. She pointed to a door that said NO ADMITTANCE. "Down the hall on your left," she said, and went back to her magazine. Just like that. And I could have been an espionage agent, sent to blow up communications in Los Angeles.

I walked slowly down the hall, listening to my high heels click on the cement floor and my heart bang against my ribs. "This is stupid," I told myself. "I know," I answered. I came to some double doors on the left, with little windowpanes at eye level. Inside was a large room with glassed-in cubicles at its center. I opened one of the doors and slipped in. A man wearing earphones stepped out of one of the cubicles, cupped his hands, and called out, "Three minutes!" I moved into the shadows and tried to blend into the wall.

Robby appeared from somewhere, running a comb through his hair, and smiled at someone out of my line of vision. He was still the best-looking man I'd ever seen in magazines or real life. He was dressed to the nines in a pale blue double-breasted suit, tie with handkerchief to match, white shoes with dark wing tips, and a standard-issue California tan. Mercy!

He went into a cubicle opposite the man with the earphones, smoothed his tie, leaned forward on one elbow, and cupped a hand around his ear. A red light went on and there was the sound of a car horn, and a motor starting up. The man with the earphones pointed to Robby.

"That," said Robby, his hand still cupped over one ear, "is the sound of a 1941 De Soto sedan."

Then you could hear a lot of people laughing, having a good time. You could make out the voices of a man, a woman, and a couple of kids.

"And that," said Robby, "is the sound of happy people—a family.

At Happy Hills Motors, we sell our cars to families . . . to people. People are individuals. Individuals live in different sorts of houses, have different numbers of children, eat different flavors of ice cream, and . . . have different problems with their budgets."

He went on and on about the glories and sorrows of being an individual. Didn't say one word about that De Soto, not even how many miles it got to the gallon. It was clear that Happy Hills Motors didn't sell automobiles, they sold financing. Fifty dollars down and ten dollars a month for the rest of your natural life. Son of a gun! The Reverend was still in the collection business.

When he finished, he told the man in the earphones that "wrapped it up," and he'd see him next week. He waved to somebody, gave a sweeping bow, and started toward the double doors. I inched down the wall, further into the shadows.

He squinted in my direction. "Can I help you?"

I took a deep breath. "Robby?" I whispered, and moved into the light.

He paled and ducked his head. "Cleo?"

I nodded.

He smiled ever so slightly and held his hands up in front of his face, the long elegant fingers spread wide. He said, "I trust, little sister, you do not have your trumpet with you."

We went to a bar on Melrose Avenue, "a quiet place where we can talk," he said. It was quiet, and dark and smoky, with a lot of imitation tropical plants sitting around, and giant seashells, and a fishnet dangling from the ceiling. A man in a Hawaiian shirt was noodling a Cole Porter tune on the piano.

I slid into a booth and Robby whispered something to the waiter, who came back a couple minutes later with two wineglasses. I laughed. No question in my mind as to what we were drinking.

Robby lifted his glass and clinked it against mine. "To old King Solomon," he said.

I took a sip, the first port I'd tasted in seventeen and a half years. I looked at him carefully and said, "You're not mad at me?"

He chuckled. "No, little sister, I'm not mad at you. It was an honest misunderstanding all around. I thought because of your—ah—enthusiasm, you'd be interested in something other than the missionary position. But you were—as you so eloquently pointed out—a farm girl, and you assumed . . ."

I felt my cheeks warming up and broke in to change the subject. "You're not preaching anymore?"

He lit a cigarette and leaned back in the booth. "Noooo," he said. "I decided the good Lord was trying to tell me I didn't have the true calling. The instrument he chose to deliver that message was very convincing."

"You are still mad at me."

He tapped his front teeth. "Only when I remove my partial."

"I'm sorry, Robby, I really am. The rest of your face looks good, just as good as ever."

He took my hand and ran my finger over the bridge of his nose. "Feel that bump?"

"Just barely. I can feel it but I can't see it. Honest to God, I'm so sorry. I thought . . ." I pulled back my hand, which was now burning like my cheeks. I said, "I still have your teeth in a little velvet box."

"I beg your pardon?"

"Rosemary and I went back to the vestry that night. You were gone, but we found your teeth."

"And why did you return? To give me another whack for good measure?"

I squirmed around on the leather seat. I could feel the sweat on the backs of my legs. After a big swig of port I admitted I'd thought he was dead. "I thought I'd killed you. I couldn't feel a pulse or a heartbeat, and there was all that blood . . ."

"So you and the mighty midget came back to dispose of the remains?"

I nodded. "We meant to weigh you down with rocks and put you in the duck pond. It was said to be bottomless."

He pretended shock. "Hardly a Christian burial, Cleo. Hardly the proper ceremony for a man of the cloth."

I squirmed again. "Would you tell me something?"

"Depends."

"Why did you put the bottle back in the file cabinet, and wash and dry the glasses? You couldn't have felt much like tidying up. Why did you bother to do that?"

He shrugged. "I hoped it would appear I'd been abducted. I wanted to leave signs of a struggle, not a party."

"But why?"

"Because I took the cash box with me, goose, the fund for God's poor. Lila knew where it was kept. She would tell the police it was missing."

"That part wasn't in the papers."

"I know. Curious."

"You saw the papers?"

"Of course. I was in the boardinghouse. Dear Mrs. Figgs furnished me with sustenance and the news of the day."

"But there was no sign of you. And she was all broken up—had crying spells and everything. Took to her bed. We had cold cuts for a month."

"You had cold cuts. I had chicken broth, which does not require the use of one's incisors."

"You mean she was pretending? Figgy?"

He rubbed his chin and gazed up into the fishnet. "A natural actress, Mrs. Figgs. A woman in love. Splendid combination under the circumstances. I stayed in her room, which, if you recall, no one was allowed to enter, and she brought in a physician to tend my wounds. A physician who was no longer licensed to practice medicine."

"Did she know that I . . ."

"Oh no, little sister, of course not. I told her a rousing story about masked gunmen—big brutes who'd broken in and were stealing the Lord's coffers. I said I'd had supper with you then came back to the vestry to do some paperwork. I said I'd caught these ruffians in the act of burglary and had done my best to wrest God's bounty from their evil grasp." He rubbed his chin again. "I believe I said there were four of them."

"But why didn't she tell the police?"

"I convinced her that publicity of that nature would damage my career in the ministry. I told her I wanted to start afresh in a new place. I implied we could start afresh together."

"So what happened?"

"She loaned me the money to go to Seattle and have my face repaired. She had old friends there with whom I could stay until she settled her affairs and joined me."

I nodded, remembering how poor old Figgy used to watch for the postman, the look she'd get when the telephone rang. I said, "She didn't join you."

He said, "I didn't go to Seattle."

"What was her first name?"

He shrugged. "Dearest . . . darling . . . sweetheart . . . muffin . . . Most women are like puppies, they respond to any and all endearments." He grinned and added quickly. "Except you, of course, Cleo."

"Sure thing," I said. "Little sister? Goose?"

"Marks of respect and genuine affection."

I just looked at him.

"So how did you find me?" he asked. I told him how Rosemary had recognized his voice on the radio. He looked pleased. "It is still distinctive, isn't it? What do you think of the commercials?"

I shrugged. "I don't know anything about commercials."

"Perhaps not, but you have a discerning mind and a good ear. I mean, do they—ah—work for you? Do they cause you to want to hurry on down to Happy Hills Motors?"

I thought for a minute, gave the question serious consideration, then I said, "You're persuasive, but it seems to me you limit yourself to customers with financial problems. You know, folks who can't get a loan at the bank. Seems to me you ought to say something about the car." He was playing close attention and I warmed to my subject. "Take that '41 De Soto, for example. If it's in good condition that's one fine automobile you've got there, a good all-around family car. It's got a four-speed semiautomatic transmission. The wife would like that. If you talked about the car you might get somebody in that could afford to buy it."

Robby frowned. "We make most of our profit on the paper we carry, and the repos."

"A few cash sales can't hurt. And it would make Happy Hills sound like a higher-class place."

He sat back in the booth and looked gravely insulted. "You mean it sounds like a low-class place?"

I was sorry I'd opened my mouth. "You asked me what I thought, Robby."

He smiled and I saw he'd been pretending, that he knew exactly what kind of place it was. He said, "I'd forgotten there are people in this world who give honest answers." He glanced down at his empty glass, motioned to the waiter, and held up two fingers.

I looked at my watch and shook my head. "I have to go to work."

He called to the waiter to never mind, and turned back to me. "Work?"

"I play my horn three nights a week at the Sundowner in Studio City. It's a bar."

He gave a condescending little smile. "Still at it, huh?"

"It's a living." What a dumb thing to say. Made me sound like a somebody with no aspirations to improve herself. Still playing my horn at the same old stand, for the same old twelve-and-a-half cents. But I sure didn't want to tell him I was a tomato packer.

"Ah," he sighed. "And I too have an appointment." He turned up his palms as if to say it couldn't be helped . . . such is life . . . two ships that pass in the night and all that. He pulled out his billfold and put money on the table, then touched the wedding band on my right hand. "I see that you are a widow?"

"Yes." I didn't want to talk about that.

"The war?"

I shook my head. "It's a long story, and we both have . . ." I searched my mind for something clever to say, something wry or world-worn or philosophical. I couldn't even think of a snappy Bible saying.

". . . promises to keep?" he finished for me.

We looked at each other while the piano man, who could read minds, noodled along on "Bewitched, Bothered and Bewildered." Neither of us blinked or looked away. I suppose we were trying to decide if it was worth it. It occurred to me that no sane person would take up with a man who admitted to treating a woman as shabbily as he had Figgy, not to mention the first Mrs. Endicott, who he said, straight out, he'd married for her money and hadn't even grieved when she went to her reward. Lord only knew how many Dearests and Darlings and Muffins there'd been since.

On the other hand, he hadn't lied about it, or tried to excuse himself. There was a wide streak of honesty in the Reverend, and he had a kind of merciless view into his own rotten character. I admired that.

For his part, surely he had grave reservations about a girl who'd bashed him senseless with her trumpet.

I looked at my watch again. "Well," I said.

"Well," he echoed. "And where are you living?"

"Glendale." I was about to reach in my pocketbook for pencil and paper so I could write down my address and telephone number.

"Out in the sticks."

"I like it," I said. "It's neighborly, reminds me of home." I inched along the leather seat, giving him time.

He stood up, smiled, and ran his hand through his hair. He said, "I have no doubt our paths will cross again."

That was the kiss-off if I'd ever heard it. George Brent telling Bette Davis he had other fish to fry.

On the way back to my car he talked on and on about the unseasonable weather we were having while I nodded and pondered the great mystery that is the human heart.

I *knew*. Oh, I knew what would have happened seventeen and a half years before if only I had been more wordly as regards matters of the flesh, if only there had not been that grievous misunderstanding when we pleasured each other in the vestry. I would have, without so much as a backward glance, abandoned all hope of a journey to Lhasa, along with my pure and uplifting love for Ed Shannon. I would have climbed into that big truck Robby meant to buy with the stolen church money, and I would have played "The Battle Hymn of the Republic" at tent meetings all along Route 66. And when we got to the Pacific Ocean and built our tabernacle on the cliffs, I would have stood behind an altar across from him just like he said, wearing a long white robe, disgracing myself and God Almighty while we made a vaudeville act out of the Song of Solomon. I would have done that at the risk of walking barefoot on hot coals throughout eternity.

I started up my car, turned on my chilliest voice, and helped Robby along with his weather report. "We tend to expect too much of June," I said. "We always forget that June is a gloomy month here."

And I drove off, my head high, didn't even look in the rearview mirror. Mam said she had never once lifted a hand to a dead horse. Good advice.

30

ROSEMARY AND I WERE AT OUR STATION
when the news came, the news the whole world had been waiting for
since August 6. The conveyor belt stopped dead and we could hear the
yelling and screaming from over in Puree and Sauce. Then Mrs.
Thornton came to the middle of the footbridge and stood there with
her hands raised for attention. Tears were streaming down her cheeks
and she was laughing—first time ever to my recollection.

"It's over," she shouted. "Praise the Lord, it's over!" She wiped her
eyes and said the company was giving us the rest of the day off at full
pay so we could attend our respective houses of worship to thank God
for granting us victory.

We didn't go to church as directed. Our whole neighborhood went
down to Brand Boulevard and we marched up and down, singing
songs, hugging and kissing wild-eyed strangers, dancing in the street,
filling the air with all those hats that had to be swept up the next day.

At some point I got separated from the Malones. After a time I'd
had all the frenzy I could manage. My feet had been stomped until I
was almost crippled, my lips were raw from vigorous kissing, and the
two top buttons were torn right off of my good linen blouse. I limped
over to a doorway and sat down on the stoop to gather my breath and
my sanity.

While I sat there, quiet and apart, watching the celebration, I remembered what I'd read in the *Los Angeles Times* editorial section.
The writer said the war was over when we dropped the bomb on Hiro-
shima. He said it took our leaders nine more days and another bomb
to make certain. He was reminded of what had happened in World
War I, and how we waited to end it so it could be the eleventh hour of
the eleventh day of the eleventh month. He wondered how many people died for the sake of symmetry. I remembered what Mam had said
about General Watie, how the War between the States had been over
for almost two months before he surrendered his Creek regiments. *I
don't know what took him so long,* Mam said. Mam said you never

brought anybody around to your way of thinking by killing them. Mam said whites and Creeks bleed the same color blood, scream in the same language, have the same salt in their tears. I knew in my heart that at that very moment there was a dark-eyed woman crouched in a doorway in Nagasaki wondering if the leaders were ever going to learn to talk to each other. If she and I could sit down together, woman to woman, I'd have to tell her—honestly—that I didn't hold much hope for our leaders when I couldn't even make peace with my own momma.

A marching band came down the street, playing "It's a Long Way to Tipperary." The trumpets were flat, all four of them. I was cheered by that, by those flat, off-key notes. *If the trumpet give an uncertain sound, who will prepare himself to the battle?* I closed my eyes and prayed that the world would spawn generation unto generation of uncertain trumpet players.

After the tubas and the bass drum passed by, I was greatly relieved to see Raymond waving to me from across the street. I stumbled through the crowd, clutching the top of my linen blouse, puzzling on the effects of peace.

We lost our jobs at the cannery in late September. Mrs. Thornton said we didn't lose them, that we'd just been holding them until the rightful owners came home. It was beyond me why any man would want to come back to that conveyor belt when he had the chance to go to college and improve himself on the G.I. Bill. Raymond said after all the misery our boys had been through, probably some of them just wanted to do something mindless for a while.

That suited me fine. I was relieved to be forced into a change. I'd been dragging my feet because of the regular paycheck, which has been known to cause foot-dragging for fifty years and more. And I was happy to be out of there before we got to pumpkins and yellow squash.

Not even a week later, another rightful owner came for my three nights at the Sundowner.

Raymond said business at Western Auto Supply would go right through the roof now that Detroit was back to making automobiles, so Rosemary decided to stay home and be a housewife. I went to the employment office, where I filled out a mess of forms and learned I had about as many useful skills as ten dead flies. Here I was, less than a month away from my thirty-fourth birthday, out of work, unmarried with no prospects, no visible family ties, and no skills.

I took this as a sign it was time to resume my long-overdue journey to Lhasa.

In the next two months I did research in the public library. When I left home in 1927, I'd planned to follow Alexandra David-Neel's own footsteps, whose footsteps themselves were a source of confusion. She made five tries before she finally got to Lhasa, and the map showed all five routes—dots, dashes, asterisks, straight lines, that sort of thing, intersecting and paralleling at certain points. In 1927, I'd meant to start from Peking, buy a mule and hire a holy man, then follow the route to Lanchow, due south to Suifu, west to Likiang and northerly to Giamda, which was near my destination. I was a good deal younger then and more heedless. By 1945 I'd developed occasional prudence and a more practical sense of geography. Peking was either sixteen hundred or two thousand miles from Lhasa, depending on your crow.

This time I meant to make my approach by way of Calcutta, from where it was almost a straight shot to Gyantze; then you looped back to Lhasa. As this route also entailed crossing the Himalayas, I began to spend time climbing in the San Gabriel Mountains outside Glendale to get myself in shape.

The major difficulty, as Libby the travel agent explained, was that Tibet was closed to all foreign visitors. I could get a permit for Calcutta but not for Tibet. One of my main sources of information, besides Libby and Alexandra's book, was an article in the *National Geographic* magazine that told of how a certain Lieutenant Colonel Tolstoy went to Lhasa looking for a new route to China after the Burma Road was lost. His "passport" was a letter from President Roosevelt and lavish gifts for the Dalai Lama.

Jody said, "Maybe President Truman will give you a letter, Cleo. And you can have my arrowheads to take to the king."

The Malones, except Jody, thought I was plain crazy, and said so most every night at the supper table, when I wasn't away camping and freezing my butt in the San Gabriels. For Jody, I was a subject of awe and reverence, and I, in return, adored him. He was a serious little boy, quiet as rocks, intense as August sun. Like my Eddy.

I said, "That's sweet of you, Jody. But he's not the king, remember? He's the living Buddha, he's like God."

"He's just a kid," said R.J., who was fifteen at the time and knew everything. His mother told him not to talk with his mouth full. He swallowed and gave a majestic shrug. "You told us yourself the Dalai Lama's not much older than Jody. Everybody knows that God has a long white beard."

I set about to explain reincarnation, which caused Rosemary to shift in her chair and push seconds all around. I ignored her discomfort and prattled on in that way folks do when they've harvested a new crop of knowledge and haven't yet baled it up tight. I told how, when the thirteenth Dalai Lama died, the holy elders investigated thousands of omens and traveled hundreds of miles before they found his reincarnated soul in a two-year-old peasant child.

R.J. speared a carrot and pointed it at me. "So this two-year-old became the fourteenth Dalai Lama?"

I nodded.

"And he had the same soul as the thirteenth guy had?"

"That's the way I understand it."

"And the twelfth? And the eleventh? All those old souls crowded into this two-year-old peasant boy?"

"I think it's the same soul each time," I said, hearing my voice start to pull up lame.

"So the soul remains the same even after living in all these different bodies?"

I frowned. That didn't sound quite right. R.J. had a real gift for making a person feel weak-minded. "The point is," I said, "that earthly life isn't important to the Buddhists. They have no fear of death because they know they'll be born again as something else."

"Like what?"

"Like even the Dalai Lama. It depends on how pious you've been. Everything is a reincarnation of something or somebody, maybe even somebody you know. If a fly falls into a cup of tea, it must be rescued because it may be your old grandmother. And in wintertime, they break the ice in pools to save the fish."

R.J. gave me a cagey look. "Why?"

Jody said, "To keep them from freezing, dumb-head."

Rosemary said, "Who wants dessert?"

R.J. folded his arms on his chest. "If the fish freezes, maybe it'll be your dopey little brother next time around. If the fly drowns, it'll just come back as something else." He spread his arms wide. "If it's a pious fly maybe it'll turn into an eagle. Come on, Cleo, if they're not afraid of dying, why go around picking flies out of the teacups?"

"It's fudge brownies," said Rosemary, "with whipped cream."

"Good point!" said Raymond, and he beamed proudly on the family's snotty candidate for law school.

I said I'd love a fudge brownie with whipped cream, and that maybe I'd have to read up some more on Buddhism.

Jody started tagging along with me to the library, and was allowed to go on one weekend campout in the San Gabriels, but when it got to the point where his supper-table conversation centered exclusively on things Lhasan—when he lost his passion for model airplanes and forgot to listen to "The Lone Ranger"—Rosemary began to fret in earnest.

"It's just a phase," said Raymond. "Don't worry about it."

I said, "I don't see what the fuss is about."

Rosemary rose up to her full five feet and said she did not mean to raise an atheist. I said Buddhists weren't atheists, that Buddha was the same as God. She said she was not going to argue with me over her son's religious education, and she'd thank me to mind my own business. I watched her just long enough to see the skin whiten around her mouth; then I put my tail between my legs and slunk off to my garage apartment. This was the first time in our long friendship that Rosemary had spoken harshly to me. Another campout had been planned for that Saturday, but the she-wolf said her cub would stay home.

After that we began to tiptoe around each other. She was polite. I was someplace between aloof and humble—the uneasy stance of a hypocrite. I spent more time at my own place but still came in for supper. Then one evening when we were cleaning up, Jody came into the kitchen and poked his mother on the shoulder. She turned around. He stepped back, brought up his thumbs, stuck out his tongue, hissed, then gave a low bow.

"What on earth . . . ?"

I sighed. "It's a Tibetan greeting."

"You stop that this minute! You hear me, Jody Malone?"

Jody went on bowing and hissing.

I explained to Rosemary how this was a mark of respect. "The higher the respect, the lower the bow, the longer the tongue, and the louder the hissing."

She gave me a stony look, threw down her dishtowel, and stalked out of the room.

Then there was the rice. Jody took to carrying it around in his pants pockets and would throw a few grains over his shoulder from time to time to appease the evil spirits. And the hornet he trapped and kept in his room in a fruit jar so he could observe the changeover. And the Tibetan buttered tea he brewed up early one Sunday morning: Boil a handful of leaves, add a piece of yak butter the size of your fist (Jody substituted oleo, yaks being scarce in Glendale), a tablespoon of soda, and a handful of salt. Churn and serve scalding hot.

I told Rosemary, "I swear to you, he's not getting it from me. He's doing his own research, he's really interested."

Rosemary hooded her eyes. "Um-hum," she said.

"It's a phase," Raymond insisted. "It will play itself out."

Things came to a head over a Friday-night pot roast. Jody sliced off a hunk and began separating it into stringy pieces.

Rosemary said, "Don't play with your food."

Jody said, "I been reading about the Porus."

I cleared my throat and gave him a little warning look.

"What's that?" asked Raymond, who was always attentive to his children.

Jody frowned. "I guess you could say they're something like under- takers. Would you say that, Cleo?"

I explained that the Porus people were similar to the Untouchables of India. I said I didn't think the supper table was the place to discuss the Porus.

Rosemary put down her fork and gave me a look that would have wilted a cabbage, one that said clearly, *I am the mother here. I will decide on what's fit conversation.* "Go on, Jody."

He pushed his meat around in the gravy. "Well, you see," he said, importantly, "they don't bury their people in Tibet. . . ."

Rosemary stiffened. "I thought you were talking about India. . . ."

Jody went right on. "The Porus take the dead bodies up on a hill- top. They have these real sharp knives, see, and they cut the dead bod- ies into little pieces—" He demonstrated on a hunk of pot roast.

"—blood and flesh and guts and bones all over . . . so they can be devoured by the vultures."

After a silence like no other, Jody was banished to his room. I said I guessed I'd get started on the dishes and was finishing up when Raymond and Rosemary came in and sat down, stiff as pine boards, at the table. Usually, after supper on Friday nights, they took mixed drinks into the den, where they held hands and listened to their cowboy program. But here they were in the kitchen, a grim posse of two.

Raymond said they wanted to talk to me. I hung up the dishtowel and sat down. Before I even got my elbows on the table, Rosemary said in an aggrieved voice that she wanted me to stop talking about my trip. "Especially in front of Jody," she said. "I just can't allow it any longer." I opened my mouth to protest my innocence—well, my partial innocence—but she went on. "You're giving him dangerous ideas. It just isn't healthy for a boy of his age to be caught up in . . . well, in foreign ideas and practices."

I thought about Momma and the Egyptians. I said, "He's *exploring* ideas, Rosemary. He's learning to use his mind."

Rosemary held up her palm. "I'm not going to discuss it. He's abusing his mind, that's what he's doing. I mean it, Cleo, I don't want to hear another word about Lhasa spoken in this household. Or the Buddhists!" She leaned forward and looked me dead in the eye. "You know what he asked for for Christmas? A prayer wheel! A Buddhist prayer wheel!"

Raymond pulled out his pipe, filled it, and tapped it down. Rosemary looked at him impatiently. He lit the pipe and gazed around the kitchen.

She put her hand on his arm. "Well?" she said.

He started. "What's that? Oh. Oh, yes." I could see his discomfort. Raymond was as out of place in an argument as Noah's dove at a cockfight. "Ah, Cleo?"

"Yes, Raymond."

"Rosemary and I have given this a lot of thought." He looked at her and she nodded. "We think you're doing this—this Lhasa business— because you don't have anything else on your horizon. We could say you're bobbing around on the surface of life."

"No plan for your future," Rosemary translated.

"No goals," added Raymond.

"Lhasa's been my goal since I was fifteen years old. You know that, Rosemary."

"But you were a child then," said Raymond. "What's that old saying? I put childish things away . . ."

" 'When I became a man, I put away childish things.' First Corinthians 13:11. You may have noticed, Raymond, that I have not yet become a man."

He lit his pipe again, filling the kitchen with great puffs of smoke. It wasn't easy to have a conversation with Raymond. There were these long dead silences while he tried to get that pipe going. Finally, he put down his lighter, satisfied, and said, "Rosemary and I think you should go to secretarial school. If you learn typing and shorthand, I think I can get you on at Western Auto. Maybe in the advertising department. One of the secretaries is due to retire next spring. If you worked hard you could have your speed up by then."

"Who's retiring?"

"No one you know."

"Humor me. What's her name?"

He looked puzzled. "Adams. Phoebe Adams."

"How old is she?"

He waved his pipe around. "Oh, I don't know, late fifties I'd guess. Why? What does that have to do with it?"

"*Miss* Adams?"

"Yes. Miss Adams."

"How long's she been there?"

He laughed. "I don't know. Forever, I suppose."

"And she's been a secretary forever? Her goal in life was to take dictation and type letters about auto supplies?"

Rosemary said, "Don't be like that, Cleo. It wouldn't be forever. There are a lot of good, eligible men back from the war. You'd find somebody you liked if you'd just let yourself. You could get married and have a child of your own. Oh, Cleo! There comes a time when you have to settle down and accept life on its own terms."

I looked down at my hands, twisted my wedding ring around, and thought about that. It seemed to me I had accepted life's terms with considerable grace under the circumstances.

Raymond reached over and squeezed my shoulder. "Wait a minute, Rosie. Maybe we haven't looked at this matter from Cleo's point of view. Why? Why, Cleo, is it so important for you to go to Lhasa?"

I stared down at the tabletop, white and pristine. There was no grain there to harbor beasts and mythical birds that would help you puzzle out difficult questions. I had never thought about why it was important. It was something that had always been there for me, since that day when Miss Hawkins handed me the book and said, "It has your name written all over it, Cleo." When I commenced to read it on the way home, letting the mule have his head, Alexandra's words went straight to my heart. *I craved to go beyond the garden gate, to follow the road that passed it by, and to set out for the unknown.* I knew right then one day I'd go to Lhasa. It was a given. You don't question a given.

I pushed back my chair. "I won't say anything more to Jody." I looked at Rosemary and added, "But you'll have to tell him it's your idea." I got up and started for the back door, feeling like a somebody who's been sent to her room to think on her sins.

"Good night, Cleo," Rosemary called after me. "Oh, Cleo, we *do* love you!"

When people tell you they love you right after they've hurt your feelings, they deserve to be ignored. "Raymond," I said.

"Yes, Cleo?"

"When you see Phoebe Adams, would you ask her something?"

He brightened and leaned forward. "Sure thing," he said, probably imagining I wanted to know about her duties or qualifications.

"Would you ask her if being a secretary at Western Auto is all she ever wanted out of life. Just ask her. Ask her if she would have gone to Lhasa if she'd had the chance."

Raymond chuckled. "She'll probably say, 'Where's Lhasa?'"

"Yeah," I said. "That's what I mean."

31

THE MALONES SAW ME OFF AT THE TRAIN
station in Glendale. Jody's eyes filled up with tears he could not shed
in front of his smart-mouthed brother, and Rosemary and I hugged
each other so tight I feared for our breath.

We had not spoken about what was between us. We pretended it
was sisterly concern for my welfare that caused the rip in the fabric of
our friendship. We knew better. We knew it was jealousy and resent-
ment on her part and loneliness for long dead children on mine. Nothing evil, just human, but neither of us had the courage to sit down over
a pot of coffee and talk it out. By the time I returned from my journey
we would have forgiven each other; you can mend the rip if the cloth is
strong. Jody would've gone back to his model airplanes and the Lone
Ranger, or on to other passions. Maybe I'd be gone a couple years or
more—who knew? By that time he'd discover girls, and even science.
No question he had the right stuff for both. When I came back I'd just
be his mother's oldest friend again. I'd be no threat to family harmony
or thief of affections.

I went to San Francisco a week early and treated myself to a stay at
the St. Francis Hotel, which Libby, the travel agent, said was grand
and elegant. She said more old money stayed there than at the Mark
Hopkins, which was for tourists. I was not a tourist. I was an honest
traveler, a sojourner, and since I'd started collecting the Lhasa money
nineteen years before, I figured it qualified as old.

There was no question the St. Francis was elegant, by any standards,
but it didn't have anything on the Mayo in Tulsa. No Blue Boy on the
wall. No Pinkie. And the drapes didn't even match the bedspread. But
the room didn't matter, as I didn't plan to spend much time there. I
meant to see the sights, and keep myself in shape by trekking up and
down all those steep hills until time for my liner to embark for the
Orient. How I loved the feel of those words on my tongue, and spoke
them at every opportunity. I told the desk clerk and the bellboy and
the waiters and the maid who came to do up my room and the gentle-

men in the bar where I had a Manhattan cocktail every evening before supper. "I am stopping at the St. Francis until Saturday, when my liner embarks for the Orient."

Miss High and Mighty herself come to call, Mam would've said, and we would've laughed ourselves silly. In truth, my "liner" was a freighter that took on a few passengers in addition to its regular cargo. That was the cheapest way to go. Of course there'd be no orchestra or badminton on deck, or gambling tables, which was just as well considering my woeful lack of skill as a poker player, but Libby said the food was as good as on the *Queen Mary*.

Libby, a nice middle-aged woman who wore her spectacles on a chain and used a long silver cigarette holder, had taken a personal interest in my trip, above and beyond the duties of a travel agent. She said she had never known a lone woman to undertake a trip so fraught with danger. She arranged for me to meet with a man from the British Consulate in Calcutta who would try to get permission for me to go on to Lhasa. No guarantees. Just the possibility. Which is about all you can expect of life. On the brightest, clearest day of the year, it can always cloud up and rain bullfrogs and yearlings.

The hills of San Francisco were surely good for the leg muscles and the diaphragm; the latter had gone a bit flabby since I'd stopped playing my horn. I caused something of a stir in the lobby of the St. Francis when I trudged in and out in my war-surplus outfit. But the raised eyebrows came down after I explained to the desk clerk that I was in training for the Himalayas. I had a shoulder pack filled with twenty-seven pounds of personal gear, which was the exact same amount Lieutenant Colonel Tolstoy carried. Alexandra had little more than her faith when she set out from the Mission House in China—just tea and a revolver and gold and black ink for her hair, all concealed in her peasant robes. I didn't figure she would think less of me for being properly equipped.

On the night of January 22nd, I'd been at the St. Francis for five days. I'd returned early from my daily hike and was all showered and dolled up and ready to go down to the bar for my before-dinner cocktail. I checked my appetite and decided it wasn't time yet. I allowed myself only one drink at the bar, not wanting to give the wrong impression to the management or the other patrons. So, I called room service and asked them to send up a scotch-and-soda and some salted peanuts. This was the first time I had availed myself of this luxury. I expected it would be dear, my only experience being with Willis Henderson at the Mayo, where he pulled out a fistful of bills every time he answered the door.

I was wearing one of the two dresses I'd brought with me—a black sheath that folded up like a handkerchief and you could rinse out in the washbasin. Libby, who helped me with my travel wardrobe, said if you were strapped for time you could get in the shower, dress and all, then drip yourself dry in the sun. I'd pulled my mess of shiny black hair into a tidy bun on the nape of my neck and wore only pale lipstick in the way of makeup. I looked like a somebody much too pampered and fragile to get to base camp in the Himalayas.

After my drink came I settled down in the easy chair by the windows and went over my itinerary, which was unnecessary as I could quote it like the Old Testament, but it gave me pleasure to read it over, to listen to the soft music of the words, words you'd play on a flute or an oboe. Phari Dzong . . . T'ang-la . . . Chomo Lhari . . . Lhasa . . . Laaah-Saaaaaah . . .

I sipped the scotch-and-soda, and watched myself get down off my mule and gather fagots for the hot buttered tea I would prepare for myself and the holy man. We are outside the village of Dochen, beside the Ram Tso Lake, which reflects the great wild peaks of the Himalayas and is lined with thousands of geese along the shore.

I say a roasted goose would surely be tasty for our supper. Since we left Gangtok we've had nothing but barley flour and yak-butter tea. But the holy man reminds me that all life is sacred in Tibet. Buddhists are vegetarians. They also abstain from strong drink. At least in theory, says my holy man. He tells about the Buddhist monks who must keep not only the vows of vegetarianism and abstinence, but also those of celibacy.

He stirs the fire and tells this story: Once an evil spirit caused a particularly pious monk to choose between the three sins. After much anguished consideration, the monk decided he could more easily take a drink than he could kill an animal or lie with a woman. So he drank and became quite drunk. In this condition he lost all control and took a woman. Then, drunk on love, he killed a sheep to make a feast for her.

Who could help but admire a people with such a highly developed sense of humor?

279

We push on, enduring cold and deprivation with stout hearts. We are good company for each other. He says I am a brave traveler. Now we are camped just five miles from Lhasa and the Dalai Lama has sent an escort to greet us. There in that vast wilderness, a telephone rings. It was like when you wake up in the middle of a dream and can't get your bearings. One foot's still in the dream and the other's gone lame.

I picked up the receiver. "Hello?"

"Cleo?"

"Where are you?"

"In the lobby?"

"What are you doing here?"

"I want to talk to you."

"How did you know I was here?"

"Rosemary told me."

"How did you find Rosemary?"

"I went to the Sundowner. They gave me the number."

"Took your sweet time."

"I know. I had . . . I had matters to settle, of a personal nature."

"That's too bad. I'm leaving Saturday. I'm going to Lhasa."

"Yes, Rosemary told me. May I come up and try to talk you out of it?"

"No."

"Will you meet me in the bar?"

"No. I've not thought about you for six months. Go on home."

"Ah, little sister, surely you'll allow me to wish you Godspeed?"

"Consider it wished."

"Cleo? Cleo, please. Just five minutes? For old times' sake?"

So I met Robby in the bar, like I knew I would when I first heard his golden voice on the telephone. He didn't recognize me at first. When he did, he came over and without saying one word took the pins out of my tidy hairdo. An intimate act, right there in the public bar of the grand and elegant St. Francis Hotel. A gentleman I'd had my Manhattan with for two nights running shrugged and turned back to his drink.

Robby helped me onto a bar stool and ordered port. He took my hand in both of his and kissed it while he looked up at me out of those lilac blue eyes. He said, "We can go to Tibet later, my love."

We? I felt myself begin to tremble like some rabbit. Rabbits spend their whole lives trembling, waiting for a hawk to drop out of the sky.

"I'll take you to Lhasa, Cleo. Or Shangri-la. Or Xanadu. Or the moon if I can book passage."

This romantic declaration from a man who wouldn't even ask for my telephone number six months ago. A man who went on and on about the weather while I suffered the miseries of a woman scorned. I said, "What was the personal matter you had to tend to? If I may ask?"

He let go of my hand and picked up his glass. "A frayed and tattered commitment of the heart."

I thought about all those probable Muffins scattered around in his past history. "I didn't think you were the sort to be troubled by commitments—of the heart or otherwise."

"Ah, little sister. That was another Robin Endicott."

I looked him up and down. "And this is a leopard with brand new spots?"

He sighed. "Once before I asked you to come with me. To share my life. I'm asking you again. Marry me, Cleo."

I almost fell off the stool. I expected him to try to get me into bed, which in truth would probably not be much of a chore, and to engage in a short affair to more or less finish off what we'd started so many years before in the vestry. But marriage? Robby?

I said, "This recent commitment of the heart. Was it—ah—sanctified? Was there issue, so to speak?"

He shook his head. "No to both questions." He smiled and took my hand again. "I was waiting for you, little sister. What extraordinary children we'll have! What coloring! What bones!"

"But I don't know anything about you." Of course I knew him. I knew him all too well. I stared into the mirror behind the bar. I said, "I think I'm dreaming. I think I'll wake up soon."

He frowned and rubbed his chin. "Let's see, how can I plead my case? I'm in excellent health for a man of forty-five. There's no baldness in the family. You know about my teeth, but I recently got a permanent bridge so there's no partial in a glass on the bedside table. What else? Ah, my tangible assets. I'm solvent, have a thriving used-car business. I own a small apartment house in West Los Angeles. Four units, I live in one of them; two bedrooms, two full baths, Spanish style, wood beams, nice little garden patio. But if you don't like it, we'll find something else. My parents are alive and well and living in

Philadelphia. I have three older sisters who doted on me and spoiled me rotten. I'm being honest, little sister. What else? I can't cook, can't even make decent coffee, and I'm not handy around the house, but I'm neat in my personal habits. I don't leave dirty socks about. I put the top on the toothpaste and the lid down on the toilet." He smiled. "My sisters' influence. What else? Oh yes, I'm thinking of running for public office."

"What sort of public office?"

"Councilman. Then . . ." He turned up his palms. "Then perhaps mayor . . . governor . . . president . . . King of Siam?"

"Oh, Robby."

"Why not? The new Christopher Robin Endicott has given up avarice, but not ambition."

I thought about that. I couldn't imagine Robby kissing babies and glad-handing prospective voters. He'd been a stern and unforgiving kind of preacher who'd caused weeping women to rip the flowers and feathers off their hats because fancy raiment was unsightly in the Lord's eyes. I didn't see that kind of high-handedness going over with voters. A servant of God is one thing, a servant of the People quite another.

"But why," I asked. "Why politics?"

He looked down at his empty glass, then up at me. "Perhaps we could continue this discussion in your room?"

"No," I said firmly. "I don't want to be distracted."

He waved at the bartender and pointed to our glasses. "It's this voice," he said. "A gift. I believe it was Mark—or perhaps Matthew—who said every good gift is from above. It's too late for me to go back on the stage, and I've lost my taste for the ministry. That leaves public service. It would be a sin to continue to use this voice to sell used cars when it could work as an instrument for the betterment of the people of California."

Ah, now he was beginning to sound like the old Robby. I half expected the pink spotlight to flood down and make a halo around his head. I said, "So you just throw your hat in the ring at City Hall?"

He looked disappointed. "You haven't been listening to the Happy Hills Radio Theater."

"True. I've been climbing up and down the San Gabriel Mountains to get ready for my journey. Besides, when I was all set to give you my telephone number, you just talked about the weather. And you . . ." I made my voice sonorous and put one hand on my breast. "You said, 'I have no doubt our paths will cross again.' Well, I just put you right out of my mind. I'm a practical woman."

He leaned over and whispered in my ear. "Our paths have crossed again. Come this way. Come with me. I love you, little sister. I need you as green grass needs rain and sunshine."

I hardened up my heart. How smoothly the words slipped off his tongue. He could as easily promise undying love for me as he could eternal life for a congregation or an automobile. I said, "So what did I miss on the Happy Hills Theater?"

He frowned and lit a cigarette. He said, "You didn't used to be cynical, Cleo."

I shook my head. "Just older and wiser. What did I miss?"

He shrugged. "Oh, I've included some current issues in the commercials. The transportation problem, principally, how our fair city needs a system to accommodate the rising number of drivers." He smiled, like someone about to get in mischief. "Then I do my part to assist in that increase. I talk about how people who work hard deserve to drive their own automobiles to the job—and not have to take the bus or the Red Car. Amazing thing, human nature! You tell a man he's entitled to something and he'll rush right out and get it, whether he wants it or not. Amazing! Anyway, I've been approached by some people who have a vested interest in freeways. They're impressed with my style, they call it." He made a banner with his hands. "Freeways for the Angels. How 'bout that for a slogan?"

Suddenly it all fell into place. "So, that's why you need a wife? Somebody to sit beside you at fund-raising dinners? And wave from platforms and convertibles?"

He looked genuinely hurt. "Ah, now, Cleo, you know if it was just any wife I needed, I'd have no problem locating one by noon tomorrow."

"What a modest man you are."

He looked me straight in the eye. "I am not a modest man. I have none of the traditional virtues. Save one."

"And what's that?"

"An honest woman at my side. If she will have me."

I glanced over toward the door that led into the lobby. The escort from the Dalai Lama was turning back. My sad-eyed holy man had doused our campfire and was shaking his head as he faded away behind the smoke.

PART IV

Behold, how great a matter a little fire kindleth.
—JAMES 3:5

32

OURS WAS NOT A FRUITFUL MARRIAGE. The doctors couldn't explain it. As far as they could determine we were both fit breeders. Robby developed a passion for medical books and journals, and he read everything he could lay hands on about infertility. It was his idea I take my temperature on a daily basis so we could locate my fertile time. We had a chart on the foot of the bed. I'd call him at the office and he'd rush home when I went over 98.2°. We tried everything. We tried vitamins, exercise, rest-cure, and odd positions. He even found an old Inca woman who dealt in herbs and spells. Finally, he read in a journal about "old eggs" and concluded the problem must lie with the age of mine. He said it kindly, regretfully, but I felt as if I had failed him in the worst possible way.

I told him it wasn't fair. A woman got her lifetime supply of eggs the day she was born, and it was a countdown from then on. She was expected to get them paired up with little fish-tailed suitors before she was even old enough to have good sense. A man went on making nice new sperm until the day he drew his last breath. What was the use of an old geezer fathering offspring he wouldn't even live to support and direct down life's path? What kind of a system was that? Robby kissed me and said I could get the answers from Charles Darwin. He said it had nothing to do with fairness.

We talked about adopting. We even went to an agency, where we filled out forms and looked at pictures, but we didn't follow up on it. I knew Robby wasn't really keen on the idea, but I suppose if there had been a picture that looked like Eddy or Em, or even Flynn or Jody, I would've said, "Yes, that's the one. . . ." But no child struck a chord. If they're not yours, they have to strike a C-minor chord.

As it turned out, Robby and I were sufficient unto each other, and lived in a state of rut for five long besotted years.

Even after we stopped the temperature business, he'd still sometimes come home in the middle of the day, shedding his clothes the minute he crossed the threshold, howling like a lovesick hound as he took the stairs two at a time. Or, I'd show up at his office and we'd lock the door and make love there on the carpet, or the desk, or standing up in the supply closet. We were not quiet, furtive lovers. We embarrassed his secretary, who told another secretary, who told the office manager, who told Robby it was improper for married people to practice nooning. Especially on city time.

Robby did become a councilman, and he enjoyed unprecedented popularity among his constituents, if not his cohorts. The first legs of the new freeway system (which Robby claimed as his own invention) opened in 1950 and he rode loftily on that laurel leaf.

He asked little of me as The Councilman's Wife—no waving from platforms or convertibles. I was not required to go to luncheons or charity events, or to play bridge with the other wives. On a rare occasion he'd ask me to be involved in some good-works-thing that was likely to get a lot of coverage in the news. "Goose," he'd say—he'd stopped calling me little sister because it caused people to look at us funny—"Goose, I'd appreciate it. It would be politic. But only if you want to." He did love to entertain, so we often had people to little Friday-night suppers and Sunday brunch. As a result I achieved some small fame as a cook and hostess. I was a crackerjack when it came to the human appetites.

The big thing he asked of me as The Councilman's Wife was that I be beautiful, charming, and desirable. He said men judged each other by that standard.

So mostly I did nothing, and discovered I had a talent for doing it well. Well, not nothing. But after my experiences as a strewberry farmer and tomato packer, everything was so easy it didn't seem like work.

A typical day went like this:

I got up before Robby, fixed my face, did my breast exercises, put on cologne and a snazzy morning outfit that showed off my legs, then cooked him a small, healthy breakfast, high in protein. Robby worried about his own waistline almost as much as he worried about mine. And when I saw him off it was not with a quick peck on the cheek. He went to work every morning with passion in his eyes and traces of lipstick on his face.

I did a few chores around the house, not real work as I had a woman come in once a week for that. Robby worried about my hands. He said a woman's hands give her away.

I managed the three apartments in our building, which is to say I made a phone call if the rent check was late and called the plumber if a drain was stuck. I allotted about ten minutes a day to apartment managing.

Then I'd read. I had a system. One of the characters in *A Tree Grows in Brooklyn* had a notion to read all the great works of literature in alphabetical order. That kind of tidiness appealed to me; to start with Aeschylus and work my way through Stefan Zweig. So, I'd go back to bed, or if the weather was fine take a pot of coffee out to our garden patio and put my nose in a book until around 11:30. I'd take a cold shower to tighten my pores, and if Robby was coming home to lunch, which he often did, I'd slip on another one of my little "at home" numbers designed to drive men crazy. Lunch. That's what we called it. I sent him back to the office looking like the cat that's just had a whole bowlful of heavy cream. Robby said we were responsible for a new sociological trend at City Hall—men sleeping with their own wives.

I'd call Rosemary in the early afternoon. We talked weekdays on the phone and got together for lunch at least twice a month. In the beginning we tried being couples, but the chemistry was wrong. Robby found Raymond bland and Raymond found Robby arrogant. They were both right, of course. It was just as well. Rosemary and I weren't ourselves in a foursome. It was enough just knowing she was on the other end of the line in Glendale. I didn't need any other friends. I needed only Rosemary, who knew where all my mislaid memories were stored.

Next I'd do a little wifely correspondence for Robby and tend to my own mail. There wasn't much of the latter anymore. Mildred passed on the year after I got married. Rosemary and I talked about flying back to Boston for the funeral but, in truth, I was uneasy about leaving Robby to his own devices. I wasn't blind or dim-witted. I'd seen the way women looked at him, and I was well acquainted with his lack of moral integrity. I could see that even his secretary, who tattled on us, wouldn't be averse to a romp in the supply closet. It was Mildred herself who said there were people born without scruples. Missing scruples were like missing fingers. I knew she would have understood. Mine was not a marriage built on honor and trust.

My other old correspondent, Emma Hawkins, said her arthritis was so bad it was hard for her to use her Smith-Corona, and writing by hand was even more difficult, so her notes were brief and to the point. *Moby's fine. I'm fine. Your momma's fine. How is Jessie's history progressing?*

I wrote to Momma every month or so. I got a card from her at Christmastime, and another either before or after my birthday. I sent a regular check to Seth Mackenzie, who had his own gardening business now with two employees, but was still tending the graves personally. He'd send photographs when the new planting bloomed. He was still studying philosophy in night school.

Then I'd change clothes again. Robby liked for me to look like nine hundred dollars even if I was just going out to get the paper. I had these outfits I bought at Bullocks Wilshire—tweed skirts and cashmere sweater sets and shoes with Cuban heels. I'd get all decked out like Miss Astor's librarian and go shopping for the dinner I'd prepare out of one of my foreign cookbooks. This trip included a long serious conversation with the man at the Bottle Shoppe about what wine to serve with what course.

Robby fretted about our waistlines at breakfast and lunch but he contended the future of civilization depended on its leaders dining well of an evening. He even slipped into his preacher voice and cited Scripture in this regard: "Proverbs tells us," he said, "a man hath no better thing under the sun than to eat and drink and be merry."

I said, "That Ecclesiastes. There's a lot of stuff like that in Ecclesiastes."

Twice a week I went to a beauty parlor in Beverly Hills that specialized in the maintenance of the human body. Robby practiced maintenance at a men's club downtown where he could get everything from a manicure to a steam bath and write it off as a business expense. He touched up his hair at home, not wanting the word to get out. And was he quick! Quick to spot new lines around the eyes or a grey hair at the temple or puffy places. He would glare at the mirror and say, "That's an incipient sag." So for my part I warded off nature with all the defenses money and free time could buy.

Back home after my big afternoon outing, I'd read some more, then organize dinner, put the martini pitcher in the freezer, have a long milk bath and get myself perfumed and oiled like some French whore for the advent of my husband. I'd put on yet another little outfit. By the end of the day I'd changed clothes maybe five or six times from the skin out even though the only sweat I'd worked up was when I was naked.

And I reveled in it! I was an alley cat that had found a place by the fire and a seat at her own supper table. It was a Roman feast far into the night. Babylon before the fall. I never once imagined the future would be any different. The future was the present, moment by moment. The same fine wine, the same fatted calf, the same delicious Song of Solomon. There was no future because there was no growing child to measure time by. Robby and I did not grow. He would not even allow us to age.

But my passion for him never flagged. This is not to take away from the pure love I'd felt for Ed Shannon. My love for Robby was not pure. It contained no high regard and uplifting selflessness. I accepted that, and saw it as my due.

33

ROBBY LEFT BEFORE SEVEN FOR A BREAK-fast meeting. It was early summer, mild and sunny. I was in the patio pruning the roses and trying to decide between Cold Chicken Isabel or medallions with a raspberry sauce, before I settled down with *The Divine Comedy*. At this rate I wouldn't live long enough to get to Stefan Zweig. The phone rang. It was Miss Hawkins with the news that Momma was bad sick, a case of weakness that had not responded to her curatives.

"What does the doctor say?" I heard the impatience in my voice. Robby had invited a visiting fireman from Canada to join us that night in our box at the Hollywood Bowl. That's why I was thinking about the picnic basket while I pruned the roses. The Isabel or the medallions?

"Are you there, Cleo? I've been trying to reach you since last Friday."

"I'm sorry, we were away. What does the doctor say?"

"I told you. He says Ethan should have called him sooner."

"Ethan?"

"Ethan, your brother Ethan. Do we have a bad connection here?"

"He's in prison."

"You've heard of parole? I just wanted you to know. Sarah's here and I've left messages in three different places for Fidelity." She paused, waiting for me to say something. "Are you there?"

"Yes, yes, I'm here."

"Well. Are you coming? What shall I tell them? Cleo, I can't stay on this telephone all day, it's long-distance."

I came to my senses. That it took so long says something about how self-struck I was. I'd never thought of myself as the sort who regarded a call about serious illness as an infringement on my plans for the evening.

First I called the airlines, then Robby, then Rosemary.

"What does the doctor say?"

I told her.

"That doesn't sound good," she said with a *tsk*. "When they say you should have called sooner . . . Oh, Cleo! I'm so sorry. I'd offer to go with you but with R.J. at Harvard, things are tight here."

"My sisters will be there. Sarah anyway, I'm not sure about Fidelity."

"Sarah's the one . . . ?"

"Yeah, she's the one."

"Is he coming with her?"

"I don't know. Oh, I wish Miss Hawkins had called me afterward!" I listened to what I had just said, and ran it through my mind again. "Lord! What a mean, awful thing to say." Rosemary made soothing sounds in my ear, the sounds of a true friend who knows every fuzz ball in every grimy corner of your soul. I let her go on until I felt a little better, then I said, "I guess I should go pack my suitcase."

"I'll pray for you, Cleo. Maybe it won't be as bad as you think. Families come together at times like these."

"That's what Reverend Shoemaker said when Mam died. Ten years ago. The last words my momma said to me were, 'It was just failed jelly.' "

"What?"

"It doesn't matter. . . ."

"But you write to each other?"

"I write to her, she sends me cards. 'Merry Christmas' and 'Happy Birthday—Momma.' Not even 'Love, Momma'—not even 'Kiss my foot, Momma.' "

There was a long, heavy silence. Rosemary's momma in Drumright called her every Sunday after dinner and talked for fifteen minutes. "I'm sorry," she said finally. "You didn't tell me. I didn't know."

"Some things are just too shameful to share, even with your best friend."

"It's not your shame, You hear me? Don't go back there wagging a load of useless guilt. You've been a good daughter. Remember how you sent money home? Remember how you farmed her land for her? You hear me now?"

"I left."

"Well, of course. That's what children do. They grow up and they leave home. That's nature."

Or they don't grow up. But they leave anyway. I gave out a long sigh. "Thank you, Rosemary. I'll call first thing when I get back."

She cleared her throat. "You want me to invite Robby over to dinner?"

I thought about that. Wouldn't hurt. Keep him occupied for an evening or two. But I heard duty, not pleasure, in her invitation. I said, "No, that's okay. He'll manage."

Robby came right home, helped me finish packing, and drove me to the airport. He was kind, considerate, and full of New Testament comfort. At the gate, I told him how sorry I was about the picnic basket for the Bowl. He said no problem, he'd pick up something at Jurgensen's. I asked if he'd be all right. He smiled and said no he wouldn't—that he didn't know how he'd get from one hour to the next. "Don't spread that around," he laughed. "People are under the impression I'm self-sufficient."

My flight was called and I flung myself into his arms. "I don't want to go."

He held me close. "Then don't. Don't go."

"I'd never forgive myself if . . ."

"I know. Of course you must."

I pulled away. "I'll call you every night."

"I'll wait by the telephone."

He handed me my train case and I started down the red carpet to the airplane.

"Cleo?" I turned back. Robby was frowning. "Is that cotton?"

"What?"

"Your suit, is it cotton?"

I looked down at myself. "No, it's linen. Why?"

He seemed truly puzzled. "The skirt. Did it shrink?"

I looked at him closely, trying to find signs of some harmless joke in his face, but what I saw was real alarm. I made my eyes into slits. "Robby, I swear! This is not the time to be measuring your wife's hips!" The man coming along behind me smirked and that made matters worse. I got on that airplane feeling about as broad as I was long. If there's anything more of a trial than a vain and handsome husband, it's a vain and handsome husband who's just come kicking and screaming from his fiftieth birthday.

When I got to my seat he was scanning the windows, one hand behind his back, holding on to his other arm like the new kid on the playground, looking downcast and sheepish. I waved but I couldn't get his attention. I wanted him to see me smile, to see I wasn't peeved at him. I wanted to tell him I understood. I understood that he didn't know where he left off and I started. He expected me to be grateful for sincere criticism, in the same way the Lord lays the sinners low so they can learn to walk upright.

At the Tulsa airport I rented a 1951 Ford, and set out for Robina. Concrete had replaced the old asphalt since I'd last driven the road, but the air that blew in the open windows was the same as I remembered it, heavy with the sweet dusty smells of cornfields and alfalfa and buffalo grass.

Either you love the plains or you don't. It's that simple. There's no place there for ambivalence any more than there's a place for forests or mountains. Either you feel small and swallowed up, or you want to stretch out your arms all the way to Nebraska and pull it all in, suck it into your lungs, roll it around on your tongue, read its tracks and lairs, sniff out its waterholes, stare at it until you're blinded by the blueness of the sky and turned stone deaf by stillness and longing.

Then the crows fly over like an angry black cloud, hollering Hawk! Hawk! And you remember why you've come.

I stopped at the cemetery to pay my respects to Mam. She wasn't there, of course. She was taking her ease by some calm and placid river in Paradise, fanning herself with her dewdrop fan, listening to sweet Juan play his Spanish guitar. But she would come, I knew that. She'd come from anywhere in the universe if I called her.

I hiked up my skirt and sat cross-legged opposite the tombstone. Her grave was a solid bloom of wildflowers, the only grave so graced. I wasn't surprised.

"I'm here," I said.

"Been expecting you."

"How's Momma?"

"Failing. But she'll hang on till you get there."

"Why? So she can fuss at me?"

"That's not the only reason but, yes, knowing Frances, she'll probably fuss at you."

"What am I to say to her?"

"As little as you can get away with. Just sit there at the bedside with your hands folded and your eyes trained on the floor. Look glum. Your momma likes it when folks are glum."

"I didn't come all this way just to stare at the floor."

"Read aloud to her from the Bible—she'll like that."

"But I want to tell her something."

"What's that?"

"I want to tell her that I love her."

"No, you don't. You want to hear her say it to you. You figure because she's dying she might have softened up some. You want her to say she loves you and you want her to call you by name. Right? You want her to say your name just once before she goes on. Don't turn away, Cleo. No point in lying to the dead. I can see square into your heart without my reading glasses."

"Then what is it I feel? I feel something."

"What's it like? Describe it to me."

"It hurts, Mam. It hurts right here."

"Oh, that. That's hope. Causes leaky valves. You keep the little doors open just a smidge so whatever you're longing for can trickle through. After a while they don't shut proper anymore. You give up hope and those little doors will swing shut like they're supposed to. Your heart will get healthy again in no time."

"Is that what they teach you in Heaven?"

"Don't smart off, Cleo. When I went on did you stand around wringing your hands and going on and on about how much you loved me?"

"No, I don't think so."

"No, you didn't. You didn't have any time for that what with stoking the fire so I could keep warm and making tea and soup and lighting up my Buglers. And did I carry on about how much I loved you?"

"No. We talked mostly about what you wanted—the ceremony I mean—and what sort of domestic arrangements they had in Heaven."

"See?"

"See what?"

"Are you blind, child? The love between us is understood, we don't have to drag it around and wool it half to death."

"It's not understood between me and Momma."

"That's right. Now you're getting it. . . ."

"Getting what?"

"How you feel about her is your business. How she feels about you is her business. You can't change how somebody else feels."

"Are you saying she doesn't love me?"

"As much as she's able. Can't get honey out of a hornet's nest."

"She doesn't love me? Doesn't love her own firstborn child?"

"Don't whine, Cleo. I cannot tolerate a whiner."

"Tell me the truth."

"I told you. As much as she's able. Frances truly loved only two people in her whole life. Her daddy and her worthless husband. When her worthless husband got hisself shot, she found she had a little left over, maybe half a pint's worth that wasn't lowered into the grave. She doled that out to poor Ethan, and when he went to prison, she dredged up as much as she could carry and put it in her letters to him. It's easier to love somebody that doesn't track up your house and get on your nerves."

"There must be something I can say. . . ."

"You can tell her you love her if you think it'll make you feel better. Just don't expect anything back, that's all I'm saying."

"What's the other reason? You said there was another reason she'd hang on until I get there."

No answer.

I waited.

I sat perfectly still with my elbows on my knees, my chin in my hands, watching the late-afternoon breeze move through Mam's wild-flowers. I heard the *chupp dzrrt* of a confused meadowlark in Garrity Fields behind the cemetery. When folks visit Robina—usually because they've made a wrong turn—they say, "What's to do around here?" And somebody tells them, "Read the tombstones and listen to the meadowlarks in Garrity Fields." In Garrity Fields the eastern and western meadowlarks cross over each other's ranges. They learn each other's songs, do both the western flute and the eastern whistle with ease, or they sing a medley of the two. *Spring of the year, Hip hip har-rah! Oh yes I am a pretty little bird.* Two different kinds of birds, probably with two different viewpoints on life, living here together singing each other's songs. Mam always said there was a lesson to be learned in Garrity Fields.

I waited.

It began to cool off. I heard the 6:15 freight train announce itself as it neared the crossing east of town. I was quiet and calm. I was prepared to wait long into the night.

"Cleo?"

"I'm here, Mam."

"You been away among the Philistines for too long. Your momma'll hang on so she can rest easy, that's why. It's the worst kind of humiliation if your own kin don't show up for the funeral."

34

I WOULD NOT HAVE RECOGNIZED ETHAN ON the street. His face was lined like a farmer's, but pale as lead, and his hair, which had been blond and silky like our daddy's, was pure white. He was stooped, had a gimpy leg and a withered arm—from when he was shot trying to escape—and there was no light behind his silver-rimmed spectacles. He wasn't even forty years old, poor soul.

I reached out my arms to him but he just bent over and picked up my bag. "Cleo," he said, with a polite nod, and turned away.

"Sit down," said Sarah, brisk as a broom. "I'll get you a cup of coffee." She smiled and kissed my cheek, as if we'd parted just yesterday and on friendly terms. She motioned toward the bedroom. "Momma's sleeping."

I said, "I'll just look in on her."

Ethan said, "Wait till morning. She's strongest in the mornings."

"I just want to see her, just for a minute."

Ethan nodded. "Don't wake her up."

The blinds were drawn and the room was almost dark. Momma's face was a still outline on the pillow. But I could hear her breathing. I could hear her waiting for me. I eased the door shut and went back to the table.

Sarah said, "Miss Hawkins finally found Fidelity. She'll be here tomorrow with the baby."

"Fidelity has a baby? Miss Hawkins didn't tell me."

"Two-year-old, a little girl. Felicity. Is that something? Baby Fidelity and Baby Felicity. Don't know where we'll all sleep. You'd think she would've had the good sense to leave her with somebody, under the circumstances. I mean a two-year-old? The terrible twos?"

She turned to Ethan, who was standing there with my suitcase like some patient porter. "You can take that out to Cleo's old room for now. We'll figure it all out after supper. Miss Hawkins said she'd send over a couple cots."

"Thank you, Ethan," I said. Then I eased into a chair at the table and watched Sarah bustle around at the sink counter.

"I got a hen in the oven," she said. "I tell you there was not a bite of anything in this house when I got here, not a crumb. I been shopping and cleaning ever since I walked through that door. I'm about wore out, I can tell you that." She set a cup of coffee down in front of me and glanced toward the lean-to. "Doesn't raise a hand," she said in a low voice. "Let Momma's garden grow up in weeds. Just sits in Momma's chair and rocks and reads, reads and rocks. Sounds like a poem, don't it—*doesn't* it. Lord, it's hard to get Oklahoma out of your mouth. Willis is always after me about my grammar. But it does, doesn't it? Weeds, then rocks and reads?"

I nodded. Sarah's tongue had always been swifter than her mind.

"Or he plays Sol," she went on. "Shuffles those cards till I'm about wild. Doesn't open his mouth unless you ask him a question face-to-face. Imagine having to pay good money for fresh vegetables!"

I poured cream into my coffee and stirred it while Sarah zipped around the kitchen, fast as a ferret. It was hard to believe that ten short years could make such a difference in a person's appearance and attitude. Her long blond hair, the glory of her youth, had been cropped and permed. She'd gained weight around her bottom. Her face was still as pretty and smooth as ever, but all the grand sensuous languor had gone out of her. And her fingernails were plain and short as a nun's.

I decided I might as well get it over with. "Is—ah—did Willis come with you?"

She brought a bowl of potatoes to the table and handed me a paring knife. "Couldn't get away, he's short a man, and anyhow it's so expensive to fly." Again she nodded toward Momma's closed door. "Besides, there's no love lost there, as you well know. As it is I had to hire a girl to come in and help out at home. Flynn's a treasure but it's too much to expect."

I smiled at the mention of Flynn and wondered what was too much to expect, but I didn't say anything, just grunted and picked up a potato.

"Ruby says she'll drive down on the weekend if I still have to be here."

"Ruby?"

"Willis's first wife. You remember. She was a Leighton, was in your grade. I don't know what I'd do in this world without her, just like a sister to me." I about fell off my chair but I kept my mouth shut while Sarah went on about Ruby's virtues and helpfulness. "She let Flynn and me stay at her place till Willis could get out the Merchant Marine. He got out early because he was wounded—nothing bad, nothing lasting. We moved down to San Jose in their old house."

"Yes, I remember now, Miss Hawkins mentioned it in a letter. . . ."

Sarah looked off toward the window and smiled her sweet smile. "Ever time I'd have a new baby, she'd take part of her vacation time and come down to help out. Like family—just like a sister."

I wondered if that was some kind of veiled complaint, that she'd had to settle for Saintly Ruby because I, a blood sister, wasn't available to change diapers and boil bottles. I stabbed another potato with my paring knife.

"And I can tell you they were coming thick and fast," she went on.

"Are they noisy?" I asked. Willis had said he wanted a big noisy family around the supper table, that he wanted to sire loud people, politicians and opera singers.

Sarah closed her mouth, first time since I'd arrived; then she revved up again. "Well, of course they're noisy, Cleo. They're kids, aren't they? But everything is fine now. Willis got himself fixed, for which I can tell you I am truly grateful." She leaned toward me. "Had to threaten him with a lock on the bedroom door. Oh well, things work out, that's what I always say. Life has it's ups and downs."

I sighed and nodded. I said, "You wake up one morning and there's the sun shining in a bright blue sky."

She looked at me sharply, then her mouth spread into a smile. "Why yes, Cleo. Real sweet of you to remember. Sarah's Philosphy of Life, Willis calls it." She fixed her eyes on Momma's door. "Don't know about this dark cloud, though. I just don't know. If this is going to be one of those lingering things . . . On the telephone Miss Hawkins gave me to understand . . ." She gave a heavy sigh. "My youngest is just turned five. You know how it is, a five-year-old needs his momma. Flynn's an angel, pure stock, but like I said . . ."

I felt my face break into another fond-auntie smile. Flynn. My sweet vice president in the strewberry business. I said, "And how is Flynn?"

"Six feet four inches, can you believe it? And still growing with every rain. Plays point guard on the basketball team. Probably get a scholarship to San Jose State. Should I make Momma's scalloped potatoes or you want them mashed?"

"What do you suppose Momma wants?"

"She can't keep anything on her stomach but broth and dry toast, sometimes a little poached egg. That's what I mean, Cleo, if she lingers somebody'll have to look after her. I can stay the week, maybe longer if Ruby can get time off. Willis understands family duty, that's no problem, but to tell the unvarnished truth, my family is out there, in San Jose. I mean, I have a five-year-old. Miss Hawkins says you're married to somebody high up in Los Angeles politics, so you probably have to be back at his side. I understand that. And Fidelity . . ." She rolled her eyes. "Well, who knows about Fidelity? But I sure wouldn't count on her."

I pointed to the stove and the Servel. "Miss Hawkins said Fidelity brought those. She must have had gas and electricity put in."

Sarah put her hands on her hips and made her eyes narrow. "Now, why is it, do you suppose, that we have to get all our news from Emma Hawkins?"

I shrugged. "She's the librarian. A librarian's job is to spread information and knowledge."

Sarah thought for a minute, then stretched out her neck and made a pronouncement. "It's one thing to spend a few dollars. I'm talking about being here. What if it gets to the point where she loses her senses and—you know—messes herself?"

I shook my head. "Momma wouldn't let it come to that, she's too proud. Anyhow, she has Mam's gift, she can go on whenever she wants to. She can will it."

"Oh Lord! Don't tell me you believe all that Indian hocus-pocus?"

"Yes, I do. But anyhow, Ethan's here."

"Didn't you hear a word I said? Ethan's not worth twelve dead flies."

"Ten dead flies. Mam always said ten dead flies." I was beginning to feel light-headed and silly. I said, "Maybe dear Ruby could come and help us out."

Sarah looked at me closely. "Cleo, are you all right? You seem a little strange, you really do. I mean, we may be called on to make— well, what Willis calls hard decisions here. And you're the oldest."

"What does the doctor say?"

"What can he say? She won't let him touch her. You can't make a diagnosis from the doorway. I made some coleslaw and we got the hen and the dressing and the potatoes . . ." She pursed her lips. "What else? That don't seem like much. Nothing from the garden, not even a green onion. You should see my garden in San Jose. You want biscuits or cornbread?"

"Biscuits. I'll make them."

"You oughta change first, don't want to muss that pretty suit. Looks expensive. And watermelon pickles from the fruit cellar."

Ethan limped in and went straight to the Servel. He took out a Mason jar and poured half its contents into a pot, then set it on the stove.

I said, "What are you making, Ethan?"

He spoke with his back to me. "Momma's supper."

I lifted my eyebrows at Sarah. "Doesn't raise a hand," she'd complained. Said he wouldn't answer unless you asked a question face-to-face. Sarah favored our daddy, yes, but she had our momma's own brand of self-righteousness.

I changed my clothes and came back just in time to see Ethan disappear into Momma's room with a tray. He closed the door behind him. Sarah was leaning up against the sink, her arms folded and her eyes on her feet. "I'll give him that," she said. "He makes the broth and the medicine. It's a secret receipt, not written down, she's only told Ethan. She lets me put her on the bedpan. That's only 'cause Ethan's a man."

"You think I should go in now while she's awake?"

"No. She won't eat if anybody's there but him. Just waits for you to leave. Oh, Lord, Cleo! I don't even know why I'm here. Far back as I can remember, the only times she ever touched me was to see if I had a fever."

I crossed the floor in big strides and put my arms around her. I was tired of feeling mean. She melted against me for a moment, then stiffened up again.

After supper Mr. Hawkins dropped off two army cots and said Emma would try to get by the next day. It was decided I would sleep in my old room, Ethan would take one of the cots out on the front porch like he used to when we were kids, and Sarah would set up the other one in the kitchen. I said we'd scare up another cot tomorrow for me to use—there was room in the walkway to the add-on—and Fidelity and Felicity could have my room. Sarah said when the baby cried and fussed she'd be least likely to disturb Momma from out there. We spent a lot more time and thought on sleeping arrangements than was necessary.

Later, when Ethan took his pipe and went out on the front porch, I sniffed the brown bottle of medicine and found at least one secret ingredient to be paregoric.

Sarah was drying the last of the dishes and I was wondering what to do with myself when I suddenly realized I hadn't called Robby, hadn't even given him a solid thought since I landed in Oklahoma. I looked at the wall over the dry sink. "Where's the telephone?"

"Momma took that out years ago."

"Why?"

"Miss Hawkins said . . ." She pulled up short and we both laughed. "Momma told Miss Hawkins that bad news came quick enough by mail to suit her. You can use the phone at Mam's. Agnes Mary won't mind."

I said I'd wait until tomorrow. Tomorrow was going to be a busy day.

Ethan came in from the porch. I knew he'd been sitting in the swing because we'd heard it creaking all the time we cleaned up. He sat down at the table and picked up the cards.

Sarah said, "Oh Ethan, I got my bed just right over there. How'll I get any sleep with all that shuffling going on?"

Ethan set the deck down, like a sullen, obedient child.

"You can sleep in my room," I told her. "I think I'll read awhile."

Sarah sniffed, took a towel and the basin from the washstand, and headed for the add-on.

When we were growing up in this house we fell all over each other like puppies, took a Saturday-night bath in the same water. Now we were trying to parcel off little spaces and put walls around them. We didn't sing each other's songs.

35

FIDELITY ARRIVED EARLY THE NEXT MORN-
ing. "Drove straight through," she said. Her station wagon was so
jammed full you couldn't see in the windows. I asked her if she was
moving in. "Moving on," she said.

Ethan took her suitcase in the same grave way he'd taken mine the
day before, didn't even smile at the baby. He said we could come in
and visit with Momma after breakfast.

Fidelity told her story over sausage and eggs while the baby sat quiet
as a Boston fern on her mother's lap. Either Felicity had skipped the
terrible twos or they had not yet set in. Without a sign of regret
Fidelity told us she'd left both her job and her husband, and was on
the way to Colorado. "I was leaving anyway," she said, "so when I got
word about Momma I figured there was no time like the present."

I hadn't seen my baby sister since she was five years old. Miss Hawkins was certainly right. She did favor me. She was me all over again
except ten years younger. But Fidelity was the one complaining about
the drawbacks of aging.

She said, "They took me out of bras and panties when I turned
twenty-four. I did negligees and full slips for a while, then after the
baby they put me in grannie gowns and housecoats."

"Weren't you embarrassed?" Sarah asked, her eyes wide as the Missouri.

Fidelity reached for another biscuit. "Nope. I was enlightened.
Housecoats is the end of the line."

"I mean about being photographed in just your—your, uh, undies. I
think I'd die."

Fidelity looked her up and down. "Not if you lost a few pounds and
exercised and watched your diet." She shrugged. "It's just like wearing a two-piece bathing suit."

Sarah flushed and sucked in her stomach. "Too bad you lost your
husband," she said.

Fidelity handed the baby a sausage link. "He's not lost," she said solemnly. "I just got fed up with being his welfare office." Sarah leaned forward, all set for the details. I changed the subject and asked Fidelity what she meant to do in Colorado. She grinned. "See the Rockies."

I knew right then and there this was a sister after my own heart, and as forthright as the rock in those distant mountains. I opened my mouth to mention Lhasa and the Himalayas but Ethan came in and said we could see Momma now. Fidelity shot up, kissed the baby, and put her in the rocker. She handed her a stuffed rabbit that had seen better days and said, "You read to Mr. Rabbit while I go visit with Gramma." She picked up a stack of books from the floor. "What would Mr. Rabbit like to hear this morning? *A Apple Pie? Ask Mr. Bear? Cowboy Small?*"

Felicity wound strands of her long dark hair around her finger and considered the alternatives. *"Madeline,"* she said. Fidelity gave her the book and said she wouldn't be long, to stay in Gramma's rocker till she came back. The baby smiled and nodded. Sarah looked dubious.

Ethan followed us in and sat like some guard dog in the straight-backed chair by the door. Momma was propped up on pillows and wearing a pink quilted bed jacket. Her hair was combed back from her face and braided into one long, neat plait. There was the smell of English lavender in the room and a Mason jar filled with fresh flowers.

Sarah and I hung back but Fidelity never broke step, went straight to the bedside and sunk down on her knees. "We're here, Momma. We're all here."

Sarah pulled up the chair by the other side of the bed and I stood at the foot. Fidelity took Momma's hand. "Would you like to see my baby?"

Momma blinked. "You have a baby?"

"I wrote you. Remember? She's out there in your rocker. Can I bring her in for just a minute?"

Momma narrowed her eyes. "Your baby have a father?"

Fidelity laughed, quick and cheerful, not in the least cowed or bothered. "Oh, Momma," she said, "there are no virgin births in Chicago."

And then came the main surprise of the decade. Our momma chuckled at this piece of irreverence. I couldn't believe it. I said, "I'll go get her."

Sarah frowned. "I would've brought one of mine if I'd thought you'd be up to it."

Fidelity laughed again. "She's just going to look at her, Sarah, not baby-sit."

"Another girl," Momma sighed. "No sons to work the land."

"I have boys," said Sarah. "Five boys. I brought pictures."

Momma nodded and closed her eyes. I started for the kitchen but Ethan shook his head. "Not now," he said, "she's tiring." No question who was running the show in the sickroom.

Sarah leaned closer, looking glum just as Mam had advised. "Could I fix you a poached egg? Does that sound good?"

Momma shook her head, then opened her eyes and took us in, one by one. "Thank you for coming," she said. "I'm tired now." An ailing queen might've dismissed her court in just such a manner.

We filed out and Ethan closed the door behind us. Sarah began clearing the table, making a lot more racket than was necessary. She said, "It's like you have to make an appointment. I don't know why he should have so much say-so, he's not even the oldest. You're the oldest, Cleo, you should be in charge."

"Of what?"

Fidelity said, "I think Ethan's doing a swell job. Didn't Momma look nice? And the flowers!" She took another biscuit and lathered it with butter and jelly. "I can eat anything I want to. If I want to I can make a skilletful of sausage gravy and pour it all over this biscuit. I can get big as a barn if I want to."

I laughed. "Is that what you mean to do?"

"No, but I'll have the time of my life putting on ten pounds. I can carry it, I'm tall enough. They made us weigh in. Can you believe it!"

I thought about our bathroom scales at home, and Robby clucking as he peered over my shoulder. I could believe it. I picked up my pocketbook and said I was going into town to use the telephone. I asked Sarah if we needed anything from the store and said I'd be "in charge" of buying the groceries.

She gave me a puzzled look. "I'll make a list."

Fidelity handed me a twenty-dollar bill. "For my part," she said, "and pick up some beer, would you?"

"In Momma's house," Sarah gasped. "Absolutely not! And I don't think you should've said what you did about the virgin birth."

Fidelity said, "Don't be such a pain in the butt, Sarah." She lifted her shoulders, rolled her eyes, and said in a wheedling little voice, "I have boys. I have *five* boys."

Sarah's back went stiff. "Well, I do. That's so. I just wanted to make her feel easier, to let her know there's somebody in this family that cares about carrying on the line. I like married life and raising kids—I can't think of any higher calling. I sure wouldn't leave Willis high and dry just so I could go see the Rocky Mountains."

I said, "Now, Sarah. That's not what Fidelity said."

"That's right," Sarah broke in. "Take her side, you always did."

"Take her side? Against what? She was a baby. . . ."

Sarah put her hands on her hips and gave me a look that would've grown icicles in a tropical forest. "I may have been his second choice but he never had cause to regret it. You were only interested in sex, not in family life. You were a big disappointment to him, Cleo. He truly loved you. You were his first love. Well, I'm his last love and I can tell you, you sure missed something. Willis is a boy-maker."

Fidelity's chair scraped the floor. She held up her hand. "That's enough, Sarah."

"One lone girl," Sarah sniffed. "When you're looking after a family you don't have time to do exercises and go to the beauty parlor." She turned to me. "And you," she said. "What ails your fancy politician?"

Fidelity whirled Sarah around by the shoulders and shook her, hard. Suddenly, Sarah's eyes grew wide and she covered her mouth with both hands. "Oh, Lord, I'm sorry, Cleo. Oh, Lord! It's been so long . . ."

I smiled at her and nodded. "That's all right," I said. "We're all a little on edge." Big Sister, the Peacemaker. But I really meant it. It was all right. It hadn't occurred to me that Sarah's old sun shining in a bright blue sky might travel with those old storm clouds, jealousy and envy.

I told her to finish the list, then went to my room to change. When I came back, Fidelity and Ethan were sitting across from each other at the table. Ethan was shuffling the cards. Sarah ducked her head and handed me the grocery list. I put my hand on her shoulder and said, "I mean it, Sarah, it's all right, you hear?"

First I used the pay phone at the gas station. Robby was out of the office and his city-bred secretary couldn't understand why I could not leave a number where I could be reached. Twice she said, "The phone is out of order? Have you reported it?" I suppose if I'd mentioned the lack of an inside toilet she'd have asked if I had called the plumber. I told her to just please give Robby the message I'd called, was fine, and would try again later.

Then I made the rounds.

As far as I could see, very little had changed in Robina except those alterations brought about by birth and death and an occasional gallon of whitewash. Neddy Wadkins had stepped into his father's shoes at the bank when Mr. Wadkins passed on. Neddy was now called Mr. Wadkins and his oldest son was called Neddy. Julius had retired from the grocery. Leon, his youngest, said he still came in rain or shine on Saturdays to run the register and keep up with the local news. Mr. Krause, who had been such a help to me in my strewberry business, had lost both his children to the war—the son in the South Pacific, and the daughter, a nurse, in France. His sister's boy moved back from St. Louis to operate the hardware store after Mr. Krause had his heart attack. Madie's twin girls, Lee Anna and Dee Anna, ran Madie's café—still called Madie's and still serving up the same specials: CHICKEN FRIED STEAK MWF and SHEPHERD'S PIE TTS; CLOSED ON THE LORD'S DAY. There was only one newcomer. Dr. Hodges' shingle had been replaced by one that read, A. KARAJIAN, M.D. With no first name, and a last name that was clearly foreign, I could see why he couldn't get past my momma's doorway.

But it was mostly business as usual, a forward surge of the bloodlines. Hail and farewell. The king is dead, long live the king.

Except. Except for the passing of Robina's own royalty, her legend, her patriarch, her Abraham. Towns, like nations, need abiding heroes. Madie's daughter said at least seven hundred people attended Gideon's funeral service, and the wake lasted for forty days and forty nights. She said the old men formed a Gideon Society and met every Saturday afternoon at the Community House to pitch horseshoes and swap tales as tall as Gideon himself. She said two shelves in Miss Hawkins' library had been dedicated to Gideon's memorabilia and personal papers, and that the papers were bound in leather and had gold lettering.

I thought about Mam's unfinished history and felt a rush of shame that almost brought me to my knees. You wonder how you get through the days with broken promises hobbling along behind you, or sleep through the nights with them sucking at your life's blood like wood ticks.

I tried Robby again but he was in a meeting. Again I left the message that I was fine.

Miss Hawkins grinned from ear to ear when I walked into the library. She told me to pour myself a glass of lemonade, and pointed to the armchair opposite her desk. She swiveled her chair around and faced the shelves behind her. "I've been saving one for you," she said. "A new one. Has your name written all over it. Now, where'd I put it?" She poked and squinted and finally came up with *The Town* by Conrad Richter. She held it cupped in both hands as she tended to do with books she revered. "Have you read it yet?"

If I had I would have lied about it, not wanting to spoil her pleasure. I told her about my project, reading the classics in alphabetical order. "That's mostly what I've read the past five years. I'll soon be finished with Dante."

She wrote a date in the book and filed the card in the same oak box that had held her library cards for thirty years. "That's an admirable pursuit," she said. "But you shouldn't neglect your contemporaries."

I settled back with my lemonade, which hadn't changed either. It was tart and icy cold, with pulp and memories floating on top. I said, "Remember the day you had the Lhasa book waiting for me?"

"I do indeed, Cleo. Only book this library has ever lost."

I came out of my comfortable slouch, alarmed. "I sent the money."

"Yes, and I was able to get a replacement. That isn't always possible with first editions. I hope you don't make a practice of that."

"I treasure that book," I said in all earnestness, hoping to make amends. "Alexandra David-Neel is just like one of my family."

She sniffed and nodded, far from mollified. In Robina, the eleventh commandment is Honor Thy Library. "And speaking of your family?"

"We're all here. Fidelity drove in this morning. She has a baby girl and is fresh out of a husband."

Miss Hawkins sighed. "Yes, I know."

"About the husband?"

"I could see it coming. Between the lines. Is Frances eating any solid food?"

"A little dry toast. I didn't see her until this morning and then for just a few minutes. She's very weak but Ethan's taking good care of her."

"No question your brother is devoted, and him not well himself."

"What's wrong with him?"

"I don't know, Cleo. You girls expect me to know everything. Whatever it is, he has to stay out of the sun. He was brokenhearted about your mother's garden."

"Sarah said he let it go because he's lazy."

"Oh? What does he say?"

"Hardly anything. Hardly opens his mouth."

"More the reason you should encourage him. One can lose one's conversational skills in prison, you know."

"I hadn't thought about that," I said. I looked at her closely. I had no idea how old she was—a hundred, maybe. Since I could remember she'd had white hair, and deep smile lines in her face, but there was an ageless erectness about her. Maybe next time I came home she'd be gone, and there'd be no one to take her place. A childless woman and her bachelor brother—the end of the line. I said, "I visited Mam's grave when I got in yesterday."

She smiled. "Isn't it beautiful? What a nice thing for that young man to do."

"What young man?"

"The Indian."

"What Indian?"

She ran her fingers over her forehead. "I've forgotten his name, I met him only once, that first time he came. For years now he's been coming every spring to sow wildflowers on Jessie's grave. The first time he came to me for permission, he said your friend in Tulsa told him to see me, told him it would be best not to disturb your mother about it."

"Seth Mackenzie," I said.

"Yes, that's right. Tall, well-spoken, fine eyes."

Then I told Miss Hawkins about the ceremony. I hadn't breathed a word to anyone but Rosemary. I told how Billy Rule and I played "La Golandrina," how Seth Mackenzie read from the Bible and Henry David Thoreau, how he'd asked for the blessings of strange gods, and surrounded himself with owls and elephants and buffalo. I told how Mam had risen in a mist, gathered, and soared off on a winged white horse Seth Mackenzie called down for that purpose.

She smiled in a vague, distracted way. I sat quietly and pondered this act of generosity—these yearly wildflowers. Then I said, "I wonder why he didn't tell me? I pay him to tend the graves in Tulsa."

"Perhaps that's why," she said. "We are most truly ourselves when other people aren't looking."

I was giving that hard thought when the clock on the wall chimed the hour. I picked up *The Town* and said I better get going.

"Did you say hello to Moby?"

"Moby? I thought she'd be gone, she's older than God."

Miss Hawkins reached in her desk drawer and handed me a box of fish food. "I would have written you, Cleo."

"Of course. I'm sorry."

"I have to keep the food locked up. Everyone loves to watch her eat."

She walked with me to the front of the store where the tank sat on an ornamental stand in the alcove, a place of honor which in the old days accommodated the big dictionary.

I said, "She must be a foot long!"

"Eight and three quarter inches to be exact."

I wondered how you got a fish to stand still so you could measure it, but didn't ask. I admired the tank. Someone had added new appointments—a frog with a crown, a castle with a drawbridge—but the old stuff was still there, the pretty rocks I'd collected from the creek, the sunken galleon, the treasure chest, the deep-sea diver.

"How old is she?" Miss Hawkins asked. "Do we have any idea?"

Oh yes, oh yes, we have an idea. I said, "Eddy got her at a school carnival shortly before the accident. Eddy would be eighteen this August." Did I hear myself say "accident," I wondered. Did I really say "accident"? "Odd, isn't it?"

"What's that, Cleo?"

"That so many people have gone on and this goldfish is still here.

Eddy didn't even get her on purpose. She was one of those prizes you win tossing rings or something."

She put her hand on my shoulder and gave it a squeeze. "I think she recognizes you."

I laughed. "Oh, Miss Hawkins . . ."

"No, I mean it."

I tapped the glass and showed Moby the box. She came to the surface and did her dance. I lifted the hood and sprinkled in the food. She bowed, came up to the glass, and kissed my finger politely before she began to eat. I watched her gather up the flakes, grace itself, and I realized I wasn't mad at her anymore, mad at her for being one of the promises that hobbled along behind me.

"Maybe she does. Maybe she does know me."

Miss Hawkins followed me to the door. She said, "If we can believe that Jessie went off on a winged white horse—and I do believe that, Cleo, I sincerely do—then what is so remarkable about a goldfish with a good memory?"

I stopped at Mam's. It was still called "Mam's"—not Cleo's place or the Tiptons'. The house was painted yellow now, the door and windowframes a clean shiny white, and there was a bright green swing on the porch. A new chicken house had replaced the one that sagged and fell under the weight of the great snowstorm of '41, and there were random shingles that had not yet darkened on the barn roof.

Sonny came out to greet me, followed by three barefoot, towheaded replicas of himself. He invited me in for a bite to eat, but I said I had to get on home, that I'd stopped to see if I could borrow a cot or small rollaway. Sonny nodded, went into the house, and was back in no time with a folded army cot. He said he'd been meaning to write me, that he'd bought some land and they'd be moving soon. "Sometime in the fall," he said, "as soon as I get the house built."

I said, "I'll be sorry to see you go, but I'm glad you got your own place."

Agnes Mary came out on the porch, wiping her hands on her apron. She frowned. "Sonny says you can't stay. Not even for a cup of coffee?"

About the rudest thing you can do in Robina, Oklahoma, is to turn down hospitality. I explained how I'd been to town on errands and needed to get back for the next time my momma was awake.

Agnes Mary nodded sympathetically and said, "Wait just a minute." She went inside and came right back with a pie. "For your supper," she said. "Sonny got those old peach trees to bear."

I took the pie, still warm, and thanked her. I said to Sonny, "They must've turned you into some kind of magician down at Tahlequah. There's been no fruit on those trees for as long as I can remember."

He rocked back and forth on his heels and looked pleased. "Just have to keep at it," he said. "They just needed pruning and a little fertilizer."

We talked in low voices about Momma's poor condition; then they walked me to the car. Sonny put the cot in the back and said he'd keep his eye open for a good reliable tenant. Agnes Mary told me to stop by anytime I could, that she wanted me to see the new wallpaper in the parlor. Then they both said to let them know if they could be any help to us. Any help at all. On the way home I thought about how kindness seemed to come so natural to country people. To neighbors, anyway. Not necessarily kin.

Ethan helped me carry in the groceries. He was wearing a long-sleeved shirt, buttoned at the collar even though it was ninety in the shade, and a wide-brimmed hat. I thought about what Miss Hawkins had said about him having to stay out of the sun. But I didn't ask about that. I asked about Momma. He said Sarah and Fidelity had each had a private visit with her, and the next time she woke up it would be my turn.

I took the cot out to the walkway, then began to put away the groceries. "Where is everybody?"

Ethan hung up his hat, sat down at the table, and started to shuffle the cards. "Sarah's resting. Fidelity's gone over to the Warwicks'."

I opened the Servel and tried to decide whether it would be best to hide the beer in the vegetable drawer or set it next to the milk in plain sight.

Ethan was still shuffling the deck. *Don't shuffle the spots off,* Mam used to tell us. I turned to Ethan, put my hands on my hips, and said, "Well now, boy, don't shuffle the spots off."

He scowled, making even deeper creases in his old man's face. Then he shook his head—getting the joke—and smiled. He said, "I tried to get permission to come for the funeral. Sometimes they allow that. But it was too soon after the trouble. . . ." His voice trailed off and he began to lay down the cards in a neat row.

"Miss Hawkins says you're out on parole now."

"I don't like to talk about it if you don't mind, Cleo."

"Is there anything you'd like to talk about?" I was thinking about what Miss Hawkins said regarding conversational skills.

"No. Talking makes my tongue thick."

"How 'bout a game of rummy? All you'll have to say is gin."

He nodded to the chair across from him, scooped up the cards, and dealt them out.

I looked over at the Servel. "Want a beer?"

He shook his head. "She'd smell it on me. Sometimes she thinks I'm Daddy, wants to smell my breath."

I took a lot of time arranging my hand. "Mmmmm. Mam would say this hand looks like a foot." Ethan smiled again at the mention of our grandmother and his face got younger. So, for the second time that day I told the story of Mam and her white winged horse.

When I finished, he said, "I don't believe in that kind of thing." But he was still smiling. I discarded and he picked it up. We played quietly for a while; then I said, "I don't know what to say to her."

"Can't help you there. I don't know what to say myself. Fidelity knows. Ask Fidelity. I picked up your last queen, Cleo, didn't you notice?" He took my discard and laid down his hand. "Gin."

Sarah came in and stood by the table. "I hope you're not playing for money. You know how Momma feels about gambling."

"Hundred bucks a point," said Ethan. "Want in?"

Sarah screwed up her eyes and I thought she was going to cry. Then she let her shoulders slump and arranged her face into that smooth, stoic mask our momma put on when she was offended. She took down the colander and began cleaning vegetables.

Ethan and I looked at each other, both of us a little sheepish. We were only ten months apart, and close as Siamese twins when we were growing up. That lasted until Ethan discovered automobile engines and I discovered Willis Henderson. But until then we did everything together, which included ignoring our little sister. We were good to Fidelity, of course, because she was the baby and had a sweetness about her. Poor Sarah was simply underfoot, and worse, a tattler.

I got up from the table. "Can I help you, Sarah?"

She shook her head. "No, you all just go on with your game. I need to keep my hands busy."

I turned back to Ethan. "You suppose she's awake yet?"

He looked at the clock and said it was about time for her medicine, that he'd get the medicine ready, then look in on her.

I put my hand on Sarah's shoulder. "Agnes Mary sent a pie."

She sniffed. "That was thoughtful."

I tried again. "Hot day for soup making. We could have cold chicken or sandwiches."

"I told you I need to keep my hands busy. You don't have to eat my soup if you don't want it."

I sighed and got a paring knife out of the drawer. "What did you say to her?"

"Who?"

"Momma, when you saw her by yourself. What did you talk about?"

She stared out the window for a minute and took an idle bite off the carrot she'd just cleaned. "Well . . . not much, I guess. I asked if there was anything else I could do for her—besides the bedpan, you know. I showed her the pictures of the kids, Flynn in his basketball jacket—he's a letterman, you know."

"Did she talk about—well, about going on?"

"She said the grave was never satisfied."

I nodded. "And the barren womb, and the scorched earth."

"What?"

"Proverbs. Momma's especially fond of Proverbs. Has anybody read to her from Scripture?"

"Not me."

"Ethan?" He glanced up from the evil-looking potion he was mixing. "Have you read to Momma from the Bible?"

"I don't read the Bible."

So, Mam was right. I could read to Momma from the Bible. That was my purpose here. It was just a question of which passages would give her comfort. I got down the old King James Mam's mother had given her when she married Harlan. It weighed maybe five pounds and was published in 1817, back when the Apocrypha was still allowed in the same binding with the canon.

In a sudden fit of inspiration I turned to the concordance and looked under *Mother*. There were not many choices. From Genesis there was, of course, Eve, the "mother of all living," but not much was said about her good points. From Judges there was the story of Deborah, "mother of Israel." When I was a girl Deborah had been one of my heroines. She didn't weep and wail and fall down on her knees as Bible women tended to do. I liked it that people came to her for advice and she bossed grown men around. She told Barak to go to Mount Tabor where she would deliver unto him the enemy—chariots, multitudes, and all. Barak whined and groveled and said he'd go if she went with him. So Deborah had to do all the work. She caused the captain of the enemy army to be slain by Jael. No slouch herself, this Jael. She hammered a big nail right through the captain's head. I took a slip of paper and marked the spot in Judges. Momma liked a good story.

From Job there was the "worm" mother. That wouldn't do, and besides Momma had no patience with Job. From First Kings the old "wisdom of Solomon" story about cutting the baby in half. And from Samuel, one of Momma's favorites about how the wise mother saved her city by causing the head of Sheba to be tossed over the wall into Joab's hands.

Not quite right. None of them.

Finally, I resorted to the method Momma herself had used in those long ago nights around the supper table. I closed my eyes, opened the Bible, and brought my finger down on a passage. Surely, the Lord guided my hand.

Who can find a virtuous woman? For her price is far above rubies. The heart of her husband doth safely trust in her, so that he shall have no need of a spoil . . .

Best leave out the husband part.

She seeketh wool and flax and worketh willingly with her hands.

Good. That was my momma all right.

She riseth also while it is yet night, and giveth meat to her household. She layeth her hands on the spindle and her hands hold the distaff. Strength and honour are her clothing; and she shall rejoice in time to come.

317

Oh! I liked that!

She openeth her mouth with wisdom; and in her tongue is the law of kindness.

Better strike that last part; she might think I mocked her.

She looketh well to the ways of her household, and eateth not the bread of idleness. Her children arise up, and call her blessed.

I felt a great excitement gathering in me. It was so perfect. Just take out the verses that weren't appropriate, rearrange the others a bit—no large liberties taken, just comfort added. I got a pencil and made faint checkmarks in the margins.

Ethan said he'd take the medicine in now, and call me when she was ready. I nodded and went back to studying the verses. I didn't want to stumble over the words I was leaving out. I wanted to ease my momma's mind—I wanted to please her. I could close with *Many daughters have done virtuously, but thou excellest them all.*

And Momma would smile then, and she would remember that I, too, was a daughter.

When I looked up, Ethan was standing over me. He kneeled down, took my hand, and patted it gently. He spoke in a strangled whisper. "She's gone. Momma's gone."

His words didn't register at first. I thought he was saying she had risen up from her bed and gone about her business. Gone out to consider the fields. Gone like a merchant ship to bring food from afar. Gone to seek wool and flax.

And then it hit me like a hard slap in the face. "But I didn't get my time with her. I was to have my time!" I began to weep and pound the table with my fists. "She could have waited if she'd wanted to. She could have waited for me. She had the gift."

We buried Momma two days later. We put her next to Daddy, so she could keep an eye on him, and Reverend Shoemaker kindly agreed to read my edited version of Proverbs 31 at the graveside. I rewrote it to leave out the verse about the virtuous daughter.

There wasn't much in Momma's will. She'd been a spartan woman as regards her possessions. Ethan got the farm, of course, and Momma's small savings. Sarah got the sewing machine, Fidelity the photograph album and Momma's wedding ring, and I got the Bible and the wooden box of recipes. Sarah went back to San Jose. Fidelity and Felicity took off for Colorado, and I went home to the Divine Comedy.

36

ONE HOT NIGHT IN LATE AUGUST, WHILE we were making love and minding our own business, Robby suffered a shortness of breath. I told him I thought it was natural, given the circumstances, but the next morning he asked me to drive him to Dr. Jacobson's office. The doctor pronounced him fit, said it was nothing to be overly concerned about, said a lot of people had been adversely affected by the heat wave, but—come to think of it—given Robby's age and habits, he might well look upon this incident as an early warning signal. He might consider slowing down. He slowed down for about a week, and geared up again. Then, the call came in the dark of morning—as those calls are wont to do—that his father had died in his sleep of apparent heart failure.

When he came back from the funeral in Philadelphia he not only slowed down, he stopped in his tracks. He stopped martinis, stopped cigarettes, stopped butter and cream sauce, stopped coming home in the middle of the day.

And he went back to God.

In the beginning I didn't mind. I rather enjoyed our new quiet life. For the first time we seemed like a normal ordinary couple, instead of people in a television sit-com. I went with him to services at the Methodist church on Sunday mornings and to Fellowship Wednesday evenings. I even thought about shining up my trumpet, getting my lip back, and offering my services to the choir director.

I got up in the mornings, dressed, and wore the same clothes all day long. No cold showers to tighten the pores, and instead of going to the beauty parlor twice a week, and making daily trips to the Bottle Shoppe in my librarian outfits, I volunteered at Children's Hospital.

Robby stopped touching up his hair. He also stopped looking over my shoulder at the bathroom scales. This is not to say we let ourselves go. He was still as trim and handsome as ever—when his hair grew in grey at the temples he looked distinguished—and I was still what they used to call a fine figure of a woman. I told him we were finally letting ourselves grow older, and doing it with grace and good intentions. I told him I suspected Ponce de León felt relief rather than disappointment when he learned there was no fountain of youth. He laughed and gave me a chaste peck on the cheek.

That was the problem with our new quiet life. At first I thought it was just a temporary lapse. But it wasn't. That primal urge, which had always been so strong in him and was the foundation of our life together, was dead on arrival from Philadelphia.

One night when he was pretending to be asleep, I said, "But Dr. Jacobson said there was nothing wrong with you."

After a long moment he sighed, turned on his light, and picked up one of the many medical magazines that sat on his bedside table. "Dr. Jacobson told me to be careful."

"He said no such thing. He said you should slow down. He was talking about alcohol and long hours at work and French food."

Robby gave me a what-do-you-know look. "I've been researching this, Cleo. If you'd ever read anything of a scientific nature, you might possibly learn that sexual intercourse is the most strenuous of man's domestic activities." I laughed and said I never thought of it as a domestic activity. "It affects the left ventricle," he went on, instructing the dull student. "That's the big pump, Cleo, the big pump in the heart. You won't find that sort of practical information in—" He raised up on his elbow and squinted at the book lying facedown on my stomach. "—in Euripides."

I reached out and touched his cheek. "I wish you'd read it," I said, making my voice gentle. "I think you might find you have something in common with Admetus. Admetus is troubled by truths he can't bring himself to recognize. . . ."

"Oh, please, goose—not now." He gave a great sigh, turned off his light, and rolled over on his side.

I took my problem to Dr. Jacobson. He patted my shoulder and told me not to worry. "It's temporary, Cleo."

"How long is temporary?"

"As long as it takes him to reconcile himself to his father's death. That's what this is all about, my dear. Impotence in the face of mortality."

"I didn't say he couldn't. I said he doesn't want to."

"Even so. A normal, natural response under the circumstances. His father is dead—Robin is now the father—but he has no sons. That confounds the problem. Do you see?"

"My mother died. I have no daughters."

He held up a forefinger. "It's different for a man. Women are more—how can I put it?—more attuned to the natural rhythms of life. More accepting—yes, that's the word. Women are more accepting of the process." He put his palms flat on his desk and gave me a smile of dismissal.

I said, "Alcestis died for her husband. In his stead, I mean." I could see the wheels turning behind his eyes. Alcestis? Do I know Alcestis? "I'm reading the Greek Tragedies," I explained.

He waved his hand. "Oh, my dear, it's been a long time since my undergraduate days. At any rate, I can assure you that no such sacrifice will be required of you. Just a little patience. Robin will come around. Bear with him."

I nodded and went on with my story. "At first I thought it was about Alcestis' bravery and loyalty. Then I decided it was about his—Admetus'—cowardice, letting her give her life for him. Now I'm not sure. I think maybe Euripides is talking about the death of a marriage. And how nobody noticed."

Dr. Jacobson glanced at his watch. "This is all quite interesting, Cleo, but it's really out of my line. I could refer you to a counselor."

I shook my head, got to my feet, and told him I was sorry I had kept him. "I'll be patient," I said. And I was. I didn't see that I had any other choice.

In November Sonny wrote that he and Agnes Mary would be moving out the first of the year. He hadn't found a renter yet, but was still looking. As I read the letter I wondered why it hadn't occurred to me earlier about Ethan. I worried about him. What good was a farm to a man who couldn't farm it? What crop could you tend after dusk and before sunup? I wrote and suggested he move over to Mam's after the Tiptons left, and rent out Momma's place. That would give him a small income, and maybe he could find somebody to sharecrop at Mam's.

Ethan wrote back to say he appreciated my concern and my offer, but he was doing fine. He'd found Momma's diary where she kept her secret receipts and her thoughts on various subjects. He was making the curatives, selling them to her regular customers and to Mr. Hawkins at the pharmacy, and with that and the egg money he was getting by. He said I might want to have a look at that diary next time I came home. I wrote back and told him I didn't have that kind of courage.

In December I heard from Fidelity. She'd seen all of the Rocky Mountains she needed to, and was coming to California to look for a job. She would stop off in San Jose. Sarah had invited her for the holidays, then—if it was convenient—could she spend a week or so with me while she went on interviews and looked for an apartment. I wrote that same day and told her our downstairs bedroom had twin beds and its own bath. I told her she was as welcome as good weather.

The day they arrived I was sitting at the desk in the living room, circling apartments-for-rent in the classifieds and growing more excited as I divined the future. I saw that Fidelity would find something close by, a nice little furnished one-bedroom apartment with laundry facilities and a walled-in patio where Felicity could play safely in the sunshine. They would come over for supper two or three times a week, and I'd drop in over there for coffee on Saturday mornings. When it got warmer we'd go to the beach or take a quilt and a picnic and go over to the park. The baby would build sand castles while my sister and I talked about the Rocky Mountains and Lhasa and new clothes and old boyfriends—all those things sisters talked about that we'd missed out on. My sister. My sister's daughter. Blood kin—well-loved—just two streets over, or even down the block.

And when Fidelity went out on dates, she'd leave Felicity to spend the night with her Aunt Cleo. Maybe Fidelity would go away for a weekend now and again. With a really nice man, of course, one who paid his bills on time. But what about the days? Who was to care for this child while Fidelity was at work? Maybe I could give up my volunteer work at the hospital, just until the baby was old enough to go to nursery school. Baby-sitters came and went. A child needed consistency. I needed to get the name of a good pediatrician. I needed to redecorate the downstairs bedroom. It was so plain for a little girl. I needed to get some stuffed animals. I needed to ask Miss Hawkins for a list of the best children's books. I needed to go to the bookstore and stock up. I needed to get a first-aid kit. And a dog.

But why couldn't they just live here with us? Plenty of room. We could be a family. I was working on the details of this possibility when I glanced out the window and saw the station wagon parked at the curb. Fidelity was standing by the open tailgate, frowning, her hands on her hips.

I hurried out to greet them, calling out, "I expected you'd have to call for directions. Been waiting for the phone to ring."

Fidelity grinned and said they hadn't made the map she couldn't read. I opened the door on the passenger side. "Felicity! It's so good to see you. And look here, why it's Mr. Rabbit."

She looked at me solemnly. "City," she said.

Fidelity came up beside me. "She calls herself City. It's just as well. We sounded like a Christian circus act. Come on, honey, crawl out and take your stuff." Fidelity had a duffel bag almost as big as the child herself. I reached for it. Fidelity shook her head. "No, City carries her own baggage. She likes it that way."

I looked back at the bags and boxes on the tailgate. "How 'bout her mother, can she use a hand?"

Fidelity smiled and nodded. "I know it looks like we're moving in for the duration, Cleo, but don't panic. It's just that I don't know where anything is and I need to repack this stuff. I wish I could talk to a real gypsy about how they manage."

We stood there for a minute, just looking at each other while City wrestled her duffel bag across the grass and up the walk. I felt stiff and shy, and it occurred to me that maybe Fidelity felt that way too. We hadn't had much of a chance to get reacquainted in Robina. I said, "I used to take care of you. You were a good baby."

Fidelity looked me in the eye. "I cried when you left home. I'd go out to the road and sit on the log and wait for you to come back. Momma said I'd sit there for hours."

"I'm sorry. I had to leave."

"You taught me to whistle with two fingers. I'd sit out there on that log and whistle till all my spit was gone."

I smiled. "I guess I finally heard the whistle."

City called from the front door. "I'm hungry. Mr. Rabbit is hungry."

Fidelity picked up the bags. "Poor Momma," she said. "We all got out of there as quick as we could. Ran away, all of us. Not one of us was able to leave in the daylight." City called out again that she was hungry. Fidelity said, "We're coming, honey, hold your horses."

I lifted a box from the tailgate and followed up the walk. I had forgotten that part when I was divining the long conversations we'd have at the park while the baby built sandcastles. That's what we'd talk about—Momma and old injuries. It's not the grave itself that's never satisfied, it's the restless inhabitant.

We were in the kitchen when Robby came home. City sat at the table with a coloring book, consulting from time to time with Mr. Rabbit about the choice of a crayon. Fidelity was at the sink putting together a salad, and I was bent over the oven checking the roast and thinking about how happy I was to be at the center of all this warm domesticity. I closed the oven door and turned around just in time to see Robby lean over and plant an absentminded, husbandly kiss on Fidelity's lips. He took a quick step backward and his eyes grew wide. He looked at Fidelity, then over at me, then back at her again.

Fidelity's cheeks turned a pretty rosy pink. "Well now," she said, "I call that a real welcome."

Robby said, "I don't believe this. This is uncanny." Again, he stared at us, first one and then the other. I began to feel uncomfortable as I watched him narrow his eyes to weigh and measure and pass judgment.

"This is Fidelity," I said. "My sister, Fidelity. And this is City and Mr. Rabbit."

City held out her hand nice as you please and said, "How do you do." Not yet three years old and she carried her own baggage and had social graces.

There was a brief, disjointed conversation about what City would call Robby. He laughed and said he didn't mind being an uncle but he'd rather not be called one. He said his sisters' children called him Rob. Fidelity argued she didn't want her daughter to get in the habit of addressing adults by their first names. It was disrespectful, she said, and I was struck by how much she sounded like our momma. Robby smiled his vote-collecting smile and said this would be an exception, not a habit, and that no disrespect would be intended or taken.

He had his way. Some people are born and raised to have their own way. He sniffed the air with appreciation for the smells that were wafting around the kitchen and said he would build us a before-dinner drink after he got rid of his tie.

I opened my mouth to remind him he was on the health wagon but he was staring at us again, shaking his head like he was confronted with a miracle. He leaned his elbow on the doorjamb the way you lean up against a fence post to admire the fruits and the fields, his eyes coming to rest on Fidelity's face then moving slowly downward. "Just like you, Cleo. You again."

He left the kitchen wagging his head, and took the stairs two at a time like he used to when he'd come home in the middle of the day. We listened to him move around overhead, then Fidelity said, "You didn't tell me."

"Didn't tell you what?"

"That he was so good-looking! I got the idea from what Miss Hawkins said that he was old. And that voice! Was he a singer before? An actor?"

I took plates down from the cupboard, handed them to her, and pointed toward the dining room. "He was a preacher," I said. "The silverware and napkins are in the buffet." I wanted to add: *He is old, he's fifty, he's a hypochrondriac.* I didn't. I had a soft spot for Robby's vanity.

I watched Fidelity walk away from me, moving the way women do when there's an interesting man on the premises, with that slight sway of the hips, shoulders back, chin lifted—an unconscious, primitive response that goes back to the first flowers showing off their pollen to the insects. I thought about my grand plan for us to be one big happy family under the same roof, and realized it would be just about as smart to invite Rity Hayworth to move in with her wardrobe of strapless gowns.

Robby was back in no time, his light blue shirt unbuttoned to show the blond hair on his chest, the sleeves rolled exactly three turns against his year-round tan. He looked like an ad for men's cologne.

"One can't hurt," he said cheerfully, as he got the martini pitcher from the top shelf to which he'd banished it in late August. "I read in a medical journal that a drink before dinner is good for the red blood cells." He reached into the cabinet where we kept the liquor and got a bottle of gin. "Besides," he said, "this is a celebration. Give us something from Scripture, Cleo—something appropriate."

What came immediately to mind was, *No man having drunk old wine, straightaway desireth new,* but that did seem a bit obvious and had a whimper in it, so I fell back on trusty Ecclesiastes. "Eat thy bread with joy and drink thy wine with a merry heart."

He nodded approval and told Fidelity that her sister was a walking version of the King James Bible.

She said she knew that. "We all had to read the Bible, but Cleo was Momma's best student. Momma always said so."

I almost julienned my finger instead of the green bean. "She said that? She never told me."

Fidelity shrugged. "You know Momma."

Robby said something about the complex nature of family relationships, smiled at City, and ruffled her hair on his way to the refrigerator. He got the ice, filled the pitcher, apologized because it wasn't cold, and carefully added the gin, then the vermouth with an eyedropper we kept for that purpose. Then he put the pitcher in the freezer. "For a couple minutes," he said. "To get a nice frost on it." He poured 7-Up over ice for City, added grenadine and a maraschino cherry, and set it in front of her, bowing from the waist. He asked Fidelity if she wanted an onion or an olive. She said she'd have one of each, thank you, and Robby nodded like that was the wisest decision he'd heard all week.

Two more martinis and considerable merriment later, Robby opened a bottle of red wine and the three of us sat down to dinner. "Fashionably late," I said with a silly giggle. City—smart kid—had already eaten, before the salad got soggy, the meat dry, and the vegetables woebegone. She cleaned her plate and announced that Mr. Rabbit was sleepy and they were going to bed. I had watched her go off through the silvery haze of juniper berries, and later, at the table, asked Fidelity if her daughter ever made a fuss.

"Not often. She doesn't have much to fuss about."

I considered that and it seemed to be the case. "Maybe you ought to write a book on raising kids. I've never seen one so easy. I thought my Em was easy, but at that age she wanted somebody to put her to bed and read her a story." I heard myself being slyly critical of my sister who'd sat with her drink at the kitchen table, laughing and talking, while her poor little child went off alone into a strange dark room.

Fidelity said, "I put her to bed whenever she asks me to. I read her a story if she asks me to. I do most anything she asks me to—if there's no harm in it. That's why she's so easy." Fidelity sawed away on her roast beef, then chewed it with pleasure. Not a word about how the cook was laughing and talking at the table while the meat burned. She took a sip of wine and said, "I learned about easy children from Momma."

"Our Momma? Not our Momma."

"In a roundabout way. Because of one of the books Miss Hawkins gave me to read. I don't remember the name of it—a little book of wise sayings. There was one about how you learn to be quiet from people who talk too much . . . and tolerance from bigots . . . and kindness from mean people . . . that sort of thing."

She turned to Robby, who was listening to us like there'd be a quiz later, with prizes. That was part of his charm, this ability to listen and not have to stick his oar in the water every time a voice dropped. She explained how our momma believed a person should work for everything, including and especially affection. "So I decided when I had my own child, I would give that child anything and everything that child asked for. I don't mean the moon or making myself penniless. I mean everyday things. And you know, it's amazing how quick we learn what's not good for us, given half a chance. City got sick on candy only once. That's all it took. I told her beforehand. I gave her my honest opinion about how many Hershey bars it took to make a person sick. She remembers that. She trusts me. She thinks I have good judgment."

Robby laughed, then reached over and patted Fidelity's hand. "Ah," he said, "but what will you tell her later when that sweet little child's body blooms and she discovers boys? How will you handle that? How will sex fit into your theory of having anything you want?"

Fidelity frowned and tried to get some limp green beans onto her fork. "I'll tell her the truth. I learned that from Momma too. She never told us anything straight out. We got our sex education from our corn-bread muffins."

I explained to Robby about the muffins, about how Momma baked Bible sayings into them and packed them into our school buckets. I said, "Momma was very fond of Proverbs 6:26."

Fidelity said, "I got that one too. And Sarah. I don't know about Ethan. I think Momma had double standards." She put her hands together prayerfully, lifted her eyes and quoted: " 'For by means of a whorish woman a man is brought to a piece of bread, and the adulteress will hunt for the precious life.' " She lowered her hands and looked over at me. "That's it, isn't it?"

"Word perfect," I said.

She turned to Robby. "You were a preacher. Now tell me, just tell me, what's a fourteen-year-old virgin to make out of that?"

Robby pursed his lips and poured more wine from the second bottle. Fidelity and I held our forks in midair, waiting for his answer. It seemed to me that we were all growing more wise by the moment, and more beautiful in the candlelight with our flushed faces and bright eyes. Robby pondered his wineglass. "The Egyptians," he said finally, drawing it out in his golden voice. "The Egyptians." He swirled the wine in his glass and held it up to the candlelight. "The Egyptians believed that the earth was a graveyard—one vast, wide, deep, eternal graveyard, where men had hunted prey and made war."

Fidelity put down her fork, leaned on her elbow, and listened intently as the words rolled off Robby's tongue like he was speaking from the pulpit. The light from the candles reflected in the mirror behind him and made a halo around his head. He was young again, following the slanted sunlight across the floor of the church. Then the light fluttered and I saw Momma heaving the jars of strewberries at the wall, shouting *Burn the Egyptians! Burn the Egyptians!* As I watched the light dance in the mirror and the shadows move across our faces I suddenly understood the meaning of it all. I saw that everything has the same starting place, the same ending place. Here we sat at this table in this timeless candlelight, these timeless shadows. We were some kind of gods, a trinity ordering the world. Of course Fidelity could stay. Stay and sit at my right hand.

Now Robby was talking about grapes, swirling his wine again, working up to some blazing insight. I could hear it rumble in the distance, bearing down on us with its gift of astonishment. "The Egyptians," he said, "believed that the grapes of their vineyards gathered unto themselves the blood of all the dead. The dead from the battlefields from the beginning of time. Not only the great battlefields but those that lie in our parlors and kitchens and bedchambers. When the grapes are made into wine, so too does the wine harbor the blood of the dead. When we drink the wine we become intoxicated with all the violence of the past. All the avarice, the foolishness—and ah yes, the passions of all those who have gone before."

I shivered and looked over at Fidelity. She was nodding, her lips parted and shiny. "I see," she whispered.

I shook my head to clear it. I saw too. I saw that Robby, the actor, was up to his old tricks. I said we could all use a good strong cup of black coffee. When I came back with it the spell was broken, the grapes and the graveyards and Proverbs had gone the way of all mysteries. Fidelity was telling about her life in Chicago. She was to the part about being put into housecoats, the end of the line.

"But it was a good living," she said. "There was a regular paycheck and you didn't have to worry about creeps. Not in catalogue work, they don't allow it."

I poured coffee and asked what kind of creeps she meant.

She said when she first started in the business she worked as a photographer's model. "We wore sheets draped around us every which way, showing a lot of skin but nothing anybody'd get arrested for. Guys—and a few women, too, I'm ashamed to say—would pay to take pictures of us. They were learning to be professional photographers." She stumbled over "professional photographers" and pretended to push her upper teeth into place with her thumb; then she laughed and said she guessed she did need some coffee.

"So what happened?" Robby looked like he was about to take a stick to somebody.

"Well, I found out those people didn't even have film in their cameras. Can you imagine anything creepier? I told my boss I'd rather work in a whorehouse where people were honest about their needs. I quit that day and went into catalogue work."

She talked on and on about the catalogue business. My eyelids began to droop. But Robby was fascinated. He'd ask a question. She'd answer him. Then he'd lean forward with a rapt expression on his face and ask for more details. Then he'd laugh or groan or look amazed—whatever reaction was called for.

For five long years I'd watched him flirt with women. It came as easy as breathing. He said so himself that night in the diner. *I flirt with all women, all sizes, shapes, colors, and ages. Doesn't mean a thing. It's my nature.* He hadn't changed a whit since the old days at the boardinghouse when he'd wound up poor old Figgy like he was using a skate key. And Betty Anne, who he charmed out of second steaks and apple pie à la mode on the house. And the pale, peaked little Prayer Partners at the church, meekly waiting their turn to commune with him in the vestry every third Wednesday. Not to mention the sad souls in the congregation whose hearts and pocketbooks he speared on the beams of light from his violet blue eyes.

But I had convinced myself there was no harm in a mild flirtation now and again, that it was just a form of exercise he needed to keep himself alive. We all have habits we're not proud of.

At some point I noticed I'd been left out of the conversation all together, and might as well be at some dinner table on Jupiter. Their heads came closer together and their voices got low and silky. Robby would reach over and touch Fidelity's hand or shoulder, then pull back like he'd just burned himself. Fidelity would run her tongue over her lips, toss back her hair, lift her chin. The air fairly glowed with pollen. You could hear the insects' wings. After this display and two cups of black coffee I had to admit I was dead wrong about the trinity business. Not only did I not want my sister in my house, I didn't want her in the neighborhood. New Jersey would be just about right.

It was after midnight when we all turned in. Before I went upstairs I got the classified section from the desk in the living room. I tore out the page where I'd circled all the nearby apartments for rent, wadded it up, and put it in the basket by the fireplace.

37

Robby WAS UP AND DRESSED BEFORE THE alarm went off. He woke me and said he'd put on the coffee and squeeze fresh orange juice. When I came downstairs he was pacing the kitchen floor, glancing first at his watch, then at the door to the guest room.

"They're not up yet," he said. "I have an early meeting."

"So?" I asked.

"I was going to suggest to Fidelity you get a sitter and the three of us go out to dinner tonight. Show her the town."

"I don't know if she'll want to do that."

"Of course she will. Why wouldn't she?" He shook his head. "What a hard life that girl has had! The least we can do is give her a small vacation before she has to leap back into the fray."

"She had a vacation in the Rocky Mountains."

He gave me a puzzled look and said he was running late. "I'll check around," he said, "see if I can get a line on a job for her—a respectable job."

"She's going to see some people she used to work with in Chicago."

He frowned. "Surely you don't want your little sister working in the skin business."

"My little sister is way over twenty-one."

He smiled and put his arm around me. "Sure, goose, sure she is, but that doesn't mean we can't help her, can't show a little Christian concern for her welfare. And the welfare of our little niece."

I looked over at the kitchen table, where two crystal glasses of fresh orange juice sat waiting on a silver tray. There were two white linen napkins beside the tray, and a basket of my homemade sticky buns.

I said, "Where's mine?"

"Your what?"

"My orange juice."

"Sorry, goose, I told you I was in a hurry. . . ."

"This is the first time in the history of our marriage you made a pot of coffee. Or squeezed any orange juice except to put in a screw-driver."

He took his arm from my shoulder. "If I'm not mistaken that's our arrangement—you make the coffee and I pay for it. I was trying to be helpful. I thought it would be nice if Fidelity woke up to the smell of perking coffee."

"The perfect host. Robin Endicott, the perfect host. Admetus was a perfect host too."

"Is that supposed to mean something to me?"

"It would if you ever read anything besides medical journals. You could find a lot of your own symptoms in Euripides."

He looked at me closely. "Cleo, are you still drunk?" He glanced at his watch. "Listen, we'll talk about this later. See if you can get a baby-sitter."

I trailed along after him, nipping at his ankles. I told him the City of Los Angeles could spare his services for another five minutes. My voice was shrill and witchy, like the nagging wife in the movies. All I needed was pink hair curlers and a flannel bathrobe.

He sighed and opened the front door. "What is it, Cleo? What *is* it?"

I slammed the door and planted myself in front of it. "When his friend Heracles came for a visit Admetus didn't tell him the house was in mourning. Good manners would've obliged Heracles to go some-where else. So he stays, drinking and carousing and shaming the household."

"Absolutely fascinating. I am late for an appointment."

"When Heracles learns the truth—that Alcestis is dead—he goes off to some fair and gets Admetus a new woman. In those days they threw women in as prizes along with horses and oxen."

Robby sighed again. "Personally, I would have settled for the horses and oxen."

"Admetus says no thanks. He says no woman will ever sleep in his bed again, but Heracles convinces him it's the will of the gods."

"Get to the point, Cleo. I have an appointment with an executive from General Motors."

"The point is that after Admetus stops weeping and sniveling, he notices this new woman looks strangely familiar. Heracles finally con-fesses she's really Alcestis, that Alcestis isn't dead after all."

"Bravo! Fantastic! And they lived happily ever after. A touching story." He reached for the doorknob and I knocked his hand away.

I said, "That's not the end. Heracles says he rescued Alcestis just as she was about to cross over to the underworld, but Admetus isn't sure he buys that. He says, 'If this is my dear wife, why doesn't she speak to me?' "

"Ah hah!" said Robby, as he took me firmly by the arm and pulled me away from the door. "Because her tongue has been cut out. That's what they did in the old days to wives who talked too much and made their husbands late for work, a practice we have—unfortunately—abandoned." He jerked open the door and stepped out onto the porch.

I followed along after him. "Heracles says she isn't allowed to talk until the third morning. He says that's the deal he made with the gods of the underworld."

Robby was slapping the side of his leg with his briefcase. "Lord," he sighed. "Dear Lord in heaven I wish I had a cigarette." He looked at me and narrowed his eyes. "You're not dressed, Cleo, that gown shows everything you own. Go back in the house. Call Dr. Jacobson, maybe you're having a nervous breakdown. Maybe it's early menopause."

"Dr. Jacobson doesn't know anything about Alcestis either. Dr. Jacobson is just as illiterate as you are."

He turned on his heel and hurried toward the driveway, grumbling and shaking his head. I yelled after him, and caused a neighbor out walking his dog to stop and stare at us. "But what if it wasn't Alcestis?" I called out. "What if this woman Heracles won at the fair just looks like Alcestis? What if this woman is—in truth—Alcestis' sister? That would be incest, wouldn't it? Reverend? Wouldn't that be incest?"

Robby gave me a look as cold as a Nebraska winter, and got into the car. I watched him until he'd pulled out of the driveway and into the street; then I walked over and picked up the paper off the lawn. The neighbor—a man from down the block who always let his dog shit on our grass—was still gawking. I hoped Robby was watching in the rearview mirror. I hoped he was grinding his teeth over the nightgown.

I put the paper on the kitchen table, next to the orange juice and linen napkins and sticky buns. I wished I was the sort to throw dishes around or point my nose at the ceiling and howl like a hound or have a drink at eight o'clock in the morning. I was giving that third alternative serious consideration when I heard signs of life from the guest room, and a few minutes later Fidelity came in, yawning and stretching, looking rosy and rested and about eighteen and a half years old.

"You sure do get up with the chickens around here," she said. "Ummm, I thought I smelled coffee. Oh, my poor head! You guys live like this all the time?"

"No," I said, making my voice calm and easy. "Last night's rumpus was in your honor. Robby wants you to enjoy yourself because you've had such a hard life." I excused myself and said I'd be back after I'd showered and dressed.

I lingered in the bathroom, where I tried on words and said them to myself in the mirror:

—It would be more convenient if you found a place in the Wilshire District.

—I'm sorry, Fidelity, but as it turns out Robby's mother is coming for a long visit.

—Robby and I are going on a cruise tomorrow morning.

The woman in the mirror looked pained and said, "Why not tell her she looks too much like Alcestis for comfort? Tell her there's no room here for a woman won at the fair. Tell her this is not the place to hunt for the precious life."

When my pulse had slowed to a trot I took myself back down to the kitchen. City was at the table eating sticky buns, wiping butter and brown sugar syrup all over my white linen napkin. Fidelity had the classifieds spread out on the counter, and was talking on the telephone and writing on a note pad. I asked City if she'd like some hot Ovaltine to go with her buns. She would, thank you. I got the milk and craned my neck trying to read the address Fidelity had just scribbled on the pad.

She hung up, turned and smiled. "Sounds good," she said. "Four places to look at and they all sound good."

I poured the milk in a saucepan. "Today?"

"Wouldn't want to miss out on a good place. I really need to get settled. You can't spend your life just passing through." She picked up the pad and read off the addresses—none of them close by.

I watched the milk make little bubbles around the side of the pan, then poured it in a mug. As I set the mug down in front of City I noticed the suitcases and duffel bag on the floor in the doorway. I felt a grievance rise in my chest. How could you throw somebody out if they were leaving on their own legs?

"But you were going to repack your boxes," I said, sounding like somebody's reliable secretary.

"They're already in the wagon. Better I should get settled, then worry about it."

"But what if you don't get one of those places?" I wanted her to say in that case she'd come back here and try again tomorrow. Then I could stiffen up my back and hood my eyes and say she must think I'm blind as a post. Then I could really light into her. I could say she had lusted after my husband in my own house at my own supper table, that she had committed adultery in her heart. I could say that the adulteress eateth and wipeth her mouth, and saith she has done no wickedness. I could say her wickedness had set my house asunder. I was not surprised to recognize the voice in my head as our momma's.

Fidelity studied the floor and said, "In that case I'll go to a motel." When she looked up, there were teeth marks in her lower lip and big tears in her eyes. She said, "I can't stay here."

"Why not?" I asked. Now she would apologize. Now she would ask my forgiveness.

"Because I feel like I've been offered up on a platter," she cried out. "How could you do that, Cleo? To your own sister?" The tears were rolling down her cheeks now. Truly baffled, I handed her the other linen napkin and told her not to cry.

City climbed down from her chair and wrapped her arms around Fidelity's leg. "Why you crying, Ma?" She looked over at me, her eyes wide and worried. "Is Ma hurt?"

"My feelings are hurt, honey," Fidelity said quickly. "I'll be just fine after I cry for a bit." City nodded, satisfied. I could see she understood the usefulness of tears. She patted her mother's leg and said she was finished with breakfast and was going to her room to read to Mr. Rabbit, that the kitchen was too noisy. City, it appeared, was not ready for Greek tragedy.

Fidelity wiped her eyes, sniffed a couple times, and squared her shoulders. "I know I had too much to drink," she said, "and I guess I was kicking up my heels, but honest to God, Cleo, I kept thinking you'd say something."

"Say what?"

"That you'd tell him to cut out the funny business. When you didn't—when you just sat there blind as a post and ignored the whole thing—I decided you didn't give a damn. And then I thought, Merciful God, is that what these people do?"

"No," I whispered. I felt my legs begin to wobble, and I sank down at the table.

"I was awake all night, thinking there might be a little tap on my door . . ."

"How could you think such a thing?"

"How could I not think it? I know for damn sure if I had a husband I cared anything about, I wouldn't let him try to seduce somebody right in front of my very eyes. Right in my own dining room!"

I shook my head so hard I could hear the bones in my neck creak. I said, "You don't understand! It wasn't serious! Robby flirts with all women. It's his way. He flirts with our eighty-two-year-old tenant next door. It's his nature." I turned up helpless palms and said, "We all have habits we're not proud of. Oh, maybe things got a little out of hand last night. Too much good wine—you said so yourself. But what really happened, I mean, what this misunderstanding is all about is that you look exactly like I did when I was younger. Don't you see? Robby wasn't trying to seduce you. He was flirting with me, a younger me. Our lost youth and that sort of thing."

I talked on and endlessly on about the passionate nature of our marriage and Dr. Jacobson's diagnosis concerning its decline, until I finally began to pay attention to what I was saying. It came to me I had never before in my life heard such nonsense come out of a grown woman's mouth.

I gave Fidelity a sharp look and said, "Do you believe a word of this?"

She reached over and squeezed my hand. "It doesn't matter what I believe."

I looked down at our hands, folded into a bundle; our momma's long, narrow hands. They might have belonged to the same woman except one was young and smooth, the other showing signs of wear. *A woman's hands give her away.* Robby meant age, just age, not whether they had raised themselves to useful tasks.

I felt an urgent need to unburden my mind and at that moment my sister's face was the kindest sight I'd seen in this century. I said, "We haven't made love since last August." Her expression didn't change, except to soften even more. "That was all we ever had together. We aren't friends, you know what I mean? Ed Shannon and I were good friends. We didn't move the earth and the stars, but we held each other in high regard."

Fidelity gave me a wry little smile. She said, "The second time around there's always more than two people in the bed. You start making comparisons and somebody's bound to fall short."

"But it's the truth. Robby and I have a life of the flesh, no more than that, and the flesh has no high regard or kindness. Oh God, oh God, Fidelity! He makes me feel so old and ugly."

She squeezed my hand again—hard. "You're beautiful, Cleo. You'll be beautiful when you're ninety—just like Mam. We've got Mam's bones."

I shook my head. "I'd rather have her good sense."

"What would you do with it? Her good sense?"

I thought about that, tried to envision myself walking around on the earth, giving my feet directions instead of trailing along after them. I took a deep breath and said, "First off, I'd acknowledge this poor creature lying here in the middle of the road as the sick horse it truly is. Then I'd go from there."

Fidelity nodded, reached over, and smoothed back my hair. I glanced at the clock above the stove. "You better go, hon, you'll miss your appointment. I'm fine. I really am."

"You sure?"

"I'm sure. You go on now, you hear."

"I'll let you know where we are." She stood up and tore the top page from the note pad. "Come on, City," she called. "We're going now. Oh my! Look at your nice white napkins. You suppose that syrup stain will come out?"

"Doesn't matter."

"I'll just put it to soak in a little bleach."

"Don't bother. We've got extra. Robby likes to have extra of everything."

"Cleo?"

"Yes, Fidelity?"

"You could come with us."

"To look at apartments?"

"To live with us. We could look for a bigger place."

I took the napkin from her. "Thank you, Fidelity, you're a good sister, good and kind. I think I'd probably like that, but I have matters to tend to here. Just because somebody lies about something doesn't mean it isn't true."

38

T HAT EVENING WE SAT IN THE LIVING ROOM, erect as polite visitors, and had ourselves a civilized fight, the kind where the people involved would much rather be chasing each other around the room with big sticks, but can't allow themselves anything more wounding than words.

He said I was lazy and self-satisfied. I said he was selfish and arrogant. That was for starters: general, low-level complaints any couple might fling at each other then laugh about—even find a reason to be proud of—after they'd kissed and made up.

For maybe half an hour we sat at opposite ends of the coffee table, in our comfortable blue velvet chairs, and assessed each other's shortcomings like we were filling out government forms. During all that time, not one word was said about my sister, or the events of the night before, or of that morning.

Someplace between my woeful lack of interest in his work, and his failure to pick up his socks and underwear, he called time out to fix us a drink—a friendly drink, he said. He set my glass down on a coaster and nodded toward the kitchen.

"Have you planned something for dinner?" he asked. "The cupboard looks rather bare."

"I haven't thought about it. I haven't worked up much of an appetite today."

The words weren't out of my mouth before he pounced on them. "That's all fine and good for you. You could benefit from a bit of fasting. I, on the other hand, do not have your ample reserves. You think you might rustle up a little of the bacon I bring home? A crust of bread for the breadwinner?"

Robin Endicott was the only person I ever met—besides my momma—who could spit in somebody's eye while he was asking them to oblige him.

"No," I said. "I wouldn't want to risk it."

He set his glass down and brought his fingertips together. "I would no doubt be wise to let that slide, but I suppose you should get a point or two to keep things interesting. Risk what, Cleo? Speak right up, goose."

"The gas chamber. For poisoning the breadwinner. It means flesh, by the way. You didn't know the answer last night so you just made up that stuff about the Egyptians."

He held up one hand, pretending horror. "Oh now, I do sincerely hope we're not going to hear more nonsense from your good friend Euripides."

"Didn't you learn anything at that seminary? It's *our* good friend, King Solomon. Proverbs. A man is brought to a piece of bread. It means he's brought to a piece of flesh. Just flesh, Robby, no heart or soul, just raw meat."

He smiled his smile of great and everlasting tolerance. "Another drink?" I shook my head. He sighed and stood up. "It's been a long day, Cleo. I'm tired and I'm hungry. I'll settle for scrambled eggs. Don't worry about the gas chamber. I'll keep my eye on the cook."

I followed after him into the kitchen. "You mean that's the end of it? End of discussion?"

He opened the refrigerator and poked around. "Well, I certainly don't want to hear about my absent heart and soul. That's where you were headed, isn't it?"

"I'd hoped we might get around to saying something real for a change. I hoped we might talk about whether there's anything here worth rescuing." He took the pitcher from the freezer and began making another drink. He hummed. Earnestness bored Robby. I said, "Did you hear me?"

He swung around, his face straight as rails, and said, "I told you I was tired. I told you I had a long day. Every day I hear about rescue. Rescue the school system, rescue the city parks, the old folks, the infirm, the poor motherless children." He glared at me. "If you had come with me when I asked you, I wouldn't be in this miserable business. I'd still be God's man. I should have charged you with assault and battery." He frowned and began pulling out drawers and opening cupboards. "Where did I hide my cigarettes?"

As I watched him rummage around like some confused retriever, I tried to remember what it felt like to love him. I said, "What about the childless mothers? If only we could have had children."

"Ah!" He cried out, and dumped a stack of clean dishtowels out on the floor. "There they are. See what you've done, driven me back to my bad habits." He tore into the package and lit a cigarette from the flame on the stove. "Now," he said, breathing out the smoke, "what was it you were going on about? Oh yes, rescue. And the little children. If only we'd had children. Well I can tell you, goose, there was never any danger of that."

I felt the hairs rise on the back of my neck. I said, "What do you mean?"

"I mean I had this little procedure done when I was still in the ministry. Sex is an occupational hazard for a man of the cloth. The world is full of weak-ankled women wanting to bear the preacher's child, wanting to entrap God's servant. It was a prudent move. Besides, I don't like children."

I took hold of the counter with both hands. "But you said you wanted them. All that business with the temperature and the chart and you coming home in the middle of the day . . . the articles in the medical journals . . . the fertility doctor. You had yourself tested. You said the problem was my old eggs."

He gave the great sigh he reserved for tiresome situations. He said, "Oh, goose, you are such a fool. I also told you, many times, that I do not always tell the truth."

And that was when it happened. The poor creature in the middle of the road rolled over, shuddered once, and gave up the ghost. I felt as light as air, as giddy as a new angel. I felt like I could float right out the door. I said, "I'm going to pack my things now."

"Please, goose, no melodrama. You can't leave now. You'll stay until after the election. Divorce is not good for votes. We'll settle up after the election."

"I don't want to live with you."

"You can move into the guest room. Otherwise, it'll be the same easy job you've enjoyed for the last five years. Sit on your ass all day and read—if you put your mind to it you might get to G or H." I turned away from him but he caught me by the arm. "On the other hand," he said, in a soft, even voice, "you leave, and I'll sue you for desertion. You won't get a penny, not a red cent, not one stick of furniture, not one china cup . . ."

"There's the money I brought with me."

"Dowries are nonrefundable." He smiled, let go my arm, and stubbed out his cigarette. "Come on, goose, let's try to make the best of this. Couldn't you fix a little something for a starving man?"

I stared at him for about one hundred years. What I felt was so far beyond anger, beyond rage, I couldn't even put a name to it. I went to the refrigerator and took out the eggs and butter. I said, "Now, listen very carefully, Robby."

He leaned against the counter, folded his arms, and put on the haughty expression he wore in the presence of inferiors.

I said, "You need two bowls. You break an egg into the first bowl, smell it to make sure it's fresh, then transfer it to the second bowl. Check for pieces of eggshell. Okay? Then you beat the eggs with a fork till they're light and fluffy. My grandmother always added a pinch of baking powder. Put a tablespoon of butter in a skillet and turn the flame on low. Melt the butter slowly, don't let it burn. Add the beaten eggs and let them cook for about ten seconds, then stir them gently with a fork. Some people use a spoon, but my grandmother was partial to a fork. Meanwhile you put two slices of bread in the toaster and push down on this lever. The object is for the toast and eggs to be done at the same time. If you want bacon, that's another story."

Robby was still smiling, showing off his infinite capacity for tolerance. But when I reached into the cabinet and came up with my cast-iron skillet, the smile left for parts unknown in a big hurry, and Robby leaped back out of range.

I said, "Remember to use the two bowls. And remember to smell the eggs—make sure they're nice and fresh. No old eggs for Robin Endicott!" Slowly, carefully, I set the skillet down on the burner. "I hope you got all that, Robby, because those are the last words I am ever going to say to you."

PART V

We spend our years as a tale that is told.
—PSALMS 90:9

39

SOME WISE OLD BIRD SAID WE STAY BECAUSE
we've got no place to go, and we go because we've got no place to stay.
I didn't come back to Robina because I had no place to stay. There
was Fidelity's little duplex on Franklin Avenue, and there was R.J.'s
old room in Glendale, which Rosemary said I was welcome to. I came
back to Robina because of a pull as strong and natural as gravity. It
was that simple.

I stayed a week at the duplex. Every evening after City had gone to
bed, Fidelity and I took Robby Endicott apart up one side and down
the other, until he was just a pile of chewed bones at our feet. My last
night, made wise on a good cabernet, I treated Fidelity to my notions
about the male animal, my observations on love and its surrounding
countryside. I concluded there were two kinds of men in the world.
There was the kind you wanted to go down to the creek with, and the
kind you wanted to father your children. I said the first represented
passion and the second, pure love. Fidelity said she didn't see any reason why both couldn't come in the same package. I said I didn't either
but that had not been my experience. She laughed and said she suspected there was more to it than that. I said if we could figure it out we
might win the Nobel Prize.

I spent one night in Glendale at the kitchen table with sweet Rosemary, who stayed up until three in the morning listening to my sorry
tale. She said, "Look on the bright side of this, Cleo. Now you can
finally take your trip to Lhasa."

I said, "Not on seventy-five dollars and fifty-three cents." And I told
her how I'd given my money over to Robby to be invested in something safe. Just before I left, Raymond gave me a hundred dollars, a
long-term loan, he said, from him and Rosie. I told him I'd only been
angling for a little sympathy, not cash. I said I had enough to get there.
He said it was for the possibility of car trouble.

*

347

Once again I arrived in Robina with little more than my satchel, my trumpet, and Alexandra's book. I looked out on that endless prairie. Patches of snow turned to ice while I watched. The wind whistled out of the north—the bitter kind that cuts through bone. *I went out full and the Lord hath brought me home empty.* I considered the woeful sound of those words inside my head and had to laugh. This was not one I could saddle on the Lord.

The house was cold and unfriendly. The Tiptons had left it clean and neat, but the electricity was off and the woodpile amounted to a few sticks of kindling. Not a soul to holler out a welcome, not even the yowl of a hungry barn cat. So what did I expect? Mind readers and marching bands? I realized I would have been smart to let Ethan know I was coming and ask him to kindly make arrangements about the phone and utilities. I told myself I wasn't smart yet, just working on it.

I locked up and drove over to Momma's, where I was gratified to see smoke rising from the chimney. Ethan opened the door before I could knock, grunted, and took my suitcase as if it was the most natural thing in the world for me to show up unannounced on the doorstep.

He poured me a cup of coffee first thing and said, "You hungry?"

"Starved," I told him. "Haven't eaten a bite since Elk City."

He looked me up and down. "Out of choice?"

"Careful bookkeeping. I'm fresh out of a provider." I smiled. "That part's out of choice."

He nodded as if he understood the whole pitiful mess and didn't need to hear about it. I was glad of that. I was tired of hearing myself tell it.

He said, "I was about to heat yesterday's rabbit stew. Maybe you could stir us up some biscuits. My biscuits are like rocks. Momma always said, 'Ethan, your biscuits are like rocks.' And sure 'nuf, I'd oblige every time."

I said I understood how expectation worked and told him I'd be happy to make biscuits light as clouds as soon as my hands thawed out. He patted my shoulder and I felt myself begin to loosen up. Things would work out. Tomorrow, I'd locate my old leather gloves and chop some firewood. Then I'd drive into town and see about the electricity and telephone. I'd talk to Neddy at the bank about a small loan, just enough to keep me going until harvest, and to buy some chickens and a mule, maybe a milk cow.

I would call Sonny Tipton and ask him if he could teach me something of what he learned at Tahlequah about farming in poor soil. In early spring I'd put in a crop of strewberries and have another go-round with that Suspension. Maybe Fidelity and City could come home for a visit and we'd put up pretty little jars of the Fruit of the Gods, and sell it to that company in Tulsa. Maybe we'd get rich—rich as the tombs of Egypt.

But as Miss Hawkins said, you can't plant in January. Maybe I'd get out my notes and work on Mam's history until good weather set in.

Meanwhile, here I was in my brother's warm house. I had a roof over my head and the prospect of a fine supper, and after that a few hands of draw poker. I told myself to try to remember the nines. *Don't stay with a measly pair of nines.*

40

January 31, 1952
Dear Mr. Mackenzie:

Due to temporary reduced circumstances, I will not be able to have the luxury of your services as regards my family's resting place in Tulsa. Perhaps that is just as well, as I feel the time has come for me to assume that responsibility myself. No words can adequately express my gratitude for the devoted way in which you've performed this duty in my stead.

Miss Hawkins told me how you come to Robina every spring and sow wildflowers on my grandmother's grave. I believe you do this, not for me, but for Mam, and, I suspect, for yourself. I remember clearly how moved you were by the success of your ceremony. Our mutual friend, Mildred Ashcroft, once told me how, when she was a girl back east, her whole village went to the cemetery in spring and fall to spend the day. She said they raked and mowed and planted, and that after they finished their work they had a picnic right there in the cemetery. "The living and the spirits," Mildred said. That's what I'm writing about. I hope when you come this spring with your wildflower seeds you will allow me to assist you. I propose to bring a picnic for us to share, and for any spirits who should care to join us.

I look forward to your reply.
Yours sincerely,
Cleo Endicott.

I stared at Robby's name at the bottom of the page and realized I needed to do something about it. I certainly didn't want to wag it around with me as an ever-present reminder of poor judgment.

February 2, 1952
Dear Mr. Tompkins:
  My friend, Emma Hawkins, has suggested I contact you in regard to changing my name. She says further that everybody should have a lawyer just on general principles due to the growing complexities of our times. My current married name is "Endicott" and I would like to be rid of it as soon as possible. Mr. Endicott is a resident of Los Angeles, California, and, the last I heard, plans to divorce me on the grounds of desertion, which suits me fine.
  My question is this: Can I get rid of the name before the divorce? As soon as possible? Regarding a new name: I was widowed in my previous marriage. I would be proud to bear my first husband's name, but the thing is, "Cleo Shannon" doesn't exist anymore, if you know what I mean. The same applies to the name I was born with.
  My next question is this: Can I take any name I choose? I would like to be Cleo Alexander. (It's Cleopatra on the birth certificate but I've never felt that suited me and besides it caused my mother great distress.) I don't know any Alexanders personally. The name comes by way of a woman who wrote a book I've treasured since I was a young girl.
(I hope) Cleo Alexander

February 5, 1952
Dear Mrs. Endicott,
  According to the Farmers' Almanac, the last frost is in early March. I plan to be at the Robina cemetery around noon on the 18th, providing that day is a convenient one for you. I look forward to the picnic with you and the spirits.
Yours,
Seth Mackenzie

February 8, 1952
Dear Mr. Mackenzie:
  If at all possible, the 25th would be a better day for me. I hope this is not an inconvenience.
Cleo

February 10, 1952
Dear Mrs. Endicott,
   No problem. The 25th it is.
S.M.

February 15, 1952
Dear Mrs. Endicott:
   I'm pleased to report that a name change is a simple legal procedure. Enclosed is a brief questionnaire and a checklist of information you should forward to this office. The charge is $20. Yes, Emma is correct, ours are complex times indeed. When you receive papers from Mr. Endicott, please feel free to send them on for my perusal. If action is required in your behalf and self-interest, I will first advise you of the fee.
Sincerely,
R. C. Tompkins, Esq.

March 1, 1952
Dear Fidelity:
   I'm tickled to hear the job is going so well for you. Now you will be the one who decides if somebody gets demoted to grannie gowns and housecoats. And you get to keep the ten extra pounds you're so fond of. I just hope you don't become such an important executive you won't have time to come home for strewberry season. I found the receipt for the Suspension. Strange thing is, it's clear Momma meant me to find it. It was right there in plain sight in her old wooden box which, as you will remember, she left me along with Mam's Bible. I was looking for the rhubarb custard pie when I came across it. Written on the top of the card in big red letters it says, "What took you so long, Daughter?" As usual, I don't know how she meant it, whether it was a complaint or she was somehow holding her hand out to me. What do you think?
   Yes, I did hear from Sarah about Flynn. But maybe we'll be lucky. Maybe it'll all be over by the time he graduates. I swear, it seems to me it was just yesterday when I stood on Brand Boulevard in Glendale and watched a band from the VFW

come marching down the street playing a tune from the First World War. I remember how the trumpets were off-key and how I took heart from that circumstance. *If the trumpet give an uncertain sound, who will prepare himself to the battle?*

Every Sunday at the service, Reverend Shoemaker offers special prayers for our Robina boys, both here and abroad. I asked him to add Flynn to the list. Sarah said she and Willis were deeply touched by that. Well. I'm still taking farming lessons from Sonny Tipton and am pleased to report that I am making gradual progress.

I finally persuaded Ethan to see the new doctor in town. (A. Karajian, M.D. has been in Robina for more than five years now but he's still called the new doctor.) Seems that Ethan has an allergy to sunshine that was aggravated by his use of Lifebouy soap. He still has to stay out of the sun but the good news is he doesn't have lupus or leukemia. The other good news is that the awful itching and painful blisters have been relieved just by a change of soap and a salve the doctor has given him. Ethan is trying to determine what's in the salve so he can make it himself and add it to his curative business. The result of all this is that our brother often smiles and carries on long conversations.

That's all. Miss Hawkins sends her best to you, and the enclosed book for City.
Love to you both,
Cleo

March 18, 1952
Dear Cleo Alexander:

I am pleased to tell you that the above salutation contains your official, legal name, as per your request. I have sent the proper forms to Social Security, but you will now need to advise your bank, the DMV, etc. All that is required is a new signature.

It has been my pleasure to serve you, and I stand ready to do so in the future, should the need arise.
Sincerely,
R. C. Tompkins, Esq.

I sat down at the table and wrote my new name one hundred times on a yellow lined pad. It flowed out of my pen as swiftly as the stream runs after a hard rain. That surprised me. When I became Cleo Shannon, I wrote the Cleo part in the old way, with the same big curlicue on the *C*, the same long, loopy *l* and a cheerful hat on the *o*. "Shannon" looked sedate as a heron by comparison, but I soon got a flourish into it and made it mine.

On the other hand, I often misspelled "Endicott," which should have told me something.

I got to the cemetery a little after noon. A pair of meadowlarks were perched on the fence, working on each other's songs, and Seth Mackenzie was there with his garden tools. He looked up, put down his rake, and called out he'd give me a hand, which I sorely needed for the grand feast I'd prepared. I had the cooler, the ice-cream freezer, two baskets, and a blanket for us to sit on. The cooler contained two big frosty Mason jars of Ethan's excellent home brew, and Momma's rhubarb pie. One of the baskets held cold fried chicken, deviled eggs, baked beans, stuffed celery, carrot sticks, radish roses, and sweet pickles—nothing fancy except the radishes, just good, plain Oklahoma picnic fare. In the other basket I'd packed Mam's good dishes and silverware, and an embroidered tablecloth with matching napkins. I hoped Seth Mackenzie had brought his appetite.

He took the ice-cream freezer and one of the baskets, and pretended to sink under the weight. He said, "Just how many spirits you expecting?"

I smiled and looked at him closely. He was just as I remembered him even though I'd seen him only briefly in the yellow light of the café, and later here in the darkness of the cemetery. Strong white teeth, fine black eyes, a face built of good lasting bones, big capable hands, and a tall, rangy body—no fat. Good stock. Good Creek stock.

We set the picnic under a tree, out of the sun, and went to work. He'd already finished the weeding so we were ready to plant. He began to make rows with his rake.

I said, "I thought you just broadcast the seeds."

He shook his head. "Better to give them a little protection while they germinate. They have a better chance that way. See, you just

354

loosen the soil with the rake to about a half inch deep." I watched while he accomplished this in long, fluid strokes. "Then," he went on, "you sprinkle the seeds around evenly. Here." He handed me a jar filled with seeds, then stepped back and leaned on the rake. "No," he said after a moment, "try to separate them, give each seed a little space of its own. There. That's it. Now you've got it."

"It's such a dainty operation," I said. I was thinking of all those rocks I'd beat up on with my shovel.

He nodded agreement. "You have to be gentle when you cultivate something wild. Now, you just barely cover the seeds and pat the soil down with your hands. You don't mind getting your hands dirty, do you?"

I said, "Remind me to tell you about my experience growing strewberries."

"Strawberries?"

"The proper name is strewberries—because they strew. You talked about Thoreau's beautiful bug at Mam's ceremony. Remember his beans? How they were impatient to be hoed? Well, I had impatient strewberries."

He gave me a wide smile of recognition. "Thoreau said his beans attached him to the earth. He said he disturbed the ashes of old nations when he hoed." He stood up and dusted off his hands. "Now all we have to do is water them. If you can come and water every day for about a week, they'll do better. I've asked for rain, but you never know."

"Which god did you ask?"

He chuckled. "Whoever's on duty."

"Are there more seeds?"

"We've planted more than enough. You'll be able to pick some. You'll have your grandmother's wildflowers for your windowsill all summer long."

I spread out my arms to take in the whole plot. "These are my folks here," I said. "I'd like them all to have wildflowers."

He nodded and said he would send me more; then we watered the seeds and washed up at the faucet. I spread the blanket under the tree and began to empty the baskets. I was surprised at how calm I felt, and how peaceful. It was as if some out-of-work angel had passed over and blessed me on her way to a new assignment.

While we ate, I told Seth about my plans for my strewberry crop and he expressed interest in looking at my fields. I told him about my farming lessons and how I meant to make a living from the land. I said, "I don't expect to get rich, but I mean to prosper."

He poured us both more of Ethan's home brew, then helped himself to more beans and another deviled egg. "Where was that place you were headed that night? Ever get where you were going?"

"Lhasa," I said. "No, I didn't get there. I was barely into the Panhandle when the Japanese attacked Pearl Harbor. I almost went after the war ended. Hired a holy man and paid for my passage. But I got married instead." I added, in an offhand way, "You married?"

He reached for a radish and held it up to admire. "Too pretty to eat," he said, then sprinkled it with salt and popped it in his mouth. "I was married, but I'm not at the moment. I have a lady friend."

"That's good. Save room for pie and ice cream." I topped off his glass with more home brew. "Is it serious?"

"Is what serious?"

"You and your lady friend?"

He rubbed his chin and looked at me sideways. "Well, we have an understanding. More or less."

"Are there children from your marriage?"

"Two boys. In high school now."

"They healthy?"

He gave a nervous little laugh. "You know, ma'am, I feel kind of like I'm being interviewed for a job."

"Ready for pie? It's rhubarb." This was not going as smoothly as I'd envisioned it. I was sorry I hadn't brought more home brew. He said pie would be fine, and I felt his eyes on me while I dished it up. "One or two scoops?"

"Two, thank you." He cocked his head. "My sons are healthy, yes. Fine boys, smart, they'll go to the university in the daytime. You want to tell me what this is all about?"

I fingered the edge of the tablecloth and tried to line words up into sentences. It had been much easier when I'd rehearsed in front of the mirror. Finally, I looked up and said, "I hope you won't be offended. I mean this as the highest compliment." His face was patient and interested. I took a deep breath and said, "While I was in California, my tenant wrote me about buying the farm. I wrote back and told him it wasn't mine to sell. It came down to me from my grandmother but to begin with it was tribal land. Creek land. So, I have this deed to this sacred piece of earth, but I have no one to inherit, no one to be its caretaker when I go on."

I cleared my throat and steadied my voice. "I'll be forty-one in October. I want to have another child. I don't want another husband, just the child."

Seth Mackenzie's jaw dropped about to his knees, and I held up my hand asking him to hear me out. I said, "I know in my heart it was some gracious spirit that came to me in the middle of the night and gave me this idea as a great gift. I've talked it over with Mam, and she approves. I hope you don't see it as a moral issue—what with you being spoken for, I mean. I don't think of it as a carnal act in this instance, but a religious one. Like a ceremony, do you see?"

He looked bewildered and shook his head. "Mrs. Endicott, I think you've got me mixed up with the Holy Ghost."

"Cleo," I said. "Please call me Cleo. If it would make you feel easier I'd be happy to sign a paper that says I have no claims against you."

"Ma'am . . . Cleo, I am deeply honored to be chosen for this . . . ah . . . this honor, but I'll need to give it some thought."

"I hope you won't need to think long on it. I've been taking my temperature and now is the best time."

His eyes widened. "Today? Here?"

"Not in the cemetery," I said. "My momma's right over there." I got to my feet and said, "Why don't you think about it while you have your pie—the ice cream's melting. I'll just go rinse off these dishes."

I took my time and when I came back he was staring off toward Garrity Fields, looking bemused and troubled. He looked up and said, "This isn't like wildflowers, Cleo. This is not a seed a man plants then abandons."

I said, "I appreciate that sentiment, Seth, but I don't want to interfere with your life."

He sighed deeply. "You already have."

I folded the tablecloth and the napkins and began to pack up the baskets. Very carefully, deliberately, we touched on other matters—the weather, the war, his classes at T.U., my potential strewberries, the meadowlarks' curious overlapping ranges.

We were quiet as we walked toward the road. I could hear all the philosophers from night school consulting in Seth Mackenzie's head. I waited. I had presented my case as clearly and as truthfully as I knew how, and I felt at peace.

41

I KNEW IN APRIL BUT DID NOT ALLOW MY-self the joy of certainty until May. I also knew that the Beulah Baptist Auxiliary would do a lot of counting on its collective hands and soon run out of fingers, and that the party lines would fairly sizzle with speculation. Nonetheless I planned to brazen it out and claim this baby had been conceived in lawful wedlock before I left California; before my dear husband, a former Methodist preacher and highly respected Los Angeles politician, was cruelly taken from me by way of food poisoning. I planned to speak knowledgeably and mysteriously of a rare phenomenon called delayed implantation. I planned to move about in a state of grace and wonderment, like one who has been visited by a miracle.

Seth Mackenzie sent a large can of wildflower seeds as he'd promised, but he did not enclose a message, nor did he telephone, nor did he write any letters. This was what we agreed to after we admitted we took entirely too much pleasure from the ceremony to try and pass it off as a religious experience. The carnal nature of the act was readily apparent, as was the danger of trying to pretend otherwise.

He did stay the night. I didn't ask him what lie he would tell when he got back to Tulsa, or even if a lie was necessary. We spoke very little, except when I was moved to tell him something more of my heritage. I assured him he could be proud to mingle his blood with that of my grandmother's ancestors. I said my family on that side was old and distinguished. I said it was descended from kings.

I probably sounded unduly self-important because Seth Mackenzie laughed out loud and said the Scots, too, were descended from kings, and even the Irish. He said old kings didn't matter anymore. Then he took me in his arms and we didn't speak for a very long time.

Even back in January when I first wrote to him, I had already determined that the ceremony would be performed in Mam's bed, under her old Cross and Crown quilt, a place of proven fruitfulness and goodwill.

But I had not expected to feel passion. In truth, I had vowed to give up passion as it had never done anything for me except get me in trouble. When it came over me, and took my breath, I looked it square in the face and said, Oh, I know you. Careful! Easy!

For this reason, and in everyone's best interests, Seth Mackenzie and I agreed to leave each other's lives undisturbed in the future. There would be no invitations disguised as business letters, no meetings by chance, no wildflower picnics to mark the day. No reckless stones skipped across the creek to make ripples that might come to shore.

When he left the next morning at first light—when lovers leave—I did not follow him out. He did not look back. I stood at the kitchen window, folded my arms and held myself gently, like something fragile, and watched him go. I wondered. Given the human condition, I wondered if we could be trusted to keep our word.

Now there is much to do. My strewberries are impatient to be hoed. Fidelity is coming next month, and we will put up the Suspension. I've hired pickers, and ordered the jars and the labels from Mr. Krause's nephew. These labels will not say Fruit of the Gods. These labels will say Momma's Strewberries. I continue to court her favor. I understand this failing in myself, and in her, and I accept it.

I've gone over my mess of notes for Mam's history and have put them into order, and made an outline and a chronology. This project awaits me in a clean white box. I will begin it the first time I feel this child move. That will be a sign that the time is right and the work is blessed. Mam says there is no big hurry. Mam says she'll be around as long as I am. Maybe longer if I tell a good story.

Last night after supper I took up my Lhasa book, which sits like an old brown monument on the sideboard next to my trumpet. I said to Alexandra, "Well, I didn't get to Lhasa. It looks like I may never get to Lhasa."

I considered these words as they floated around me like a cool breeze off the river. They did not seem to have in them the sound of defeat. Or disappointment. Or regret. Just a statement of fact and probability.

I said, "But every day of my life I have traveled to the unknown, and have often found welcome and astonishment there."

I said, "On the other hand, it took you five tries. I'm only forty. You didn't get to Lhasa till you were fifty-five years old."

Alexandra said she would brew us a pot of yak-butter tea and we would have a good long talk on the subject of journeys—of departures and arrivals—of the wide plains and the high passes along the way.